NOTHING SACRED

NOTHING SACRED

'A Divine Comedy'

Martin J Featherston

Matador
Unit E2 Airfield Business Park,
Harrison Road, Market Harborough,
Leicestershire. LE16 7UL
Tel: 0116 2792299
Email: books@troubador.co.uk
Web: www.troubador.co.uk/matador
Twitter: @matadorbooks

ISBN 978 1803131 566 (Paperback)
ISBN 978 1803139 098 (eBook)

British Library Cataloguing in Publication Data.
A catalogue record for this book is available from the British Library.

Printed and bound by CPI Group (UK) Ltd, Croydon, CR0 4YY
Typeset in 11pt Adobe Jenson Pro by Troubador Publishing Ltd, Leicester, UK

Matador is an imprint of Troubador Publishing Ltd

For Douglas

PREFACE

Throughout history, attempts have been made to decipher the perfect day of the week for God's ultimate return. The methodologies used were as varied as the cultures and religions applying them and had little in common with each other, except for the fact that each conclusion became piously set in stone, without compromise, sanctified by theological logic and propagated through means of rigid dogma.

Ironically, it's this uncompromising nature that inevitably leads to counter-arguments designed to bring about compromise. These alternative views, generally labelled heretical by the culture affixing the label, are typically dismissed out of hand and banished to the scrap heap of fanciful ideologies. This became known as the '*my God is the only God, and He says you're a dick*' theory of divinity.

Generations of human ancestry, primarily living in isolated cultures around the globe, became very sensitive to outsiders questioning their entrenched dogma or claiming to know the mind of God and expressed these sensitivities in a variety of ways. Some innocuous, such as lively debate followed by snacks and refreshments, while others, less benign, usually resulted in collective rock-throwing or similar unpleasantries.

The crux of the overall problem looks something like this: A theistic scholar proclaims either a Sunday, Saturday or Friday as the only acceptable day for their deity's arrival. The conclusion is based on the interpretation of scripture, more commonly referred to as holy writing, and touted as the only authentic word of God. Almost instantly, the decree is attacked by others, insisting that the day in question was exclusively designed for rest and worship. Therefore, it was implausible God would blatantly disregard his own laws by conducting miracles, sermons or partisan pep rallies on the Lord's Day.

Vociferous debate ensues until a different day is proposed by a different scholar from a different religion, and the cycle begins anew with a freshly insulted party filing protests based on their specific interpretation of what *their* God wants.

The process continues, adding twists, turns and interpretations over generations until the entire concept is mired in sacred quicksand.

Modern-day thinkers suggest that these attempts to define the holiest of ETAs have irreparably segregated religions, leaving the chances of Christianity, Islam, Judaism and Hinduism agreeing on a common day as likely as a Pride parade breaking out in Tiananmen Square.

So, with the three holiest days hopelessly lost to disagreement, the faithful are left debating the merits of Monday through Thursday, the only remaining options for a workable consensus. Although well-intentioned, the devout inevitably overlook the fact that the unfaithful, or secular as they prefer to be known, might also wish to weigh in on the subject. After all, even an atheist can opine about the most suitable day for a non-existent God to drop in. Surprisingly, these unaffiliated souls are pretty vocal on the matter and most adamant that Monday through Thursday should not be considered equal in any way.

The heathen viewpoint looks like this: There's a general consensus that Mondays are off the table because they're Mondays, and Mondays suck. Nobody likes Mondays. The last thing anyone wants to do is dress up in formal attire and meet God on a day so universally loathed and fundamentally flawed.

Tuesdays aren't much better, having their own unique challenge. Tuesdays are generally set aside for employees to call in sick with faux illnesses and/or medical appointments. Mondays are rarely used for this purpose because it looks suspicious – creating a sudden three-day weekend via instant flu bug, dentist visit, or, for the truly inventive, a great-aunt's third funeral. So, by default, Tuesday has been entrenched as the optimum day for skipping work, a day set aside for mental vacations usually triggered by the depressing reality Mondays tend to induce. And since nobody wants God to return while they're at the spa, golfing or playing video games in bed, Tuesdays are off the list.

This takes us to Wednesday, which simply cannot be an option. Throughout the western world, Wednesday is known as hump day. This is an inappropriate term, and therefore an inappropriate day for God's homecoming. God (he, she, or it) is renowned for having prudish attitudes towards sex or anything capable of turning the mind toward the subject. So, dropping in on a hump day seems implausible, even if the hump in question is a harmless reference to the middle of the workweek. Thus, Thursday wins by default.

And who doesn't love a Thursday, the penultimate workday before TGIF festivities? Clearly, the most suitable day for God's grand entrance.

However, timing aside, even the most inept PR agency would balk at the choice of Phoenix, Arizona, as the quintessential point of arrival, likely opting for the global impact of the Vatican, Dome of the Rock, or the Las Vegas strip.

So it was that on this particular Thursday morning in the year 2005, pre-brunch, the man who would soon be known worldwide as 'God Almighty' received a somewhat less than enthusiastic welcome. Just another forgettable face, stretchered through a set of opaque hospital doors to the unbridled apathy of the attending physician, Dr. Rory MacMann.

O N E

Earl Grey had not been created for winter use. His pale skin reddened in extreme cold, his nose suffering the most, blossoming into crimson hues every October as the last crinkled leaf plummeted to the ground. Alcohol didn't help improve the situation either, nor did his tendency to blush brightly at the first sign of embarrassment or shame. Reasonably fit despite a sedentary lifestyle, he did have a roundish face – 'chipmunk cheeks' his mother would call them when she reached out for a pinch. Others said it was a soft, kind face, albeit a sad one. Thin reddish-brown hair hinted at his Irish roots while disqualifying him from any legitimate attempt at growing a beard – clown-red stubble emerging three days into every effort. Otherwise, Earl was a forgettable thirty-eight-year-old man of average height, average brown eyes and an average nose. His above-average ears stuck out ever so slightly, requiring sideburns to conceal the flaw.

As a newspaper reporter, a real journalist, Earl would say, his greatest skill was observation. A skill he knew was wasted in his current role as a lifestyle reporter for the *Toronto Telegraph*. A keen eye or cunning investigative talent was rarely needed to grind out stories about snow tire selection, local hockey results or retirement home craft shows.

The aftermath of a messy divorce had reduced Earl's forward momentum to a crawl. Mass graves of fear, anger and bitterness had been exhumed, leaving him in a constant state of reburial.

Winters made everything worse. The darkness and cold amplified Earl's negative emotions, reducing his desire to fight to Tibetan Monk levels. *Thank Christ Dad can't see me now,* Earl thought, wrestling the car around a snowbank and correcting the skid. *I'd never hear the end of it.*

When Earl was ten, Charles Grey delivered the classic, *what will you do with*

1

your life speech to his son. Earl recalled how his father stressed the importance of making a name for himself. But he couldn't remember why.

This father-son chat, or more appropriately, the unidirectional speech, took place on the back deck of their cottage in Muskoka, Ontario, where Earl planned to spend the entire summer doing varying degrees of nothing in the humid, hazy sun. However, upon arrival, Charles Grey presented him with a report card that had recently arrived by mail. The report highlighted Earl's academic achievements from the previous school year. He remembered how deeply it cut as his father read out every negative comment recorded by the teacher.

"Capable of greater results!" Charles loudly pronounced as if they were his very own words. "Could do better!" his eyes leaving the yellow paper, locking onto Earl's expression like a bear-trap springing on a chipmunk. "Sometimes Earl daydreams when he should be paying attention. He is often distant and seems unwilling to participate in class." Charles Grey straightened in his chair and prepared to deliver the fatal blow. "Young Earl is a bright boy," he pronounced with an exaggerated thespian delivery, "capable of much more than he is currently delivering. He can easily handle the work but seems unwilling to challenge himself. Instead, Earl chooses to *observe* rather than *participate*. While he seems interested in the lessons and class discussion, he does not engage, only watches and scribbles in his book. This behaviour borders on antisocial, and I fear, if left uncorrected, Earl may become reclusive. In summary, Earl is merely observing the world around him instead of participating in everything it has to offer."

Charles concluded the recital by opening the can of Molson Export his wife had gingerly placed on the side table. "What do you have to say for yourself, Earl?" He forced the question through clenched teeth. "Is this how I raised you, not caring about your work?"

Earl caught a glimpse of his mother peeking out from the kitchen. "I care," he meekly protested, then studied his running shoes, "my marks were... good."

"Marks will only get you so far in life, my boy; you've got to stand out from the crowd, make yourself heard, or else you might as well start driving a truck right now." Charles flicked the report card towards Earl, displaying how valueless and unworthy it was of keeping.

Of course, at aged 10, Earl loved the idea of driving a truck. It looked like fun. And you could do it alone, without people around you, without pressure, just your little universe of thoughts and country music. He hated country music, but being so young, he assumed it was mandatory listening for all eighteen-wheel professionals.

He'd watched *Smokey and the Bandit* a dozen times on DVD, and while all his friends desperately wanted to emulate Burt Reynolds's Bandit character, Earl identified with Cledus, the truck driver played by Jerry Reed. Seemed like the perfect life. Zipping across the country without a care in the world. *What's wrong with that life*, Earl thought, *driving about the countryside with my own hound-dog. Soam-bitch!*

Young Earl sat on a homemade wooden bench overlooking the water near the front railing of the deck. Sunshine dodged through the leathery green leaves and tickled his shoulders, casting deformed shadows on the deck boards in front of him. He instinctively knew to sit still and wait out his father's lecture before commencing a jam-packed summer of wilderness exploration via the boundless imagination of an only child. However, this lecture was well into overtime, longer than any previous, and grinding at his very will to live. Something about its direction was disturbing: the more Charles Grey spoke, the more Earl felt the need to run like hell.

"So, here's what we've done," Charles stated abruptly, interrupting his son's trance. "You'll spend next week here with your mother and I on vacation. After that, I'll drive you up to Camp Wiccappoo for eight weeks of youth assertiveness training and leadership skills." Charles's face was beaming as if he'd just handed Earl a cup of coffee in the Holy Grail.

"W… w… *what?*" stammered Earl.

"It's pardon," corrected Charles, "and you're going to love it. Mrs. Newman's son Miles went there last year; now he's class president."

"But I wanna play here this summer… with you," Earl pleaded, recalling how much everyone hated Miles.

"Nonsense, this will be the best thing that ever happened to you," Charles insisted. "Your mother and I had to save a lot of money all year to give you this. Try to look a little more grateful." Charles Grey rose, indicating that the discussion had ended, and headed inside, his crushed beer can rocking in the breeze, a memorial to young Earl's independence and free will.

Earl sat on the bench, disbelief pinching at his spine, leaving him paralyzed for three hours – long enough for the afternoon sun to set on his hopes, dreams and summer plans.

*

The faded black Ford Taurus ran over a clump of hard snow, bouncing Earl's head into the side window and back to reality. He smacked his hand against the steering wheel. "Assertiveness training!" Earl mumbled with a bitterness usually reserved for presidential runners up, steam from his hot breath briefly frosting the car's windshield. "Why couldn't I drive a goddamn truck?"

A hundred yards beyond an all-night donut shop, awkwardly named The Big O, Earl turned left down a poorly lit street lined with thick maples. The shortcut brought him out in a neighbourhood renowned for payday loan stores and pawn shops. Passing under a streetlight, he knowingly nodded as it popped out of existence, tossing the nearby homes into darkness. Blown streetlights had become so commonplace that Earl simply assumed the technology was dirt cheap and undependable, just another example of his tax dollars in action. Another left, and he pulled into the parking lot of the Excelsior Townhouse complex, coasting into his spot as he unbuckled his seatbelt. As he reached for the door handle, dull vibrations from a holstered Blackberry 8700 spasmed through his hips and up to his brain. *An email at this hour?* He popped three buttons in the middle of his coat and reached inside for the smartphone. After skimming the lengthy email from his editor, Earl focused on the last few paragraphs in horror.

> *…so, I've got no choice. I've already notified Travel, they'll have a ticket waiting for you at the airport. You'll need to rent a decent camera. I want as many pictures as possible, the hospital grounds, the turmoil, the throngs of believers. Everything you gain access to. As for your press credentials, we'll drop them at the airport tomorrow using a runner; they'll be at check-in. I'm gonna need regular updates and any side stories you can dig up during your downtime, anything to justify this enormous cost. No extraordinary expenses – no room service and NO minibar.*
>
> *Since there's no chance in hell of getting on the inside, work your angle around the religious nuts who flock to these fucking things. There's little chance the other rags in this town will send anyone, so we may be able to sell a few exclusives.*
>
> *Call in twice a day, and don't fuck it up, Grey.*
>
> *Kindest regards, Ed*

This is a joke, concluded Earl, anger filling the space between his ears. He attempted to calculate the odds that a nobody like him in charge of local interest stories would be chosen to report on the crowds of religious nuts surrounding a Phoenix hospital. Mathematics complete, he concluded that the odds were pretty damn good considering every other reporter at the *Telegraph* refused to go.

Earl sat still in the dark of the car, the overhead dome-light long dead. He stared down at his phone, urging it to light up and reveal a 'just kidding' from his editor, or 'wait a sec, we found a night janitor who's willing to go. And he can write and has his own pen.'

The Blackberry remained dark and unhelpful. Rereading the email, Earl mumbled, "Send an atheist to report on religious nuts. Great plan, guys." Holstering the phone, he shook his head in disbelief and frustration.

T W O

Friday, November 13, 2:15 p.m. MST
Phoenix General Hospital, Doctor's Lounge

"How did this happen?" Frank moaned, his fingers intertwined and clasped behind his head, elbows embedded in a white plastic cafeteria table. He raised his eyes to the tall physician towering over him.

Dr. Rory MacMann, Phoenix General Hospital's Chief Medical Officer, looked down upon his temporary boss, Acting Chief Administrator, Frank Shedmore, and offered a highly rehearsed look of sympathy. "My guess is the EMU lads leaked it, but, let's face it, Frank, we're not the friggin' CIA, word travels fast like shit through a goose, anyone could have leaked it." The doctor's mild Scottish accent rose in step with his annoyance. "Besides, it's nothing. Typical John Doe amnesia case. Psychosis and delusional symptomology. Happens all the time. This one thinks he's the Almighty. So, some dobber makes a quick score by shopping the story to a gossip site."

"That gossip site got the attention of network news shows," said Frank. "Now, my friggin' lawn looks like Woodstock." The administrator's words were emphatic, spit projectiles arcing across the table, landing on various parts of the doctor as he tried to ignore the deluge. Frank Shedmore, career bureaucrat, appeared small, consumed by an ill-fitting dishevelled black suit, his hands barely protruding from the sleeves. He carried a sickly pallor, despite living in the sunniest place in America. His choice of short black hair and round-rimmed glasses were a tribute to a bygone fashion that had never looked good on anyone. After years of managing medical clinics and smaller hospitals, the stress had left him hunched and fragile, his arms hanging off his shoulders like shanks in a butcher's window. "I've already got the Board all over me about sloppy security issues, personal privacy infractions, bad national PR, and a host of religious community complaints. I'm in deep shit – a big six-foot shit-grave. I can see the headlines now. 'God's not dead, just recuperating at Phoenix General. Acting Chief Administrator buried in shit-grave'."

MacMann tried to jump back into the conversation like a kid boarding a spinning merry-go-round. "Frank, Frank, do you know how many delusionary deities get admitted every year in this country?" He didn't wait for a response. "Thousands! It's the most common manifestation of a psychotic episode. Religion plays such an intense underlying role in society that it becomes the most common persona when the mind breaks down and reinvents itself. Frankly, I don't understand the media interest in this particular... patient."

"There are hundreds of reporters outside," Frank literally spat back, "all demanding access to 'God'. The press is already saying he's healing people here in the hospital. Four people have already gone to the media detailing their miraculous healing at the hands of this man. Apparently, even on a stretcher, all he does is reach out to touch a fellow patient and say, 'trust me, everything will be fine'. And boom, several hours later, everything's friggin fine. They leave with no symptoms. Nothing wrong at all. Friggin healed!"

"Healing? Not bloody likely," MacMann spat. "John Doe's a charismatic man who, judging from the Armani suit he was wearing when he arrived, has many skills, but healing's not one of them. I assume one of these so-called miracles you're referring to is Mrs. Ballister?"

"We're releasing her today. Heart checks out fine." Frank frowned, suggesting he would have preferred major cardiac complications or a severe bout of death.

"Gas, Frank, it was just gas, no miracle."

"Not according to her. Severe chest pains on admission. Tells everyone she's dying. Huge drama. We park her on a stretcher next to Doe and boom, miracle-friggin' city. Doe says, 'Hi, I'm God,' touches her hand and says she'll be fine. An hour later, she checks out with nothing wrong. Not a goddamn thing."

"Of course she did. Nothing *was* wrong, Frank. It was just gas."

"She had a history of heart problems. Swears that when Doe touched her, she felt a warmth in her chest, along with some peace and love crap."

"Ridiculous, more like the burrito she had for lunch," snapped MacMann. "So, Mrs. Peace and Love races off to the press and sells her story to the highest bidder. Financial gain via gastroenteritis. Next, it'll be the Madonna's image in the cafeteria tapioca."

Bedside manner had never been a top skill for Dr. Rory MacMann. Hospital Administrator manner was even lower on his list of core competencies. Born and educated in Edinburgh, his father and professors never once stressed the importance of human interaction. In fact, MacMann had spent twice the time studying billing techniques than patient psychology and communication. After residency, he left Scotland and moved to America, marrying in his late twenties a younger girl who he saw from time to time whenever she fit into his schedule. New York, Chicago, Baltimore, and Phoenix were all stepping-stones on his road to glory. A glory that of late seemed harder to define than actually attain. Phoenix would be his last opportunity to achieve something beyond the norm. A place where he could elevate himself beyond the mechanical tedium of healing the sick. Where he could discard the degrading moniker of 'employee' and become a high-profile leader, maybe a politician, best-selling author or overpaid speaker. Being a physician was no longer enough. Doctors weren't worshipped like they once were. It was time he achieved the notoriety he knew he deserved. All he needed was the opportunity, a suitable catalyst, a flashpoint. Until then, Phoenix offered a plethora of exceptional golf facilities and zero possibility of snow-shovel ownership.

Of the many unpleasantries associated with his profession, the unavoidable postings to Emergency were the worst. Despite his general revulsion for people, Rory MacMann remained confident in his ability to mimic enough sincerity to endure typical medical interactions. He could tolerate the sick and needy as long as his situational control remained absolute. However, introduce the frenzied turmoil of an emergency room, and all bets were off. Unbridled commotion would raise his temperament to a boil, overflowing in a simmering cesspool of derogatory opinions. He loathed the arrival of a new patient, flanked by their immediate family, co-workers, and top ten Facebook friends, insisting on priority attention. The previous day's posting had supplied the additional irritation of a meandering group of hospital employees, feigning purpose, eager for a peek at the incoming 'deity'. Word had travelled fast among the hospital staff, beginning, as usual, with Shirley Figgis in Admitting. Her seasoned curiosity quick to pique at the news of an incoming 'cartoon' – hospital humour for a 'looney tune'.

John Doe had arrived in a conscious state, with vital signs weak from dehydration and lack of food. The paramedic was quick to point out the considerable bruising and lacerations of the torso as if the patient had fallen down a mountain several times. He added that the hiker who'd found the body reported no ID or documents of any sort. The patient spoke with an American accent, in other words, no discernible accent at all, and reserved his comments during the ambulance trip to, 'pleased to meet you, I'm God'. According to the hiker's statement, the old man was found holding a small Nike shoulder bag in a death grip. The bag was near empty, more sand than valuables, an empty water bottle smelling of gin, a few meaningless golf gadgets, and a small sack of desert rocks with an estimated value of diddly-squat. Despite the mystery, the man was not without style, sporting an Italian designer suit and Fendi shoes. Improper, to say the least, for unexplored Arizona.

"It's no joke," snapped Frank, "this is spiralling out of our control. We should transfer John Doe to St. Luke's immediately. Wash our hands of the whole godforsaken thing. For Christ's sake, we can't even get an ambulance up to the emergency entrance without some news crew blocking it with their trucks."

MacMann paused for a moment and stared at the floor, an idea percolating like coffee. "What's wrong with a little PR," he purred. "We've certainly had our share of bad press lately. Those same goddamn reporters hounded us day and night over your predecessor's salacious indiscretions. They waited outside for us every day, remember? They even showed up at my house, Frank. But now the tables have turned. They need us, need access for their story du jour. They need to see God, Frank. And if we handle it correctly, we could use this to restore the hospital's reputation and maybe even," MacMann paused, glanced around, then whispered, "personally benefit along the way."

As if clipped by a passing semi-truck loaded with stunning revelations, Frank recoiled. "Personally benefit?" He edged forward in the cafeteria chair.

MacMann expanded on his idea, visibly formulating a plan as he spoke. "Think about it; why should we confirm or deny anything? Simply blocking access to Doe, coupled with a few well-placed no comments, would build this stupid little story into a nationwide phenomenon. We could upgrade our image by holding press conferences and interviews. And you might become very famous," MacMann leaned further over the table, "very much in demand, Mr. *Chief* Administrator. No more *acting* for you…"

"Admitting a cartoon doesn't translate to a promotion, Rory. Come on, at best, I'd be a laughing stock nationwide." Frank scratched his stubbled chin.

"Miracles, Frank, that's the key." MacMann grinned. "I could ensure the hospital retains a professional image while strategically opining on these strange events, stoking the flames of journalistic skepticism and maintaining interest and intrigue. You'll get the press you need to improve the hospital's battered image and secure your role as Chief Admin, and I'll get the front-page coverage I deserve. Everybody wins!"

"Except the poor delusional bastard in the psych ward."

"Are you kidding," snapped MacMann, "he'll be friggin' famous. When he gets his mind back, he'll be the bloody CEO who spent a week as God. This country thrives on stories like this. They'll bombard him with TV offers, book deals, even movie rights. But we'll have to act *quickly*."

"This is nuts," spat Frank. "Even if I agreed, I'd have to quarantine the patient and hire guards to ensure his privacy." He paused. "Why... quickly?"

"These cases have a nasty habit of remembering who they are in a few days. Poof, there goes the party. You'll have no trouble with ambulance access then."

MacMann's cold eyes pierced Frank's like a prison shiv. Frank wondered why the man ever became a doctor in the first place – politician, lawyer, maybe sniper, but healer of humankind? Puzzling.

"What do we..." Frank paused mid-sentence, forcefully slowing his breathing and carefully reselecting his words, "... how do we ensure there's time to make this happen?"

"You hire some building security and get Doe a private guard. I'll write some media notes and official statements, which you and I can alternately release. As for that swarm of reporters, I think I know a way to corral them. Just relax, and leave everything else to me," said MacMann, draining his coffee in one shot.

"Everything else, what's everything else?" Frank snapped. "If Doe regains his memory or sanity, or whatever, we've got to let him go. There's no medical reason to keep him here beyond a couple of days to strengthen and hydrate. Need I remind you, you report to me, doctor, not the other way around." Frank lowered his eyes to the table. "So, this is not a request, OK?"

"When he's physically and mentally capable of leaving under his own power, I'll personally sign the discharge papers," MacMann replied softly as a grin formed.

"Very well," said Frank sliding back in his metal chair. "Where do we start?"

"Leave that to me," said MacMann, standing up and collecting his saliva-soaked papers. "All we need are a few more miracles, and we're off to the races."

"What?" Frank bolted to his feet.

"Jesus, relax," MacMann strode toward the double doors of the doctor's lounge and pushed them apart with the confidence of Moses, "miracles are my department." With that, he disappeared down the dimly lit hall, white doctor's gown floating majestically behind him.

THREE

Friday, November 13, 6:35 p.m.,
Toronto. Earl's Townhouse

Stepping from his Taurus with the finesse of an Inuit native, Earl's dress shoes sank several inches into new powder, making a Captain Crunch noise, *sans* milk. Drawing a deep frosty breath that whistled slightly like a poorly played F# on a plastic recorder, he slammed the car door out of necessity, not anger. Immediately, a sharp blast of wind assaulted him. Flustered, Earl attempted to palm-comb his hair back into something stylish, only to have a second gust instantly rework the do into something asymmetrical and European.

The front door to Earl's townhouse yielded with a squeak, and the hallway lights blinked like a nervous gambler. Dropping his gloves and hat on top of the heating grate, he back-kicked the door without a glance. Skating to the living room, he searched the usual hideouts for the TV remote, hoping to find additional information about the phony God who'd stolen his weekend.

As the TV burst to life, Earl scrambled to turn down the volume, inexplicably preset to stun, then rapidly clicked around the channels. Eventually, he found *First Edition*, just in time to hear the host announce, "In tonight's last segment, the story you've been waiting for – God Almighty. Right after these words from Playtex."

Only mildly interested in the Playtex commercial, Earl stepped into the kitchen. A quick scan of the refrigerator confirmed that it was, in fact, devoid of food but reasonably stocked with alcohol. Grabbing an American beer and Polish pickle, he moved back into the living room, shedding his coat along the way and vaulting over the chair arm.

"Deranged or divine?" the television host questioned in an authoritative voice. "Examples of phonies and mentally unbalanced faux creators are plentiful in our world, a world deeply yearning for signs or messages from the great beyond. So why is this one considered different? Why the sudden interest in *this* particular

11

man, found unconscious in the barren Arizona desert? Miracles!" the talking head snapped at his own query. "Yes, true, proven, medically certified miracles." He nodded at the viewers convincingly. "In the brief time since his arrival at the Phoenix General Hospital, three miracles have occurred, including the Lazarus-like healing of a woman near death."

"Crock of shit," Earl yelled, already angered by the pretty-boy anchor.

"Tonight, we'd planned to air an interview with the man claiming to be God. However, circumstances have changed. At this time, Chief of Medical Services, Dr. Rory MacMann, is refusing to allow reporters and camera crews into the room where God is said to reside." A screen appeared above the left shoulder of the anchor, displaying a photograph of a pale man in his mid-fifties, sporting a stethoscope and a huge Hollywood grin. "A growing number of reporters have been camped out, waiting for access to God. However, Dr. MacMann has announced the cancellation of all interviews previously granted due to the overwhelming demand from media outlets, independent press, government agencies, and the Catholic Church. He's confirmed that a member of the Church *will* be permitted to see God, after which only one member of the press will be granted an audience. That member will act as a liaison to the media at large. The doctor believes this will relieve the overcrowding and accessibility concerns faced by the hospital."

Earl grunted in annoyance. *So much for getting a look at this phony*, he thought.

The news anchor continued: "The member of the press will be chosen by way of random media lottery and have strict conditions applied to them. Since the Hospital's Ethics Committee forbids the selling of visitation rights, they cannot receive payment for access to or information from the patient. At this time, Dr. MacMann has received over nine hundred applications from news organizations around the world, each hoping to get the scoop on this miraculous story."

Earl watched the screen behind the announcer's head as it changed from the doctor's picture to a stock photo of the hospital, then file footage of the Pope waving at a gaggle of nuns.

"In addition to reporters, the faithful have arrived in droves. We now go live to our on-the-scene reporter, Mary-Lynn Wu, for an update on the pandemonium surrounding the Phoenix General."

Earl sat transfixed as the scene transitioned to a circus-like atmosphere on the lawn of a large hospital.

"Thank you, Eric. Yes, it's certainly a sight here in Phoenix. Hundreds of people are standing, sitting and lying around the grounds of the hospital. Worshippers and protestors mingle with the sick and injured. Placards welcoming the saviour, intermix with *End is Nigh* signs and anti-religious slogans." The camera panned around the grounds, eventually settling on an impromptu food stand selling Godburgers.

As the camera returned to Wu, she leaned in towards a physically challenged pilgrim. "Excuse me, Ma'am, you've recently arrived here from another hospital in search of healing, is that correct?" A middle-aged, heavyset woman with screaming red hair looked up from a wheelchair. "Yes, I knew it was a sign when I heard he was here, a second chance for me, a chance to walk again. He does that ya know. He makes the crippled walk again."

Wu knelt down in front of the wheelchair for effect, her tight skirt riding dangerously high on the hip. She thrust the microphone towards the woman in a stabbing motion as if shining a flashlight up inside an elephant. "Please tell us your name and your condition?"

The wheelchair-bound woman placed her hands around the microphone in a casual Karaoke manner and leaned forward. "Esther Spitzberg, of the Cincinnati Spitzbergs. I'm here for my bunions."

Due to bad timing on Mrs. Spitzberg's part, Earl's beer exited his mouth like a misting machine at Disneyland.

"Bunions," Wu asked with a skeptical smirk.

"Yes."

"The feet bunions?"

"Yes, the feet bunions. You think it's funny? They hurt like shit…" was all Earl heard before the scene went from blurry to confused.

Instantly, and with Blair Witch precision, the cameraman scurried after the frazzled reporter. She fled up the grassy knoll, spiked heels sinking in the soil, far from the fading profanities of Mrs. Spitzberg, from Cincinnati.

The cameraman stayed glued on the pretty reporter as Wu improvised. "We're now going to move inside the hospital to await a briefing. Until then, we'll send it back to you, Eric." She stared at the camera for an unspoken five-count, then said, "And we're out." She raised her head to the blue sky and shouted, "Jesus tap-dancing Christ! Why do I always get nut jobs? Seriously? Bunions? Look at this fucking place. It's like Starbucks sponsored a leper convention."

"Ummm, thanks, Mary-Lynn." Eric the anchor's voice crackled nervously in her earpiece. "And apologies to our viewers for the profanities due to the time delay in our satellite feed from Phoenix. We'll be right back after these words from Crest brand mouthwash."

Earl chuckled. He felt a little sorry for the reporter, mostly because she was cute. Still, he couldn't help but take a little shameful joy the death spiral of improvisational live reporting, accelerated to light speed by the laws of Murphy.

With *First Edition* wrapping up, Earl shut off the television. He needed a moment to process the recent news of his pending migration from Ontario to Arizona. In the dark, he could feel his anxiety rising, well beyond the ever-present five-pound bag of gut angst representing his normal state of mind. A state capable of producing existential fear even in the middle of a grand-mal orgasm. But, luckily, since his divorce, those were few and far between.

FOUR

The Story of Nog: Part 1
Friday, November 13, 12,042 BC, 11:18 p.m.

Fridays were of little importance circa 12,000 BC. The concept of a five-day workweek was even more unfathomable, much less the notion of a weekend. A weekend, meaning the workweek was over and one could relax, was a strikingly stupid and dangerous concept. Anyone trying to unwind for forty-eight hours would likely encounter one of several grisly deaths, the slowest of which being starvation.

It was a typical Friday night, alive with ancient sounds, amplified by the calm thin air that evenings always bring. Ubiquitous calls of the hunter and the hunted. The game had begun. A game that scared the living shit out of Nog, squatting in the corner of his cave, back against the wall, chewing on a giant bug he'd found earlier in the day. Outside, millions of stars and galaxies raced above in the darkness as if starved for attention. But Nog knew nothing had actually changed from the daytime. Everything remained the same – a lush valley, choked with trees, split by a meandering river and surrounded by cliff walls, dotted black with cave entrances. Night-time simply added a nocturnal radiance, an ebony backdrop for the evil moon-waltz across the sky. A sky itself in full motion, non-stationary, non-regular, sweeping toward an unknown horizon. All of this was very bad.

Nog, typical of most prehistoric homo sapiens, was a massive fan of monotony and stability. He preferred his world to be highly predictive, cast in concrete and anchored deep in the ground. Any break in the norm created uncertainty and undependability. Therefore, should instability arise, he kept a wooden club and a sharpened rock-tipped spear by his side. Trustworthy companions should matters escalate into happenings of the clusterfuck variety.

Nog was a passionate cave painter by profession and a deep thinker – a prehistoric renaissance man with no time for mundane activities. Little escaped his attention without prompting a thought or two, unlike the other human-like

15

inhabitants who shuffled about in a daze, possessing no discernible philosophy to explain their existence. Not Nog. He pondered everything, and not just in simplistic terms such as *why am I cold*, or *I wonder what makes that growling sound*, or *didn't I used to have five fingers on this hand?* No, his brain ventured much further, questioning the whys and what-ifs of each situation while dissecting each cause and effect.

A statuesque five feet in height, Nog possessed thick forearms and muscular legs, completely covered with thick matted hair inhabited by several species of insects. His long black locks, contrasted by a greying beard, were common in elderly males beyond their thirtieth year. Three decades of sticking his bulbous nose into the open for signs of impending death had resulted in a deep-brown complexion. Although dirt played an undeniable role in the finished product. His teeth, well, his teeth were not in the best condition, especially the ones he kept in a little bag attached to his loincloth. But the teeth he kept in his mouth were more than sufficient to rip and grind small furry dinners, though fruit remained his preferred choice as it rarely required a struggle. Nog's eyes were a deep, piercing black. Once again, this was due primarily to dirt and charcoal soot, but when scrutinized, a mischievous stare and devilish squint lurked just below the surface. A long crescent-shaped scar moved down from beneath his hairline and curved over his right eye – a permanent reminder to track animals smaller than oneself, preferably toothless, with massive bonus points for being pre-dead.

In this era, one could not expect to reach the rank of senior citizen without applying considerable attention to their surroundings. Nog, not the lean, strong hunter type, discovered that observation was his greatest survival skill, and he applied it well. For future reference, he compiled a mental list of scary things capable of triggering bouts of spear swinging and urination. Consistently high on his list were the unseen animals of the night. Further down the list came the daytime animals, their blatant visibility removing much of Nog's anxiety (especially when they turned out to be squirrels, birds or just dead). His list also included people – physically similar hominids living in the nearby village adjacent to the river. These creatures made Nog's shitlist not because they were particularly dangerous, mainly because they were irritating. That's why, long ago, he'd chosen to stay clear of their encampment, opting for an antisocial life, alone in his cool, dark cave.

Although the shitlist had been continuously updated over decades, Nog's perennial chart-topper had never changed – thunder. The explosive clatter of thunder shook his cave without mercy, necessitating the invention of a protective maneuver he deployed in the deepest corner of his home. He called it an ass-ball, and so far, it had kept him safe on those nights when angry thunder gods stomped about the heavens.

Tonight, like most nights, Nog would sleep on the sand, club and spear beside him. He'd dream of a world without thunder gods, evil moons or anything in the pointy-teeth category of his shitlist.

FIVE

Saturday, November 14, an ungodly hour.
Toronto, Earl's Townhouse

"Christ, what planet is this?" Earl mumbled, his face buried in his pillow, ensuring minimal oxygen supply. "Why do I hear Bananarama?"

After a pause, he thought, *how do I know this is Bananarama?*

"It's 5:09 a.m. on this frigid Saturday morning, and that's Bananarama folks with 'Venus'. The traffic's coming right up, but first, let's go to Angie for a look at today's weather."

"Aw, come on!" said Earl, as his focus landed on the luggage sitting at the end of the bed. He tried but failed to control his breathing.

*

The cab ride to Pearson Airport was uneventful. After checking in, Earl picked up the waiting courier package containing his press credentials and proceeded to completely forget about the camera he was told to procure. Entering the cattle-herder at U. S. customs, he kept a tight grip on his wallet and passport should a thief attempt to steal his identity and buy nuclear arms via Earl's Rainy Dayz Savings Account.

The flight was on time and boarded as usual – muckity-mucks first, then plebs like Earl with seats at the back. And Earl's seat could not have possibly been further back. He claimed the two armrests, a universal right of centre seat ownership, and watched as the passenger in the aisle seat began untying his shoes. The guy in the window seat was already asleep, his window shade down and snoring like a woolly mammoth.

With five and a half hours of flying time in front of him, Earl could feel his shoulders rising. Needing a distraction, he unfolded a newspaper he'd brought along, a competitive rag he preferred over his own employers. The front page was choked with headlines. The world remained in shock over the unexpected reelection of George W. Bush – a man many suggested was the dumbest president America ever had or would have.

Other headlines spoke of the tumultuous year so far – stories about the Catholic faithful, still in mourning over the April death of John Paul II, or the inexplicable marriage of Prince Charles to Camilla Parker Bowles. While the summer had been a chaotic combination of Asian bird flu, Hurricane Katrina, and the Olympics.

Turning to page three, Earl scanned a short article about the launch of an internet company called YouTube. Snickering, he considered how many suckers would buy into this particular craze. The sudden introduction of video sites, online news and social media irritated Earl. Slowly shaking his head, he rubbed the newsprint between his thumb and forefinger. *Nothing,* he mulled, *will ever replace the good old newspaper.*

The lead article in the Business section stated that texting, another fad according to Earl, had become more popular than email and suggested it would replace phone calls within a year. Earl smirked and rolled his eyes, trying to imagine a cohesive thought constructed from 140 characters. He shook his head and moved on.

Eager to read the movie review for the newly released *Brokeback Mountain,* Earl flipped to the paper's Entertainment section. He loved a good shoot-em-up Western and planned to catch the movie in Phoenix during his considerable downtime. However, merely three words into the review, the overhead light flickered and died. Earl reached up and tapped the plastic light cover with his middle finger, which, surprisingly, did not fix the problem. Slumping back in his seat, he pinched the part of his nose between his eyes and slowly exhaled. ETA, five hours and twenty minutes.

SIX

Saturday, November 14, 9:30 a.m.
Phoenix General Hospital, Media Room
(formerly the Phoenix General's Chapel
and interdenominational Prayer Room)

Organized chaos. Microphones perched atop gleaming metal poles, their wires strewn about the floor like a snake pit. Crushed humanity, obnoxious and aggressive, pushing for better vantage points or audio sweet spots. Cell phones ringing, buzzing, or playing chirpy ring-tones. Conversations, loud and ubiquitous, merging into one giant glob of human jackhammering.

Such are the makings of a press conference.

Phoenix General's hospital chapel had been hastily converted into a media room, the pulpit doubling as a podium. Ironically, all religious symbology had been removed or hidden. In their place, lights, reflectors, and a six-foot cardboard sign denoting the hospital's name along with an overlay of Dr. MacMann's face, partially blocking a photograph of the facility. The room came conveniently equipped with a direct exit door to the visitor's parking area, enabling controlled entry to the building. This configuration allowed thirty or so lucky journalists from big-name outlets to stand, packed together, in the little room. However, the remaining reporters were left to occupy the parking area or the hallway to main reception, where speakers had been set up so they could listen to the proceedings.

A little man took to the pulpit and spoke at half-volume to no one in particular. "Hello. My name is Robert Hand, and I'm the assistant to the Acting Chief Administrator, Mr. Frank Shedmore, who is currently unavailable. However, our Chief of Medical Services is here, and he will provide you with an update on our famous guest's condition. Ladies and gentlemen, Dr. Rory MacMann."

Silence.

MacMann crossed the mini stage in slow motion, his white hospital coat fully buttoned. A stethoscope hung from one shoulder, partially obscuring the nametag over his breast pocket, the visible part read, *D Mann*. Arriving at the podium, the doctor arched over the crowd like a crane. Six-foot-five and slender, his beak-like nose and bushy blond eyebrows highlighted his clean-shaven face, pale as a West Island Terrier. MacMann gripped the edges of the pulpit like a snake oil salesman and surveyed the tightly packed audience as they jostled for position. Clearing his throat, he pulled his shoulders as far back as possible without popping a coat button, then waited for camera clicks that never materialized. "My name, as you already know, is Dr. Rory MacMann. M, small a, small c, large M, small a, n and n." He grinned. "I've been personally treating Mr. John Doe since his arrival. His current condition is listed as stable but guarded."

MacMann flipped a page on his clipboard. "A desert hiker discovered Mr. Doe just north of Scottsdale, not far from the Cave Creek Regional Park. An EMT was dispatched to the scene where a sheriff's deputy had a brief conversation with the patient and concluded that this was not a matter for the police. John Doe was in a state of severe dehydration, confusion, and extreme fatigue. After admission, he was treated for dehydration; however, so far, he has not regained his strength, and there may be internal damage to his organs. We're running tests as we speak. As for his identity, Mr. Doe insists that his real name is, and I quote, 'unpronounceable by humans'. As such, the moniker John Doe has been assigned until the patient is more forthcoming."

"Can you tell us if you witnessed the miracles?" a tall blond reporter from the *Chicago Tribune* shouted from the first line of reporters.

"Excuse me?"

"Did you witness them? The miracles?"

"I'm sorry," MacMann glanced at the ceiling to intentionally inject a little drama. "I can't comment on these claims. My responsibility is to treat Mr. Doe for physical ailments."

"So, you admit there were miracles, healings?" a man wearing a bow tie piped in.

"No, I'm simply stating that God's actions, sorry, I mean, Mr. Doe's actions are those of a private citizen. It's not my place to comment or opine."

MacMann smirked at his calculated slip of the tongue.

"When will we have access to God?" a reporter from the back of the room yelled.

"Access to Mr. Doe will be allowed for only one member of the press, and that member is being chosen by lottery as we speak." MacMann glared across the sea of faces, a pre-emptive challenge, should anyone question his credibility.

"This is highly irregular, doctor. So, you alone will decide who gets this story first-hand. Meanwhile, the rest of us get second-hand pot-luck" a tall Hispanic TV reporter said, pointing at MacMann for effect.

"Not at all. In fact, we have every right to conclude that no visitors are permitted whatsoever. We are simply reducing the frenzy *you* people created, decreasing it to something manageable while protecting Mr. Doe's privacy. Let's face it, ladies and gentlemen, if Mr. Doe is who he claims to be, then the *random* selection of a journalist will hardly be random at all, correct?" A Cheshire cat grin spread across his face.

"Excuse me, but could we go back to the miracles? Were there any medical examinations to substantiate the healings?" inquired Mary-Lynn Wu, glancing into her camera.

"All individuals who've claimed an *experience* with John Doe have been released and are in fine health." MacMann chose his words with extreme care.

"So, they were healed?" Wu added, over-shouting a short, arrogant woman from Fox News.

MacMann smiled at the attractive reporter. "Let me assure you, anything God-like occurring in this hospital is the result of highly-trained physicians like myself and our exceptional facilities. We do not believe in voodoo, goblins, or pixies, Miss…?"

"Wu – *First Edition.*"

"Miss Wu First Edition. Patients who have made claims of a healing most certainly owe their thanks to this hospital and my staff. Any further questions regarding divine intervention will not be substantiated or validated by any member of my team."

"So, you're saying you don't know?" Mary-Lynn Wu smiled.

MacMann retaliated. "I'm saying…"

"Doctor, when will we have the name of the press representative, and how many press conferences will you hold each day? And will there be video and audio feed from God's room?" shouted the Fox News reporter.

Distracted, MacMann regrouped. "The name of the press representative will be announced later today. We'll try to conduct at least one daily press conference. I will co-host these events along with the media representative."

MacMann glanced at his notes to see if he'd missed anything. "Ah, yes. The press representative will conduct all interviews with Mr. Doe in private. Your questions are to be submitted in writing only."

"Doctor," said Wu, "for someone who claims to have no interest in the situation beyond medical care, you seem to be building quite a bureaucracy."

*

In room R2112, Nurse Abigail Morallas was changing John Doe's intravenous drip when he opened his eyes and smiled at her.

"Hi, Abby."

Startled, the nurse juggled a clear plastic bag in her right hand before regaining control. "Whoa, Jesus, you scared me."

"Oh. Oh no. You've got me confused with someone else," laughed Doe. "I'm not Jesus, although I met a Jesus once. Mexican fella. Super nice guy."

"I'm so sorry," said Abigail. "I didn't mean to offend." Her face reddened around the cheeks.

"Not at all, don't say another word. Totally my fault for startling you."

"Are you comfortable, Mr. Doe? Do you need anything?"

"I'm a bit light-headed, but the newspaper would be nice. I like to keep up on the goings on. It's been a while. I've been out of touch, you know. The last time I was here was... many years ago."

Abigail flicked her long hair back and straightened her uniform with the palms of her hands. "I'm honoured to meet you, sir. Are you who they say you are?"

"I'm not sure of this *they* of whom you speak, but if *they* say I'm God, then they're not far off." Doe giggled like a five-year-old.

Abigail gasped and dropped to one knee, bowing her head and letting both her arms hang by her side.

"Ummm, what are you doing?" Doe peeked over the rail of the hospital bed.

Without moving, she replied, "Humbling myself."

"Oh, why's that?" asked Doe.

"Because I am not worthy of attending you."

"How come?" he laughed. "Flunk the nursing exam?"

"Scuse me?"

"Oh, are you one of those trainee nurse-type candy-striper gals?" He leaned on one elbow. "Great tan, by the way. I see you work out."

"I, err, well, I..."

"Oh, please stand up, Abby. You've been reading that Old Testament stuff again. I'm not like that, my dear. I certainly don't require worship. That would be quite the ego trip, huh? Create a universe, evolve some monkeys, then insist they worship me? Diva-Ville, am I right?" Doe sang with jazz hands up high.

Abby's face narrowed in surprise and confusion as if she'd bit into a lemon while expecting tofu. "You sure don't sound like *Him*, and I doubt *He* would be checking me out."

"Oh, I'm sorry. I need to catch up to this year's level of political correctness. I meant no harm. I am, after all, just a man, and you're very lovely. Like an angel."

"Look, Mr. Doe, or Mr. God, or Mr. whoever you are, I wasn't placed on this earth for your visual satisfaction. I worked hard to get where I am, and I did it without any support from anyone, just me and Jesus."

"Ahh, yes, the Mexican guy."

"No, not the stupid Mexican guy. The Son of God. The saviour of mankind. The King of Kings and Lord of Lords – Jesus Christ!"

"Oh," said Doe in full recollection, nodding rapidly. "Him. Yes, I remember him, but that was long before your time, Abby. As I recall, he was a fantastic carpenter. Very talented. He made me a rocking chair! Imagine. Two thousand years ago – a rocking chair. I mean, how cool is that?"

"You're loco, mister. Nuts."

"Oh, good idea, some nuts with the newspaper would be great. Full of protein, you know? The nuts, that is, not the newspaper. Now, what was that you were saying about why you were placed on this earth?"

Abby stared at Doe in irreverent silence, trying to formulate an answer that wouldn't betray her professional training yet accurately convey her belief that he was a looney.

"Mr. Doe, my purpose in life is of none of your concern. At this moment, I'm here to ensure patient treatment is successful, and we can return you to society as a healthy citizen. My job ends with your physical rehabilitation. As far as your mental condition, that's between you and your therapist. Now, I need to take these read-outs to my station and enter them in your charts. Press the red button if you need anything. Your clothes and personal belongings are in the right-hand cabinet." She pointed.

"Wonderful." Doe clapped his hands in front of his chest. "Such service. And my little bag with the shiny stones?"

Abby rolled her eyes. "We should have thrown it out. Disgusting germ-infested thing. But yes, it's there."

A grin erupted on Doe's face. "Excellent."

"Now, if you don't mind, sir, I'll be on my way." Her emphasis on 'sir' denoted a significant loss of respect.

"Abby?"

The nurse stopped and half turned. "What?" she said flustered, trying hard not to look into Doe's eyes.

"Your mother and father are very proud of you." Doe smiled and leaned back, closing his eyes.

Abby's bottom lip quivered. "You know nothing of my parents," she whispered with a tremble. "How dare you…"

"True, I never met them directly, but all they ever wanted was a daughter who'd make a difference in people's lives. And that's what you've done, my dear. You're strong yet caring, meek yet determined, but most of all, you honour them every day by remembering them."

Bursting into tears, Abby threw her hands to her mouth and ran out the door, smashing arms with the security guard and knocking a milkshake out of his hand.

SEVEN

Rory MacMann swaggered into Doe's room like a tourist. He scanned the table-tops and floor space, looking for the various machines he had ordered.

"Hello again, Mr. Doe."

Doe struggled to prop himself up on his left elbow, rubbing his sunburned neck with a manicured right hand. Something inside him creaked a little, then popped like a champagne cork. "Hey," he grunted, a hint of a smile creeping to his weathered face, another crack among dozens.

"How do you feel?" MacMann quizzed, briefly glancing up from his clipboard.

"Shitty," replied Doe, closing his eyes and rolling his head in slow rotation, "like a one-legged goat on an alligator farm."

Ignoring the wisecrack, MacMann began scanning the clipboard notes. "Mr. Doe, the results of your blood work are concerning. It seems the prolonged dehydration has damaged your liver and kidneys. The extent of the damage will be better understood once we do an ultrasound. At this point, it looks extensive, but I won't be able to offer you a full prognosis until we perform additional tests. Do you understand?"

Doe stared straight ahead, consumed every word but offered no emotion. "I'm dying!" he said matter-of-factly, then proceeded to pick at something lodged in his nose.

"That's perhaps a bit extreme, but I won't mince words; you appear to have severe internal damage from whatever happened to you. It's possible the damage is irreversible," MacMann spoke with arid emotion, drumming his fingers on the back of the clipboard. "Are you sure there's nothing you can tell us about what happened in the desert? Maybe an accident, something that might explain the additional organ damage?"

"Sorry, Doc," said the old man before a dry and raspy cough took hold, a retched sound like someone was sanding a hedgehog.

"Alright, well, for now, you rest. I'll keep you on a heavy IV drip while you keep that plastic bottle between your legs. We'll keep an eye on that cough and think positive thoughts," said MacMann while robotically searching his pockets for a small pager that was vibrating wildly.

"No problem. Positivity's my middle name."

"Yes, about your name," MacMann added hesitantly. "Any luck coming up with a few clues beyond Positivity?" MacMann's eyes widened as he read the new message on his electronic pager.

"It's not important," Doe replied, "you see, my name..."

MacMann nodded his head and briskly exited the room, with no parting pleasantries.

*

Most hospital hallways were designed for speeds under two miles per hour, glossy wax surfaces and tight corners capable of producing disastrous human train wrecks. MacMann, knowing a sprint might prove fatal, opted for a speed-walk, heel-toe, heel-toe, down the hall toward the elevators, away from Doe's room. Looking ahead, he spied Frank pushing through the slowly parting silver doors and making a nervous but cautiously controlled beeline in his direction.

The two met with a glancing blow mid-hall. "He just arrived," whined Frank. "Black gown, purple sash, the whole deal. He told the nurse at the front desk that he's a Monsignor or some such bullshit. He says he's got an appointment to see God. Right now!"

"What?" MacMann roared. "No one told me of a firm appointment with the Church. We're not ready. What dobber set this up? Is the press aware? Shit, did they see him come in?"

"That's just it, it's weird, no entourage, no assistant, the Monsignor just walked in and said he had an appointment. I thought you'd arranged it?"

"Jumpin' Jesus, no, I'm not ready. I need more time with Doe. Damn it! Where's his royal highness now?"

"My office," said Frank, looking down at the ground. "I got him a coffee and said I'd be right back. He seems impatient to meet Mr. Doe. Which, you know, is understandable."

MacMann grabbed Frank's arm, and the pair sprinted back down the hallway toward the elevator, sliding into the wall in unison. MacMann smacked the call button with the back of his clipboard, then nervously watched as the numbers descended. As the doors squealed open, MacMann pushed through first, dragging Frank behind while completely ignoring the presence of a young orderly and a white-haired woman in a wheelchair. Using two fingers, the doctor simultaneously hit the floor and 'close' buttons.

The orderly interjected, "Umm, could we just…?"

"No," said MacMann sharply, staring down the young man, then turning to face the closing steel doors. The elevator had an unpleasant stench of disinfectant and death, with a tiny hint of vanilla pudding.

"Rory, let's just tell the priest that Doe's not mentally stable. No miracles, just a big misunderstanding. Tell him to be on his way," Frank whispered while giving MacMann an upward sideways glance.

"Just shut up for a second, lemme think." MacMann drummed his fingers against his chin. "We need the presence of the Church to maintain the story, but they need to remain skeptical. There's no chance they'll ever endorse this, but their ambiguity keeps the press here."

"I think he's just wonderful," a frail female voice wafted from the wheelchair. "You know, I'd planned on visiting him today for my healing. He's given out so many."

"What?" MacMann snapped as he spun around, fixing his gaze three feet below on the wrinkled but grinning Mrs. Herrington. "What are you talking about?"

"Why, God, of course, young man. Isn't he wonderful, coming back like this for us folks here in Phoenix?"

"Jesus!" MacMann exhaled some spittle while turning his back to the elderly woman. "Frank, we need to leave doubt. Skepticism's the key."

"I've got a bad feeling," said Frank.

"Oh, I'm sure he'll fix it for you too, young man. He can fix anything." Mrs. Herrington tugged at the hem of Frank's suit jacket.

"Frank, it'll be fine; leave it to me. I won't lie, but I won't be specific either. Besides, if Doe's chart is correct, we'll only have to do this another week or so."

"How so?" Frank whispered.

"Can't see Doe lasting longer than that," MacMann said dispassionately.

"What?" Frank accentuated his challenge with a Cirque du Soleil maneuver to the side, forcing Rory into the corner of the elevator.

"What are you planning? What the hell are you going to do?" Frank was frantic, his words and spittle rebounding off the metal walls like hail through a moonroof.

Cornered, MacMann raised the clipboard, creating a personal dry space between him and the serial spitter. "Keep your bloody voice down. I'm not doing anything," he whispered through his teeth. "Doe's sicker than we first thought, that's all."

Frank peered carefully into MacMann's eyes, looking for sincerity. It was like gazing into binary black holes of emotion. "You did nothing to cause this?"

"For Christ sake, Frank, are you serious?" MacMann hissed while rolling his eyes.

Shedmore thought about this as he watched the digital read-out above the doors. Four floors worth of thinking. The delay irritated MacMann, who pushed his way out from the corner and returned to a ready position, facing the crack in the metal doors.

"Rory, I trust you, I think, but just yesterday, you said he'd be fine?"

MacMann sighed, keeping his eyes on the doors, anticipating an imminent escape while mumbling under his breath. "The test results were bad. I'm amazed he's not in more pain. Looks like kidney failure and liver damage, plus internal bleeding on the lower right side near the kidney. Not good at all."

"Probably where the spear got him," said Mrs. Herrington.

MacMann lifted his eyes to the tiled ceiling. "Dear God, what?"

"Where the Romans pierced his side at the crucifixion. After the Jews sold him out," she continued. "Stigmata, the wounds of Christ. Poor man. Must hurt like a bitch."

"Is there any chance you're Mel Gibson's mother?" MacMann's face was crimson. "Surely to cow tits, if he was God, he'd heal himself, right? It's people like you that drive me friggin…" The elevator doors slid open, and it was Frank's turn to grab an arm, pulling Rory away from Mrs. Herrington and the marginally insulted orderly, Steven Cohen.

"Jesus, Rory, hold it together."

"Stupid cow!" MacMann moved at a sideways gait, peering over his shoulder at the closing elevator doors. "Probably a bloody Catholic."

The duo's trip to the administration office to meet the Monsignor was a short one, expedited by several ill-advised jogs on the straightaways. Luckily, the halls were empty, but for the occasional garbled announcement crackling from the ceiling speakers.

Pushing open the glass doors, Shedmore led the way. He maneuvered around the pointy coffee table and re-greeted his robed guest, who'd risen to meet Frank without smile or emotion.

"Pleased to meet you, your... eminence?" said MacMann. The doctor stretched out his hand to greet the stocky emissary while maintaining a defensive yet respectful distance across the glass table. As he sized up the priest, MacMann keenly observed the heavy use of purple sashes, quite different from the clergy he'd seen as a child.

"It's my pleasure, Doctor. I'm Monsignor Anthony Del-Monte, of the Los Angeles diocese, special investigations department." With that, he bowed ever so slightly, never breaking eye contact with MacMann.

"My goodness, that's impressive," said MacMann, unimpressed. "Can I get you a beverage, maybe a Fanta?"

"Umm, no, no, thank you. Can we just proceed to the matter at hand: my access to the one claiming divinity?"

Del-Monte smirked most unpleasantly. His yellow teeth stood out against his weathered skin.

MacMann repositioned himself. "Yes, of course. However, your Excellency, nobody informed us of your visit, and I'm afraid Mr. Doe is unfit to receive visitors at the moment. You see..."

"Doctor, I'm a busy man. I don't have time for pleasantries or your earthly excuses. There's no reason why I can't be in the company of either our Lord or an imposter, immediately and without delay. I'll be the ultimate judge if my visit is futile. Awake or asleep, available or indisposed, willing or unwilling, I'll have an immediate audience with this man, and I assure you, I'll know instantly if our saviour's returned."

"OK, look, so here's the deal," MacMann said, dropping all air of protocol. "There's only one true way, one true path to this patient, and that's bloody-well through me. And I don't care if you're the Pope's personal fucking fluffer. I'll decide when access is granted when and if my patient is capable of handling visitors. And I'm telling you right here and now, he's currently unfit, so why don't you take your funny hat and your Prince and the Revolution costume and walk it back to your parish. Go pound back some Blood O' Christ with an altar boy and cool your Catholic ass for a spell? We'll let you know."

Without shock or hesitation, Del-Monte stepped around the glass table and into MacMann's personal space, looking up at the doctor with a coldness beyond Inuit measurement standards.

"Oh shit," Frank mumbled under his breath, stepping back.

"Dr. Muck... Man," Del-Monte miraculously said between tightly pursed lips. "Your options seem clear to me, but in case you're confused, let me spell them out in no uncertain terms. If I leave without seeing John Doe, I'll go outside and immediately call for a press conference. I'll explain that I've been denied access to God by a domineering, egotistical, power-hungry hack of a sub-par medical fuck-nut. Conversely…," he paused for a breath, sucking in all the air in the room, "you plaster a smile on your pale soulless face and walk me to the patient's room right fucking now." Del-Monte paused again for effect and another rasping lung-full of holy air. "I eagerly await your decision, mister, ah, so sorry, Doctor MacMann."

MacMann's artificial smile slid from his face like snow on a tin roof. He paused before clearing his throat and straightening his white gown. "Right this way, your eminence."

E I G H T

The landing was bumpy. After half a dozen hours cramped into 36E, Earl's limp body had melded to every seam, bend and valley of the seat. The high-suction toilet, located directly behind him, infused a complex mixture of locker-room odour and outhouse fumes mixed with Old Spice and rum for a tropical feel.

After a twenty-minute wait to exit the plane, Earl weaved his way through the gate stragglers and stepped on the closest moving walkway. After five steps, he abruptly halted behind a stationary couple from Vietnam, six bags planted at their feet, discussing Turkish architecture. They seemed oblivious to the fact that people were walking briskly on the other side of the moving sidewalk.

Earl, now sandwiched between the Vietnamese couple and an entire German volleyball team, cleared his throat in a subtle attempt to point out that this was, in fact, a *moving fucking walkway*. Sadly, the Asian couple didn't understand non-verbal western messaging. They continued the entire length of the walkway in a stationary debate surrounding their upcoming Phoenix itinerary, where they hoped to see mountains, cowboys and the Empire State Building.

Stepping from the walkway, Earl raced around the couple, making a point to turn his head and roll his eyes while mumbling, "Jesus Christ!" Fully vindicated, he stormed towards the escalators that descended to the baggage claim area. After a ten-minute battle at the baggage carousel, Earl, luggage in hand, sprinted for the exits. Stepping through a set of opaque sliding doors, he emerged in the outer terminal, almost colliding with a small black man in an ill-fitting blue polyester uniform. The man held a crumpled sign reading, Gray Earl. Too much of a coincidence to go unchallenged, Earl said, "Hello, I'm Earl Grey, and I'm curious, notwithstanding the spelling error and reverse syntax, if that sign might be for me?"

The little man looked over the top of the sign and surveyed Earl up and then down. "You the reporter from Canada, here about this God thing?" he asked with a condescending frown.

"Why, yes, I am," said Earl trying his best to match his greeter's level of condescension.

"Come with me," snapped the diminutive man turning toward the main exit and scampering off.

Earl, somewhat puzzled, didn't move. The *Telegraph* had rented him a car. And, to his knowledge, rental car companies didn't typically meet their customers brandishing misspelled names in crayon on the back of pizza carton lids.

After walking the entire width of the main arrivals area, the small man stopped in front of the main exit and turned around to discover he was alone. "Hey," he shouted directly through the bellies of several fat men, "you comin'?" He flicked his head like a horse shooing flies, "They told me to step on it."

Earl strolled up, stopped, and placed his shoulder bag on the ground. "Seriously, do people just automatically follow you when you meet them in public places brandishing facsimiles of their names on cardboard?"

The short man leaned over and picked up Earl's bag, then grabbed the handle of the wheelie bag and walked away.

"Whoa, whoa, whoa," fumbled Earl, "what the hell are you doing? I could have you arrested!"

The small man stopped short. "Look, Grey, I don't have time for this shit. They said to pick you up and rush you to the Phoenix General for a news conference. Stop for nothing, they said. If I get you there in 20 minutes, I get a two-hundred-dollar bonus. So, if this is your first time in civilization, no problem, please work out the culture shock during the drive. I'm not missing that bonus. So get in the limo, or I'll place you there myself."

Earl stood bemused, albeit tickled pink that someone had sent a limo for him. Part of him was wary of leaving with a stranger while snubbing a perfectly respectable car-rental agency, one that might be worried when he didn't show up. But a limo was a limo, and for fun, he tried to imagine how the short chauffeur planned on *placing* him in a car should he refuse to cooperate. *Big gun, perhaps? After all, this is Arizona. Maybe martial arts for dwarfs or a finely-honed Joe Pesci complex?* Pausing his thoughts, Earl realized the small man had gone. Panicked, he ran toward a revolving door and entered with comic book coordination. Earl waited impatiently until the mechanism slowly arrived at the next opening, then stepped into a blazing inferno, sometimes referred to as outdoor Phoenix. Sprinting across the crosswalk, he caught up with the driver, several feet from the trunk of the biggest car he'd ever seen in his life. "Sweet Jesus!" said Earl.

"Yep, hotter than hell here in civilization," the chauffeur quipped, wiping his forehead with the back of his black cap.

"No, no," Earl corrected. "This car, it's enormous." He watched the chauffeur remotely pop the trunk and toss Earl's bag and suitcase inside with reckless abandon. Several minutes passed before they hit bottom. *It's conceivable*, thought Earl, *that the trunk is deeper than the chauffeur is tall. How does he intend to retrieve my bags when we arrive? With a pole and a hook? Maybe I'm supposed to hold him by his heels while he bobs for luggage?*

Earl stepped around to the rear door of the limo and scooted inside. His body swished across a slick leather sofa, coming to a halt midway in front of a circular minibar with crystal glasses and an unknown brand of scotch. And the angels sang.

The chauffeur closed the door with excessive force, leaving Earl alone to survey his new surroundings. Two leather couches, one at the rear and one along the driver's side, bracketed a round glass coffee table. At the front, below the driver's partition, was a smaller leather loveseat; to the left, a minibar and new-fangled flatscreen TV. *Hope they don't expect me to pay for this when they discover I'm not the Gray Earl they're looking for*, thought Earl.

Realizing he could be uncovered as a fraud at any second, he lunged at the single malt scotch. He turned the amber bottle around in his hands like a golden idol, then ran his fingers around the red wax near the cap, reading the label for clues of origin. The brand was a word he couldn't pronounce, but a valuable clue, printed at the bottom of the label, said *30 years*. A tiny girlish squeal slipped from his lips as he plucked a glass from a silver clip fastened to the bar. Opening the ice bucket, to his surprise, he discovered ice. Dropping two perfectly square cubes in the heavy crystal glass, he simultaneously poured a double as the limo pulled away from the curb. To his left were buttons, many buttons, but not a label or explanation in sight. One of them must be for the TV, Earl decided.

After several minutes of lowering windows and repeatedly opening and closing the driver's privacy panel, Earl finally found the TV controls. With a click, the limo's interior was drenched in a cable news channel glow. The volume came up slowly, as did Earl's alarm and anxiety.

"… is on his way from the airport now. We'll have more details as soon as he arrives at Phoenix General, where we hope to get a word with Mr. Grey."

Earl's eyebrow lift was Vulcan-esque.

"Dottie, do we have any background on this reporter or reason why an American reporter wasn't selected for this assignment? After all, this is American soil."

Earl shot the scotch and poured a second with shaking hands.

"No clue, Dan. I guess God is multinational."

"Well, Dottie, keep us updated. Next, we'll be going to Professor John Stavorie of M. I. T. He joins us to discuss the statistical improbability of a media lottery selecting an obscure newspaper reporter from Canada, beating out over 1000 American journalists."

Dottie responded from off-camera with a meticulous blend of sarcasm and incredulity, *"I'm guessing one in a thousand, Dan?"*

"Shit!" Earl turned off the TV.

NINE

Saturday, November 14, 1:10 p.m.
Phoenix General Hospital

Three men walked briskly down the hospital hall, shoulder to shoulder, elevator doors clanging shut behind them. Frankincense and myrrh were absent, but a generous selection of bling was on display.

On one end, a tall man, his paleness accentuated by a white doctor's gown, looked nervous and agitated; his only colour, a pink glow radiating from his eye sockets – the classic albino bunny look. On the trio's other end, the man walked with a death-row gait, no posture at all, just a barely functioning skeletal system supporting slabs of disconnected meat, draped in a dishevelled suit. With every other step, a glance to his right confirmed his inquisitor's ongoing presence. God's emissary from L. A. proudly marched in the middle – a short, portly man of Mediterranean descent, sporting a slicked collar-length haircut and traditional purple zucchetto. Was one to replace this skullcap with a yellow construction helmet, all authenticity would have remained intact. On occasion, a butter-brown Gucci shoe appeared from under the robe, the source of the tap-dance clicks resonating down the hallway. Embedded in the priest's chubby brown fingers were several large rings, scratched and worn. A perfect complement to his thick, scab-covered knuckles. As he walked, he grinned; the triumphant smirk of the victorious.

"So," said Frank, clearing his throat when the sound came out a bit girlish. "How long have you been a priest?"

Del-Monte continued, pace unbroken, smile intact, without acknowledging the question.

"My mother wanted me to be a priest," Frank continued, struggling for something to counter the clickity-clack torture. "But us being Protestant made it a bit tricky."

"Jesus Christ," said MacMann rolling his eyes and spinning his head towards Frank.

Del-Monte briefly glanced at MacMann, the smug grin never leaving his face. "Sorry," said the doctor, realizing the name he'd vainly taken.

"Oh, yes, good, here we are," Frank said. He was delighted to have the non-conversation cut short as they arrived at John Doe's private room fronted by an enormous security guard. "I'll just ask Dr. MacMann to pop in first and make sure Mr. Doe is awake and decent."

As MacMann edged towards the door, the priest abruptly morphed into a running-back, splitting the guard and doctor and bursting through the door in one belligerent motion. "No more stalling," he shouted over his shoulder as he headed toward the bed. Fast on his heels came MacMann and Frank. Moments later, springing to action, the massive security guard jogged into the room. His left hand gripped a canister of pepper spray while his right held tightly to a McDonald's banana milkshake.

The three wise men caught up to Del-Monte at John Doe's bedside. The patient was alert and smiling, sitting upright with a look of expectancy on his weathered face.

Del-Monte, his grin expanding to Grinch-like proportions, placed his hands tightly around the metal railing of the bed and stared intently into John Doe's eyes. "Good day, my Lord," he said with sarcasm. MacMann and Frank looked at each other puzzled.

"Hiya," said Doe.

Instantly, Del-Monte spun around on one heel, so fast that Frank leapt back in shock, and commanded the men to leave the room. "Out! Now!"

"Scuze me?" guffed a startled MacMann, not at all clear on who the priest was addressing or what the command was intended to convey.

"Did I stutter?" asked the priest. "Get out of this room right now. I will be left alone to converse with this… man… and I will not be disturbed under any circumstance. Am I quite clear?"

"Yes," said Frank looking to MacMann, "perhaps we should give them some privacy, all things considered."

"Not a chance, Monty," MacMann said, planting his feet and crossing his arms. "Lest ye forget, this is my patient. I have jurisdiction. You have the privilege but not the right to visit him. A privilege I can revoke at any time should I feel the patient's well-being is at risk. That means I stay and observe, *capiche?*" MacMann's Scottish accent thickened as it rose in decibel.

The guard, still confused, stepped forward from the doorway and crossed his arms in solidarity, spilling a little yellow milkshake down the sleeve of his blue uniform.

Del-Monte upped the ante. "Listen, let's drop the pleasantries, shall we?"

MacMann raised an eyebrow, indicating he was not aware there'd been any pleasantries up to that point.

"This is not a road you want to embark upon, doctor," Del-Monte said, stepping one foot closer to his prey. "I can be your greatest ally or your greatest nemesis. The choice is yours. I only wish to talk with this poor man to understand who and what he is. If you're in the room, I cannot ensure his answers are genuine and unaffected by your intimidation. Your earthly plans for this man are no concern of mine, nor will I interfere with your actions or statements after this visit, that is, if I'm left alone. If you choose to stay, I'll have no choice but to leave, and my comments to the public will be short and concise. They'll guarantee your removal from this patient, along with your tenure at this hospital. In fact, by the time the Church is through with the American Medical Association, you'll never practise medicine on humans again… *capiche?*"

MacMann's head was swimming, a poor attempt at the butterfly stroke, mostly gulping water and sinking at the nether regions. Still, fighting for a just cause, if not a lost one, was his heritage, and a bloody good fight was a bloody good fight. Ever the hawk, it suddenly dawned on MacMann that the priest's aggressive demands could create the perfect bargaining chip. "If I leave you alone with him, will you agree to make no public statement for at least a week?" MacMann whispered.

Doe's face went back and forth between the sparring men.

"If he is who they say he is, then none of this matters, does it?" smirked Del-Monte. "Conversely, if he isn't who he says he is, I'll need some time to compose a suitable statement to the press, one that the Vatican can accept. Should take about a week." The priest's Grinch-esque smile returned.

MacMann looked at Frank, who simply shrugged.

"Well, I do have some rounds to make," said MacMann. "Why don't I pop back in 30 minutes?"

"Marvelous," said Del-Monte with mock sincerity. "Don't worry, I'll show myself out when I'm done. I have a car out back. No one will see me leave."

"Good." MacMann half-grinned as he backed out of the room. "Frank, shall we be on our way?"

Lost for words, Frank grabbed the guard's wet forearm and marched him toward the door, not entirely sure what had just happened.

"Your… eminence," said MacMann, bowing ever so slightly to his adversary, as the door slowly closed under its own weight, latching with a click.

Doe, smiling and propped up in bed, turned his attention to the priest, who, in turn, locked eyes on the bedridden man like a python accessing a newborn kitten.

"It's nice to meet you, Father. I didn't catch your name?" said Doe.

"Shut up," Del-Monte hissed, flushing any remnants of a smile from his face. "Stop the fucking games. It's me. I know exactly who you are. And you sure as hell know who I am."

TEN

The limousine traced the curved driveway toward a large overhang jutting from the main doors of the hospital. The sun pounded the pavement like a bully, its glare bleaching every colour, leaving a faded version of nature, utterly devoid of contrast. The sheltered arrival area shimmered like a mirage, a sanctuary for wayward travellers in search of shade and sub-solar air. Grey concrete covered every unoccupied surface, and what little grass existed was perma-brown and angry.

Earl's face pressed against the limo's tinted glass like a hobo at a liquor store, his eyes frantically scanning the sea of reporters, media equipment and police. The limo moved a foot or two at a time, then stopped, repeating the process over and over as reporters peered in the windows and camera crews focused on the black stretch testament to indulgence. The driver repeatedly honked the horn in short bursts, attempting to part the sea of humanity that had engulfed the limo like zombies at a sweetbread buffet. His right hand worked the accelerator and brake controls, allowing his feet to hover in mid-air over the floor mats.

Earl sat back and tapped his fingers on the armrest. *Well, isn't this a lovely predicament, my free vacation, rudely interrupted by an unscheduled and very public mind-fuck.*

As the limo came to a final halt, Earl swigged the remainder of his third double scotch. Returning the empty glass to the table, he placed his right hand on the chrome door handle, then froze, staring indignantly at the device.

While most people measured comfort zones in inches, Earl's lifelong struggle with social anxiety had led to his use of yards as the ideal measurement for interpersonal dialogue. Charles Grey's systematic eradication of Earl's self-confidence throughout his childhood left one-on-one conversations as the only bearable form of social interaction. Earl could handle a single person within a foot or two, making the job of interviewing people a little easier. However, add more to the mix, and his brain would begin to liquefy, curtailing his ability to focus and dropping his senses into a blender of garbled surround-sound. A thick fog would descend, smothering him like a heavy wool blanket soaked in chloroform. It wasn't until his twenties that Earl realized he needed to construct a defence mechanism for times like this, a safety net of sorts. He chose a time-honoured process utilizing copious amounts of alcohol and deep meditative breathing brought on by the copious amounts of alcohol.

Earl placed his hand on the door handle and whispered, "I can't breathe!" Lungs constricted, he stared out the limo window, aged scotch busting through the big iron gates of his brain where he stored his childhood anxieties. With no desire to exit and his mental safety gates wide open, a distant memory barged into his frontal lobe and insisted on attention.

As a young boy, on Sunday mornings, Earl would lie in bed, listening to the sounds of hurried preparation echoing throughout the house, mixed with shouts of, "Are you up and dressed yet, boy?"

Church was a chore of immeasurable sacrifice and pain. Earl spent his Saturday mornings watching cartoons, wrestling and roller derby. So it was logical that he believed Church was robbing him of similar pleasures on Sunday mornings. He hated his stupid uniform – church clothes, a polyester leisure suit from Sears that fit nicely three years ago. Now it was just a weekly reminder of his numerous awkward growth spurts, squished and highlighted for public viewing. The polyester black and grey checkers made him itch, and the extreme tightness made it impossible to sit still in a pew, much less walk with any dignity. He was sure the entire congregation could hear the squeak of his thighs rubbing together whenever he made the slightest move. Young Earl feared that a day would come when his crotch would ignite in friction-based hellfire, leaving him smouldering and naked on the church floor with four pounds of melted plastic to hide his shame.

Earl, even as a young boy, never bought into the whole God business. He just knew that, short of a sudden bout of emancipation, he was stuck with his parents' philosophy for years to come.

By far, the worst part of Sunday mornings was the procession from Church at the end of the service. Earl would shuffle, head down, polyester whisps and whistles emanating from his groin, inching toward the exit. To add insult to injury, the minister, Reverend Tickle, a man whose mere name could induce painful bouts of suppressed laughter, would crush his hand and tell him how lovely it was to see him. Reverend Tickle would squeeze his shoulders and deliver a weekly charge. And every week, Earl had the overwhelming desire to bolt and run, push through the crowd and head for the trees. But he always managed to resist the urge, returning a polite smile to the reverend. Only then could he leave, pinballing his way through the grazing sheep on the stone steps, and bolt to the getaway car.

Earl's head bobbled as the limo rocked against the weight of the crowd, reminding him of his unpleasant reality. His white knuckles gripped the chrome door handle as sweat formed on his forehead and neck. The irony was obvious. "Same clusterfuck – bigger pants," he sighed. Resigned to his fate, Earl pushed open the door and stepped into the congregation of photographers and journalists surrounding the limo.

Merely two short strides into the multitude, a lamb to the slaughter, Earl came to a complete stop. The circling wolves moved in for the kill, stabbing at him with microphones as their cameras stole his soul.

"Mr. Grey. Mr. Grey, will you be speaking to God this afternoon?" A disembodied voice pierced his ears. "Will we have an opportunity to present our questions today?"

"Mr. Grey, Danny Viscount, WNRB national public radio. Will you be recording God's voice, and will you be providing the audio files for us?"

"Sir, sir, how can you be sure all of our questions get tabled, and in what order will you ask them? Will TV networks take precedent over radio and web, or will you opt to deliver each inquiry randomly?"

Earl pushed another three hundred millimetres into the lion's den, but with no one to run a block, he quickly sank into gridlock again.

"Will you be wearing anything ceremonial or religious before entering God's room, Mr. Grey?"

"Are you a believer, Mr. Grey? Do you adhere to any particular religion, and will that religion guide your questions, or will you treat all faiths equally?"

"What?" Earl stammered, using his empty scotch glass to wedge his way between a camera and a tall man with a notepad. "Secular," he said to no one in particular, as if well prepared, having a full eight minutes to digest the fact that he was no longer on vacation.

"Danny Viscount again, Mr. Grey, will you be taking pictures of God, and, also, regarding the audio files, will they be in .AIFF format or .WAV format, and will you be posting them to a landing page or passing them out on flash drives?"

"What?" Earl put his knee into something soft, and it yelped, providing him considerable satisfaction.

"Emily Dawson, ABC News Phoenix. Mr. Grey, can you tell us what you know so far? Are you intimidated by this meeting?"

"Intimidated?" said Earl with surprise. "Umm, I…"

"Mr. Earl, JPEG or GIF picture formats, and can we have the full spelling of your name?"

"What do you know so far?"

Earl was making slow progress through the throng of journalists, although he could still feel the heat from the limo's engine, now a full yard behind him.

"Well, after my extensive briefing, I understand there's a man in there who says he's God," murmured Earl. "Apparently, I'm going to chat with him and determine his theistic credibility. I'll let you all know the result after the water boarding."

"Do you know God's nationality? Is he black?"

Earl chuckled, "I wasn't aware *black* was a nationality. However, I believe I'll be able to determine said blackness during my first meeting, if not, then by the second encounter for sure."

"Mr. Grey, what was that about waterboarding?"

"Mr. Grey, Ann Gerrie WNBC. Will you be able to determine if God is a virgin?"

With a bewildered glance over his shoulder, Earl pushed on, stepping on feet for better traction. "Of course," he said with a sheepish grin. "I'll conduct a virginity test as soon as I can, plus a blood test for STDs."

"Is the CIA involved, and are they employing torture methods?"

"I can't comment," replied Earl in his best authoritative voice, "about the clandestine aspects of this investigation. However, I can assure you that Interpol is *not* engaged at this time. The situation is currently being handled as an American concern until we establish proof of divinity, upon which time, we'll get the universal police involved."

"Sir, sir!"

A mad scramble was developing as microphones beat down cameras for better access. "So you're not denying the CIA is involved, and you're withholding comment regarding interrogation techniques?"

Earl abruptly turned around. "Look, I just got here, OK? I can't answer your questions, primarily because they're stupid and vacuous, and I may have had too much to drink." He nodded and turned back, scraping his shoulders on a few camera lenses and pushing all the harder to get through.

"Mr. Grey, have you always had a drinking problem?"

Earl rolled his eyes as his arm stretched for the main door. It swung open before he could grab the handle, leaving him staring down at the limo driver. "Where the hell have you been?"

"Waiting for you to finish your love fest with the paparazzi," said the diminutive driver.

"Well, aren't you supposed to be delivering me to your boss or something – not abandoning me to the jackals?"

"Dude, I tried. I was right there with you until I got elbowed in the face. So, I said, screw it and walked over here to wait."

"Oh, well, you make that sound easy. I'm guessing there's less traffic down there."

"Funny!"

The driver grabbed Earl's sleeve with considerable strength for a man of his stature, pulling him inside the hospital. Instantly, two uniformed guards stepped forward and closed the door, then stood, arms crossed, staring through safety glass at the throng of reporters still slinging questions.

ELEVEN

Saturday, November 14, 2 p.m.
Phoenix General Hospital

Earl's Blackberry buzzed. He ignored it. The man standing in front of him looked like a weasel, albeit taller, less hairy and not as attractive.

"Mr. Grey, my name's Frank Shedmore. I'm the acting Hospital Administrator. A pleasure to meet you, please follow me?"

Frank shook Earl's hand. It was damp.

"Yes, that's nice…" Earl began, then switched gears. "Listen, there's been a mistake. I need to quit this thing or abdicate or something? This is all very confusing. I didn't sign up for anything or apply." He tried to match pace with Frank, double skipping a few times to keep up.

Frank made no effort to slow. "Mr. Grey…"

"Earl's fine."

"Earl, this is a great honour for you. You were selected from over 1,000 entries in our media lottery. It would be most awkward and embarrassing for you to say no at this point. Besides…" Frank continued undaunted down the hall, "this will be great for your career and exposure. Imagine the number of people hanging on your every word, your every expression. You'll be in every newspaper, on every news program 24/7."

"Sounds ghastly."

"Earl, Earl, you're missing the big picture. Think of the opportunities you'll have. Why you could even write a book. Wouldn't that be nice?"

Earl wasn't sure if the man was belittling him or just a sarcastic dickwad. "Seriously, I'm not even American. I've no face for television. And truth be known, I only wanted a little time in the sun to medicate my complexion and toss back some cheap American beer."

"We'll get you some beer."

After a short elevator ride, the pair reached a set of glass doors and a sign touting the Hospital Administration Wing. "You're perfect for this role, Earl. Just

45

follow our lead, and you'll have a great time here. We won't require much at all, my friend." Opening one of the big glass doors, he ushered Earl inside.

"Earl, this is Dr. Rory MacMann," Frank continued, gesturing with an extended arm toward a gowned man standing in the middle of the foyer, sporting a Hannibal Lector-esque grin. "Rory, this is our Canadian friend… Earl."

"Good day, eh?" MacMann said, stressing his version of a Canadian accent. "How's it going, eh?"

Jesus, thought Earl, *here we go*. He wiped his hands on his trousers and reached over the coffee table, shaking the doctor's hand. "Hi," he said with no expression.

"Now, Earl," MacMann began, "here's the situation. As liaison to our patient John Doe, you will be granted a daily visit, which will last for one hour, perhaps a little longer if the patient is strong enough. After which, you'll meet with us, then proceed to the press room where you'll deliver a daily update and answer any questions about John Doe. It's not a big deal. After all, I'll be handling all the difficult medical questions. All good?"

"All bad," said Earl. "You're missing the bit where I'd rather perform my own prostate exam with a coat hanger than speak to the media."

MacMann glanced at Frank and then back to Earl. "Mr. Grey, we don't want to do this either, but when your name was picked, we couldn't think of a better, more suitable candidate. You've no baggage, nothing to prove, and no network producers to serve. You can say whatever you wish, with no need to make friends, maintain affiliations or protect some Hollywood persona."

"You mean I'm a nobody, I don't matter, and you can get me to say what you want, correct?"

"Now you're getting it, a win-win situation. You'll probably make a few bucks when you get back to Canuckville while we restore the image of this fine hospital."

"Listen," Earl stiffened. "You got the wrong sock-puppet, OK? Find another patsy to play PR pooner. You seriously expect me to toe the line at the expense of some poor bastard in a hospital bed?" Earl turned towards the door.

"Your editor's very excited, Mr. Grey," Frank said pleasantly.

Earl stopped short of the big glass door and turned back. "What?"

"Your editor, Mr. Thompson, correct? He's extremely excited about the opportunity. After all, he's the one who submitted your name to the pool in the first place."

Earl thought of his Blackberry phone, unchecked since landing. "Um, he called you?"

"Oh no, we called him the moment we drew your name," said Frank. "What a pleasant man, so passionate. He was delighted to hear of your selection and feels it will significantly boost your paper's international readership back home."

Earl pulled out his smartphone and glanced at the screen. He noted the 23 messages in his inbox, all from his editor. "Well, I'll be damned," he said, eyes wide like his fingers had just pushed through the bathroom tissue. "Didn't you guys just think of everything?" He re-holstered the smartphone like a six-shooter.

"We did, and we will," said Frank.

"If you don't mind, I need to make a phone call."

"Go right ahead, Mr. Grey. Use our office phone if you wish. Dial nine to get out." Frank gestured towards the credenza.

"If it's all the same to you, I'll use my cell out in the hall."

"Of course, but I suggest you take those stairs up to the roof. You won't get a signal in here. It's blocked in the halls and rooms because it interferes with medical devices."

"Those stairs over there?" Earl pointed.

"Yep," Frank said. "The roof door is open. Some doctors have a quiet cigarette up there."

"Makes perfect sense," lied Earl, pushing open one of the glass doors with his shoulder.

Reaching the white metal stairs, Earl climbed carefully. The steps had been designed to inflict maximum pain should anyone slip and fall – raised jagged studs protruding from each tread to facilitate traction or cheese grating. Reaching the door, which was ajar, he could already feel the heat streaming through the crack. "Well, this was a bad friggin' idea," he mumbled to himself.

And it was, in fact, a really bad friggin' idea. On the best of days, the roof was twenty degrees hotter than ground level due to the exceptional ability of black tar to suck up heat rays.

Earl looked around the roof, flat as a trucker's ass, not a chair in sight. Hardly the ideal spot for a heart-to-heart with an irate editor. Wading out on the sticky surface, he pondered why anyone would voluntarily live in this heat. *Satan himself would surely head home for the cooler climes.*

*

When Earl was young, his parents would take him to a local beach on humid July days to sit by the water and let the breeze do what their antique air conditioner could not. Their plans usually coincided with those of a thousand other city dwellers, who invariably snagged all the best spots – primo sandy ones for sunbathing, shady nooks for relaxing. Young Earl was forced to sit on an itchy wool blanket near the parking lot in the open air, directly under the scorching sun. Making matters worse, his mother insisted on frequently applying a full-body sunscreen, slathering every square inch of his body despite his objections.

The family picnic spot was a half-mile from the water, indeed closer to the highway ramp, so swimming required the stamina of a hiker coupled with a massive dose of public shaming. The sand, slightly under the ignition point of glass, provided Earl with the excuse to run like hell, like a snowman sprinting through the set of a Coppertone commercial. To complete the humiliation, his mother made him wear the only pair of swim shorts he owned. Like his Church suit, the shorts were far too small, crushing his genitals and providing that tapered androgynous look, alluring to neither girl nor guy. Many a beachgoer returned home with stories of the topless transvestite geisha, bobbing and weaving her way through hordes of sunbathers.

Earl would stand in the water for hours, hoping the tanning oil would dissipate without killing all the fish. His only pleasant memory of these torturous outings was the sensation of his broiled feet as they slowly sank into the ooze at the bottom of the lake.

*

Earl's feet sank into the tar and stone mixture on the roof. It was not a pleasant sensation.

"That's what I've been trying to tell you, Ed; send someone else." The sweat ran between Earl's Blackberry and his cheek, dripping from his jaw and onto his arm. He could barely move, each step requiring extreme effort just to escape the stringy globs pulling on his soles like Jupiter's gravity.

"Listen, Grey, there's no second chance here. If I pull you out, they'll just pick another journalist, and you can bet your hind-tit they won't be from Toronto."

"Try to see it my way, Ed. They want me on TV and radio and quoted for national newspapers. The anxiety's already blocking my colon," he said as he paced. "Besides, this is a total scam. God? Sitting in a hospital bed in Phoenix? Ridiculous! Think of my reputation."

"You don't have a reputation, Earl."

"OK, think of your reputation, or the *Telegraph's*."

"Look, Earl, this is great exposure for us. It's a shitty time to be in the newspaper business. So consider this a lifeline, Earl. A literal gift from God. Everyone gains here, along with our stock. And need I remind you, you hold a few options yourself. Hypothetically, if you do your fucking job, you could cash out and disappear."

"I'm not feeling very hypothetical, Ed."

"Grey, I'm ordering you, begging you. It's an hour a day, followed by a short press conference. I'm not asking you to cure cancer. You're a reporter. This is what you do for a living. Just get in there and do it."

"I don't understand why this is happening to me," Earl sighed rhetorically.

"Why is the ocean salty? Why is the sky blue?"

Earl pondered for a second and shifted his feet to avoid permanent adhesion to the roof. "Yeah, why is the ocean salty?"

"What?"

"Why is the ocean salty?" Earl repeated.

"It's just a figure of speech."

"I mean, if rivers are freshwater and they run into the oceans, why would oceans be salty?"

"Earl, you might want to go inside now and get some water."

"There's no humongous salt lick at the bottom of the ocean, and rain isn't salty, so where does all this magical salt come from?"

At that point, Earl figured he must have lost cell signal as all was quiet. Holstering the phone, Earl headed back to the sketchy stairs and sanctuary from the oppressive heat and perhaps a fire extinguisher.

TWELVE

Moments later...

Frank and MacMann, sporting impish grins, waited as Earl stepped from the metal stairs. "Shall we get started, Mr. Grey?" said MacMann, gesturing toward the elevators.

Earl took a deep breath. "Let's get it over with."

"Excellent, very wise choice," said Frank.

"Can I get a drink?" Earl asked dejectedly.

"Frank, get this man a drink while I take him downstairs to the media room. Earl, we've scheduled your first conference for the top of the hour, so we've only got a few minutes to prepare your statement and approach. The world is waiting to hear from you." MacMann led Earl towards the elevator by the elbow.

"That's in fifteen minutes," exclaimed Earl. "So, you knew I'd agree to this little scheme, huh, Doc?"

"Since we're friends now, call me Rory."

"I'm not your friend." Frank was scurrying behind MacMann like Frankenstein's Igor. "What would you like to drink, Earl?"

"Scotch, rocks, and damn you if she's under eighteen."

"Gotcha." The administrator stopped, pondered for a moment, then scurried down a side hall.

"He's a useful idiot, Earl," mumbled MacMann as he pressed the elevator call button.

Earl stared at the doctor, trying to discern his species.

As the elevator doors closed, MacMann abruptly turned to Earl. "So, here's the deal, lad. Just field a few questions from the press today, then meet with John Doe. I doubt he'll have any helpful answers, but we can whip up something after if necessary, OK?"

"So why see Doe at all?" asked Earl. "Why do you need me?"

"Because too many nurses and doctors have access. It would be too obvious if you didn't visit him. Some prick would spill the beans, then the conspiracy theories would explode. Just spend an hour in his room, then see me before the daily conference so we can craft a plausible story for the press. Simple, even a Canadian can do it."

Earl stared in disbelief. "So, we're gonna make up the answers?"

"Earl, the man's not in his right mind right now. When he recovers, he'll read about everything he said, but he won't remember. And he'll be too busy counting money. Someone's gonna pay him a ton for this story."

"It's all about money, isn't it?" said Earl.

"Now," continued MacMann, ignoring the comment, "after I introduce you, here's what you have to do. One: tell the press who you are and the name of your newspaper. Two: explain that you'll try your best to represent everyone equally and fairly. Three: say something nice about me. Four: ask them to submit their questions in writing. Simple."

"Say something nice about you? I don't like you!"

The smile returned to MacMann's face. "Aye, and I don't like you either, wee man, but that's what you're going to do, right?"

A mischievous grin slipped from Earl's lips as the clarity of the moment impacted him. It seemed likely that the whole God thing would be over and done in a few days once the man in the hospital bed recovered his health and sanity. However, in the meantime, there might be some fun to be had squashing MacMann's plans for media exposure. Plus a few jollies at the expense of the A-level reporters, suddenly under his thumb. In fact, other than the dreadful thought of being on TV, there was really no downside to any of it. He could protect the poor, unstable bastard who thinks he's God while gaining a little public awareness, maybe just enough to move him from lifestyle reporting back to the front section of the *Telegraph*. All at the same time.

"Earl?" MacMann's face pruned.

"Look," said Earl. "If I do this, it's got to be my way, my style. I won't be some trumped-up fictitious character you invent during a three-minute ride in the slowest elevator in the galaxy. Besides, I think you need me more than I need you. Or would you prefer I walk to the microphone and blow the lid off this whole charade?"

The doctor looked up at the elevator's digital read-out, then quickly glanced at his watch. "Earl," MacMann switched to a softer tone. "We both need each other, right? Imagine! You could become so successful that you could retire down here, enjoy the rest of your life doing sweet dick all. Hey, we could even golf together."

Earl stiffened. "Doctor! I don't like you. And you *do* need me more than I need you. So, it's your call. Once you introduce me, there's no turning back. It's my show. Right now, your choice is to either present me or pick another candidate and let me go. Of course, I'll leave in full knowledge of your intentions – but that's your risk to take, isn't it?"

The elevator doors opened slowly, and the two riders stared directly into the face of an out-of-breath Frank Shedmore. The hospital administrator stood grinning with a glass full of ice and a bottle of MacMann's finest scotch from his office cabinet.

"How the hell did you do that?" said MacMann.

"Delightful," said Earl. "See, Doc, he's not an idiot, after all."

"Um, thank you?" said a bemused Frank, handing the glass to Earl and pulling the cork out with a squeak. "Say when."

Earl watched in silence as the glass filled, then, with almost no room left, said, "When."

MacMann closed his eyes as if a stomach cramp had reached up and grabbed his throat. "Alright, fine. It's your show, but I'm still the director."

"Sounds good to me, Mr. Demille. Oh, and we should start looking into tee times pretty soon."

MacMann stared as Earl took a huge grinning gulp of the golden liquid. "Ohhh, that's good stuff, boys."

"Glad you like it," said MacMann insincerely. "Follow me, let's get you introduced to the press, then you can pop up and meet Doe."

*

In the makeshift press room, murmurs echoed with a ubiquitous drone, pierced by random shouts of frustration or command. "Try the feed now. Give me a level. Hold it up higher. I'm live in two." Anticipation was palatable and bitter.

At 2:59 p.m., a side door opened. A small procession consisting of Frank, MacMann and Earl marched into the room and onto the stage, gingerly stepping between wires and microphone-stands. Frank walked directly to the podium and cleared his throat, sending spittle into the front row. "Good afternoon, everyone," he said with no response. "Today, Dr. MacMann will provide an update on the condition of our patient, Mr. Doe. Following that, I'll introduce your media liaison who, as you know, was chosen by lottery, a fair and supervised lottery," he added for no discernible reason. "And he'll take your preliminary questions at that time. Dr. MacMann?"

MacMann floated majestically across the stage to the podium.

"Good afternoon, everyone. In case anyone doesn't have a copy of my bio, I've left copies at the door. Please feel free to take one to include in your articles," he said, beaming. "Now, regarding Mr. Doe. He is currently resting comfortably, his condition listed as serious but stable. He continues to receive intravenous fluids and is being monitored twenty-four hours a day by the best healthcare team in America." MacMann turned his head and gave Frank a nod. "In addition, I have assigned myself as the attending physician to ensure the patient and you, the press, are directly connected. Our primary concern is his liver. Although rare, the dehydration may have caused complications, which could be life-threatening, but we're doing everything we can to address this. Mr. Doe's comfortable and alert, and he's quite the personality, I might add."

Thirty hands shot up in the air as the room morphed into a New York deli at lunchtime.

"Doctor, is he dying?"

"Have there been more miracles?"

"Does he show any desire to heal himself?"

"Does he have a Bible, a Torah?"

"Can you release his medical charts?"

"What are the names of the staff members attending him?"

"Will there be surgery?"

MacMann remained stoic. "Now, it's my pleasure to introduce our media liaison. He joins us from the prestigious *Toronto Telegraph* newspaper, where he's a well-known contributor, beloved by millions of, um, Torontites. Ladies and gentlemen, Mr. Earl Grey." MacMann took one step to the side of the podium, then posed with a grin, anticipating a slew of camera clicks, which did not come.

"Hi," said Earl, donning his church smile. "My name is, in fact, Earl Grey. Yes, like the tea. Um, and I'm Canadian, and I am quite honoured to be chosen for this nice, umm, thing."

MacMann rolled his eyes.

"Rest assured, I will represent your inquiries to Mr. Doe with the highest degree of professionalism and zeal. To do so, I'm gonna need you to write down your questions in English, good English, so I can accurately relay them to Mr. Doe. I'll convey as many as I can within our allotted time and deliver the responses back to you at our next meeting."

"I see there's some sort of bucket over there," Earl continued, pointing to the door, "which I presume is for your inquiries. So, please write them out as I asked. Penmanship counts. I'll get back to you later with an update. Okey-doke?"

Not a single discernible phrase could be heard through the ensuing roar.

Earl beamed. "Very good, so if there's nothing else?"

As the crowd surged forward, MacMann grabbed Earl by the arm and marched him offstage toward the side door with Frank Shedmore in tow. Arriving at the exit, one Mary-Lynn Wu and her cameraman, James, faced the three-man exodus head-on, blocking the door, microphone thrust forward like a dagger. "Mr. Grey, what will be your first words to God?"

"Come on, Earl," said MacMann pulling on his sleeve while wedging past the reporter.

Earl stopped inches away from Wu's face and froze, his mind blocking the enveloping maelstrom. "Umm, hi, Miss?"

"Mary-Lynn Wu," replied the reporter.

"Miss Wu. Mary-Lynn, such a nice Catholic name." He blushed to a hundred camera flashes. "Well, I think I'll introduce myself to Mr. Doe first, although I suspect he knows I'm coming, and ask him how he's feeling. I mean, after all, no matter who he is, he's sick and needs our help, right?"

Mary-Lynn's expression softened. She slowly moved the microphone back to her mouth. "That's so true, thank you, Mr. Grey."

"Call me Earl," he replied in a whisper. "I saw you on TV, but you're so beautiful in person... oh, shit... I didn't mean... not that you're ugly on TV." *Jesus, Earl, could you possibly shut your mouth?* Screamed the exasperated voice in his head. He stared at the pretty reporter for what seemed like a millennium. Stars ignited and died, galaxies flew apart as civilizations sprouted from algae then perished in political ideology. Earl's universe soared from middle age to senility, then shattered under the aggressive grip of a man's hand, dragging him through a door with extreme prejudice and releasing him into a tiny office.

MacMann slammed the door against the onslaught of microphoned jackals, then turned his back to the door, leaning against it for effect. "Jesus Christ!"

Frank sat on a desk and stared at the floor. "We're in way over our heads. They're gonna eat us alive."

"Nonsense, they're just reporters," MacMann said, pacing. "No worse than lawyers!"

Earl stared out a small window into the parking lot. "Wow, she's gorgeous."

"What?" barked MacMann.

"The reporter, at the door – stunning. And smart too. Who'd have thunk to block the door where we entered, ultimately getting the best exit interview."

"Would you concentrate, Grey? This requires more finesse than I thought. We can't be dodging questions like that. That was a bloody shit show."

Earl didn't hear a word.

The outer door opened, and two nervous men squeezed in, the first clutching a large file folder. "Doctor, I've got the lab reports for Mr. Doe. You need to look at them right away."

MacMann flung out his arm, demanding the file with a finger snap. After flipping through the first two pages, he closed the chart and tossed it on the desk beside Frank. "Shit!"

"What?" inquired Frank, gingerly picking up the file.

"And just what the hell do you want?" MacMann shouted at the other man, meekly frozen near the escape door.

"Umm, I was asked to tell you that you've got important visitors upstairs." The young man made no eye contact with anything living.

"I've no time for visitors right now," said MacMann before pausing. "For Christ's sake, who is it?"

"Haa," snickered the young man, the irony of the question dawning on him. "It's the delegation from the Catholic Church, here to see Mr. Doe."

MacMann froze, one eyebrow moving skyward as the blood drained from his face.

THIRTEEN

The Story of Nog: Part II

Saturday, November 14, 12,042 BC, 8:15 a.m. Nog's Cave

A rainstorm awakened Nog. He lay still, listening to the rumblings of a distant God and the more urgent rumblings of his empty stomach. The air inside his cave was thick and dank. Echoes of dripping water mingled with gusting wind, peaking and receding like the waves.

Rising to all fours like a post-kegger freshman, he considered which of his breakfast options required the least amount of effort. Just north of the cave, toward the mountains, a serene patch of grassland stretched for miles. A tasty variety of wild berry grew there, and competition was sparse. The morning's plan took shape: exit the cave, circle around the village, hike the escarpment, and feast on the low-hanging fruit.

Spear in hand, Nog poked his head from the cave. Once certain that all was clear, he scampered up to the rocky high ground, darting between predetermined hiding spots along the way. Arriving at the meadow, he slowed, gingerly creeping through the long grass and up a slight hill toward the yellow trees and their forbidden green fruit that, if consumed, robbed one of a restful night's sleep in lieu of squatting in the nearby aloe bushes.

*

By 11 a.m., the high sun had chased the evil shadow people away and was busy baking the sand to a subtle shade of untouchable. Relief had arrived in the form of a pleasant breeze blowing in from the west, although the swirling dust made long-range scanning difficult.

Nog sat comfortably on a flat-topped rock adjacent to a large bush laden with red succulent fruit. As he feasted on the soft berries, red juice stained his fingers and dripped from his beard, pooling beside the image of a two-foot-long arrow carved in the dirt. *This is new*, thought Nog. *It looks like a tiny spear.*

The spear appeared to be pointing at something, and Nog assumed this probably meant it was in-flight, sailing toward an unseen quarry. However, the pointy bit led away from the bushes and toward the foothills of the nearby mountains. Not that pointing into the bush made much sense either since berries rarely needed spearing before consumption. *That's a pretty long throw*, thought Nog, and then he ate another handful of berries, staring in confusion at the odd pointless carving.

*

An hour passed without incident until Nog heard the sound of several village women coming closer, up the hill, towards the berry picking area. Not wanting to engage in any way, Nog clambered to his feet again and moved into the long grass where he could hide. Thirty steps in, he stopped at a clearing where the elders had piled rocks and rubble years ago in an attempt to relocate the centre of the village to a more upscale and panoramic neighbourhood. This impressive undertaking ended quickly after a big cat ate them. Now it stood as a sombre monument to urban sprawl.

As Nog approached the rocks, he spied a second mystery. A series of small stones, pebbles and sand, arranged in the shape of a spear. *Well*, thought Nog, *isn't this a coincidence. Just over there sits a spear-shaped hole in the ground where dirt should be, and now I find a spear made from sand and hundreds of tiny rocks. But there's no way to pick it up, much less throw it since it would instantly fall to pieces.* He sat down beside it, thinking. *Apparently, whoever made this, just left it here, likely out of massive embarrassment.*

Nog listened carefully as the village women collected berries. Although close, they couldn't see him, and since he was downwind, it was unlikely they could smell him, so he sat motionless, staring at the ground and the shitty rock spear.

Time passed, and the big yellow sky-ball moved a bit to the left. After a brief discussion, the ladies elected to move to another site that offered different coloured berries, agreeing that a nice fruit salad would be perfect for the evening meal.

As Nog pushed himself to his feet, a thought occurred. The virtual spear and the rock spear were pointing in the same direction. With nothing better to do, he moved into the grasses towards the mountains.

Mere minutes passed when Nog stumbled on yet another spear, ten feet long and made out of tall grass, bound together in bundles forming the shape of spear tip and shaft. Nog laughed. *This one is just lying here, not even complete. No sharp point and only dried grass for a shaft.* Then a terrible thought ambushed him. *Who builds ten-foot grassy spears? Ten-foot people, that's who.*

Nog dropped to his knees. *I'm in trouble*, he thought. *Just what kind of monster builds a ten-foot spear? Granted, pointless shitty spears, but still, gigantic.*

Nog mustered enough courage to continue toward the mountains, passing two more feeble attempts at spear manufacturing, each one pointing to the same destination. Finally, emerging at the base of the grey and purple foothills, Nog scanned the flatlands for further signs of half-assed spear construction. Seeing none, he sighed, disappointed that his little adventure had ended with no explanation for the spear mysteries.

"*Doooo cha!*" shouted an old man standing directly behind Nog, scaring the living snot out of him.

*

The old man chuckled, holding out his arms, palms up – a gesture of pacification and benevolent welcome.

Nog, still rattled, neck-hair erect, straightened a little and forced a closed mouth smile since open-mouthed smiles were often mistaken for the baring of one's fangs. He followed up the smile with his own palms-up gesture of peace.

All was well. A moment passed, and a breeze slipped between the two men, whistling over the tips of the long grasses and whipping them into a vast circle. Nog used the moment to inspect the stranger who appeared quite old. Long grey hair and scraggy white beard set against a leathery face, heavily bronzed from considerable time in the sun. He was shorter than Nog by several inches and appeared to be missing several toes. He wore a passé light-skinned hide, draped around his midsection like a layered miniskirt, forgoing the more seasonal loincloth. Not nearly as hairy as Nog, the old man also lacked any semblance of dirt, grime or dust. He was, in fact, clean. Most curious was the little pouch hanging from a leather strap around the stranger's belt. The bag was encrusted with beautiful polished stones that sparkled with many colours.

The old man broke the silence, tapping his chest many times and saying, "Numa, Numa, Numa." Then he pointed at Nog, inquiring, "Sarraa char jarr?"

Nog nodded in understanding. "Noo-gah," he shouted, then patted his chest repeatedly.

Numa smiled with delight, purposefully blinked twice, and motioned with his right arm for Nog to follow. "Noo-gah, Noo-gah," he sang, moving out of the grasses and up a gradual slope of gravel and weeds like a geriatric gazelle, avoiding the sharper rocks by memory. Using his spear as a walking stick, Nog followed the old man, partly out of curiosity but mostly because he had no other pressing appointments.

Wild grasses of purple and bronze dotted the lower slopes, quickly transitioning to scattered rocks and a stony shale mixture as they climbed. Jagged blades of razor-sharp rock protruded at menacing angles, necessitating a head-down, highly focused gait for fear of slicing a toe or ankle. Numa selected a serpentine route, attesting to his familiarity with the climb. He sometimes slowed to catch his breath or boost himself onto boulders or a ledge, then waited as Nog caught up. The process pained Nog, not so much from the climb itself, but mostly the continuous exposure to Numa's geriatric junk.

Arriving at a plateau, mid way up the cliff, Numa stopped, smiling as the higher winds blew through him, drying his sweat. As Nog caught up, the stranger turned and pointed to a grouping of two large boulders bracketing a fifteen-foot natural monolith. Over the decades, wind and rain had sculpted the natural tower into a somewhat embarrassing salute to manhood. Near the base of the two round boulders, a cave entrance was visible, well-hidden at first glance, with small rocks and dry bushes surrounding the flat approach. "Glaaaaaa," Numa said with a grin.

The entrance was too small to walk upright, requiring both men to go quadruped on the entry, once again exposing Nog to Numa's dangling participles. *I've had about enough of this*, thought Nog, squinting in disgust.

Once inside, he stopped abruptly, still on all fours, his face pruning as if someone had just poured warm marmalade down the crack of his ass. "*Da Maagaaa?*"

The cave was like nothing Nog had ever seen. Sunlight streamed through small openings in the rock ceiling, creating spotlights that flickered and roamed as if controlled by an unseen stagehand. The beams spotlighted artwork on the cave walls, framing paintings of animals or people, seemingly animated, popping into the room as if they were alive. Ghostly figures in full motion – hunting, fishing, even fighting.

I'll be damned, thought Nog. *Numa's an artist. Like me.*

FOURTEEN

The most recognizable trait of the Catholic Church is its commitment to ceremony. Pomp and ceremony. This has remained constant throughout the ages. Nothing half-assed is permitted. Any hint of humility is met with the sternest of punishment and rebuke. If there's an absence of opulent bling or entourage, then it's not the Catholic Church. It's not even a respectable street gang, although there are similarities.

In the central foyer of the hospital's administration wing, a flock of black-robed elderly white men and one stern-looking nun stood in a tight circle around a payphone. Some with arms crossed, while others flipped through their Bibles for guidance or inspiration. In the middle, on the payphone, a dark-skinned portly priest spoke slowly and loudly in Italian. It was evident that he was having difficulty hearing the replies.

Into the group strode MacMann, clipboard in hand, devilish grin on his face. "Good afternoon everyone, my name is Dr. Rory MacMann, and how can I be of service today?"

The tallest priest stepped forward, apparently chosen to address MacMann at the same altitude. "Good day, doctor, I'm Monsignor Matthew Bellecourt, and we have an appointment with you, remember?"

"I remember seeing a request for a meeting, but one of your gang was already here yesterday, and he spoke with my patient. So, you're a little late, I'm afraid."

"Late?" The priest turned to his co-workers. "What is he talking about? Who is this man he speaks of?"

The posse murmured briefly amongst themselves, then the nun replied on everyone's behalf. "Nobody from our diocese, Monsignor."

The Monsignor turned back to MacMann. "What are you up to, Doctor? What's the meaning of this?"

MacMann was puzzled. "Well, maybe you lost track of a priest, or he was a freelancer. Nonetheless, I assure you, I introduced him to John Doe, and they had a friendly private chat. So, if you don't mind, I've got rounds to perform," MacMann said, taking a step toward his office.

"What was his name?" asked Bellecourt, ignoring the doctor's desire to leave.

"If I recall correctly, it was Monsignor Del-Monte of the Los Angeles detachment, or God-squad, or whatever you call it."

"Diocese," growled Bellecourt, frowning. "And I know of no one by that name."

"Catholic CIA?" MacMann pushed through them towards the administration office.

"Look, doctor, can we simply proceed from here and visit with the patient? We need to begin our investigation?"

MacMann partially opened the large glass door, ensuring nobody could follow him inside. "I'll see what I can do. In the meantime, grab a seat in the waiting area and try not to frighten the children." He shut the door behind him and jogged into a private office, closing and locking the door.

*

"So, this is the room, Earl," said Frank, pointing toward Doe's guarded door. "Now, Robbie, this man, Mr. Grey, has full access to the patient, so make sure he's not impeded or disturbed in any way. Got it?"

"Impeded?" inquired Robbie, scrunching up his face.

"No one goes in, OK?"

"Ohhhh, gotcha."

"Eleven bucks an hour," Frank mumbled.

"Nice to meet you, Robbie," said Earl holding out his hand.

The guard looked at Frank for approval, then shook Earl's hand vigorously, a dopey grin crossing his unshaven face.

"May I go in now?" asked Earl.

"Oh sure. Mr. Shedmore said you could go in at any time, not im-ped-ded-ed," said Robbie with pride, pushing the door open and holding it for the two men.

Earl stepped into the bright yet chilly room and stopped hard. A familiar smell rushed his nasal passage and slammed into his brain. His mind got straight to work, digging and wrestling for the associated memory. Many floral offerings lined the nearby counter, but they were not the culprit. This smell was from long ago. Childlike and innocent, triggering overwhelming feelings of serenity. With the emotion came a clear, benevolent message that said, *you are safe here.* And with the message came physical weight, like a blanket, engulfing Earl, wrapping him tight. An immediate sense of belonging and the inexplicable feeling that everything was exactly the way it should be.

"Earl!" exclaimed John Doe, breaking the moment. "At last, you're here." Doe stretched out a hand from the bed even though Earl was ten feet away, forcing him to perform a piddle-skip over to the bed. Grabbing Doe's hand, Earl shook it gently for fear of breaking the poor man.

"It's an honour to meet you, Mr...?"

"Anything's fine," chirped Doe. "My real name would sprain your cheek muscles."

"I see, right, well, my name's Earl Grey, but I see you already know that," said Earl, a pending scotch hangover dawning on his cranial horizon. "I'll be interviewing you for a few days. Please feel free to decline if you wish."

Earl glanced over at Frank, who glared back. "But before we start, I can't say I like this John Doe moniker they've given you. And since you're concerned that your real name could cause unnecessary damage, how about I just call you JD?"

"I quite like that," said the elderly man. "JD it is. But if we're going to chat, I suggest we hurry. You see, I'm dying."

"What?" said Earl, glancing at both men.

Frank interjected. "Mr. Doe's tests have uncovered considerable damage to the liver and kidneys. Likely a result of extreme dehydration from his time in the desert."

"I see," said Earl, "so is he, you know, gonna... um... depart?" He held his eyes on Frank's gaze as he motioned upwards towards the ceiling.

"That's unknown, but we're doing everything possible." Frank seemed genuinely concerned.

Earl returned his gaze to Doe. Doe was staring intently at Earl and smiling the way one does when handed a large slice of cake. "Well, JD, whatever happens, I'm honoured to spend a little time with you... we'll make the most of it."

"Brilliant," beamed Doe, his eyes transfixed on Earl's. "When do we start?"

"Well, the global press has a bunch of questions for you, but I don't have them in my hands just yet," Earl explained apologetically.

"Oh, I see," said Doe. "Then, when will you be back?"

Pulling the chair over to the bed, Earl sat and opened his notepad. "Frankly, I'm exhausted from the flight and several exceptional beverages, so probably first thing tomorrow if it's all the same to you? I'll have the list of press questions by then, I think."

"Do we actually care really about press questions, Earl?" Doe said, propping himself up on an elbow. "Isn't there something of a personal nature you'd prefer to discuss?"

"Sir, I've no intention to bombard you with all, or even any, of their stupid questions, but I've got a role to play here, charade that it is, and I've got to follow their rules. But I'm happy to discuss anything you want."

Frank cleared his throat, opening his eyes wide toward Earl.

"I know, I know," Earl glared, "gear down big-rig, the jackals will get their answers, one way or another."

FIFTEEN

Thirty minutes later...

Frank ushered Earl back to the executive offices where they both convinced MacMann, found barricaded in a vacant room, that the new Church representatives were, in fact, who they claimed to be, and not Catholic Special Ops. Once inside, the pair watched MacMann pace by a window overlooking the emergency arrivals area. The horizon had disappeared, replaced by menacing black clouds barreling toward the city. "How did it go?" inquired MacMann, staring intently at the biblical scene.

"Not bad," said Frank. "Just an intro. But they seemed to hit it off."

"Oh, saints be praised," said MacMann, sarcasm thick as molasses.

"He's quite sick, you know?" Earl interjected.

"Thank you, Dr. Grey," snapped MacMann.

"We'll need the press questions this evening," said Frank.

MacMann turned from the window. "I've already got the questions, but they're somewhat irrelevant, don't you think?" He pointed to a bucket on the floor, choked with paper, spilling over next to a black garbage bag that sat upright under its own weight. "No feasible way to navigate that lot." He turned to Earl. "I suggest you ask him the questions *you* want answered as a professional journalist." MacMann rolled his eyes at his own words. "Your questions will likely mimic ninety percent of those in the garbage bag. Suitable receptacle, don't you think?"

"Very," said Earl, nodding.

"So, tonight," continued MacMann, "jot down a few answers to satiate the vampires. Make sure they believe we've read their cards with due diligence."

"Piece of cake," said Earl, fully intending on a quiet evening of doing nothing at all, followed by a good night's sleep.

"Alright! Frank, I need you here with me. There's a multitude of priests skulking around who say they've no idea who Del-Monte is, suggesting he's an imposter. So, I've no clue who we were talking to yesterday, but we need to find out." MacMann sat down on the desk, trying to ignore Earl. "In the meantime, those penguins are insisting on seeing Doe, but I can't risk it. I've got no idea what Doe's told Del-Monte, or where that information's gone, and I can't risk letting those choirboys get conflicting info."

"Did he have an official church ID, maybe a tattoo of the Virgin Mary?" asked Earl to no response. His question triggered thoughts of Mary-Lynn Wu.

Frank shook his head, "So, who *was* that guy yesterday?"

"Hmmm," said MacMann, raising his voice to boil and marinating it in sarcasm. "Danny DeVito, Jack Black, maybe it was Jesus Christ himself, Frank, how the hell should I know? Why don't *you* find out?"

Earl continued knowing full well his colleagues were ignoring him. "My guess is he's a reporter, dressed as a priest. One-upped you guys. Got the scoop, and he's long gone. You'll find out soon. It'll come out in the *Enquirer* or the *Star* or maybe the *Washington Post*."

"Just how the hell am I supposed to find out?" Frank fortified his words in an attempt to match the doctor's bluster. There was a great deal of spit.

"Well, you could start," MacMann closed his eyes, clenching his teeth to control his anger, "by asking Doe who the hell was in his room yesterday and what they talked about?"

Frank backed off, feeling a little stupid. "Valid point."

"Can I go now?" said Earl.

"What?" said MacMann, flipping out of the conversation. "Yes, go. Fuck off!"

Frank continued. "I'll ask Doe. In the meantime, what do we do about the priestly entourage?"

"Stall them," said MacMann. "Just find a way to keep them from Doe until I figure out what's going on."

"Where should I fuck off to?" asked Earl, halfway out the door.

"Stall them? How do I stall a bunch of priests and a nun? Pentagrams? Inverted crosses? Pitchforks?" said Frank.

"Look, it's dead simple, they don't know where Doe is, and they couldn't get past the bloody guard even if they did," said MacMann.

Earl snickered at the notion of Robbie tackling a swarm of priests.

MacMann paced, his arms flailing. "Tell them it's a privacy thing or paperwork or that I ordered rest. Do I have to think of everything around here?"

"Excuse me, but where am I supposed to sleep?" said Earl stepping between them.

MacMann turned his head. "I thought you'd fucked off?"

"Well, I was going to fuck off, but then I realized I had nowhere to fuck off to. I figured you guys must have booked me a hotel or something?"

MacMann turned to Frank. "Gonna kill him!"

Frank intervened. "Earl, your car's waiting downstairs. We booked you a room at the Marriott just down the street. Just eat there and put it on your room tab. We'll look after it, OK?"

Earl grinned, picturing a minibar with his name on it. "Sweet! And how do I get out of here without the press spotting me, or getting wet, for that matter? It's pouring out there. I thought it didn't rain in this part of the world?"

"Just go down to level three and head west. There's a side exit to the garage, your ride will be there, and there won't be any press around. Get some rest." Frank shot Earl a weak smile.

"Yes, yes," said MacMann, "and if you need a massage, pedicure, scented candles or a bloody Belgian rim job, please feel free to charge Frank's Visa. We wouldn't want you inconvenienced in any way."

Earl couldn't contain his laughter. "Gotcha, Doc. Alright, see ya'll tomorrow. Oh, and if it's not too much trouble, I'd like some good coffee. I'm Canadian, remember? Can't handle Dunkin's. Maybe a Starbucks latte with a little cinnamon?"

MacMann stuffed his hands in the pockets of his gown and stormed back to the view from the window.

"Splendid. Sleep well, everyone." Earl sympathetically patted Frank on the shoulder, then opened the door and left.

"I hate him," spat MacMann.

"Let it go, Rory, bigger things at stake." Frank locked the door, then sat in the leather chair behind the desk. "Just how sick is Doe?"

MacMann pondered the question for a few seconds. "Very sick. And that may be our way out of this."

*

Earl stepped into the administration floor's public area. Although deserted when he'd arrived, the holy men and nun had returned, sandwiches in hand, looking for answers. "You're that press fellow, right? The guy with access to the patient?" asked Monsignor Bellecourt.

"Hi there," smiled Earl. "I'm your man." His neck was beginning to ache from talking to so many incredibly tall people. He rubbed it with his hand, moving his head around in circles like a bobblehead doll.

"Why are we being kept from the patient? Have you seen him?" Bellecourt asked.

"Well," Earl grimaced. "Question one, that's up to the dynamic duo in the office behind me. As for question two, yes, I've met him, and he seems like a genuinely nice man, albeit a sick one."

"This makes no sense," interrupted the diminutive Sister Donello. "If he's our Lord, then why's he sick? Surely he can heal himself?"

"Maybe," Earl interjected with a theory, "he's doing that whole dying for our sins bit again."

The portly priest rolled his eyes. "That was Jesus, sir. God didn't come here to die for our sins."

"Sorry," said Earl insincerely, "I get that whole father, son and spooky ghost thing mixed up. It's like a Scooby-Doo mystery to me."

The nun broke the silence. "You're not Catholic, are you, Mr.....?"

"Grey, Earl Grey."

"Mr. Grey. You see, to us, this is not a laughing matter. We do not wish to perpetuate this absurdity one minute longer than necessary. However, in the infinitesimal chance that this man is God or even a messenger from God, we must be the first to verify it. Do you understand?"

"Sis, I get it, but I'm only doing my job, you know, same as you guys. Works both ways."

"Can you take us to him?" implored a priest, gripping his Bible tight in a chokehold.

"Ooo, ahh, no, that's not a good idea," Earl said. "Besides, I'm just leaving for the evening. I have a date with a minibar, room service and a kingsize bed."

"One way or another, Mr. Grey, we'll meet this John Doe," threatened Bellecourt. "And we're not leaving until we do."

"Awesome," said Earl. "I admire your spunk. Now, if you'll excuse me, I haven't had a drink for several hours, and I'm concerned I might be losing my buzz."

The entourage blankly stared as Earl pushed through them and walked to the elevators.

Pressing the down button, Earl shouted back, "Keep the faith, fellas, oh, and you too, Sister." He held his fist high in the air as the metal doors closed around him.

SIXTEEN

Saturday, November 14, 9:15 p.m.
Downtown Phoenix

Rainwater streamed the exterior of a blackened drainpipe, forming a pool where decayed brick met heaved concrete, deep in the bowels of an unnamed dilapidated alley.

An expensive car stopped at the mouth of the lane and ejected a shadowy figure wearing a black trench coat, his head shrouded by a wide-brimmed short-topped hat. The shadow braced himself against the elements, pulling the leathery hat forward, allowing the warm rain to orbit the brim and cascade off the front, blurring his face.

Partway into the alley, the figure paused and reached into his trench coat for a flashlight. White light pierced the blackness like a dental tool, painful and probing, coming to rest on a rusty green garbage bin where a rain-soaked figure stood, shielding his eyes from the rays. The beam dropped to the ground but remained on, pre-selecting footsteps, several feet in front of the shadowy stranger and side to side like a radar beam.

"Fucking weather," said the figure by the garbage bin. "We should have done this on the phone, sir."

"It's him," said the shadow, drawing closer, sidestepping each puddle exposed by the flashlight. "I thought it never rained in this fucking place. Do ya know what these shoes are worth?"

"It's him?" gasped the man by the bin. "Are you sure? You talked to him, saw him up close?"

"Are you questioning me?"

"No, no, sir. I'm just shocked. It can't be."

The dark figure switched off and re-pocketed the flashlight, waiting several seconds for his eyes to adjust, his pupils vast pools of blackness. "Why's he back, Warren? I thought this place was all mine now?"

"I guess I'll just have to kill him again," Warren Peel chuckled nervously,

68

fumbling for a pack of cigarettes in his jacket pocket.

"Not that easy now. Everything's changed," growled the man in the hat. "There's a guard at the door, security cameras everywhere, people in and out constantly. Plus, he's gone and told everyone he's God. Every journalist on the planet has the place surrounded. If you'd done your job, this would be over, and I wouldn't have had to come back to this shit hole."

"Sir, he was miles from anything. He was dead, I know it. There's nothing out there, no ranger station, no shade. It's not even on a flight path. If he's alive, it's a total…" Warren held his tongue.

"Go on. You were saying?"

"Umm, a total, um, fluke." He offered an uneasy grin.

"You were going to say miracle, weren't you, Warren?"

"Miracle? No, of course not."

"Would ya like to see a real miracle, Warren?"

The stranger pushed Warren back against the rusty bin, hands in front of his chest, one open, the other clutching a crumpled pack of cigarettes.

"I'm sorry, sir, I meant no disrespect," Warren pleaded.

"Warren, I was wrong to think you could handle such a simple job." The figure pulled one hand from his pocket, brandishing a black knife with a serrated black blade. An instant later, it was under Warren's throat. "Let me tell you about miracles, Warren. It'll be a miracle if I don't slice your fucking head off. That's why we don't do these things on the fucking phone, capiche?"

"Please," Warren begged, one hand firmly grasping his attacker's wrist. "I'll fix it, gimmie a chance." Droplets of sweat mingled with rain and ran down Warren's face, dripping from his chin and landing on the blade where they danced like beads of blood. Despite having a gun tucked into the back of his pants, Warren knew he'd be sushi before he could reach it.

"What's that smell?" asked the shadowy man.

Trembling, Warren tried to compose himself. "Wha, what… smell?"

"It suddenly smells like piss here."

"It's the dumpster, sir. This whole place stinks. Please put the knife away."

"No, no, this is fresh." He raised his head like a wolf to the sky, sniffing deeply. "Fresh human piss. Warren? Did you piss yourself?"

"I don't think… no, I don't think so." Warren stuttered, watching as a Cheshire cat grin oozed from under the wide-brimmed hat.

"You pissed yourself." The man erupted in laughter. "And I suppose you shit your pants too?"

Warren closed his eyes, turning his head to the wall. "Please, sir."

Suddenly, nothing happened. Then, ever so slowly, the knife pulled away, Warren's grip easing proportionally. *In the movies, this is the part where you think it's over*, thought Warren. *Then the bastard shoves it in your gut a dozen times.* He winced at the visual.

"Warren, perhaps I'll kill you tomorrow. How does that sound?" The shadowy figure wiped the rainwater off the blade by dragging it back and forth across Warren's shirt collar. "Or, if you're keen to avoid a headless eternity in hell, perhaps you'd assist me with another easy job. If you think you can handle it?"

"Yes, yes, of course, sir!" Relief spewed out with each word. "Anything!"

"Go to the hospital, find out where they keep the security videos and take them, or erase them, whatever, burn the place down for all I care, just make them disappear. Make sure you get everything from this week and any backups if they exist. And be goddamn discreet about it."

Still shrouded in darkness, the figure backed up a few steps and turned without waiting for a reply. "Oh, and Warren," he said, dodging puddles on his way back to the street, "do something about that bladder problem, would ya? Wouldn't want-cha slipping on those slick hospital floors and hurting yourself." He burst out laughing again.

Warren watched as the dark figure disappeared inside the equally dark BMW. As the car pulled away, he opened his left hand and examined the soggy crushed cigarettes. Frowning, he tossed them on the ground, two feet in front of the garbage bin, then walked deeper into the alley, and total blackness.

SEVENTEEN

Exhausted, Earl fell into a dream-filled sleep, conjuring many disjointed yet vivid memories, the last of which was a forgotten but familiar interaction from his days at university. For Earl, the dream felt very real.

Slumped at the back of lecture hall 4B, Earl watched as the enigmatic Professor Harold Sawchuck summarized the topics likely to appear on Friday's final exam. A rugged, hairy man, the professor carried his weight well, disguising it with tweed sports coats, always worn open. Earl suspected they wouldn't close even if Sawchuck wanted them to, but, somehow, they made him look thinner and hip for his age. Faded blue jeans and dress shoes always rounded out each ensemble. Sawchuck's buzzed white hair looked like frost on the side of his head, and his dark, rugged skin suggested a skillset connected in some way to lumberjacking. But, contrary to first impressions, the professor was a renowned expert in the field of investigative journalism, publishing several books and appearing on local radio and TV when expertise was needed.

Earl liked the professor a great deal, even though he was averaging a C in the class. But this was due to his *laissez-faire* attitude and not because Sawchuck was a biased or harsh marker. College was exhausting. It took so much effort to keep up with the parties and sex and non-needle drugs – who could expect him to add creative writing and still perform at a high level? As Earl left the lecture hall, he passed Sawchuck, who was mercifully looking the other way.

"Earl," said the professor with his back turned. "Can I assume you'll impress me on the finals this week?"

Earl froze. "Oh, yes, sir, absolutely. Massive study awaits."

Sawchuck turned, smiling. "Really?" He sounded incredulous. "Frankly, Mr. Grey, I'd be impressed if you managed not to oversleep on exam day."

71

*

Earl bolted up straight in bed, in full panic mode, shooting glances around the pitch-black room. "Jesus," he exclaimed, rubbing his eyes and checking the alarm. 5:45 a.m. *The exam*, he thought, *I'm late for…*

Reality crept in, reminding Earl that he was in a hotel room and that the only exam he was late for was a prostate he'd been putting off for months. He moved to the edge of the bed, wide awake, his internal clock at 8:45 a.m. The room was dark, but the clock's read-out illuminated a tray of plates, glasses and bottles discarded near the television – remains of a bountiful feast ordered from the Marriott's late-night room service menu. On the floor beside the bed lay a heap of clothes where he had disrobed and two damp towels from his evening shower.

After an unsatisfying hotel shower, like all hotel showers, Earl stepped out onto the cold tile floor with a small towel over his head as a sudden knocking echoed through the room. "Housekeeping!"

"Are you fucking kidding me?" He tried to find something more extensive than a hand towel to cover his nether regions, but there was nothing. "Yes, hello, someone's here," he shouted.

"Housekeeping!" A key card slid inside the card slot.

"There's someone in here!"

"Housekeeping!" The door cracked open, mercifully banging to a halt on the sliding chain lock. A single eye peered inside and questioned, "Hello?"

"Goddamit," Earl shouted, hands over his genitals. "It's six-fucking-a.m.! Who the hell does housekeeping at six-fucking-a.m.?"

"Hi, Earl."

Earl paused, pondering the odds of a hotel maid knowing his first name, or for that matter, introducing herself through a door-crack. "Who's that?" he said, positioning himself behind the bathroom door and peering around.

"It's me, Mary-Lynn," said a soft whisper. "Mary-Lynn Wu."

Earl froze in soggy silence, droplets from the tip of his johnson splashing in a small pond at his feet.

"Earl?"

"Ya, it's me. I was in the shower. Like, a minute ago. So, I'm wet. As in damp, um, from the shower."

"I'm so sorry to intrude, but I must speak with you. Can I come in?"

"What, like, right now?" Earl frantically tried to dry himself off with his hand towel. Glancing in the mirror across from his hiding spot, he cringed at how pale his body looked in the harsh lights. Straightening up, he critiqued his physique. *Not bad for my age. Still got some mojo working.* At which point, he noticed a long vertical slice of amber light in the mirror. Hallway light, bleeding through a three-inch crack down the side of his front door. "Shit!" he shouted and scurried to the opposite side of the tiny bathroom, certain he'd heard a muffled giggle through the crack.

"Now's not the best time, Mary-Lynn. May I call you Mary-Lynn?"

She giggled more. "Yes, Earl, Mary-Lynn's fine. I'm so sorry to track you down like this, but sometimes it's the only way to get the scoop. You know the game, right? You're a big city reporter?"

Earl thought about the pressures of his job back home. The unrelenting stress brought on by his endless investigations into the Toronto underworld – toboggan races, children's zoo walks, shopping mall ribbon cuttings, raccoon infestations, yoga for the blind, and a thousand school plays.

"I know what you mean – it's hell out there."

"So, can I come in?" Mary-Lynn said sweetly.

"Um, well, ya, but I've still got this naked thing going on." He scrambled to find a way to save the opportunity. "How about after the press conference, maybe a late lunch?"

"Awesome, Earl, that would be amazing." She slipped a card with her personal cell number through the crack, and Earl watched it bounce on the carpet.

"Earl, I submitted a question for God that, well, I really hope you'll ask it for me. Did you see my question?"

Panicked, he threw out his first thought. "Of course, but I read so many, I can't remember which one was yours. Can you refresh this old guy's memory?"

She paused a moment. "Oh, well, it did say 'Hi Earl, it's Mary-Lynn' on it."

"Goddamnit!" exclaimed Earl under his breath.

"It may not be the most impactful or pragmatic question," she continued, "but I wrote it for me, not for my stupid producers. It just said, What's the point?"

"Oh," said Earl, lost for words, "I see." He sat with his bare ass on the counter, waiting for an intelligent response to ride in like the cavalry, which never happens to anyone. "I'm guessing you've been through some tough times?"

Silence. The crack in the door closed slightly, then reopened. "I'll see you at lunch, Earl."

"Oh, I'm sorry, I didn't mean to pry or offend." He smacked himself in the forehead, a little too hard. "It's just, well, I ask myself that same question every day, and I thought…"

"It's OK, Earl, all good, we can chat later. Call me. I'm looking forward to it." The door almost closed this time, then sprang open yet again. "And cute ass, by the way." She giggled again, closing the door firmly.

Earl sat in an ass puddle, feeling the grin on his face slowly widen. Genuine emotion arose, a feeling he hadn't felt in a long time. Desire.

I have a cute ass, and I have a lunch date, he thought. The grin widened.

After dressing in a black suit and white shirt, top button open, Earl tied his conservative blue tie loosely below his collar. Moving to the bed, he sat at the end with his notepad and a hotel pen, thinking about his upcoming visit with JD.

What's the point? How appropriate, Earl thought. All the other questions were probably, about miracles, or the afterlife, healing, and rewards. He wrote on his pad, *What's the point? What's the point? Mary-Lynn Grey. What's the point?* His mind repeated the mantra over and over, soothing him into a trance.

Then, the bedside phone erupted with the subtlety of a blind burglar in armour.

"Christ!" Clamouring across the bed and lunging for the phone, Earl's Canadian politeness failed to keep pace. "Shit, fuck, what?"

"Aren't you in a good mood this morning, sunshine?" the caller laughed.

"Who's this?" Earl could feel his heart exploding.

"It's me, Orlando."

"Who?"

"Orlando, your limo driver?"

"Ohhh, right, I didn't get your name yesterday," Earl said apologetically.

"Ya, well, whatever, too low on your lofty radar, I guess."

Earl ignored the obvious opportunity to take a shot. "Where are you?"

"The kitchen downstairs. Take the elevator to the sub-basement and turn right. The lobby's got a bunch of reporters milling around. Pretty sure they don't know you're here, but they will if you go anywhere near the main entrance."

"OK, be right down." Earl shoved the phone into its receiver, grabbed his shoulder bag, checked for his room key, and took another peek at himself in the bathroom mirror.

How on earth did she find me? How did she even get up here?

Earl stopped at the door. *Was she wearing a maid's uniform?*

He shook off the thought with a flick of the light switch and speed-walked to the elevators. After a painfully slow descent, the steel doors opened, ejecting Earl into the kitchen/laundry area, where he proceeded right as Orlando had instructed. By the time he passed the freezers, he could see Orlando, hands in pockets, near the loading bay.

"We're over here, near the garbage compactor," Orlando pointed with his car keys.

Arriving at the hospital – a three-minute ride, including lights – Orlando took the limo around the side of the building, then used an access card to enter the employee parking garage.

"So, why exactly didn't we use this entrance yesterday?" Earl asked suspiciously.

"Dude, I was explicitly told to drive you to the main entrance yesterday, not the wisest choice, in my opinion, but the command came from on high. I guess someone wanted to make sure the entire planet saw you arrive."

"Ya, someone." Earl stared out the window at the line of doctors' vehicles, angled like a Paris auto show – Porsche, BMW, Cadillac, and one racing-green Jaguar with the licence plate *RorMan*.

EIGHTEEN

Sunday, November 15, 8:10 a.m.
Phoenix General Hospital,
Administration Wing

Earl and Orlando scampered inside the General's administration reception area, looking over their shoulders like politicians in a porn shop. Earl pointed to the couch. "You'd better wait there while I talk to the terrible twins. Try not to break anything."

As Earl approached the office, he could hear two men inside. "Oh, aye, sonny-Jim, send in a boy to do a man's job, eh?" The words were soaked in Scottish heritage. "Jesus, Frank, I thought you were made of stronger stuff." A book was slammed down on the desk. "You've got the stones to stand there and tell me you got nothing out of him? A feeble, bedridden, poor excuse for an adversary and all you come back with is blithering drivel?"

"He's not an adversary. Not everyone on this planet is your enemy, you know." Frank's voice was higher than usual and tinged with atypical disrespect. "He's sick, and he also happens to be a genuinely nice man. And if all he can tell me is that Del-Monte *wasn't* a nice man, then you're going to have to accept that. He wasn't hiding anything. He was profoundly disturbed by the encounter. So, don't you dare go in there and upset him."

"Don't I dare?" bellowed MacMann. "Don't I bloody dare?"

"*Déjà vu*, gentlemen," said Earl, gliding into the room and plopping nonchalantly into a chair.

"And hello to you too," said Frank. "Or should I say, *bonjour?*"

Earl laughed. "Such a beautiful day, gents. Viva Arizona, eh? Shorts weather during the holiday season. Cloudless skies, chirping birds, and a gun in every pocket or purse. What's not to like? Trust you both slept well?"

"Fine, Earl, how about yourself?" Frank replied with a marginal smile.

"Oh, for Christ's sake." MacMann threw up his hands and slumped into the leather chair behind the desk.

Frank continued: "I was just describing the chat I had with Doe this morning. I questioned him about a visit he'd had from a priest who it seems was not a priest. Mr. Doe was quite disturbed by the visit, insisting that the fake priest was a very bad man. We're looking into it, but so far, our investigation has turned up nothing." Frank tried not to glance at MacMann.

"Seems very odd," said Earl. "Did you call the cops? Or a private detective? This fake priest could have been dangerous."

"We'd rather not if it can be avoided," said Frank. "We have enough to juggle without turning the hospital into a crime scene too. We'll keep looking, but I can't say I'm hopeful."

Earl raised an eyebrow. He was already on high alert in case Frank and MacMann might be using him as a scapegoat for their shenanigans. "So what about the real priests?" he asked. "Where's the God-squad now?"

Frank shrugged. "No clue, haven't seen hide nor hair of them."

"Good, maybe they've given up. In the meantime, I guess I better head up to see Doe. Can't procrastinate forever." Earl stood up, patted Frank on the top of the head and walked out, the door clicking officially as the muffled voices erupted with renewed vigour.

"Should I come with you?" asked Orlando, awkwardly seated outside the office on the waiting room's sofa, flipping through a magazine called *Tactical Weapons for the Home and Cottage*. "It's also kinda my job to, you know, look after you?"

"I need looking after? Huh, who knew. But nah, I'd suggest you stay here. I'll be at least an hour." Earl put his hand on the big glass door of the reception area, then paused. "Hey, are you any good with security systems, you know, video cameras?"

Orlando squinted at Earl. "What are you saying?"

"Could you figure out where the security archives are kept for this hospital and get some specific footage?"

"What makes you think I've got the means to steal video footage? It's cause I'm black, right?" The driver pushed himself from the precipice of the sofa and swaggered toward Earl, expecting a confrontation.

"You're black? Huh, hadn't noticed. No, nothing like that… I just figured that with you driving all sorts of muckity-mucks around, you'd know a thing or two about security systems."

"Oh." Orlando disengaged and looked down. "I suppose I could look around and see what I can find. Whaddaya need?"

"Apparently, some guy visited JD, er, sorry, John Doe recently. He was dressed as a priest; lots of opulence. He should be easy to spot on the video. I need his picture."

"What the hell for?" asked the confused driver.

"Cause you're gonna find him for me?"

"What? Why?"

"Because apparently, he may not be a priest. And if not, that makes this really interesting. So, I figured you could put the word out, you know, in the hood, get me the goods, the down-low."

Orlando threw the magazine at Earl's head, hitting him in the kneecap.

"Come on," Earl grinned. "You're supposed to be my bodyguard, so what's a little private-eye work on top of that? I'll pay you."

"Keep up that 'hood' shit, and you will be payin'."

Earl pushed open the door to the hospital corridor and waved with his free hand. "Threat noted, now don't let me down."

*

"Hi, Mr. Earl," said Robbie in front of Doe's hospital room door, his right side leaning against the door jamb. "Beautiful morning out there."

"Indeed, it is," said Earl. "And it's just Earl, no need for the mister."

"Whatever you say, Mr. Earl. Are you spending some time with the patient this morning?"

"Yep, just an hour. I heard he had an upsetting visitor the other day?"

"You mean Dr. MacMann?" asked Robbie.

"No, no," Earl paused for a moment, processing the odd reply. "I mean the priest that was here."

"Ohh, yaa, a mean one. Lots of foul language. Kinda odd now that I think of it."

"So, what did he say to Doe?" whispered Earl, stepping closer to Robbie.

"Well, I couldn't hear much through the door," whispered Robbie without knowing why, "but he was mad, the priest. Like really mad. He kept telling Mr. Doe that he shoulda stayed dead."

"Stayed dead? That's an odd expression."

"Ya, and he kept saying that he knew who he was and to stop pretending like they didn't know each other."

"Interesting. Anything else?"

"Ummm, no, not really, but when the priest left, he did speak to me."

"Oh?"

"Yeah, he said, 'Goddamnit, get out of the fucking way.'"

Earl smiled, "Aww, isn't that just like the Church, always looking out for you, making sure you're on the right path."

Perplexed, Robbie pushed open the heavy door. "Have a good visit, Mr. Earl," he said with an uncertain smile. As the door clicked shut, Robbie removed his cellphone from his pocket and tapped speed-dial number one.

As Earl walked into Doe's sun-drenched room, he was hit with the same scent of belonging as the previous day's. It was like walking through the front door of his childhood home, except that there was an impossible majesty to the tiny hospital room. The feeling was one of security as if he had stepped into a small protected alcove in a vast desert of stark vulnerability. Doe's bed sat parallel to the window, washed in sunlight, bathing the patient in a heavenly glow that, while blinding, appeared peaceful and benevolent. An aura enveloped the blankets, dishevelled and bunched around a fetal silhouette at the centre of the mattress. On the adjacent wall, shadows formed dark grey mountains descending to the golden-hued counter, then fading away into the washroom.

"Impressive," said Earl, approaching the cot while pulling a stool closer.

Doe stirred from slumber and rolled onto his back. "Earl?"

"Yes, it's me; I just got here. Take your time."

Doe fought off a stubborn blanket and shifted himself so he could see Earl. The monitors protested with a flurry of beeps and buzzes. "That's calming, isn't it?" said Earl.

"More probes in me than a hillbilly at an alien BBQ." Doe chuckled through a wet cough.

"So, here we are," mumbled Earl. "Yes, indeed, here we are, interview time, lots to discuss."

"Earl, relax. It's not the SATs, just a chat, you know? Two would-be friends, getting to know each other."

"Sorry, I just don't think it's right what they're doing to you..." Earl paused to restate, "What *I'm* doing to you. You're being exploited. It's all a scam to gain media attention for the hospital." Earl lowered his head in embarrassment. "I'm just saying we don't have to go through with this charade. We can just sit and talk about the weather, and I'll make stuff up..."

"Or," interrupted Doe, "we can have gobs of fun chatting about philosophy and life and, who knows, maybe even develop a keen friendship. All at their expense."

"Fair point. Oh, and maybe we can deliver a message of hope for all those sheep waiting outside."

"Sheep?" said Doe. "Are you suddenly interested in their well-being? Is this the conversion of Grey?"

"Well, no. But I see no reason to hurt those people. They're camped out there waiting for a life-changing moment. They believe God has returned. I don't want to be the guy who pulls salvation out from under them."

"You don't believe I am who I claim to be?"

Earl blushed but stayed on track. "No, sir, I don't, but you see, that's not about you; it's about me, a committed atheist. Fact is, I wouldn't believe *anyone* claiming to be God. I promise you, though, it doesn't diminish my respect for you one bit."

Doe sat up in the bed and let out a small laugh. "So, the atheist interviews the Almighty. How wonderful."

Earl chuckled too, then pulled a notepad from his jacket. "Alright, so what do you want to tell them, Almighty one? What's your message to the world?"

Earl watched as Doe pondered the question. "Well, therein lies the problem, Earl. I didn't come here to answer a bunch of bullshit questions about the afterlife or sin or pathways to heaven."

"Alrighty," said Earl. "Then why *are* you here?"

Doe stretched as far as he could reach, placing his left hand on Earl's forehead. "I came here… for you."

NINETEEN

Thirty seconds later...

"You came here for me?" Earl examined Doe's expression to see if he was joking.

"Of course." Doe glowed. "You don't think I'd subject myself to all this on a lark, do you?"

"You chose... *me?*"

"Yes, nothing random about it at all. I came here so we could chat. It's been... too long. Much longer than I'd wished."

Earl looked confused. "Have we spoken before? I'm sure I'd remember."

"We have, indeed. But it was long ago."

Earl put down his notebook and pen on the small table and shifted forward. "Sir, I'm a lifelong pragmatist and skeptic. It's my nature. Nothing about your arrival indicates divinity to me, just a poor sunbaked fellow who's delirious and in need of medical help." Earl offered a benevolent smile and placed his hands on the bedrail.

Doe tilted his head to the side like a dog listening to Björk. "Perhaps I can fix this. Here we are, both of us, for whatever reason, stuck with a role to play. I want to spend time with you, and maybe, through my intervention, it's not too late to save you from the eternal sulfuric pits of hell."

"What?" Earl spluttered.

Doe howled with laughter. "It's a joke, son, to see if you're paying attention. Seriously, what's the harm in starting each day with a little philosophical debate to exercise the mind? Why the young Earl I once knew would debate the colour of a traffic light just for fun." He placed both hands gently on top of Earl's.

Earl felt a shiver radiate through his body, then warmth welled up inside him. "You're good, JD. I'll give you that." Earl left his hands in place. "Very well then, chat we shall. Life, the universe and everything. Sound good?"

"Couldn't have phrased it better myself." He laughed, then fell into another coughing fit.

"Let me get you some water," said Earl.

Doe glanced at the clock on the wall. "Don't trouble yourself. My angelic nurse is due any second now. And, oh, you'll love her, very beautiful, although not Asian… so maybe not your type." He let out a childish titter.

"Scuse me?" Earl spat his words.

"Oh, I'm sorry, is that not politically correct these days?"

"Umm, no, it's fine. But I'm curious why you'd think Asian women are my preference?"

"Oh, come now, Earl. I know everything about you, nothing to be embarrassed about. Well, maybe a couple of things…" Doe rolled over on his back with a giggle. "But all are beautiful. All are special. We want what we want, and we need what we need."

"Well, I trust our philosophical chats will plunge a tad deeper than my preferences in women?" Earl joked.

"Earl, don't overthink this. Sometimes everything you need is staring you in the face. Sprinkle your thoughts with a smattering of belief in the improbable, and see where it goes."

"Smattering, sure, but this is sipping from the evangelical fire-hose."

"Let me get this straight, Earl. To converse with me, you need proof of my claim, right? Moreover, for my words to be credible, I must be sane by your definition of the word. Correct?"

"It would help."

Doe chuckled. "Sounds fair. You want proof before you can believe."

Earl scrunched his face. "Well, it sounds kinda dumb when you put it that way."

"OK," Doe shook his head. "Maybe we should come back to this in a day or two. Right now, I doubt you'd accept my reasons for needing your help."

"You're here because you need *my* help?" Earl shifted uncomfortably in his chair. "You're the one who keeps talking about my need to believe in you."

"And believe you must, my boy. That's key to assisting me." Doe beamed as if he'd just solved the riddle.

"I'm spinning from circular logic. Keep this up, and I'll collide with my own ass."

"Alright, alright. Let's park the subject for a bit and discuss why you harbour doubts about me."

"JD, I like you, but we won't get very far if your prerequisite is my belief in the divine. I've seen what this world is capable of. There's no benevolent oversight, just pain and mindless, self-indulgent hypocrisy. Kick 'em when they're down, then pray for their salvation."

"Perhaps. But you know, Earl, many people use belief to anesthetize this pain you speak of."

"Well, that's stupid."

Doe raised an eyebrow. "Stupid? Why stupid?"

"Belief isn't genuine if it's knowingly adopted to avoid the pain of reality. Fears should be dealt with head-on, without the need for supernatural belief. Look at me; I've never believed in anything without empirical proof."

"Monkey balls!" said Doe.

"Those I believe in. I saw some at the Toronto zoo."

"You believe in countless things every day. You barely go five minutes without an act of faith."

Earl looked at Doe, scrunching his face in opposition. "Do tell?"

Doe cracked his knuckles, then stared at them for a few seconds, marvelling at the sound he'd just made. "Right, do you drive a car?"

"It's been called a car by some. I prefer to think of it as a worthless skid-mark on the underwear of society."

"Fair enough, and I suppose you follow the rules of the road?"

"Of course, well, most of the time. Almost always when someone's looking."

"So why do you drive on the right side of the road in Canada?"

"Well, I drive on the right because if I drive on the left, there's a strong possibility of becoming a hood ornament on a Peterbilt."

"There you go. One tiny example of belief, one simple act of faith."

"Um, are you suggesting my survival instinct and compliance to the law is somehow related to faith?"

"Not suggesting, proving." Doe clapped again and nodded his head wildly. "That little yellow line in the road can't hold back a two-ton car. Anyone can cross it any time they wish. You merrily drive down the street every day with the firm belief that your fellow humans will not hurtle towards you in your lane."

"That's a stretch!"

"Is it? You believe the pilot who flies your plane is qualified, but you have no proof. You believe the engineers and workers who build the bridges you drive across are capable. You believe, without any proof, that you should follow your doctor's orders to the letter."

"It's not the same. There are rules and regulations for those professions, not to mention extensive educational requirements for each discipline."

"Indeed, there are, and you believe, without a doubt, that each of those people, and many more, adhere to all of them."

Earl got a new pencil from his reporter's bag, replacing the one he'd just snapped. "All of that's different from religion."

"Earl, I see a man with massive logic-based defence mechanisms designed to protect himself. But you're a hypocrite. You spend your practical life in a state of faith." Doe clapped three times and bowed in victory.

With his elbow on the armrest, Earl supported his head with his fist. "Impressive argument, but a long way from having faith in Zeus or Space Ghost." He paused and looked in his lap. "Do you still want to continue with this?"

Doe sighed. "OK, what kind of proof do you need?"

Earl grinned. "A couple of miracles would be nice."

"Well, my Doubting Thomas, miracles are simply the absence of understanding. Instead, I propose a leap of faith."

Doe rubbed his hands together, warming them over an unseen fire. "We can't proceed with our chats unless you assume some level of belief. Nor can you honestly address the press out there. Your only genuine response to their questions will be 'He's not God,' thus ending all future chats between us. So, why not humour me a bit: pretend I'm the real deal and see what transpires from there, hmm?"

"Fake faith?"

Doe curled up his lip like Elvis. "Uh huh."

TWENTY

"Did you write out any answers to the press inquiries for Earl?" asked Frank.

"A few, but it's all rubbish. And since I'm sure Grey didn't bother to write anything last night, I jotted down some crap about creation and a nice bit about seeing your grannies in heaven," scoffed MacMann.

"Earl will never say that stuff." Frank laughed.

"He'll say what I bloody well tell him to say. The last thing Grey wants is a ticket back to his igloo. He'll play ball." MacMann handed four cards to Frank. "In case I'm late, give these to Grey when he's back. I'll meet you in the ready room before 9:30 a.m." MacMann stepped around Frank and stormed out without further comment.

*

"Who the hell are you?" asked MacMann, emerging from his office and spotting a pint-sized chauffeur seated on the couch.

Orlando glanced up from his magazine. "Why is everyone so fucking rude around here?"

"Pre requisite," said MacMann.

"The name's Orlando; I'm Mr. Grey's driver. And you must be Dr. Boss Man. I recognize the accent."

"So, you're Orlando. I pictured you a lot..." he paused, "... different. Why are you here?"

"Mr. Grey told me to wait for him."

"Aye, and I suppose you're on the clock?"

"Do I look like someone who'd hang out in a shitty waiting room on my own time?"

Dismissive, MacMann turned to leave but then hesitated. "Have you seen Grey speaking with anyone other than myself or the hospital administrator, especially outside the hospital?"

"Nope." Orlando grinned.

"You're sure?"

"I don't miss much, Boss."

"Unless it's up high, say, over four feet?" MacMann burst out laughing.

Orlando glared at the doctor as he left, waiting for the glass door to slowly swing shut.

"Haggis-sucking shithead."

*

Sitting quietly at Doe's bedside, Earl considered the old man's proposition while bathed in the warm morning sun streaming through the hospital room window. Something about Doe was compelling, magnetic. Like the benevolent attraction of the room itself, John Doe was an anomaly. Inconsistent with everything Earl expected from a patient being treated for a mental breakdown. Fraudster or opportunist didn't fit the bill either, nor did Doe's absurd claim of divinity. Regardless, the man appeared genuine, convincing, and of sound mind, if not body. Earl's initial suspicions and cynicism began to drift. The old man seemed honest and kind, certainly no threat to anyone and no ulterior motives. It appeared his only interest was in Earl's companionship.

There was a time in his life, pre-divorce, when Earl would have left no stone unturned to investigate such an eccentric character as Doe. To find out what made him tick. Could it be that there was a piece of that once-proud journalist still alive and trapped under so much cranial rubble?

As for the press, Earl could perform his media liaison role with or without Doe's input. However, Earl couldn't shake the feeling that there was more to this than met the eye.

Doe sat patiently, watching Earl, waiting for a response, rocking slightly from side to side like a child in need of the toilet. "So, what say you, young man? Do we have our bases covered? Are we ready to get it on? Is that what they say these days?"

"No, sir, that's not what they say, ever."

Earl retrieved his notebook from the table. "Alright, fake faith for our interviews, and fake faith for our chats. I'll try, but no promises, OK?"

"That's all I need, for now, son."

"OK, so let's get the business part out of the way first, since I have a press conference coming up. Let's start with a few meaningless questions that the press will be expecting answers to, such as why Phoenix, why the desert, and why does God need such an expensive suit?"

*

The elevator doors near the media room opened, spot on 9:25 a.m.

"Where've you been?" insisted Frank, cell phone to his ear, an anguished expression on his face as he scanned Earl up and down. "There's less than five minutes until the briefing."

Earl, lost in thought, stared directly through Frank. "Hmm? Oh, sorry, I've no clue where the time went. I totally lost track." Stepping out of the elevator, Earl finished off a note in his notepad. "What's happening? What are we doing now?"

"Damn it, Earl, we needed time to debrief before facing the press. Here's a few cards MacMann wrote out. They might help you answer some questions. Come with me."

Frank jogged down a darkened hallway toward the ready room. Reaching an unmarked door, seemingly aware it would be locked, Frank rapped his knuckles three times in slow succession.

"Who is it?" a small voice inquired.

"It's me. Frank," he rolled his eyes. "I've got Earl." After a metallic unlocking sound echoed from inside the room, Frank pushed the door hard, hitting something soft, then charged inside.

"Sir, we're out of time. Some stations go live in minutes," whined Frank's assistant, Robert Hand, who backed into the room as they advanced upon him.

Frank took three seconds to scan the room. "Rob, where's Rory?"

"On his way; I just got his message," replied Robert, massaging his forehead.

With perfect timing, MacMann caught the closing door and roared into the room, spinning, doorknob in hand like a jitterbug dance partner. He slammed the door as if the hounds of hell were on his ass. "Ladies, ladies, a million pardons. Long morning, plus a quick pit-stop for a squat."

Earl scrunched his face in horror.

"Right then," began MacMann. "Frank, you'll introduce me first for the medical update, then Grey can recite a few answers off those cards. Oh, and Robert, you can fuck off now."

Robert looked both ways to ensure it was indeed *he* that needed to do the fucking off, then lowered his head and walked to the exit.

"Well, no time for last-minute prayers, gentlemen, we're on, let's go," said Frank moving to the door that led to the chapel.

"Umm," said Earl shuffling through the yellow cards. "I can't read this stuff out loud! Can I assume you wrote this dribble?" he asked, looking up at MacMann.

"That I did, lad." MacMann was steaming.

"Let's go!" Frank intervened, his hand gripping the doorknob.

"I can't believe you wrote this shit," Earl said, beginning to chuckle. The cards reeked of Sunday School placation. Simple little answers to life's giant questions, parables and lessons about the need for kindness and empathy.

MacMann opened his mouth to reply as Frank opened the door. "Rory, now please, no option."

Earl winked at the doctor. "Showtime."

The trio strolled into the media room as a rippling murmur spread throughout the crowd. Frank led the procession up the small metal steps of the prefab stage, then proceeded straight to the microphone. Rory and Earl parked themselves at the darkest edge of the platform.

"Good morning, everyone. It's nice to see you all this lovely sunny day." Frank started. "Today, we're pleased to bring you two updates regarding our patient, John Doe. One from the physician in charge, Dr. MacMann, the other from Mr. Earl Grey, your media liaison. We'll begin with Dr. MacMann." Frank gestured with his right arm towards MacMann and grinned like a used-car salesman.

As MacMann walked the few steps to the podium, Frank backed away in mock reverence. "Ladies and gentlemen of the press, I have a few updates for you on John Doe's condition." He paused to survey the room. "Most of the results are back, and I'm afraid there are several reasons for concern moving forward."

Earl paid little attention to MacMann. His interest was in scanning the audience for Mary-Lynn, but she was nowhere to be seen. Suddenly, a thought prodded his frontal lobe. *That's how JD flagged me for liking Asian women. He was watching the conference yesterday when I made a total dick of myself. Clever old bugger.*

"Mr. Doe has severe liver damage, and his kidneys are not responding as they should. There are also internal injuries to the spleen and abdominal muscles, which we cannot attribute to dehydration. We're trying to understand the cause of these traumas, but so far, Mr. Doe has been unwilling, sorry, unable to provide further details surrounding the circumstances that brought him here." MacMann signified his conclusion with a nod.

A young reporter in the front row piped up. "Are you saying he is dying?"

MacMann replied tersely, "Mr. Doe is in serious condition but not critical. We're focusing on the liver and kidneys and need to locate the source of his internal bleeding. What surprises me most is the level of pain he must be experiencing, which should be extreme and necessitate sedation. Instead, he's wide awake and in fine spirits, as Mr. Grey will attest. We plan to sedate him at various points during the day, so his body can rest and heal."

"So, he's not dying… is that what you mean to say?" the same reporter inquired.

"Listen, lad. I'll not give you a definitive statement on the subject either way. My job here," he paused, "our job here is to ensure Mr. Doe recovers to good health. Dying is a relative condition, one we're all subject to. My job is to treat his immediate ailments to the best of my ability. Our business is life, lad, not predicting death." He glanced over at Frank and gave him a lottery-winning smile. "Now, with that, I'll hand you over to Mr. Grey so he can present his… spiritual… findings."

A hundred hands shot in the air as voices erupted in unison.

"How long does he have?"

"Does God have a next of kin?"

"Will he require an iron lung?"

"Will there be any surgery performed on God?"

"Can you speak about the trials and injuries he received in the desert, and were they inflicted by a human or metaphysical hand?"

"Do you believe in the devil, Dr. MacMann?"

"What colour is God's blood?"

Ignoring their cries, MacMann stepped towards Earl and offered him the podium.

Overwhelmed at the apparent feistiness of the jackals, Earl hesitated before placing his hands on the lectern and smiling. He arranged the notepad and cards on the pulpit and flattened his shirt with the palms of his hands. "Hey guys," he started, clearing his throat. "Could I ask you to settle down a bit?" He held out his arms, motioning for quiet.

There was no quiet.

"Can we have the doctor back?"

"What is the official prognosis for the patient?"

"Was there a medical examination to certify his theistic claims?"

"Have there been any more miracles?"

"Will representatives from each religion be allowed to meet with God?"

"Does God have genitalia?"

Earl looked over at MacMann, who held his palms forward, signifying, 'don't you dare call me back over there.'

Earl leaned into the microphones positioned at the front of the podium. "Um, folks, that's all the medical information we have available at this time. I'll ask the good doctor to prepare detailed answers to all of these questions before our next briefing." He turned and winked at MacMann, who appeared to be padlocking his anus. "The best I can do is offer commentary on my meeting with Mr. Doe, which lasted almost ninety minutes."

"Mr. Earl!" a young Asian man said, thrusting his voice forward from the front row. "Before that, can we have Mr. Doe's photographs for publication?"

Earl hesitated. "Um… right… I hadn't thought of that." A gasp rippled through the journalists. "Yes, I suppose you'd like to see what he looks like, right?"

General insanity ensued.

"What are you keeping from us, Mr. Grey?"

"Is God deformed or non-human?"

"Is God humanoid?"

"Are you hiding God's nationality?"

"Why didn't you take some goddamn pictures, you moron?"

"OK, that last one was a bit harsh," said Earl, trying to not raise his voice. "It simply slipped my mind."

"We need pictures, Mr. Grey; it's imperative," said a reporter from TMZ. "Our viewers prefer not to read."

Earl pushed on. "However, I do have replies to some of your questions submitted yesterday. I'd be happy to provide them at this time." The roar dialled back to a medium setting. "After spending the first part of our chat getting to know each other and setting some ground rules, we moved on to the more philosophical subjects, where I had the opportunity to present your questions…"

Medium shifted to silent. "Sweet, OK, here goes…"

TWENTY-ONE

Warren hadn't slept since his night in the alley. Wearily, he roamed the hospital's third floor in search of the MIS/IT offices labelled 3–F on the lobby's directory board. The hallways were warmer than the other floors, with a different smell, not antiseptic, more like business machines, printers and computers.

He walked with purpose – tight blue pants, an ill-fitting shirt, and a short blue jacket embroidered with the name 'Eric', just above a breast pocket full of pens. He was confident no one suspected the hidden gun stuffed down the front of his pants.

Locating the IT department, Warren pushed his way into the outer reception office, deserted but for a portly man seated at a small desk, frantically typing and mumbling.

"Hey, chief," said Warren. "Do me a solid and point me to the video storage servers, would you?"

The large young man looked up from his monitor without slowing his typing, trusting his work would continue while his mind stepped away for a moment. "I'm not a chief. Who are you?" he asked, glancing at Warren's visitor pass dangling around his neck.

"I'm here to check the video files, figure out why your cameras aren't recording complete cycles before dumping old data."

"News to me. Cameras work fine. System's up with no bottlenecks. Servers and storage are good as gold." He returned to the task at hand, completely disengaging with the stranger in front of him.

Warren stiffened. "Look, I've got a busy day and overtime to boot. Your people called us in a panic, asking for emergency service, which I might add is full rate plus fifty percent."

"Dude," said the big man, determined not to be distracted from his computer monitor. "I got no call, no alert, and no knowledge of this big friggin' emergency of yours. Believe me, I'd know, I work here. So, you got it wrong, OK?"

"Not OK," said Warren. "How about you take me to the video storage area and let me show you how a professional does it."

The techie stopped typing and looked around. "Dude, do I look like the receptionist here?"

"Actually, yes," said Warren grinning. "You're the only one out here, in the reception area, and there's a sign on your desk that reads… *Receptionist.*"

"Well, she's on a break. But, no, I'm the senior tech for the hospital's IT department, and I'd know if any of my systems were faulty."

Warren rolled his eyes. "Look, Jabba." He watched the techie's eyes pop wide. "I don't give a shit if you're some child prodigy who can wirelessly pick your nose. Either show me the server room or my report will state that the dildo at reception had no clue what was going on. If I leave now, it's gonna cost your department a two-hour round-trip penalty. That's before we address this serious issue that you apparently know nothing about."

The techie paused and adjusted the carpel wristbands on both arms. Probing for a tissue in his bulging pocket, he asked, "Let's see the work order," feeling a twinge of control returning.

"Here's your work order," said Warren, his right hand grasping his crotch. "We received an emergency call, something to do with this whole God thing you got going on here. Something about a privacy protection lawsuit. Dude's name was Shedmore. Ring a bell?"

The techie returned to a nervous, fidgety state and blew his nose.

"Mr. Shedmore," continued Warren, "said this needed to be kept quiet, and there must be no paper trail. He believes the video glitches mean someone spliced into the system to hack pics of your God guy. But it could also mean that someone in this department is stealing footage to sell to the media. That's why, my young nerd, you know nothing about this important shit. You're expendable, suspect, and maybe the perfect fall guy to make it all go away."

The techie's face went whiter than his usual shade of paste. "Jesus."

"Exactly!" said Warren.

Scrambling to his feet, the techie motioned for Warren to follow. "This way, and please don't mention my name in your report. I need this job. My mom will kick me out."

"Start by being some goddamn help, and maybe I'll forget the roadblocks you've thrown up," said Warren.

"Consider it done. We can work faster as a team. Tell me what you need, and I'll get it for you instantly."

"Now that's better," said Warren, trying hard not to look smug.

"Up these stairs, through that glass door," said the techie sliding his pass-card in the reader. "Almost there, Mr... ummm?"

"Just call me Eric," smiled Warren.

"OK, Eric, nice to meet you. My name's Arthur."

"I don't give a shit, Arthur."

*

After he finished explaining that John Doe had no recollection of how he ended up in the desert dressed in opulent clothing, Earl paused to allow questions from the media.

A reporter inquired, "Do *you* believe he's a God, Mr. Grey?"

"I think the only thing that matters here," said Earl, "is what *he* thinks. What I believe is irrelevant. The point of being a reporter is to report, and that's what I'm doing, delivering my observations without bias. Since there's no available proof to the contrary, I'm proceeding under the belief that he is who he says he is."

The room emitted a collective buzz.

"I asked Mr. Doe why he was here..." Earl continued, "... and he suggested there were people in need of help, perhaps lost, looking to find their way, or something like that."

A female reporter in the middle of the fray shouted, "This help he speaks of, is it the miracles he's already performed or is there more to come?"

"I don't think his intentions have anything to do with physical healing, although we never discussed it specifically. I think he has some... unfinished business. And chose this place, time and body, to complete his work." Earl realized his statement just helped with his own understanding.

"You're saying his body is human, but the spirit is God's?" asked a reporter near the front of the room.

"Interesting," said Earl. "A good theory. I'll dig deeper when I see him tomorrow."

"When you get us the photos, right?" asked a random voice, bustling with irritation.

"Um, sure."

"Close-ups too, and some shots of his skin, his hands, etc., you know, as much as possible, to satiate the public's curiosity."

Earl didn't like that. "That's revolting," he said. "First and foremost, Mr. Doe is a patient of this hospital, not the latest flip phone. I'll take photos if he permits, and you'll make do."

Frank cleared his throat loudly. "Aheeemmmm."

Earl continued undeterred. "I'd like you all to remember that Mr. Doe is not an object, not something to elevate on a pedestal until boredom sets in, then dump when a better story comes along. We're talking about a life here." Earl felt his face flushing.

"I think what Earl's trying to say," interjected Frank, leaning into the microphone after sneaking up from behind, "is that we have no intention of turning our patient into a sideshow attraction. This hospital believes in the highest level of patient care and respect, and this policy outweighs all other considerations. I'm sure you can see that…"

"If you'll allow me." MacMann stepped in front of Frank after his own stealthy approach to the podium. "The patient's been good enough to grant us access… and… as we spend time learning the nuances of this man, what makes him tick, we're obliged to remember the sacrifice he's making by opening himself up to the world like this."

Suddenly, MacMann stumbled sideways, becoming entangled in the many microphone wires lying about the stage and ending up on his knees. Earl, regaining his own balance after delivering an NHL-worthy hip-check to the doctor, reclaimed the podium and stared at Frank until he backed away. "That is entirely not what I'm trying to say, not in any possible respect, degree or language." He took a few deep breaths. "Mr. Doe has no desire to become a celebrity. My access is already the limit of his desire for fame."

A few audience members felt embarrassed, but they were far outnumbered by those who didn't have a clue what Earl was talking about. "So, does this mean no close-ups?"

Back on his feet and fuming, MacMann, his face deep purple, vigorously brushed himself off. Signalling Frank to join him, both men headed for the door, leaving Earl alone to deliver a few more responses from God.

In the outer room, Frank tried in vain to calm the furious doctor. "I'm sure it was an accident, Rory. Earl wouldn't intentionally knock you down. He was only trying to get to the microphone."

"I'm gonna chop up his guts for stew and feed them to a fucking goat," replied MacMann.

"Seems like a calm and rational reaction." Frank rolled his eyes, which made matters worse.

"You saw it? You saw what he did. I was just trying to spark a little interest. Bait the jackals into a higher energy state. Not like they needed it, but with Grey going on about respect and other such fuckery, I'm surprised they didn't walk out. This bloody fool's gonna cock it up before we have a chance to…"

"To what, Rory? Exploit Doe?" Frank said, a blank expression on his face.

"Nay, now don't you start that crap too. Doe is who he is, live or die; we didn't do that to him." MacMann was now launching spittle at a competitive distance, threatening Frank's record. "I'll straighten Grey out the minute he steps in here."

"Need I remind you that we have to remain distant, professional and agnostic." Frank's face pruned as he spoke, disturbed by his own words.

"Aye," MacMann spun and paced. "But, I'll not be made a fool of, especially in front of the press. We created this little performance to gain positive exposure, remember?"

"We? We created nothing. You arranged this whole thing, and I trusted you to keep it harmless. Your continued use of the plural is not only chilling but baffling." Frank did his best to straighten his spine, surprised at how far he could see at the new altitude.

At that moment, an irate Earl Grey burst into the room, barely capable of closing the door before exploding. "What the hell was that?" he yelled directly at MacMann.

MacMann, alarmed by a version of Earl he'd never seen, instinctively stepped backwards, smiling politely. "What the hell was what?"

"You know damn well what I'm talking about. 'Learn every nuance of what makes him tick? The sacrifice Doe is making'?"

Earl looked for something to throw. Finding nothing, he pushed a bunch of file folders on the floor for effect. "Have you lost your mind? Hey, I've got an idea. Why don't we speed things up by banging together a cross and doing it the old-fashioned way?"

"Earl, Earl, you need to calm down." MacMann held his palms up as an act of capitulation. "Perhaps my words were a wee bit… distasteful." He laughed nervously.

"A wee bit distasteful?" said Earl in Cyndi Lauper soprano. "You served up Doe as a well-seasoned steak to a room full of starving lions." He stepped closer to MacMann, fists clenching without his knowledge. Never in his life had Earl been in a fight, much less provoked one, yet all he wanted was one good swing at the doctor.

"Don't be daft. I was simply trying to resuscitate some interest in the story since you were in the process of drowning it in a bucket. Relax. We can walk it back next time." He smiled again.

"We?" asked Earl incredulously.

"He does that a lot," inserted Frank.

"You, Rory, my highlander of healing, *will* walk it back, or I'm out, right now," said Earl forcefully. "Quit, gone, finished – and I go straight to the press with a story they'll really sink their teeth into."

Earl's phone rang. He glanced at the call display, noted his editor's number, and pressed ignore.

MacMann took the opportunity to circle back, moving behind Frank's chair. "Alright, fine, you win, this time. I'll tone it down. God forbid we stray from your precious version of ethics."

"Do you actually care about anyone, MacMann?" said Earl, shaking his head. He flopped into a chair and cursed the fact that he didn't smoke.

"Of course, I'm a doctor!"

Earl cringed. "While that may be true, you've missed my point entirely."

Earl's Blackberry rang again, and this time he grabbed for it, stabbing at the talk button. "For Christ's sake, what?"

Sitting for a moment in silence, Earl listened, eyes pinched shut. "No, no, Mary-Lynn, I've always got time for you," he pleasantly chirped while smacking himself hard on the forehead.

TWENTY-TWO

It was half an hour of walking before Earl spotted the restaurant anchoring a small strip plaza. Dave's Diner didn't look fancy, Mary-Lynn had warned him it wouldn't, but there was no possibility of the press being there, only locals and a few tourists looking for comfort food.

Inside, he scanned the tables. *Now let's see,* he thought; *she said she'd be easy to spot.*

The diner was almost empty. Ruling out tables with two or more customers, he focused on the three booths with solo patrons. There was a big dude who looked like a truck driver, a waitress, apparently on a break, and a pretty blond cheerleader in full uniform, sipping on a strawberry float, straight out of a Rockwell painting.

Puzzled, Earl studied the empty booths in case Mary-Lynn was in the washroom, perhaps leaving her bag as a placeholder. Nothing.

"Did a good-looking Asian woman come in recently?" Earl asked as the waitress counted coins from a tip jar.

"Asian? Nope, don't think so, sweetie. You wanna booth?"

"Um. Ya, I guess." Earl scanned the room again, selecting a spot where he'd be most visible when Mary-Lynn arrived. The cheerleader was smiling at him, lifting her hand ever so slightly off the table while making a cute little wave with her three smallest fingers.

Earl stared in disbelief. *No way!*

Excusing himself from the waitress, he walked across the room toward the flirty cheerleader. "Are you kidding me?"

Mary-Lynn burst into a wide grin. "Cute, huh, you like?" she asked, flicking long blond hair over her shoulder.

Earl's mind began to float somewhere between extreme confusion and Eroticville. "What are you doing? Why the... get-up?"

"Shh," she said, "sit down before you attract attention. I didn't want anyone to recognize me from *First Edition*," Mary-Lynn began. "And I didn't want any of the other reporters following me. I have a talent for undercover work. It's kinda my thing. Pretty cool, huh?"

"Yum, ya. I mean, wow, yes, pretty cool. Very pretty," stammered Earl.

"Aww, I'll take that as a compliment," she said, placing a finger on the back of his right hand and gently rubbing it in a circle.

Earl's face flushed, and he immediately broke eye contact. His eyes, now free to wander, landed on her ample cleavage. "You went all out, didn't you? I mean, first the maid thing, now this. Are you trying to give me a heart attack?"

"You're just the sweetest. No, I found the best costume shop in town the other day. My standard M. O. Disguises always come in handy. Investigative reporting at its finest."

"OK, so were you actually at the news conference this morning?"

"No, I wasn't there. But I saw you on TV. You did very well."

"Perhaps you missed the part where I tackled the Chief Medical Officer and nearly threw up from rage on live TV."

Mary-Lynn laughed. "It's obvious what MacMann's trying to do. He's playing to the tabloids. Within days, the headlines will decry 'A Dying God's Sacrifice To The World' or worse."

"That's what I'm afraid of," sighed Earl.

"You'll fix it. You're a smart boy."

"Mary-Lynn, don't get me wrong, I'm thrilled to be here with you. You're delightful and so, so pretty, but I can't help wonder what this is all about. What do you want from me?"

Mary-Lynn pouted, causing Earl's inner strength to crumble like an overstuffed taco. "OK, mister, listen, it's true I've got a job to do, or at least I did. And I can indeed come on a little strong, but that doesn't mean I don't genuinely like you."

"And the cheerleader outfit?"

"Can you curb your libido for one second?" She flashed a sultry grin. "It just so happens that the high school behind this diner has a championship football team, and their cheerleaders practise every Sunday. I'm as invisible as a pound of electrons in here today." She giggled.

Earl nodded, albeit still suspicious. "I see. So what did you mean when you said 'I did have a job to do'?"

"Caught that, did you? Yeah, well, my editor's not too thrilled with me right now."

"Bunions?" said Earl.

"You saw that?" She blushed and rolled her eyes. "Shit."

"Not good, huh?"

"Well, I figured they'd fire me, but this is kinda worse. I'm suspended from on-camera duty and assigned to investigate the story, nothing more. F. E. is sending down a replacement for the on-air segments. Anyway, if you ask me, the underlying story here is money. Someone's after a payday, and I'm gonna get to the bottom of it."

Earl nearly coughed up a lung. He briefly thought of telling Mary-Lynn the truth but then parked the idea based on his aversion to being publicly slapped in the face. "From what I've seen, John Doe's just some poor sick man. He's not in this for fame or money, as far as I can tell."

"But earlier at the press conference… you said you believed he was God?"

"Not quite, Miss Wu. I said *he* believes he's God. If I'm to conduct a viable interview, I have to proceed on that premise. I can't just make this about mental health."

"Why not?" She looked puzzled. "If it is just about a crazy person, no offence intended, then why not call a spade a spade, and send everyone home?"

Earl, struggling to find anything wrong with her suggestion, remained quiet just a little too long.

"Earl?" She poked him softly with her index finger.

"Oh, sorry. Truth is, Mary-Lynn, it was John Doe that asked me to see it through."

She raised an eyebrow.

"Whoever he was, or is, he wants me to spend time with him. Call it a deathbed confession, or he just enjoys my company, but he only wants to talk to *me*."

Mary-Lynn smiled and tilted her head. "I can see that. OK, you're off the hook, mister. But someone's exploiting the situation, and I've got a pretty good idea who." She pondered the lines on the ceiling for a moment. "Did you ask him my question? Did you ask him, 'what's the point?'"

Earl grimaced and shook his head.

Mary-Lynn reached across the table and playfully smacked the top of his hand. "It's cool. Ask him when the time's right."

Earl nodded and meekly smiled.

Mary-Lynn settled in, elbows on the table, chin in her hands. "Alright, mister, so what's he like? Tell me everything."

TWENTY-THREE

Sunday, November 15, 11:10 a.m.
Phoenix General Hospital,
Frank Shedmore's Office

MacMann parked himself in the chair, facing Frank's desk. "What... a... morning."

"Did you see him again?" asked Frank, staring glumly out the window.

"Twice." MacMann rummaged for a stick of gum in his shirt pocket. "You'd never know he was sick from looking at him, but every test result is worse than the last. We'll have to prep him for exploratory if we can't figure out where he's bleeding. White cell count is through the roof. Ultrasound's a bloody mess. He should be screaming, but instead, he just smiles and tells jokes. Any word from Grey?"

"Nope, he left right after his shit-fit. You gonna tell him?" said Frank. "He needs to know how bad it is."

"Aye. And I'd say this gets progressively worse over the next few days."

"So, what do we tell the press when the Almighty dies on our watch?" Frank asked. "Not the best PR for the hospital, considering the press has us under a microscope... or did you not think that one through?"

MacMann shifted in irritation. "No, I didn't, OK? But, I suggest we slowly leak the idea that their 'God' might expire in the next few days due to his bleak condition and nothing to do with our exceptional care."

"Can't you do something for him? Anything?" asked Frank.

"I'm doing my best. I even brought in that tally-washer Higgins, the young pathologist who can't even grow a proper beard, but they say he's the best in his field."

"Looks like there won't be many more pressers." Frank slowly shook his head.

"We'll get a little more camera time, I'm sure."

"Can't say I care anymore," Frank said, dejected. "Now that Doe's dying, I feel like a ghoul."

"Doe's recovery or death is in no way related to or caused by your desire to advance your career, Frank. Nothing would be any different if you hadn't come up with this scheme in the first place." MacMann rose and headed for the door.

Frank itched with irritation. "My scheme, huh. I swear, if this falls apart, I'll…"

"Shhhhh," said MacMann, holding his index finger to his lips. "All will be fine, wee Jessie. Big uncle Rory will take care of everything. As usual."

The office door closed with a thump, leaving Frank alone, pondering whether he should look up the term 'Jessie'.

*

"As you can see, this is all state of the art. The system cabling and the hardware were new last year." Arthur proudly led Warren through an impromptu tour of the IT department, his arms waving in different directions, explaining the virtues of his electronic toys.

"Ya, ya, Art, just show me the digital storage," said Warren.

"For sure. Did ya bring a coat? File storage is over here in the refrigerated vault. Not the worst place to be on a hot day, but stay too long, and you'll wish you'd brought a parka," Arthur chuckled nervously.

"I don't intend on being in there that long," asserted Warren nodding toward the card-access slot.

Arthur swiped his card and stepped inside, "Tada." The smell of chilled electricity filled the air while a thousand microlights danced and flickered.

"Down this aisle over here," said Arthur. "This is where we keep the video feed." He walked backwards, facing Warren, expecting oohs and ahhs that never materialized.

"Alright…" said Warren, "… show me the security videos from the floor where this John Doe fellow is, and any stairwells and connecting hallways."

Arthur moved to the end of the shelving, where a dozen black boxes were stacked on top of each other. "These three here, they cover the entire floor plus stairwell and elevator cams. Anyone interested in our prestigious guest would want these files."

"Excellent, and where can I access them?" asked Warren. "I only need the last forty-eight hours," he said, rubbing his hands together to warm up while bouncing on the balls of his feet like a kid waiting for the ice cream truck.

"Ummm, forty-eight hours? Sorry dude, long gone." Arthur's voice warbled. "Already overwritten."

Delighted with the news, Warren smiled as he watched his own breath swirl around him. "That's quick for an overwrite."

"It is," Arthur said, trying to adopt a pleasant expression but instead looking constipated. "But with our new security protocols, since our famous guest arrived, the new maximum is twelve hours before overwrite. But, fear not, they're still backed up as usual."

"Backed up?" Warren's face puckered.

"Ya, the video data automatically dumps into a massive tape backup, big bruiser of a thing. Replaced every thirty days."

Warren placed his thumbs to his temples and rubbed in slow circles, closing his eyes. "Alright, let's start again. Can you show me the tape back up for this period?" he said with a feral growl.

"Well, no. The last pick-up was earlier than usual. I was told that it was due to our unique situation and our need to ensure security and privacy. But it's no issue, Eric. All you have to do is pop over to Iron Mountain and have them pull up the specific period you need. Easy!"

Warren cringed. "Picked up earlier, Art?"

Arthur backed toward the glass door. "I'm sure it's legit, Eric. I mean, the new guy from Iron Mountain signed off on it."

"The new guy?" Warren paced in a tight circle. "Did he have a name?" Warren's attempted smile never surpassed satanic on the pleasantries scale.

Arthur was shaking, sweat trickling down his forehead. "If you'd follow me to my desk, I'm sure I've got it written down."

"Uh-huh," mumbled Warren. He walked through the opening as Arthur held the door.

"My desk's right over here. I know I wrote the name down somewhere. Here it is." Arthur pushed a wrapper from In-N-Out Burger across the desk, a pencilled name written on the big yellow arrow.

"Vince Carter?" announced Warren while wiping ketchup off his fingers.

"Yep. Super nice dude, brand new with the company, should work out well, great guy."

"I see," said Warren in disbelief. "And I suppose you could describe him for me if I needed to track him down?"

Arthur laughed with nervous relief. "Of course, piece of cake," he replied. "After all, how many four-foot-tall black guys do you meet in a day?"

TWENTY-FOUR

Sunday, November 15, 6 p.m.
Downtown Phoenix
(The Shady Side)

"What the hell am I supposed to do with this thing?" said a scruffy, dirty-looking man behind the glass reception counter at Eddie's Adult Emporium. He rotated the heavy black box in his hands, squinting at the connection ports on the back panel.

Orlando pulled himself a little higher against the counter. "Do I look like Steven Spielberg, Eddie? Just do what you do, ya know, plug it in, or log it on, or whatever you do to see what's inside."

"You make that sound easy, dude. I don't even know what kind of port this is or what software it runs on. This could take a while."

"I don't have a while, Eddie." Orlando tapped hard on the glass countertop. "Best I can do is let you have it for a day. But you gotta get in and find me some very specific pictures."

"Look, dude, if this is some freaky messed up stuff... I mean, I ain't touchin' anything illegal. I run a legit porn palace here. My clientele ain't into that crap, and I ain't getting busted for it."

"Yes, the place is delightful. You've got that high-class brothel vibe working real nice."

"I'm just sayin I don't play with that illegal shit, OK?"

"Look, it ain't like that. It's just a security video. But there's tons of it. I need you to locate the last forty-eight hours of files."

"Well," Eddie rolled his head on his shoulders, "I guess I could give it a try; research the model and make, which probably leads to an operating system I could borrow off the dark net. But this could take forever. What are you trying to find anyway?"

"Narrow it down to Friday and Saturday, which will be at the end of the file logs, then scan them until you find a priest."

"A priest?" Eddie said incredulously.

"Yes, a priest. I'm sure you've seen them: big flowing robes, smug air of superiority. As soon as you see him, you'll know. Just get the best resolution you can and print off some images, OK?" Orlando glanced over his shoulder as if the Gestapo was on his trail.

"Jesus, dude, that's not a favour. That's a full-time job."

"Relax, you'll get paid. Have I ever stiffed you before?"

*

In a dark corner of the hospital cafeteria, five priests sat in a circle. Sister Donello patrolled the perimeter. "Let's just go room to room until we find him," she said, circling the despondent men. "It's normal to see priests and nuns visiting the sick and dying. We think he's in the psych ward. It would take ten minutes to find him, tops."

Monsignor Bellecourt interjected. "Sister, you forget the armed guard at the door. Finding the room would be straightforward, but how are we going to get past him?"

"Just walk right in," suggested the portly priest in an Italian accent. "Who's gonna stop a priest? What's the guard gonna do? Shoot us? Tackle us to the floor? I doubt the hospital wants those headlines on the front page."

"There's got to be another way, a peaceful approach," said Bellecourt. "A disguise, maybe?"

"That's a great idea," said the nun. "I could dress like a candy striper or a nurse."

"Sister, thank you, but at eighty-six, you might have some difficulty pulling that off. Besides, it's got to be me. I'm going to need a disguise no one would question."

"Hmm," pondered a priest tapping on his notebook. "Absolute, unquestioned authority around here seems to reside at the doctor level."

"Yes, you're right, Father. All I'd need is a doctor's gown, fit for someone of my considerable height."

Everybody nodded at the same time.

TWENTY-FIVE

The Story of Nog: Part III

Saturday, November 14, 12,042 BC, 4 p.m.

Numa had gone out of his way to make Nog feel comfortable, showing him around the vast and winding cave, then offering him a place of honour to sit. He served Nog a fine selection of dried fruits and meats retrieved from a natural pantry concealed inside a rock crevice. After the meal, Numa offered his guest a cider-like concoction, which made Nog wobbly but happy.

The cave darkened as the yellow sky-ball slipped below the tallest red-rock cliffs in the west. Robotically, Numa fetched an animal skin and unrolled it in a corner under a painting of a hairy two-toed *Darr-meewan*.

Nog nodded his appreciation. Staying the night suited him fine since he was now too tipsy to walk. Besides, it was almost dark, so the likelihood of being eaten on the way home was considerable.

As Numa mixed another batch of delightful cocktails, Nog took in his surroundings. Being only human, he mentally compared everything with his own cave and possessions. Numa's larger home was of no concern, but the superior quality of his artwork challenged Nog's primitive ego. Clearly, Numa was a better painter. And whatever this strange old man did for a living, it seemed sufficient to provide an exceptional supply of food and drink. Numa was clearly too old to hunt or even forage. Yet, his home was overstocked with food, enormous quantities, leaving him wanting for nothing.

Numa served Nog another drink and sat down, crossing his legs in front of his guest.

Nog, trying not to look down, turned his attention to the bedazzled bag attached to Numa's rawhide belt.

Nothing Sacred

"Maa Gaa?" asked Nog, pointing at the bag.

Numa picked the bag up in both hands and cradled it like a baby. "Noor a ween, ara Tooche, Numa Nog," Numa said by way of explanation. Then pointed to the centre of the cave and a naturally formed pedestal.

Nog was sorry he had asked. But the bag seemed important to Numa, and who was Nog to say what should or shouldn't be treasured – *more power to him.* Nog encapsulated these thoughts by replying, "Gaa!"

In under a minute, Numa had slipped into a deep sleep.

What a lightweight, thought Nog, chuckling. He reached over and snagged the clay bowl that Numa had used to mix their libations. Forgoing any further use of a cup, Nog began to lap up the drink directly from the bowl, eventually draining it in one neck-bending motion. As an immediate follow-up, he fell backwards onto his makeshift bed in a state of glee-filled delirium.

TWENTY-SIX

Monday, November 16, 6 a.m.
Phoenix Marriott Hotel,
Room 624

Startled awake by a priority email from his editor, Earl scanned the message with sleepy eyes. It was a long-winded rant criticizing Earl's public performance and complete lack of professionalism. Unable to fall back to sleep, Earl typed a quick reply. First, he assured his editor that his allegiances remained with the *Telegraph*. Then he explained that his total lack of contact was merely due to the all-encompassing workload that swamped each day. After finishing the short message, Earl briefly reviewed the words with a smirk, then stabbed the 'send' button.

Hopping out of bed, he paced the room's perimeter while scrolling down through several screens of his smartphone. It wasn't long before Mary-Lynn's name popped out like a zit on prom night. He tapped it instantly.

Hey, Earl, miss me yet? Hee. Thanks a ton for lunch yesterday. Time went by too fast, and there's still so much to talk about. You're a good man, Mr. Grey. I'm happy we're friends. Are we friends? I hope so. Your description of Doe made me sad, even though, as you say, he seems to like you and needs your company. Anyway, when's our next date? Hee. Don't keep a girl waiting too long. I know where you live.
Hugs and kisses, Mary-Lynn.

"Why would she play me like this," groaned Earl, shaking his head. "Unless she's not? OK, stop it, Earl." He mumbled louder than intended, emotion welling in his chest. In just two days, his cranial cocoon of comfort and security had been ransacked. Blindsided by instant fame, nefarious secrets, religious dogma, and a woman with a penchant for roleplay. Worse yet, his much-needed vacation had been grounded – cancellation due to an inclement existential crisis. Overwhelmed, he found himself in the bathroom, inches from the mirror. He needed a quick chat with his least favourite person in the world.

"Who are you?" he growled under his breath. "Bitten off more than you can chew again, haven't you, idiot? Dad was right." He jabbed a finger towards the mirror for effect, then turned to leave, suddenly sprinting back to the mirror for a second round. "Global media liaison." He laughed in his own face. "Global laughing stock. You said I'd never amount to anything, right, *Dad*? So enjoy the moment wherever you are. Enjoy the spectacle of Earl Grey's global crash and burn." Earl's face reddened as he tightened his grip around his smartphone. "Oh, but not to worry, Earl, at least the gorgeous girl wants you. I'm sure that's real. Asshole!"

He stormed out of the bathroom, collapsing into the only chair in the room. Closing the email from Mary-Lynn, he thumbed his way further up the list of messages in his inbox, hoping to find nothing. But there was an email marked urgent – a message from Frank. Earl felt a chill.

Hi, Earl.
We're not sure where you've got to... but we need to chat before the next press conference, without fail. You need to understand the results of Doe's most recent medical tests. Suffice to say, not good. It's vital you track me down.
Frank.

Earl slumped further in the chair. He typed a quick email to Orlando, inquiring about the pick-up time and where to meet. Once sent, he permitted his mind to wander back to Mary-Lynn's words. Genuine or playing him, she deserved a reply. One must not be rude.

Hi Mary-Lynn,
He paused for what seemed like ten minutes before writing and rewriting the first sentence.
Hi Mary-Lynn, so nice to hear from you so soon.
God no. Sounds like we just had a job interview.
Hi Mary-Lynn, wonderful to hear from you, how have you been?
"Jesus, what's next? How are the kids and Uncle Ray? Have you been to the beach house yet this year? Are you going to Mike and Nora's wedding in August?"
Hi Mary-Lynn, it was indeed a fantastic lunch. Being a newspaper reporter, I'm not very good with words, so I'll try to keep this brief. I, the person, not the media

liaison, would immensely enjoy more time together with you. Let me know what times work for you, and we'll set it up. Earl

He hesitated over the send button for several seconds. Then thought, *screw it*, tapped it firmly, then threw the smartphone onto the bed where it instantly buzzed for an incoming message.

"Goddamnit." He creaked to his feet and trudged over to the kingsize bed. The email was from Orlando.

Hey man, be there at 8 a.m., like it said on the itinerary I gave you yesterday, and you've probably lost. Anyway, meet me in the sub-basement, same spot. No one's caught on yet. Also, please score me some time today. I got stuff to tell you. See you at 8.

Earl raised an eyebrow at Orlando's vague email. He propped up the pillows on the bed and settled in, content to watch the clock slowly work its way toward 8.

*

Slumped in the back corner of the limo, Earl watched as the steam rose from the little hole in the top of his disposable coffee cup. "Orlando, why are you so quiet this morning?" he asked.

"No reason," said Orlando in a guarded tone.

"You said you wanted to chat? You found the priest?" asked Earl as the limo entered the parking garage at the hospital.

"Not yet, but I'm close. Give me a day, and I'll have a pic for you, maybe ID too." Orlando's reflective sunglasses filled the rearview mirror. "But I'll need more than an elevator ride for what we need to discuss. Can we talk when you're done?"

"For sure. Let's see, I've got Doe first thing, then the Hardy Boys. After that, the press conference, and then I'm all yours. But not too long, OK? I might have a date." Earl grinned.

Impressed, Orlando exited the limo and opened Earl's door. "Way to go, playa, nice work," he said, offering Earl a fist bump as he exited the massive vehicle.

"Yah, playa," Earl chuckled, scratching his morning stubble.

As Earl and Orlando arrived at the fourth floor, the elevator lights flickered then promptly died just as the doors squealed open. Two feet away, Bellecourt's God-squad surrounded the opening, intent on divine intervention.

"Oh, come on, guys, like I need this right now," said Earl with a long and lingering eye roll. "Don't make me sic my security man on you."

All eyes dropped on Orlando for several seconds.

"Mr. Grey," said Monsignor Bellecourt, "I assure you the easiest way to get rid of us is to let us meet Mr. Doe."

"Look," said Earl, shouldering his way out of the elevator as the doors tried to close for the third time. "I've already told you, I can't do that. Not my gig. I'm just a pion here. The only people who can grant you access are Shedmore and MacMann. Otherwise, you won't be seeing the big guy anytime soon."

"Oh, make no mistake, we'll see him," threatened Bellecourt. He and his squad surrounded Earl as he walked, like a flock of teenage groupies chasing a rock star. "This is your last chance to do the right thing. Otherwise, we play... hardball."

Earl stopped at the glass doors of the administration office. "Guys, first off, I'd strongly suggest you work on this whole intimidation thing. It's not working for you. To be quite honest, it's kinda funny. Secondly, let's be real for a moment. What do you think you'll accomplish by creating a big stir? Can you picture the headlines? 'Catholic Church Raids Psych Patient's Room!' 'God's Convalescence Disrupted By Priestly Fanboys!' Or how about, 'Dying man's last wish for privacy, thwarted by robed ruffians'?"

The priests glanced back and forth uncomfortably. "Mr. Grey," said Bellecourt, "we won't give you that satisfaction. But, have no doubt, we *will* converse with John Doe. And we will release our findings to the media, along with our comments regarding your continued efforts to block us."

Orlando snapped with anger. "Listen, buddy, I've had enough of your..."

"Orlando!" Earl intervened. "Let it go. Be cool. My penguin-esque friends are only doing their job."

"Tomorrow, Mr. Grey," said Bellecourt. He watched Earl hustle Orlando into the Admin offices.

Grinning as he closed the glass door, Earl said, "You've got quite the temper there, man. But that was seriously cool, you defending me and all. No one's ever had my back before."

"Just doin my job, Grey. Don't get all horny over it."

*

Neither Frank nor MacMann were in their respective offices when Earl arrived, which was fine with him. He only wanted to escape the Priest Patrol and have a chance to breathe before seeing Doe. Both Earl and Orlando took a seat on the official administration couch facing the glass doors – eyes locked on the priests until they finally boarded an elevator and disappeared.

"Well, I better get going… I suppose you can stay here unless you've got somewhere else to be? Some knees to break, maybe a shiv-making class to teach."

"You're a funny man," said Orlando. "It's the funny ones who die young."

"I'll remember that. Besides, I trust you," said Earl.

"You trust me, huh?"

"Well, why not. Despite that massive chip on your shoulder, you seem like a decent guy."

"Anyone ever tell you you're a shitty judge of character?" Orlando shook his head and chuckled.

"Yeah… pretty much everyone."

TWENTY-SEVEN

Monday, November 16, 8:25 a.m.
Phoenix General Hospital,
Room R2112

"Good morning, Mr. Earl," said Robbie, the guard, enthusiastically waving even though Earl was only five feet away.

Earl chuckled. "Hi, Robbie. Just starting?"

"Yep, a few minutes ago. The night watch, Hector, just left. Great guy, we go bowling together."

"Um, good," said Earl, mulling the importance of the information. "How's our star patient today?"

"The doctors prepped him for some tests or something about an hour ago. I heard the nurse say they were upping his pain meds."

Earl nodded solemnly. "I'll head in, but remember, if you see anything... out of the norm... you let me know, OK?"

"Yes, Mr. Earl. But, um, how would I go about letting you know?"

Earl slowly recited his phone number as Robbie entered it into his phone's contact list.

"Have a good visit, Mr. Earl," said Robbie with a smile. He held the door open.

As usual, the room was radiant. A sublime warmth greeted Earl, hugging him tightly, draining his anxieties.

"Earl, my friend." Doe smiled and clapped his hands three times. "Pull up a chair. I had Robbie find a comfy one for you."

"It's good to see you, sir." Earl reached out his hand, gently shaking Doe's cold hand. "I trust you slept OK? You seem in good spirits?"

"Drugs, my boy, wondrous drugs."

"I'm sure they are." Earl adjusted the padded chair and sat down. "Drugs aside, are you improving a little?"

"Oh, no, no. Dying, my boy."

"You need to stop saying stuff like that. Positive thoughts."

Doe looked puzzled. "I thought that was positive. You humans amaze me. Most of you carry this deep belief in angelic afterlives, yet you're terrified to get there. Bit odd, don't you think?"

"I see we've started?" joked Earl.

"No, no. I just find it all a bit hypocritical," chuckled Doe.

"Well, JD, we wouldn't be human if our DNA wasn't marinated in hypocrisy."

"Hard to argue that, son. So, where should we begin?"

"Well, as you can imagine, the press asked countless questions, mostly metaphysical in nature. So I figured I'd divide our chats into categories, essentially asking their questions, but from my point of view, that way, I can throw them a bone each time I see them."

"Clever boy."

Earl blushed. "OK, so, yesterday, we spoke for some time about your body, or shell, as you called it." Earl scanned the entire length of the old man, noting the multiple tubes and monitor connections. "And you said you had no recollection of your history or how you got here. So, rather than debate the topic further, why don't we start today's chat by discussing a more important beginning? In other words, how did we *all* get here?"

"Lovely..." began Doe, "... makes perfect sense. I wouldn't have expected anything less from you, pure unemotional logic."

"I think I was just insulted," chuckled Earl.

"Not at all, be proud of your mind. You're a smart guy, at least when it comes to empirical logic."

"Is that a shot at my lack of belief?"

"No. More a desire to discuss your... *animalistic...* beginnings."

"Evolution?" asked Earl.

"Yes, of course. You don't buy this whole Adam and Eve thing, right? So why step into that quagmire? You're an evolutionist, so let's chat about you and the other apes." Doe grinned.

Earl frowned. "Folks here in Phoenix won't like this one bit."

"People consumed with questions..." whispered Doe, "... don't get to choose the answers."

Earl shook his head. "You certainly don't beat about the burning bush, do you? Straight into controversy. So, we did, in fact, evolve?"

"Of course."

"Unguided?"

"Hmm, that depends on what you mean." Doe paused, looking for the right words. "Was your eventual outcome preplanned via evolution? No. That would be a tedious way to get there."

"So, unguided?"

"Well…" Doe hedged, "… as you know, evolution depends on the environment. Animals don't evolve independent of their surroundings, just the opposite. They evolve based on their surroundings."

"So, you're saying you, as God, created the ground rules, the playing field?" Earl scribbled as he spoke. "And the players made the game up as they went along."

"Not a bad description."

"But, you're also saying you had a hand in creation, the formation of the playing field?"

Doe chuckled. "Sorry, Earl, not quite. This 'God' label is a tad confining. You see, *God* is all around you, everywhere. Accountable for everything but responsible for nothing. Sorry to burst your universal bubble."

"Alright, so you did your thing, then sat back and watched what happened?"

"Pretty much. But I pop in sometimes. When I really need something."

"You have needs?"

"Indeed. God, the label you humans created, is omnipresent but not omnipotent. An important difference worth understanding."

Earl chuckled. "You're ubiquitous, and you screw up a lot?"

"A bit liberal, but yes. A mistake or two has happened."

"So, you come back here to fix things?" suggested Earl.

"Oh no, there's nothing to fix, my boy, it's all part of the same. We're all part of the big nothing." He smiled at Earl sympathetically. "You're struggling for no reason, son. It's all good in the end."

"I see." Earl didn't, but there was enough meat on the bone to formulate a follow-up question. "So, at this moment in time, *God* resides in a hospital bed in Phoenix, Arizona, because it's vital he be here and nowhere else?"

"It's clear this God-talk is leading you astray. Try to think of me in terms of a plurality, a collective."

Earl scratched his neck and wrote a few keywords on the next clean page. "That leads to a whack of new questions. But, I suppose evolution covers how we got here, although not how the universe came to be, or why?"

Doe smiled. "Well, that's an easy one too."

"I highly doubt it," said Earl, smiling back.

"No, seriously, I think I can sum it up for you with a brilliant illustration." Doe sat up straighter in the bed. "Consider for a second this collective I referred to being packed tightly in a tiny little ball. And let's call the ball a singularity, OK?"

Earl stopped writing and listened carefully. He pictured a golf ball in the middle of a fairway.

"Everything that exists, all the stuff that ever was or ever will be, is crammed into this little ball, and the ball sits in nothing. Now, I know that's tough for your brain to process, but try. The ball is not in the middle of the universe. There's no universe. Not yet. And it's not in empty space either, because the fabric of space is part of the universe, which hasn't been created yet. But the ball still exists, sitting in absolutely nothing. Got it?"

"Yep!" Earl lied enthusiastically. He wished he had some weed to help him clarify the concept, or at least make it funny.

Doe continued. "You see, Earl, a human being can know itself through many means. You can see and examine your body if you want. You can smell yourself, although I have no idea why you'd want to do that. And you can hear the sound of your own voice. What's more, other humans can tell you who you are. You can read medical articles to understand your physiological or psychological traits. But a singularity can't do that. It is a singular point with no frame of reference. The only way it can know itself is to divide into pieces and look back upon each piece."

"If you say so," responded Earl. "But for us humans, simply knowing ourselves doesn't explain our endless curiosity. Our need to know the bigger answers to life's questions."

"And what might those be?" asked Doe, fascinated by the directional change.

"You know, our purpose. Is there an afterlife? Why are *we* here?"

"Why are *you* here? Is that an important question?" Doe responded with a quizzical look.

"Yes, everyone asks that. It's the ultimate question of questions, isn't it?"

"Well, it's a silly question," said Doe. "Not really worth wasting your time on."

"Why are we here, is not worth wasting time on?" Earl blinked rapidly in confusion.

Doe shifted in his blankets. "Why does your kind so vehemently seek meaning? Why is it so important to you?" he queried. His old face was etched with compassion.

Earl lowered his gaze to his lap. "I think it has a lot to do with suffering. We want to believe there's some reason for it all, some reward, or at least a decent explanation. Some meaning beyond the perpetuation of the species." Earl sketched a picture of his first dog in the corner of his notebook.

"I see," said Doe.

Earl looked up from the book, his eyes red. "A friend of mine has a question for you. "She wants to know 'What's the point?' It's a very different question than *why are we here*. It transcends biological reasons and demands a pragmatic answer. Clearly, we *are* here, so *what's the point?* But if I may be so bold, I'd like to slightly modify her question, adding my years of personal experience, disappointment, loss, and frustration. JD… what's the fucking point?"

TWENTY-EIGHT

Two corridors away...

Nurse Abigail Morallas spun her chair from the wall of filing cabinets and back to her computer. Stacks of official documents spread out in front of her like a termite's buffet – reports, insurance forms, shift schedules and patient dosages. Her annoyance was visible. She grunted with anger and snorted with indignation. *Years of medical training,* she thought, *and half my day is filing paperwork.*

"Good morning, Nurse Morallas," said Monsignor Bellecourt.

She jumped many inches, gasping with surprise. "Oh my God, you scared me," she said, swivelling around to face the voice. "Oh, Father. I'm so sorry. But you scared me half to death. I meant no disrespect." She crossed herself.

"Quite alright," said Bellecourt smiling. "Would you have a private moment? I have a few questions for you."

The nurse peered over the priest's shoulder at a secondary flank of priests and an elderly nun, leaning in on the conversation. "A private moment, Father?"

Bellecourt glanced over his shoulder, then back to the nurse. "They're with me, my child. Just as all of us are one with God. Don't be frightened. I understand you're attending to Patient John Doe. Is that correct?"

Abigail felt a shiver. "Yes, Father, um, he's one of my patients, part of my rounds."

"And Nurse Morallas… would you consider yourself a good Catholic?"

Bellecourt widened his grin as the group leaned in.

*

"Frank, you need to use far more possessive pronouns in your speech." MacMann paced about in his office. "More, *my* hospital, *my* staff, *I've* decided, etc., to facilitate your ownership of the Chief Admin job."

Staring into the doctor's eyes, it occurred to Frank that by continually speaking on behalf of the hospital, he provided everything MacMann needed for a future defence. 'I was just following orders' would be the first excuse offered as the house of cards collapsed.

"I'll consider it, Rory," said Frank blankly.

"Aye, you do that."

"Earl's with Doe right now," said Frank, changing the subject. "When he comes in, we need to be clear about the prognosis. Let Earl use his judgement regarding future meetings. I suspect he'll want to end this little charade once he hears how serious it has become."

"Oh, we'll tell him, Frank, but I see no reason to push him to end the interviews prematurely. We need a little more time to establish our credibility and reputation before pulling the plug. That goes for Grey, too, if he ever wants to work in the media again. You heard those scathing voicemails from his editor? That boy's in for a whipping when he returns to the North Pole."

Frank changed the subject again. "What about Del-Monte? Any word on who he was?"

"Still working on it," MacMann lied, having never given it a second thought since the priest left. "Probably just a hack, imposter, most likely a reporter. I suspect he'd be in far more trouble if he went public than we would. After all, he duped us, right? We're the victims." MacMann grinned.

"I marvel at your mind," said Frank coldly. "Only you could conclude we're blameless in all of this." A little spittle flew from Frank's mouth in contempt.

*

The makeshift meeting room was sparsely decorated – no artwork or signs, just a round plastic table and scattering of stackable chairs. Nurses were known to use the all-purpose room for lunch or as a hideaway on horrible days.

Sister Donello and four priests sat lined against the long wall. The uncomfortable plastic seats creaked at the tiniest movement. In the centre, at the table, Nurse Morallas sat nervously across from Bellecourt, her eyes fixed on the gold crucifix hanging around his neck. "I understand what you're asking of me, Father, but you must realize how much trouble I'd be in if I helped you," she said, trying, but failing, to be assertive. "I swore an oath to protect my patients. I can't even tell you the room he's in, although it's not much of a secret; it's the only room with a manatee guarding the door."

"I understand, my child. But perhaps we could join you during your rounds, a spiritual pick-me-up for the patients, which would include Mr. Doe, of course.

It's not like you'd be letting us in. We'd just pop in after you're finished… without your permission."

"Father, my job is to protect my patient." Abigail looked up, searching for strength from above. "And the manatee's job is to shoot you if you barge in without permission. However," she compiled a quick thought, "if you brought him McDonald's…"

"Alright, Miss Morallas, I respect your professionalism," Bellecourt said. "We won't bother you any further on the matter. Can I trust this little conversation will remain between us?"

"Yes, Father."

"Last thing, Miss Morallas, a quick question, entirely unrelated. We've been asked to meet with Dr. MacMann. Apparently, our rendezvous location is near his locker, the area where he keeps his personal items. Unfortunately, no one told us where that was. Would you happen to know?"

Abigail raised a skeptical eyebrow. "Umm, I can only think of two places that might be. It's either the doctor's lounge, which is the private café and change room for the doctors, or his office in the administrative wing."

"Ah, yes, someone mentioned the café. That must be it. Thank you so much for your help, my child. Now, go in peace. You've been of… divine… assistance." Bellecourt stood up and gave her a fatherly tap on the shoulder.

"Thank you, Father," she said, then turned to the others. "Fathers, Sister."

The God-squad smiled.

TWENTY-NINE

Two corridors back the other way...

"Hmm, what's the fucking point?" Doe placed the fingertips on both his hands together and scrunched up his face. "Let me begin by asking what you think the point is for the amoeba, or the slug or perhaps a fish?"

"JD, Lord knows I've known a few slugs in my day, but it's too easy to suggest that since there's no point in being a slug, we humans share the same valuation."

"Earl, my question wasn't, 'What's the point of being a slug?' No, I asked you what the *slug* presumes the point to be."

"Oh, well, that's a difficult one for me, not being a slug and all. It's an unknowable answer for sure. How can we know what a slug believes?"

Doe smiled. "Your thoughts presume that slugs, fish, or birds never internalized the question in the first place. You seem to align with the prevailing opinion, outside of Disney studios, that suggests none of these creatures take a moment to think about their purpose."

"Think?" said Earl. "But that's just it, they don't think. We do."

"Who's we? You mean apes?"

Earl scratched his head. "Well, ya, evolved apes. Meaning ape descendants. Look, I'm just saying we're the only species on this planet that... thinks."

"Oh no, no, no. My, my, aren't we starting the day with a bowl full of arrogance? Thinking is simply the learned extension of experience, experimental actions, and differing results. A cultural lather, rinse and repeat, passed down in centuries of DNA, as well as words, pictures, dance and the friggin' internet."

Earl laughed.

"You're not giving the poor slug a chance, are you, Earl? At this moment in time, it doesn't think as you do. Therefore, you conclude it has no point of view. Such racism." Doe chuckled. "As for those animals who do think, by your definition, there are many, from chimps to dolphins. Perhaps rudimentary thinking, compared to yours, but thinking nonetheless."

"OK." Earl was amused at the left-hand turn the discussion had taken. "So, let's say other things think too, in some manner. What does this have to do with understanding their point, their place in the universe?"

"In many respects, Earl, they are smarter than you and the bunch you hang out with."

"Canadians?"

"No, humans. Most animals understand their purpose. Despite their instinct to eat, procreate and wander into the snowy woods after their eightieth birthday, animals do something so simple it's been rendered invisible to your kind. An activity long since lost on your so-called *advanced species*."

"Is it, eat their young? I always thought we'd be better off if we ate the dumb ones."

Doe edged towards Earl. "Life is to be experienced, Earl. Not just something you wander through, but something to *live*, every moment, every single sensory perception, noted, registered and logged."

Earl sat still, his pencil twitching in search of a sentence or valid word. "Boy, when you say simple, you don't mess around. They live! That's the answer? Just live and experience life? I suppose it's better than '42', but seriously?"

Doe took no offence. He giggled, sending tiny tremors rattling down the bed, vibrating the wires and tubes connecting him to a plethora of machines. "I knew you'd be disappointed."

"It's just a little too… simplistic, don't you think? Just live, experience every moment? Christ, I do that every time I get drunk." Earl unconsciously closed his notebook, a move keenly noted by Doe. "So, that's it, that's the friggin' point of all this?"

"There's more. But first, let this sink in: The action of living within an experience, as opposed to something that simply happens around you, was lost centuries ago. Your life is to be experienced, be it joyous or horrific. In truth, Earl, one can find the most significant experiences even at the precipice of disaster."

THIRTY

Later the same day...

It was nearly 10:30 a.m. when Earl arrived at the hospital's administrative wing, conscious of the empty foyer, having no desire for a priestly pow-wow before the 11 a.m. press conference. Frank, appearing suddenly out of nowhere, quickly ushered Earl into a small meeting room where MacMann was already stewing in the dark. "Well, thank you for gracing us with your presence, your highness," spewed the doctor.

"Gentlemen, sorry for the wait." Earl plopped down on one of two vacant chairs in front of the desk and looked up at Frank, implying he should sit as well.

Frank remained standing. "Earl, as I mentioned in my email, Mr. Doe's doing poorly. We've had to increase his pain medication… twice. He's a tough old bird, doesn't complain, but it's clear his body is in a state of extreme decay. A lesser man would have passed out. We're amazed at his composure."

Earl's face dropped. "During my visit, the smile never left his face. Is that the drugs, or is he a master at disguising pain?"

"Bit of both, I suspect," MacMann piped in. "At this point, I give him a 20 percent chance of survival. Mr. Doe's body is breaking down, giving up. It's hard to explain, but he's not responding to the liver or kidney medication, and the internal bleeding might have spread. We're scheduling a diagnostic laparoscopy. It's a camera, inserted at various points. We need to get a look at the bleeders and the state of his organs."

Earl's sadness spread throughout his deflated frame. He slumped in the chair, arms dangling. "How much time does he have?"

"Hard to say," MacMann replied. "There's comorbidity at work here. It's a race. If we can operate, stop the bleeders and find him a liver donor fast, we could buy him time – but not long. The kidneys are in bad shape, but they could wait for treatment once he regains strength. A great deal depends on his ability to hold on. Hence the 20 percent."

Earl picked out patterns on the floor.

"Earl, medicine can only do so much," Frank offered in a compassionate tone. "Sometimes it comes down to timing and luck. Neither's on Doe's side right now, my friend."

Earl sighed deeply.

"In a moment, you'll have to address the press," Frank began. "I realize this is sudden and overwhelming, but do you have any initial thoughts on what you might say?"

Earl shook his head to indicate no.

"It's simple," MacMann said, standing up. "You're a professional journalist." He rolled his eyes at his own words. "Separate yourself from your emotions. Tell them what you've learned this morning and answer any new questions that crop up. Leave the medical prognosis to me. Doe's not your friend. He's your subject. Do your job."

Frank recoiled at the statement but then proceeded to nod. "Harsh as it sounds, I think that's for the best. When we reconvene, we'll discuss how we should proceed."

Earl shook his head. "This isn't about us. It's about him. And he wants to talk, wants to tell me his story, and I want to hear it. Press be damned. They'll get what I give them, and perhaps there's something to be gained there too."

"Now you're talking, laddie," MacMann said, forcing his shoulders back.

"Jesus, Rory!" Earl threw his head back. "I don't mean personal gain. I mean, maybe we can do some good here. Atone for *our* selfishness."

"Speak for yourself, lad."

"I'm pretty sure I was," said Earl.

*

The delay in the press conference's start-time had roiled the pack of reporters, jammed together, shoulder to shoulder in the makeshift press room. The trap was primed, lying in wait for the next sacrificial lamb to drop by. Into the ambush strode the familiar procession, forced grins stretched to facial edges. Frank led the group as always, followed by MacMann, with Earl trailing glumly.

"Good morning, everyone. I'm very sorry for the delay. We've had a few... logistics... issues. Once again, my name is Frank Shedmore, Acting Hospital Administrator."

MacMann frowned and cleared his throat.

"With me today, as always, is Dr. MacMann, Chief Medical Officer, and our media liaison, Mr. Earl Grey. But first, I'd like to start with a few housekeeping issues."

Earl grimaced. A forgotten housekeeping task of his own springing to mind.

"It's come to my attention that some of you are broadcasting from the front lawn and side access points. We thank you for freeing up access to the emergency entry and ambulance ramps; however, we've been advised of another issue. It seems many of your video angles and photographs include background shots containing companies and institutions who have complained about their inclusion in this story. Their respective lawyers have contacted me, and, as such, I'm obliged to state the following. Please refrain from using any further camera angles that include: Evermore Cryogenics Corporation, Rippers Bar and Grill, Arby's, and the Arizona State Democratic Headquarters."

Frank shuffled his notes. "Alright, Dr. MacMann…?"

Earl watched the room with keen interest. The crowd was bigger than the previous day's, spilling into the halls. He spied the *First Edition* crew; two young men were busy with various audio and video duties. Flanking them was a six-foot-tall plastic Ken doll sporting a Hollywood spray tan and a peroxide smile right out of a dentist's wet dream.

"Good morning, everyone," bleated MacMann, unable to stop glancing at the throbbing glow from the orange reporter.

The crowd collectively groaned.

Disturbed by the mob's collective disdain, MacMann moved straight to business. "Mr. Doe's been through a series of tests over the last twenty-four hours. Most of these tests were lab-based, analyzing his blood and urine. So far, the results are… less than encouraging."

"Is he dying?" said several reporters in unison.

"We are scheduling an emergency laparoscopy to examine his internal organs," urged MacMann ignoring the questions. "It is my professional diagnosis that Mr. Doe is suffering from several conditions brought upon by exposure to the elements and pre-existing conditions related to the liver." MacMann looked up from his papers with the intent to smile, then thought better of it. "After an internal examination, we'll have a better idea of what's going on. We'll advise you of our treatment plan and priorities as soon as possible."

"Doctor," hailed the Ken doll. "Steve Atkins – *First Edition*. Can you state categorically if Mr. Doe is in a position to survive the treatment process and will, um… survive the treatment process?" The orange man grinned, forcing several camera operators to adjust their light metering.

"As I just explained," said MacMann. "Additional information is required before any declaration can be made. Besides, as a doctor, I've never been in a position to guarantee anyone's mortality under any circumstance. That should be obvious, even to a simpleton."

"I'm not sure what you mean," Steve Atkins responded, smiling like a poster boy for condoms.

"No doubt," replied MacMann. "Was it the mortality word or the simpleton comment that confused you?"

Frank closed his eyes and wished he was far away.

"I'm just asking if you're sure he'll survive?" repeated Atkins.

"Uh, huh." MacMann cracked his knuckles and glanced around the room. "Are there any other questions regarding Mr. Doe's condition? Questions born of logic, presented in a grammatical manner defendable as English?"

Frank's eyes shot open. Earl stifled a snort by covering his mouth.

Not surprisingly, there were no further questions, just blank stares and immobile pens on pads.

"Well, very good then," chirped MacMann. "When I return, I will present the results and analysis from Mr. Doe's laparoscopy."

Frank wedged his way in front of MacMann and took to the microphone. "Thank you, doctor. Now I'd like to bring in Mr. Grey to update you on his discussions with the patient and his interpretation of Mr. Doe's message."

Earl took the podium. "Hello. It's good to see you all again; everyone looks to be in fine spirits today." The crowd glanced back and forth at each other; a muffled 'fuck you' resonated from the back row. "However, I'm afraid I have a confession to make."

Frank and Rory shot panicked glances at each other, visibly stiffening.

"Remember yesterday when you asked me to take pictures of Mr. Doe? Well…"

THIRTY-ONE

Seconds later…

Earl's confession that he'd again forgotten to take any photographs triggered the crowd's pent-up fury. Anger spread quickly throughout the room and culminated in a crushing stampede onto the makeshift stage. Added to this onslaught were several projectiles never designed to fly – blunt objects lacking any aerodynamic quality.

Earl struggled in defence of the surge. Hands were grabbing and pulling, pushing him back and forth like a rag doll. "People!" he shouted. "People! Please! Please, just give me a minute to explain."

The thunderous noise lessened only slightly, like an interval between songs at a Zeppelin concert. But it was enough for Earl's voice to come through. "Look, it was an oversight, OK. I got caught up in the discussion, which, if you allow me, I think you'll find fascinating. But for sure, I'll take a photo tomorrow, Mr. Doe permitting."

"Describe him for us!" someone shouted. "Or didn't you bother to look at him either?"

"That's cold." Earl pouted. "But I'll try."

Decibels dropped even lower.

"I suspect Mr. Doe is in his seventies. He has white hair and a trimmed white beard like Wolf Blitzer's, and he's deeply tanned. It's obvious he was muscular in his prime, although now he appears weak and frail. He has blue eyes, a thick prominent nose and a welcoming smile."

The crowd gradually eased off.

Pausing to catch his breath, Earl straightened his jacket and pants, twisted around him like a jungle vine. "Look, I know this is hard. I'm just getting used to it myself. It's my first time interviewing a deity."

"You really believe this is God?" shouted a reporter from the third row, thrusting her voice recorder high into the air.

"That is who they introduced me to, and that's who the gentleman claims to be," said Earl, mustering his fake faith.

"Have you witnessed more miracles?" asked the same reporter.

"Maybe not by your definition of miracle, however…"

The word 'however' was enough to drop a blanket of silence over the room. The crowd hushed.

Earl continued. "The simple fact he's cognisant, mobile, and jocular, despite his severe injuries, is in itself a miracle. He's had quite an ordeal, and by rights, he should be unconscious. But that's not the case. He's delightful, animated, and highly intelligent." Earl placed both hands on the podium to emphasize his point, then scanned over the crowd, a move he'd seen many preachers perform in his youth. "Our initial discussions have centred around *purpose*, our purpose, the purpose of humanity. Mr. Doe's schooling me on the Creator's hand in guiding our evolutionary path."

Chaos returned. Reporters unleashed a torrent of ballistic queries too garbled to decipher. They bounced off the back wall then echoed throughout the room like shrapnel.

"Please, please, let me continue," urged Earl, spreading his arms. "I'll try to get to all your questions. But, you must understand, Doe is telling us there is indeed a process of evolution, and it guides every living thing on this or any other planet."

Well, that was about it for any hope of a quiet or orderly press conference. The room transformed into a three-year-old's birthday party. From every angle, the press verbally assaulted Earl with questions, barely discernible through the din. Questions were grouped into three general categories:

Category One

Now that you've alienated every creationist on the planet by confirming a theistic connection to evolution, where does God fit in? Is everything now by chance, random mutation, or was God partial to ten-ton lizards before he got bored and chucked a comet at them?

Category Two

Where does this leave divine guidance and intervention? What good is prayer now if we're all predisposed to disease, negative character traits, and outcomes based on genetically inherited qualities?

Category Three

What's this *other* planet stuff? Are we not alone? Did God create aliens? Who does he love more, us or the bug-eyed two-fingered grey blobs from Betelguise? In whose image are these aliens created? Is God a bug-eyed two-fingered grey blob from Betelguise? Are the rules and commandants the same on other planets, and what does alien hell look like?

Earl felt confident that *this* was what alien hell looked like.

MacMann grinned, bouncing on his heels like a boy watching his sister get grounded.

"Um," said Earl. "I don't have all of those answers, nor was I astute enough to think of those questions at the opportune time. However, I'll try to work them into future discussions. But, if you'll allow me to continue, Mr. Doe did explain his role within the cosmos."

That seemed to quieten the room enough to regain order.

"He said we are all one. All of us come from the one… God, if you will. It's impossible for us to be apart."

Reporters scribbled on pads and whispered into voice recorders.

Surprised at how easy it was to restore order, Earl continued interpreting Doe's words. "Mr. Doe went on to say that before everything, there was the one. And the one existed inside itself. Sort of like a golf ball. But with no golf course." Earl paused to sort through his elusive thoughts as they swarmed like bees inside his head. "OK, OK, right. And, the only way 'the one' could become self-aware was to expand. Explode the tiny ball into trillions of parts so he could look at every component. Every part, including us, but with the full intention of being whole again one day. Isn't that wonderful?"

Two levels up, a bed ridden John Doe stared at the live feed emanating from his tiny TV with delight. He grinned widely and clapped his hands, causing the TV to flicker.

*

Bellecourt confidently marched into the doctor's lounge as if he had been summoned. Without his robe and collar, his black shirt, pants and tan leather shoes screamed medical professional. Speed-walking up to the coffee machine, he poured a cup, then sat down with a lifestyle magazine, far away from three doctors sharing a coffee near the window. After twenty minutes, the three doctors got up to leave, briefly nodding as they passed their assumed peer. It was Bellecourt's time to move. He rose, tossed the magazine, left the cold coffee on the table, and headed for the locker area.

Pleased to see nameplates on doors with no padlocks, finding MacMann's locker proved easier than Bellecourt expected. After one last check for people or video cameras, he popped open the door marked MacMann, R, MD, with a firm pull. Bingo! Three white robes, neatly hung, still in their dry-cleaning plastic. Reaching up inside a transparent bag, he unhooked one of the gowns, careful not to disturb the others or tear the plastic. Conveniently hanging from the back of the locker's door was a stethoscope, the perfect accessory to complete his ensemble. Bellecourt headed for the door, stolen goods in hand, and speed-walked down the hall toward the parking area.

THIRTY-TWO

Back in the media room...

Earl watched the reporters with amusement. The press conference was as good as over. The crowd had disengaged, busily filing their breaking news stories to beat the competition to the punch. Feeling a tug on his trousers, Earl spun on his heels to find Orlando beckoning him to follow. Frank and MacMann had already taken a cue from the media's sudden bout of introspection and left the press room via the green-room door. Earl elected to follow Orlando directly through the crowd and into the hall, then made a beeline for the parking area and the limo's solitude.

"Where to, boss?" asked Orlando, adjusting his hand-controls.

"Not sure yet," mused Earl, settling in the front passenger seat. "Hey, tell me something, and I mean no offence to your height, but limo driver? Seems like an odd and awkward profession to choose?"

Orlando stared across the seat at Earl. "I do take offence, Grey. This is a perfectly acceptable profession for someone like me."

"You mean a vertically challenged individual?"

Orlando gritted his teeth. "No, I don't. Look, for your information, this job gives me the perfect place to operate my real business. Downtime for chauffeurs is enormous. Ninety percent of the time, we just sit around and wait. So it's a great front to oversee my other... interests?"

"Main business? Other interests?" Earl was intrigued.

"Look, dude. I'm not here to be interviewed. I have a lot of stuff on the go. Stuff you wouldn't understand. It's an underground economy thing. Get it?"

"So... it's illegal?" Earl grinned.

"Look, do you wanna go somewhere or not? I'm a busy man."

"OK, OK, relax. I was just curious. Let me check my messages and see what's happening. Besides, it was you who wanted to chat. You said you had something to tell me."

"Ya, I do. But I could really use a beer first." Orlando glanced at the digital clock read-out, 12:01 p.m.

"Isn't there beer in the back?" asked Earl, motioning his thumb behind him. "I mean, there's scotch. There must be beer."

Both men paused for a moment, then stared at each other, processing the same thought. Before you could say 'open bar', they had crawled through the driver-partition, raided the minibar and settled themselves into the oversized leather couch at the back of the limo.

"To free beer." Orlando raised his can in the air.

Earl cheered and clinked his can with Orlando's. "To Dr. MacDouche!" Earl added. The pair both took large gulps of their beers.

"So whatcha got for me, my friend?" asked Earl.

"I am your friend, aren't I, Earl? I mean, you consider me a friend; it's not some meaningless phrase to you?"

Earl was puzzled. "Of course. I liked you from the moment you stole my bag at the airport and threatened me with nebulous acts of violence." He laughed and took another swig of beer.

Orlando smiled and drained his can of its contents. "You're a strange animal, but I can't say I hate you."

"Well, that's the nicest thing anyone's said to me all day. Thanks, big guy."

"OK, stop calling me that or I'll murder you whether I like you or not," said Orlando, discarding his empty and opening the fridge to fetch another can.

"You realize I'm just messing with you, right?" laughed Earl.

"Keep it up, motherfucker."

Earl scrolled through his email messages. "OK," he said, changing the subject. "Check this out. Here's a message from the *National Enquirer*, offering me $100,000 for the exclusive story and rights to the first pictures."

"Take it," snorted Orlando.

"Haa, no, I don't think so. Those reporters almost skinned me alive today. Imagine if I told them I'd cut a deal with the *Enquirer*?"

"Money's money!"

"There's more to life than money, my friend. Although I could be wrong since most of mine is tied up in my collection of returnable beer cans." Earl continued scrolling through his inbox. "Here's the fourth one from my editor. Check this out," he announced, clearing his throat.

Why have you ignored my three previous messages? This morning's press conference was an embarrassment to our paper, not to mention our nation. I'm contacting the hospital administrator to propose a substitute for you. A reporter who won't forget to take pictures or mention our newspaper. A reporter with passable investigative talent who can prepare statements of substance without using comparatives to Wolf Blitzer…

Earl lowered the Blackberry to his lap, unable to stop giggling. "He goes on to comment about my speaking abilities, fashion sense and distorted evolutionary path."

Orlando was rolling on the leather sofa, teary-eyed with laughter.

"I seriously think he's having a breakdown," said Earl.

"How the hell could you work for a guy like that?" asked Orlando, straightening up to retrieve the handgun that had spilled from his jacket, much to Earl's surprise.

"Um." Earl elected to ignore the sudden introduction of weaponry, assuming everyone in Arizona likely carried, licence or not. "It's more accurate to say he employs me. I wouldn't say I ever worked for him."

More laughter. "Are we drunk?" asked Orlando through his beer can.

"No way. We've only had two beers. Although you're only, what, fifty pounds?"

"Fuck you!" Orlando snapped, then broke into fits of giggles again.

"You're supposed to be driving me somewhere."

"OK, OK, just one more beer. It's hot out."

Earl continued scanning his phone, and sure enough, there were several texts from Mary-Lynn. He read them in timestamp order, silently asking Orlando to pause their conversation by holding up his index finger.

I saw you today on camera, Earl. Looking good. Can't wait to see you, but it will have to be for dinner. I've got a meeting with the team today, including that poor excuse for an orange tree, Steve Atkins. Fuck, I hate him. Well, I don't hate him, but you know what I mean. I hate him. How's 7 p.m.?

Hi again. I mean, can you believe the stupidity of that moron? 'Duh, do you think God will…, ummmm, I don't know what you mean, doctor…' Jesus, he can't even form a sentence. Yet, they brought that sack of shit in to replace me. What's he gonna do, pose his way through the story? Total dickwad!

Hi, Earl. Sorry about the last email. I probably sound obsessed, and I'm not. It doesn't bother me at all. Fucking tool. Anyway. Is seven good?

Earl wrote back and attempted to keep it cool.

Seven's great, tell me where and I'm in.

"What are you smiling at," asked Orlando, fetching two more beers.

"Ohh, nothing much, just got a date, that's all." Earl's chest involuntarily puffed.

"Well, look at you, the great white hope. What time?"

"Dinner at seven. And since you're too drunk to take me anywhere today, I propose we stay right here and order pizza."

Orlando snapped to attention. "On it, Mr. Grey." He phoned in the pizza order, then debated with the restaurant about his odd delivery request. After assuring them he was dead serious and actually ordering from a limo in the General's parking lot, he snapped his flip phone closed with irritation.

"Wicked," said Earl with a grin. "Alright, so enough stalling. What's so secretive that you needed three beers and more than three minutes to discuss?"

Orlando nodded. "Well, for one thing, I got the videos from the hospital."

"You did? Holy shit, that's great. Let's see them."

"Not so fast. They're in some wacko format, costing me big bucks to crack," Orlando said, taking a sip from his beer. "Oh, by the way, I'm gonna need big bucks."

"How big?" asked Earl, one eyebrow arching to his hairline.

"Probably $500. Plus my fees."

"Damn, dude, did you hire IBM or something? So, how'd you get the videos?"

"Ahh, it was genius. My genius. Against the moronacity of the hospital techie guy. Is moronacity a word? Anyway, five minutes later, boom, I walk out with the box of those backup file thingies. Understand?"

"Um, sort of. So you stole a backup drive instead of just copying the files?"

Orlando slumped back down on the leather sofa. "And it was soooo easy. Child's play. You'll have your priest pics... soon-ish."

"Nobody saw you?"

"Of course somebody saw me, you dick." Orlando fought to sit back up like a turtle on its back. "I'm small, but not invisible, you know? I had to walk in there and get them. But I did have a cunning disguise. I wore a badge with a different name on it."

Earl rolled his eyes.

"Just don't worry about it, Earl, my Earl," Orlando stammered and reached for the last beer. "The techie moron won't say a word. He thinks everything's the way it should be. So shut up."

Earl laughed. "Fair enough. OK, let's talk about phase two of Operation Phony Priest."

"Impossible!" Orlando giggled.

"Impossible?"

"Yeah, you haven't paid me for phase one yet. What am I a fucking bank? Do I look like a bank, Earl?"

"Piggybank, maybe."

"Scuse-me?"

"No, you don't look like a bank. I'll get you the cash tonight. Now, can I tell you about our next move?"

Orlando drained his beer, placing the can on the small round table in the middle of the limo. "No, you can't, Grey Earl. I still haven't told you my secret. And you can't tell this to anyone, OK?" He put a finger over his mouth and shushed. "Shhhhhhhhhhh."

"OK," said Earl grinning. "Secret spy stuff, is it?"

Orlando squinted at Earl. "Yes! Yes, it is my pasty friend. And the spy in question… is me."

THIRTY-THREE

Monday, November 16, 12 noon.
401 North 7th Street,
Denny's Diner

The booth at Denny's was typical in design but had the advantage of being tucked away in a corner with no window, surrounded by empty tables awaiting the lunch crowd.

On one side sat Mary-Lynn Wu and her twenty-two-year-old senior team leader, Andy. Across the table sat her cameraman, James, violently digging into his fully expensible bacon and pancake breakfast. Beside him, a tall orange creature named Steve positioned a smartphone on the table so everyone could hear their producer's voice on the speaker.

"David, this makes no sense," said Mary-Lynn at the phone. "It should be me on camera, I started the story, and I'm leading the investigation and research. Steve's got no clue what he's doing. He doesn't even know why he's down here, do you Steve?"

"Mary-Lynn," David's voice sounded distant in more ways than one. "I take no pleasure in this decision. You know it comes from on high. You're lucky this story is so ubiquitous. Anyone who saw your profanity-laced rant has likely forgotten it by now. Unfortunately, the network hasn't. And you know we're getting a hefty fine from the FCC. You're lucky you have a job at all."

"Look…" Mary-Lynn stated, "… I've said thank you a hundred times, but the truth is, if I can't get back on camera, there's no reason to stay with *First Edition*. You've got to find a way to get me back on air… and this mutated carrot… off."

The mutated carrot didn't register that he was, in fact, the mutated carrot in question.

"Can I get the pecan pie?" asked James across the table, interrupting Mary-Lynn's train of thought.

"Just find the hidden angle here," spat David, "the story behind the story. Get us behind the scenes, and I promise you'll get the production credit."

Mary-Lynn sat back and looked at her untouched French toast. "Yeah, and golden boy here gets credit for another stunning piece of investigative journalism. Hey, Steve, can you even spell investigative journalism?"

"Mary-Lynn," David cut in with blunt force. "This is gonna take time. I can't promise you anything. Laying low's your best bet right now. It's not like another show's gonna pick you up after your profane rant on live TV."

Mary-Lynn rolled her eyes. "What happened to the three-second delay? I was supposed to have a three-second live delay. How did you guys not catch it?"

"I, N, V, E, S, T, E," Steve began to spell using his fingers.

"Bzzzzzzzzz," said James the cameraman, laughing.

"David, I'll do my best to deliver a solid backstory, and yes, I want the production credit. But you have to get me back on camera, even if it's standing beside this imbecile. I need vindication. Just get me some face time."

As Steve looked around the restaurant for the imbecile in question, David mumbled, "I'll see what I can do," then the phone went dead.

"Terrific," moaned Mary-Lynn, burying her face in her hands.

James reached across the table and gently patted her arm. "Does our expense account cover refills?"

*

Several hours had passed in the limo. The pizza and beer were gone, and the scotch supply was near critical. Orlando had delivered an impassioned confession detailing his sketchy history and his two previous run-ins with the law. But he had insisted he had been framed in both cases – once for illegal firearms possession and the other for armed robbery. He had gone on to point out how easy it was to pick out a four-foot black guy in a bogus police line-up and then explained how the 'three-strike' law worked in America. As a side note, Orlando suggested that his shady past was the only reason MacMann insisted on selecting him in the first place. The doctor hadn't been shy about leveraging the 'third strike and you're out' law to ensure his spy remained loyal. Completing the lengthy mea culpa, Orlando explained that his secret mission was to observe Earl's every move and report them to MacMann daily.

Earl had listened intently to the entire confession, never once dropping his smile. Once Orlando had finished, Earl offered instant forgiveness in the form of a high-five, allowing Orlando to decompress with relief.

"I'd say this is a lucky break," Earl said with a smile. "Now, you must continue to report to MacMann each day, mindless logistical stuff, but keep the lines of communication open. We may need it in the coming days. There's nothing more valuable than a trusted double agent."

*

Bellecourt, dressed in MacMann's doctor's gown, strutted out from the elevator and into the psychiatric ward, stolen stethoscope slung around his neck. This was a rookie mistake, as experienced physicians prefer the over-the-shoulder look or simply stuffed in the gown's pocket.

After several false starts and dead ends, Bellecourt came upon an annex leading to a new set of rooms. At the far end of the long hallway, a large uniformed guard stood motionless, seemingly entranced with the beige wall ahead of him.

Bellecourt approached the guard with a purposeful stride. "Hello, my son."

"What?" said Robbie, shaken from his trance and confused by the salutation.

"Oh, sorry, you look like my son. I meant to say hello, young man."

"Hello," said Robbie, chewing more gum than legally permitted in one mouth.

"There's a quick medical question I have for the patient," said Bellecourt, trying very hard not to lie.

"And you are?" asked the guard, popping a big pink bubble.

"Oh, the name's Bellecourt," said the priest. "Haven't we met before? It seems like we must have?"

"Can't say I know the name, doctor, and I don't remember your face." Robbie tried squinting to see if it might help identify the visitor. "Nope, I think I'd remember you. Let me call the main office and check."

"No, no, young man, mister, um, what's your name?"

"Robbie."

"Wonderful. No, Robbie, that's not necessary. This will only take a second. One of the nurses forgot to ask the patient if he had any allergies to medications. I won't be long." Bellecourt felt the sting of the lie rifle through him.

"Nurse?" Robbie smiled for the first time. "Which nurse?"

"Oh," Bellecourt spied an opening, "it was Nurse Morallas."

"Abigail?" Robbie stepped closer to Bellecourt, a smile broadening his ample cheeks.

"Yes, yes, of course," said Bellecourt, wondering how much penance he'd have to pay for this particular slice of misdirection.

"Did she say anything about me?"

"Well," Bellecourt went all in. "She said you were a nice young manat... um, man. And that you were very responsible and nice, and um, fit."

Robbie grinned again. "Sweet!"

"Yes, yes, it is sweet. So anyway, I'll just pop in and be right back."

"Oh, ohh," stammered Robbie, his smile popping like a pink gum bubble.

Bellecourt stalled and turned, his hand resting on the push plate, a three-inch opening visible into the room. "What's wrong?"

"It's just that," Robbie reddened, "Abigail's married. They've been together forever. Oh wow. This could get messy."

*

"Don't you have to be somewhere?" said Orlando, swirling the last of the scotch in his glass.

"Lots of time, big guy, dinner's not until seven."

"Where's the restaurant?"

"Let me check." Earl reached for his phone, which was sitting in the ice bucket. "Oh, she's been busy. There's a bunch of messages. Ah, here we go, Fleming's. Does that mean anything to you?"

"Jesus!" Orlando rubbed his forefinger and thumb together, indicating bags of money were required to dine at said establishment. "Pretty nice, too nice, for the likes of you."

"I could use a little pampering," Earl laughed.

"Yeah, but here's the thing. Fleming's is not just around the corner. It's almost in Peoria, and you'll need a cab since there's no way I can drive." Orlando looked at his watch. "It's already six."

"What?" yelled Earl. "After six, it can't be, no way. Holy shit, it is."

"I'm not the only one who took a nap, Mr. Grey."

"Great, so now we've slept together. And I'm late for my date."

"No, no, you won't be late. I'll call you a cab, but you'll still be drunk when you get there, so don't go saying anything awkward, OK?"

"What? Why would I say something..."

"Taxi's five minutes away," interrupted Orlando, lowering his phone. "Now, straighten up and do something with your hair. You look drunk and stupid."

"I can't believe this. Where did the time go? One minute we're drinking beer, the next, it's after six. I need to shower and change, and, damn it, I've got to pull myself together."

"Yeah, chill, dude, you're not meeting the Queen of Canada. We'll get you there early so you can clean up in the washroom."

Earl's panic grew steadily, peaking as a yellow Crown Victoria pulled up alongside the limo. The driver, an eager young cowboy, tipped his hat toward Orlando, who peered back from the rear driver's-side window. Earl gradually emerged from the far side of the limo and offered a slight nod to the cabbie-cowboy. Then, clearly drunker after standing up, he moved tentatively towards the big Ford, not at all as the crow might have flown.

"Have fun, Earl, win one for the Gipper, or Gretzky, or whatever the hell you've got up there in Canada." Orlando laughed at himself, then reached for the scotch bottle before slumping back in the seat.

Opting for the taxi's back seat, since he didn't want to talk to anyone, Earl buckled his seatbelt after carefully inspecting the mechanism and reflecting on its overall concept. "Oh, oh, I need to hit an ATM on the way," he stammered to the driver. "And no stop-and-go, OK, I get a bit car sick."

*

"Did I say Morallas?" stammered Bellecourt. "I might have misheard. I meet a lot of people every day. I think she's new. But, now that I think of it, it was more like, um, Bor... ee... alis."

Robbie placed his right hand on a can of pepper spray hanging from his overcrowded belt. "Sir, I'm gonna have to ask you to step away from the door."

"Are you crazy?" Bellecourt added authority to his voice as he tried to figure out what had just gone wrong.

Robbie was quick to sum up the situation. "Sir, I've never seen you before. You have no ID badge or name tag. You're wearing hard-sole shoes, a no-no around here, and a real doctor wouldn't be caught dead checking on a patient's allergies. In addition, there is nobody named Borealis, or even close to that, at this hospital. I know that because I study the duty roster each day as part of my job." The guard stiffened with pride, somehow growing even taller.

"Um." Bellecourt felt his gut sink to the floor. He glanced through the three-inch crack in the door, trying to catch a glimpse of Doe, but the exiting light was blinding.

"Robbie, this will only take a second, I assure you. It saves me asking a nurse to come down for such a simple task."

"Hi," said Nurse Morallas, suddenly standing behind Bellecourt, clipboard in hand.

"Ah, hell," said Bellecourt. "I mean, ah hello, Nurse Morallas, how good to see you again?"

"Father, what on earth are you doing here… and why are you wearing a doctor's robe?"

"I was, um, I was just leaving," he lied. "Excellent work, Robbie, you passed the test with flying colours. Thank you for keeping our special patient safe."

With that, Bellecourt overcompensated with a massive grin, then turned on his heels and speed-walked down the hall, click-clacking with every step.

Nurse Morallas turned to Robbie. "That was odd."

Robbie nodded, then smiled shyly as his face turned crimson. "Hi, Abigail. It's really nice to see you. Twice in one day." He shuffled his feet. "Um, so, how're things with you and your husband?"

THIRTY-FOUR

Monday, November 16, 6:40 p.m.
Fleming's Steak Restaurant

Puking on an ATM is not the worst thing in the world – unless someone's watching or you're second in line at the time. Ashamed as he was, Earl felt much better after ejecting the unprocessed alcohol and pizza over most of the machine.

The remainder of the ride to the restaurant was bearable and incident-free. However, as Earl stepped from the taxi, the queasy feeling returned to his gut. As the cab drove away, Earl stood alone in the parking lot, analyzing the sensation. It wasn't the alcohol this time; this felt different. *Is this pre-date nerves?* thought Earl. *Could this really be a date?* Earl's stress level began to rise. He had one shot to make an impression, and he would have to take that shot while straddling the line between sobriety and hangover.

Earl entered the restaurant and scanned the room, relieved to see Mary-Lynn had not yet arrived. After claiming their table, he made a beeline for the men's washroom. Standing at the sink, Earl examined the creature in front of him – paler than usual, sweaty, dishevelled, and not without a few spots of dried vomit. *Delightful*, he thought.

Despite the fancy surroundings, Earl removed his shirt and began to bathe his upper half in the sink, resulting in several patrons bypassing their hand-washing routines and exiting without comment. Earl squirted hand soap on a paper towel and rubbed it into his armpits, hoping the lavender smell would substitute for cologne. He soaped up his face, neck, and hair and rinsed off in a head-down position, splashing the fast-flowing water in every direction like a garden sprinkler. After drying off using all the hand towels, he re-dressed, palm combed his damp hair and checked his look. It would have to do.

Back at the table, he asked for four ice-waters and six Tylenol, which the waitress clandestinely provided. Mission accomplished. 7:03 p.m. Right on time. Brilliant.

*

In the back of the limo and still drunk, Orlando ended his daily phone call with MacMann. Six minutes of his life he'd never get back. Much to MacMann's annoyance, Orlando had explained that Earl was the most boring man on the planet and spoke to no one during the day. To be credible, Orlando explained that Earl had only sent emails to a girl and a couple to his editor, who was apparently very displeased with him. Beyond that, there was nothing new to report.

Unsatisfied, MacMann concluded the call by ordering Orlando to either dig up or invent some usable dirt to discredit Earl, just in case. Orlando lobbed the command into his mental trash bin and then decided a nap was in order. Stretching out on the limo's oversized leather couch, he got comfortable, still drunk, but with a growing desire to punch something.

THIRTY-FIVE

Earl glanced over the top of the leather-bound menu as the main doors opened, and a sultry angel swaggered in. She chatted briefly with the maître'd, who then turned and pointed at Earl with a frown.

Earl smiled way too much.

As Mary-Lynn approached, Earl expertly simulated eye contact while scanning his companion's dress choice in an attempt to determine how date-like the evening would be. The resulting eye bulge stabbed at his evolving hangover.

Mary-Lynn glided fluidly in black high-heels. Her white dress, perhaps created from a new type of NASA material, the integration of spandex and paint, clung to her body as if statically charged. The dress, dangerously high on the thigh and contrasting with her light brown skin tone, was sleeveless and perfectly accentuated with a black and brown striped purse hanging from one shoulder. Long black hair teased her cleavage, and a devilish grin squinted her eyes.

Earl rose. Leaving the table, he met her halfway, where they embraced in a hug normally reserved for returning troops.

"You smell wonderful," chuckled Mary-Lynn, looking him up and down as she palmed the wrinkles on his shirt.

"Oh that," said Earl, "that's just a little Eau d' toilet I found lying around."

She giggled.

"You," he gasped, "... look incredible. I'm sure every neck in the place is aching with whiplash."

Mary-Lynn blushed but took the compliment. "Looking good yourself, mister."

Once settled in the booth, Earl stared at his companion a little too long.

"What are you looking at, Earl? Do I have something on my face?"

"Oh, no, sorry." He smacked himself in the back of the head. "I've never seen you look more beautiful. But you also seem a little sad. What's wrong, Miss Wu?"

"Stop it, goof. I'm not here to dump my problems on you. Let's talk about your day."

"No," said Earl emphatically, surprising himself at the volume and zeal of the command. "You already know so much about me. It's only fair I know a little more about you. After all, you could be a spy. Apparently, I'm surrounded by them."

*

"Alright, alright, so we regroup," said Bellecourt, re-dressed in his holy garb and huddled with the God Squad in a van at the back of the hospital's parking garage. "My cover's blown," he said like a Tom Clancy character. "But we're not sunk. Good Lord, I was so close. He was right there."

Sister Donello was first to offer a solution. "It's clear you won't get in now. They'll be watching for you. So, can I suggest a new plan?"

"I'm listening," said Bellecourt.

"Let me try this time," she urged. "They'll be on high alert for another *man*, a priest. They'll assume a nun is of little concern since the church wouldn't send a woman to assess claims of divinity."

All the priests looked at their shoes.

"Rightly or wrongly, it's just a fact," she continued. "Let me try. If we're lucky, the guard's Catholic and won't risk a nun's scorn. It's our only option."

Bellecourt sat expressionless for several seconds, contemplating his options. "Very well," he frowned. "You have my blessing, Sister. May the Lord guide you."

*

"Earl?" asked Mary-Lynn from across the table, her second glass of Chardonnay in hand. "Did you ever have the feeling you were destined for something... *bigger*... but oblivious to what it might be?"

"Every day," replied Earl without thinking.

"Right?" She took a sip of wine, then frowned at Earl's multiple glasses of iced water. "Trying to get me drunk?"

"Nope," he smiled. "Just trying to keep my head in the moment."

"Anyway, it's not just my ego, Earl. It's like I've been chosen to save someone's life, rescue them from certain death, except no one's given me a name, or address, or planet."

Earl sat in silence, entranced in her beauty.

"Earl, stop looking at me that way."

"Oh, sowwy," he stumbled over his tongue. "I was trying to determine if, um, if your nose was properly curved," he snickered.

"Everything's properly curved, Earl," she whispered. She reached across the table and took his hand.

Earl had a mild heart attack, which he bravely fended off with a sip of water. "Do a lot of guys fall in love with you?"

"I dunno, maybe. Never asked." She giggled, brushing away the question.

Earl simply nodded.

"OK, OK," she offered. "I'm not very forthcoming, am I? So, here's the deal about love. It's a total mystery to me, Earl. I've never ever loved anyone. Except for my mom. And she was taken by cancer at thirty-eight." Mary-Lynn's eyes dropped to the table.

"Oh," Earl said softly.

"She was my everything," Mary-Lynn continued, her eyes locked on her wine glass. "I was her only daughter in a family with three boys and no father." She took a large gulp of wine. "When I saw her in the hospital, those last days, before they protected me from the worst, she was smiling, joking, and telling me about the amazing person I'd become. But you know what, Earl? I'm not an amazing person. I'm not even all that nice. Self-centred, grasping, manipulative. I tell myself it's necessary in the world of TV news, but I know deep down that's just… *bullshit*."

"Is this where your 'What's the point?' question came from?" inquired Earl.

"Probably. My mother sacrificed everything for me. I've never sacrificed anything for anyone, Earl." Her eyes were wet.

"When my mother passed, my brothers told me she'd gone to a better place. I know that's stupid now, but I guess they were stuck for answers to give a fifteen-year-old girl. I suppose they were grieving too, and their intent was good. Still, even then, I knew she'd died for no reason and that they had just lied to me. An angel like her, racked with pain, while horrible people get away with horrendous crimes. That was the moment I knew life was totally unfair, and if it was going to change, *I'd* have to change it."

"But that's good, right?" said Earl, wishing he could slide around the booth and give her a hug.

"Good, yes, if I'd done something about it, something *real*. But, Earl, I did… *nothing*."

*

It was nearing 9 p.m., and the hospital's admin offices were lifeless. The only light blazed from under a door at the far end of the executive hallway. Midnight oil at the ready, the Acting Chief Administrator sat in whisky vigil, sunk in a seat he dreamed of owning.

Frank Shedmore waited for something to happen. Going home would offer no comfort. There'd be no point. He'd only pace around the bedroom all night, incapable of sleeping.

From the inception of MacMann's grandiose plan, Frank had felt his control slipping away. Subtle at first, but now, mere days into the scheme, the slippage had turned into a total loss of grip.

It was time to take action. But action is typically reserved for people with healthy spines and fearless hearts, two things Frank admittedly never possessed. But all that was about to change. It took five shots of liquid courage for him to place the phone call he'd been putting off all day, and, as fate would have it, nobody answered. Without thinking, Frank had left a rambling, disjointed, and thoroughly unrehearsed voicemail that now resided on the answering machine of the only man who could make this mess go away. No matter, the dye was cast, and there was no option to un-send – only wait.

Frank crossed his ankles and planted them on the edge of the antique oak desk, nudging the office phone with his shoe, willing it to make a noise. "Come on. Call me back!"

THIRTY-SIX

Monday, November 16, 9:15 p.m.
Fleming's Steak Restaurant

"Earl…" Mary-Lynn offered, having dabbed some chocolate sauce from the edge of his mouth using the corner of her napkin. "… Are you sure you're cut out for this reporter game? You don't seem to possess a shred of arrogance or the much-needed *crush the pions* attitude to be successful. And, I mean that as a compliment."

Earl laughed. "Ever since I was a kid, I've wanted to know why things were the way they were and who the hell was to blame. Reporting, writing, and investigating the *whys* instead of the *whats* – were supposed to appease my obsession. It's all I ever wanted to do… other than drive a truck."

"Ooh, pot bellies and plaid," Mary-Lynn snickered.

"But, you're probably right. I lack the intestinal fortitude." Earl's face quickly turned serious. "I'm more the mole in a china shop type. Fact is, I've always found interacting with people to be difficult. To me, they're like something I need to deal with instead of something of value."

Earl began to tell Mary-Lynn of his former professor and mentor, Harold Sawchuck, and a revealing discussion they'd had one warm spring day…

Earl was cutting through a small windy park on campus when he came upon Sawchuck sitting on a bench, sunning himself in the breezy May air.

"Why Mr. Grey, how nice to see you. We missed you in Modern History yesterday. Sick, were we?"

Earl's already reddish complexion reddened. "Self-induced," he replied. Earl found it difficult to lie to the jovial professor.

Sawchuck shook his head. "One of the trappings of freshman life, I'm afraid. Get it out of your system, boy."

"This, I know," said Earl. "But life's a little… overwhelming right now."

"Bored with monotony, terrified of change?" asked Sawchuck.

Earl laughed. "Yeah, something like that, for sure. It's a big step from High School. Having my ignorance exposed is a real kick in the ass."

"A right of passage, more like it. It's called growth, Earl."

"Yeah. But still disappointing to find out I'm not as smart as I thought I was."

"A few dents in your perfect record?"

Earl shook his head. "No. I know I'm not perfect. But they say knowledge is power. So, any exposure of my ignorance must be a reduction in my power."

"Oh my," said Sawchuck, crossing his legs and getting comfortable. "And what do you need this power for? Global domination?"

Earl laughed again. "It just feels better when I'm in control."

"As I'm sure it does for everyone. But the question remains, is this power you seek a remedy for unhappiness or the armour protecting you from the things you don't want to face?"

"You're a wise man, professor," said Earl. His mentor's comments biting hard.

"Wise? Oh, goodness, no. If I may mangle a quote by a real wise man… 'Wisdom is what's left after we've run out of personal opinions.'"

"Cullen Hightower, right?" Earl scrambled for a lecture memory.

Before Sawchuck could reply, a young Asian man dressed in khaki shorts and leather sandals walked up and stopped directly in front of them, staring with extreme curiosity. The young man had approached through the flower gardens that separated the Science building from the Chapel and Humanities wing. As he stood frozen in silence, a wave of fear swept across his face. He opened his mouth as if to speak, but no words came out.

Professor Sawchuck offered a nod of recognition, just as Earl took it upon himself to dress down the uninvited intruder.

"What the hell are you staring at, dude? This is a private discussion. Hit the road."

The young man blinked as if Earl's words were foreign, then turned and robotically climbed the grassy slope toward a path that led to the Physics lecture hall.

"My goodness, Earl, where did that come from?" Sawchuck asked, his eyes wide in surprise. "Such anger. I'm sure the young man just wanted directions or something."

Earl felt his stomach drop. "Shit! I'm sorry. That was way over the top." He shook his head in self-disgust. "I'm just frustrated. Frankly, every day since I arrived, I've been unable to shake this surreal feeling. Like I'm a fictional character, an imposter, a fake. The dumbest guy on campus, disguised as a viable student."

"Ah, yes," Sawchuck nodded and placed a gentle hand on Earl's shoulder. "Your struggle for academic perfection and the resulting loss of power. Have you ever considered that this lust for power, for control, is misguided, perhaps a defence mechanism designed to avoid everything nasty in the world?"

Earl said nothing, quickly turning his attention to an untied shoe.

"Regardless of your reasons, son, just remember, power is something you're given by others, not something you take."

"That's good." Earl nodded over and over. "OK, so how do I force them to give it to me?"

"Earl?"

"Kidding."

"Son, I suspect your path to happiness won't be apparent until you've figured out who you are. Right now, you believe happiness is the antithesis of that which makes you sad and anxious. As such, you've decided knowledge and power will allow you to bypass the need for personal reflection and change. Allowing you to drift lazily through life without making an effort."

Earl's emotions made a concerted effort to escape through his tear ducts. "Well, sir, this has been wonderful, but I've got to get going. Class starts in five," he lied. "Thanks again, Professor. I won't forget this."

The candle on the table flickered wildly, catching Earl's attention and pulling him back to the present. He lifted his head and locked his eyes on Mary-Lynn's. "But I did forget. In fact, it's been years since I considered his words. *Power is something you're given by others, not something you take for yourself.*"

Mary-Lynn squeezed his hand again. "Earl, whatever you're running from, let me help. Maybe this media liaison role is too much pressure to handle on your own?"

A sinking feeling overwhelmed Earl.

Mary-Lynn brightened. "You know, I've always believed I was going to meet someone extraordinary and life-changing. So maybe I can help you get through this madness while fulfilling my destiny at the same time." Mary-Lynn cleared her throat and looked away from Earl's gaze. "Let me... connect... with John Doe."

Earl's outward smile belayed the fact that his heart was sinking like a basket-weave canoe. Mary-Lynn seemed genuine, but his psyche was ringing loud alarms. And not the clangy ones you'd hear at school recess, but wailing sirens, the European kind, all pompous and anally retentive. Earl caught the attention of a nearby waitress and ordered a beer.

*

It was an hour of avoiding the subject before Mary-Lynn offered to drive Earl to his hotel.

"I have a question," Earl stated, staring at the dark and empty highway ahead of them."

"Shoot."

"So, honesty being the better part of stupidity, what was tonight for you? I mean, was this about getting close to me... or Doe?" Earl kept his eyes glued on the road ahead.

Mary-Lynn turned sharply to her passenger. "Earl, I like you, OK? A lot."

Earl nodded his head, choosing to believe.

"As for my desire to meet Doe, it's destiny. He's someone I feel has... *answers*. Someone who might fix everything. Someone who won't lie to me. Someone who would never..."

"Are you crying?" said Earl, trying hard to understand the sudden emotional deluge.

"No!"

"But, you have tears..."

"Shut up." She held her right palm toward him. "Please."

"Shutting up."

A few moments passed in silence. Enough for the car to exit the highway, clear the traffic lights and pull into the courtyard of Earl's hotel.

"I believe you," Earl said, putting his hand on Mary-Lynn's arm. "However, the reality of the situation is different. I'm supposed to be the only journalist with access to Doe. People would know if you were there. The guard, the nurses, you'd be on security camera. Better if you stay away. OK? Please."

Mary-Lynn scrunched up her face. "Fine."

"Fine?"

"Fine, yes, fine."

"You don't seem fine, you look..."

"Earl, stop. I said, fine. I won't see him. Don't push it."

Earl sighed. "So, I guess this changes everything?"

"Errrr. Get out of the car, mister," said Mary-Lynn with a subtle twinkle in her eyes.

Earl popped the car door and walked around to her driver's window, leaning in. "If it's any consolation, I like you too, Miss Wu. A lot."

Mary-Lynn, her eyes still wet, offered a thin but sweet smile. "You're such a dick."

With that, she squared her shoulders, faced forward and clunked the car in gear. "Email me tomorrow. We'll figure out a time to hang, kay?"

"I will," Earl grinned. "Goodnight, Mary-Lynn." He waved as the car slipped off into the darkness.

An unfamiliar feeling grew in Earl's chest. At first, he mistook it for angina. But then a twenty-year-old sub-program, stored in the dank basement files of his brain, sent a note of clarification – *You're happy, Earl.* Followed quickly by an insistent alarm from his pragmatic sensory lobe. *Now, don't screw this up.*

THIRTY-SEVEN

The Story of Nog: Part IV

Sunday, November 15, 12,042 BC, 7 a.m.

Pinpricks of sunrise eastern sunlight streamed into the cave, much to Nog's annoyance. Although too early to get up, it felt like Mardi Gras at Elton John's house. No matter how hard Nog squinted, he couldn't find darkness. Giving up, he opened his eyes slowly, revealing Numa in all his glory, hobbling around the cave in nothing but what God gave him.

Seeing Nog was awake, Numa greeted him in Full Monty. "Toooo, Lama," he said brightly, spreading his arms wide, embracing the beauty of the beautiful morning.

Nog pushed himself up to a seated position, trying hard not to look at his new friend's package. "Roww Laa," he smiled, waving to his host.

"Roww Laa," replied Numa, struggling with morning stiffness as he shuffled to a small alcove and selected several types of dried meats for their breakfast. Numa's age was a mystery to Nog. There was white fur everywhere, and Numa's face was deeply carved like the mini canyons of the sunburned flatlands. Nog pondered what the old man could have possibly traded for all his food and such an elaborate cave. There was nothing of value, apart from the wicked-ass light show.

After eating, Numa retrieved the bag from his sleeping area and held it up for Nog to see. Full from breakfast and in need of a mid-morning nap, Nog sat cross-legged and nodded at his host, smiling the smile of misunderstanding.

Numa moved to the pedestal near the centre of the room, placed the bag in the middle, then backed away – hands in presentation mode.

OK, thought Nog. *So, the bag works as a lovely centrepiece. That's nice.*

Frustrated, Numa pointed with his right index finger to the cracks in the ceiling. Then, slowly tracing the sunbeams to the floor, he stopped at the bag. Taking a deep breath, he shouted, "Numa, Noo-ag," and extended his left arm and index finger toward Nog. Lastly, he brought both hands together in front of his chest with dramatic flair until his index fingers touched, then closed his eyes.

Yep, thought Nog. *Gotcha. That's where it's kept. Couldn't agree more.*

Numa sighed, opened his eyes and shuffled over to his sleeping area, where he promptly collapsed with a grunt, his old body cracking and popping in protest.

*

After an uncomfortable hour of small talk, Nog figured he should head back to his own cave before some dick stole it. But the mystery that surrounded Numa was intriguing. After a brief internal debate, Nog convinced himself that hanging out a little longer wouldn't hurt.

Numa stood and straightened himself, then donned a full-length robe and briskly palmed it, flattening eight of the two-thousand wrinkles. After tying the robe off with a dried and twisted leather belt, he attached the jewelled bag, letting it hang like a sporran. Once presentable, Numa moved toward the cave entrance, dropped to his hands and knees, then looked over his shoulder, motioning for Nog to follow.

Both men emerged into a beautiful morning featuring deep blue skies and a pleasant breeze. Still three hours from its apex, the sun bleached the grounds and rock faces but spared the deeper crevices, leaving them chilled in purples, browns, and blacks. Nog registered none of it. He stood with his mouth open, eyes wide, staring at a semi-circle of twenty people surrounding Numa's cave entrance and moving closer.

*

Nog chose to stay in a shaded area, twenty feet from the closest stranger, as Numa, perched directly in front of the phallic monolith, addressed the crowd. Numa spoke with great authority and was highly animated, his arms reaching for the sky then touching the ground. In an eerie precursor to Tai Chi, he rocked an unseen baby in his arms then patted the left side of his chest, the place where the sacred drumbeat resided.

Locals of all ages, shapes and sizes sat transfixed as Numa concluded his speech and pantomimes. Then, standing completely still, the old man held his arms out wide, sweat running from his face and under his scruffy grey beard.

153

"Tarra, Tarra," the crowd chanted in unison.

"Saaa-rettt," shouted Numa, appearing exhausted, dropping his arms to his sides. And there was much hugging.

After a great deal of pleasantries, Nog watched in fascination as the males in the crowd stepped forward, leaving gifts of dried meats and fruit, then leaving, presumably heading home. The women remained, gathering together at the foot of the large phallic rock between the two boulders. Sinking to their knees, they chanted something that sounded suspiciously like the chorus of Zeppelin's 'Immigrant Song'.

*

As the last few ladies departed, Nog helped Numa carry the food offerings into the cave and store them in a deep cool crevice. The old man looked winded, spent; the effects of his highly animated speech, plus the unforgiving sun, were obvious. Concerned, Nog helped the old man out of his robe and onto the soft animal skin he called a bed.

Numa forced a smile and patted Nog's hand, then became preoccupied with the jewelled bag and the various sunbeams streaking through the cracks in the ceiling. Clearing his throat to get Nog's attention, Numa pointed to the bag, then immediately to the pedestal in the centre of the room, jabbing his finger forward several times.

Nog was quick to pick up on the request and took the bag. He placed it in the centre of the pedestal, where parallel grooves had been chiselled into the surface, then looked back at Numa for approval. The old man smiled. "Gee la nooo," he said, then lay back and closed his eyes.

THIRTY-EIGHT

Tuesday, November 17, 7:30 a.m.
Phoenix Marriott Hotel,
Room 624

Earl wished he had puked again before hitting the bed. After a restless night spent in and out of consciousness, many things weren't sitting well, least of which was the shrimp scampi he'd had for dinner.

During the morning drive to the hospital, Earl paid Orlando for his private-eyeing efforts plus the cost of acquiring the pictures. Then, lost for subject matter, he briefly described his surreal dinner with Mary-Lynn from the previous night.

"Didn't get laid, huh?" teased Orlando as he parked the limo in the hospital parking garage.

"Didn't expect to," Earl said firmly, if unconvincingly. He was in no mood to be teased so early in the morning, especially while nursing the dying embers of two hangovers and a terminal case of dry mouth.

"Chill, man, just messin'."

"I know," Earl sighed, a little louder than intended. "I didn't sleep well. This whole situation is becoming… too much."

"For a white guy, you worry too much. You're not without options, you know. If you're so concerned about this going south, go north."

"Leave?" Earl mused as he stared at the bottle of scotch that had miraculously been refilled since the previous day. He glanced at his watch, 8:15 a.m., and concluded it might be a tad early to hit the sauce.

"I'm just saying it's an option," continued Orlando.

Earl needed to change the subject. "Any clue what MacMann's up to?"

"The dude's very busy with his head up his ass," replied Orlando. "He just asks me what I've seen or heard but never really listens to my answers."

Earl nodded, which hurt his head.

"We're here, man. Any idea when you want to be picked up?"

155

"Presser should be done around eleven, then a quick chat with Mork and Mindy. So, say twelve, but I'll call you if I'm out earlier…"

Orlando shook his head. "You know what you need today? A break. And I know just the place. So, don't make plans for later, OK? I've got something I want to show you."

*

"He's not in," said the front desk clerk at the Albion Hotel, a place that had seen much history, none of it grandiose or memorable.

"When do you think he'll be back?" asked Warren, glancing around the decrepit lobby, empty but for an old man playing with a cat.

"Do I look like his fucking secretary?"

"Dude, chill. He's waiting for this envelope."

"Leave it here. I'll give it to him."

Warren sized up the clerk. Forty-ish, pale face, white tee-shirt with egg stains peeking from under a foot-long beard. A hodgepodge of tattoos covered both arms down to his wrists, where they abruptly disappeared under multiple leather bands and a Mickey Mouse wristwatch. His lower half was hidden by the front desk, but Warren knew a gun was on his belt, if not two. "I'll just hang on to it, for now. No offence."

The clerk seemed perplexed by the comment. "Whatever!"

Warren fished a crumpled twenty from his jeans, then grabbed a strip-club brochure from a wire-stand on the counter. He wrote his phone number on the pamphlet and pushed it and the money toward the clerk. "Call me as soon as he comes in, OK? There's another twenty when I come back."

The clerk snatched up the crumpled bill without saying a word, then watched Warren cross the lobby and leave through the main entrance. After a pause to ensure no one was around, the clerk fumbled for his cell phone and entered a memorized number.

*

With MacMann and Frank oddly absent from the administration wing, Earl settled into the waiting room's sofa and set about to read his editor's latest diatribe.

… as of yet, I've been unsuccessful in removing you from this story, but I plan to be well-prepared when you return, and so help me, you're one dead bugger

when you do. You know something, Grey, when I was in college, journalistic integrity was a full-year course. I remember once telling my prof...

The delete button made an indignant click. As Earl pocketed his phone, a juicy thought landed on him. An inspirational idea, something akin to, *I must no longer accept the role of victim* or some such motivational bullshit. Earl attempted to focus the fuzzy thought by summarizing his real-world shit storm in his mind.

I am clearly trapped in a no-win situation in front of the whole world.

Mary-Lynn will most certainly discover my part in MacMann's scheme, after which I'll be as popular as Mormon Death Metal.

My journalistic career now parallels that of a South Pacific island – post-nuclear testing.

It's almost certain I will become the scapegoat when all of this eventually collapses.

Yet strangely, instead of fatalism, strength erupted inside Earl. Revisiting Professor Sawchuck's advice during dinner with Mary-Lynn had triggered something inside, and he couldn't turn it off.

I suspect your path to happiness won't be apparent until you've figured out who you are. His mentor's words ricocheted around his skull before finally sticking in his throat.

"OK, Earl, so who the hell are you?" he mumbled.

The epiphany hit him hard. If he opted to run away this time, he'd never have another chance to uncover his true capability. He would never discover the destiny he had so far vigorously denied himself. He would forever remain... nothing.

The thought was freeing, invigorating, and incredibly powerful. A surge of joy welled within him as he summarized. *A man with nothing to lose can do anything he pleases.*

Earl rolled his shoulders and cracked his neck as if entering the ring for a heavyweight fight. He retrieved the Blackberry from his pocket and opened the email app, forcefully typing editor@torontotelegraph.com with a C.C. to Board-of-Directors@torontotelegraph.com. An evil smile crossed his lips. *Alright, Earl,* he thought to himself, *while you're emotional and irresponsible, let's carpe the fucking diem.* His thumbs glided across the raised keys, muscle memory leading the way, finishing his reply in under a minute. After a quick review, Earl let out a gleeful squeal like a teenage girl updating her diary.

Dear Ed,
I trust you'll accept my apologies for the limited communication? Bad cell-

signal. But fear not, all is well. Today is day three of my interviews with God – and all the best stuff is in my head. I can't wait to write a blockbuster series we can sell for global syndication. Let's double that stock price, Ed.

Wishing you a great night and warmest regards from Arizona, Earl.

Earl hit send, then giggled out loud.

*

"Hello, Mr. Earl, how are you this morning?"

"Great, Robbie, and yourself?"

"Oh, pretty good, bit bored. A hazard of the job. Nothing exciting so far."

"Let's hope it stays that way," chuckled Earl.

"Mr. Doe's inside, but he's had a rough night. They had him in and out of here several times, according to Hector."

"Hector?"

"The night shift guard, Hector."

"Oh. So, what happened?"

"To Hector?"

"No, to Mr. Doe last night. What was the problem? Is he OK?"

"Well, I'm no doctor, you know?"

"I did know that."

"But, from what I heard, he set off the alarm three times. The doctor said he's stable now, but they had to increase his meds. It don't sound good. I don't think he's gonna make it."

Earl patted Robbie on his considerable bicep. "We all gotta go sometime. Maybe it's his time, Robbie." It struck Earl that using the word 'time' suddenly felt inappropriate.

"That's sad." Robbie shuffled his feet.

Earl smiled. "I'll just go in now if that's OK?"

Robbie didn't reply but stepped forward and pushed open the heavy door as if it was cardboard.

THIRTY-NINE

"The first customer of the morning, bright and early, I see. Oh, it's you again."

"Hi Stanley," said Mary-Lynn, "I'm returning the cheerleader outfit. It was a big hit."

"Great, well, if you're happy with the service, tell a friend, and come back soon. Halloween's only eleven months away, so book early." The shop owner smiled, tossing the collegiate outfit into a laundry hamper behind the counter.

"Hold on, Stanley, I'm not done yet."

"Oh, sorry, was there something else?"

"I'm looking for a medical outfit, you know, doctor or nurse. Scrubs and a gown."

"Oh," Stanley frowned. "I have both, but they're out on rental right now."

"Damn," said Mary-Lynn, rolling her eyes. She began to scan the shop, hoping to find something suitable for an inconspicuous hospital visit. "Firefighter? Cop?"

Stanley shook his head dejectedly. "All rented for the day."

"Err." Her scan came to a halt on a highly realistic Pope costume. "Hmm. Stanley? Whatcha got in a nice nun's habit?"

*

"Earl, my boy, how good to see you." Doe was propped up in bed, watching TV. A new set of monitors had replaced Earl's interview chair from the day before.

"Great to see you, too," replied Earl. "I heard a disturbing rumour about your health. Are you in pain?"

"Best of health, my boy, or as close as shite is to swearing."

Earl chuckled. "Are you up for a chat? I can come back later if you wish?"

159

"Please, my boy, sit, um…" Doe looked around the room, and the array of new machine clutter, "… somewhere."

Earl cleared the cables from the top of a squat machine, which appeared to be processing an unknown liquid. The device was just high enough to work as a stool, and the vibrating warmth offered a welcome change to the old chair.

"Earl, you've impressed me a great deal," said Doe. "Your performance at the press conference yesterday. Quite wonderful. I watched it on the television." Doe pointed to the dull, yellowed, plastic box mounted on a swing-arm to the wall and currently tuned to WWF wrestling.

"Oh, that, yeah. That was embarrassing," said Earl, running his hands back through his scruffy hair. "What did you like the most, my ninja moves during the coordinated audience assault or the keen way I bumbled your message to the people of Earth?" Earl shook his head and chuckled.

"Nonsense, Earl. You spoke from the heart and gave everyone pause for thought. You sent them away with much to consider."

"I take it you saw everything? The whole news conference?"

"Of course, wouldn't miss it. Must-see TV."

"So you know they want photos? They're being very persistent," said Earl.

"Ah, yes, and I'm sorry to put you in such a predicament, but I'm afraid that's an impossibility."

"I suspected as much."

"Earl, every Christian church you've ever been in, whose picture is prominent?"

"Jesus Christ."

"Exactly. And Jesus of Nazareth himself said he was a messenger, right? Although some say prophet or teacher. But, let me ask you this: what happened to him over the centuries, what happened to his simple message?"

Earl nodded, knowing exactly where the conversation was heading. "People now worship the messenger as *the* message."

"Precisely. And like all prophets from your past, the message faded over time, leaving only the idol. An oil painting of Jesus is no different than a sandstone sculpture of Horus or a porcelain Buddha. Humans would rather follow than listen."

Earl nodded, scribbling quickly with his pen. "That's good."

"Earl, I'm speaking to you through this broken body at some risk. If I become associated with this body, this face, anything you or I say will be forgotten in place of the image. They must never see this face or this body, OK? It has no meaning."

Earl stared, consuming Doe's expression, his tiny intricate movements and twitches, the chiselled lines, dark in hue, recessed deeply around his eyes. Doe appeared, for the first time, stoic and resolute. The brightness and depth of his eyes, alive and penetrating. His white hair, framing his head like an old-time football helmet. His face, ashen brown, angelic but fatigued.

"Promise me," Doe said sternly, staring deep into Earl's eyes.

"There'll be no pictures, sir. That's a promise."

*

MacMann sat at a small plastic cafeteria table across from Frank, spreading out medical print outs as far as he could. "It was close, Frank. Three flatlines. Everything was shutting down, like dominos."

"He's stable now?" Frank ran his pen across the pages, lining up different columns with critical vitals and counts.

"Aye, but it was touch and go. We completely lost him once. Stone dead. The emergency physician even called the time. And then *blip*, Doe was back."

Frank shook his head from side to side. "And… what do you plan to say at the press conference later?"

"Well, I won't be mentioning the code blues. I'll lead with the deteriorating vitals and a wee bit about our staff and state-of-the-art equipment."

"Fine. I intend to be downbeat myself. Make it clear this whole thing's winding down," Frank stated firmly, allowing for no rebuttal.

MacMann studied Frank's mood. "Just as well. We basically lost him last night. But barring a miracle, I'm afraid John Doe is not long for this world."

*

"Yesterday…" said Doe, "… we discussed the beginning. Today, I thought we might discuss how everything came to be. At least the way *you* perceive it."

"You mean evolution in more detail?" inquired Earl.

Doe pondered the question. "In a way, yes. But you need to understand where everything came from and, more importantly, where it's going. However, in fairness, my analogy *is* a deceptive one."

"Always the riddle, huh?" Earl chuckled. "Could you be a bit more specific? Us reporters don't do well with vague."

"I'm honestly not trying to be vague. This is not an easy concept to grasp. No offence."

161

Earl regrouped. "OK, fine. So what do you mean when you say 'came from' and 'going to' is a deceptive analogy?"

"Earl, *everything* evolves, and as I'm sure you know, biological evolution takes hundreds of millions of years, even for subtle changes." Doe paused and sighed. "If you're a scientist, you're always searching for the first mover, right? The cause that creates the effect, right back to the beginning. If you're a religious or spiritual person, you also seek the beginning, but frame it within a closer historical context."

"With you so far," said Earl scribbling.

"I'm not here to resolve this debate. Both sides of the aisle are convinced of their superior knowledge. One is based on empirical logic, the other on ancient writings. But there's something neither party is capable or willing to see."

"Hit me..." said Earl, shifting his butt to a cooler spot on the machine.

"There is no first mover."

Earl looked at Doe, expecting more. "Ohhh... kaaay?"

"Let that settle in for a minute, Earl. Try very hard to think in a larger frame of reference. Think big. And then go bigger."

"OK, JD. Thinking big," said Earl with a grin.

"Really?" said Doe, rolling his eyes. He looked out the window at the brilliant sun, bleaching everything under its watch. "It's a lovely day today, Earl. Can you see? Just look out there, look at that sky."

Earl, confused, slipped off the machine and walked over to the window for a better view. "Not a cloud in the sky!" he said.

"So predictable," laughed Doe. "I knew you'd say that."

"I'm sorry?"

"Not a cloud in the sky, really? In the entire sky?"

"It's just an expression. It's cloudless, beautiful, perfect." Earl defended his statement without knowing why.

"I won't debate aesthetics with you, Earl. One man's beauty is another farmer's curse. My point's a bit wider than that. Of course, there are clouds in the sky, just not right here, in your centre of the universe. My boy, I need you to look further, beyond yourself, beyond your programming. You glance at the sky in your tiny corner of the universe and declare it cloudless. You need to see beyond the human scale."

"There's a little puffy one over there by the mountains." Earl pointed.

"Yes. Yes, I see. But stay with me here, OK?"

Earl returned to his seat and retrieved his notepad. "OK, I clearly understand that my two square feet of universe is not everything that exists."

Doe laughed with a rasp. "Good, then you're the right man for the job."

"What's this job I'm applying for again? Does it come with benefits?"

"Oh, my yes," said Doe. "More than that human brain of yours can imagine. Again, no offence."

F O R T Y

Earl took a sip of water and flipped through his pages of notes, ensuring he'd captured everything correctly. Nurse Morallas had just left the room after stopping in to check Doe's vitals and change his IV bag. Doe teased her mercilessly as she adjusted his catheter. The poor embarrassed woman made a beeline for the door as soon as she was able. Her only words to Earl, "Get off that machine before you break it."

"Now, where were we, Earl?"

"Umm." Earl flipped back to read his last note. "I wrote down… 'Skies are not cloudless', and 'Don't be so shortsighted'. Before that, I wrote, 'There's no first mover.'"

"Ahh, yes." Doe seemed rejuvenated after orange juice and bed adjustment. "So, there's your answer – the solution to the cause and effect enigma. There was no first cause. So there's no need for a beginning, a creation. Time doesn't exist."

"No time?"

"No time."

"Give me a minute to write that down," joked Earl.

Doe laughed. "Earl, I've got a thought experiment for you, if you're game?"

"As long as it doesn't involve algebra."

"Oh, we'll find X, but let's start with a question. When does the past become the past? At what point does your present morph into your history?"

Earl put down the notebook and crossed his arms over his knees. "I see; OK, let me think. Interesting. I suppose the very second something happens, that very instance it becomes history. Is that right?"

"Pretty good. But you still had to use the word *second*, implying a measurable time between present action and previous. Let's reverse the question, shall we?

How about the future? When does the present end and the future begin? What's the time frame between what *is* happening and what *will* happen?"

"Well, again, I'd have to say it's instantaneous, although I think I'm backing myself into a logic corner."

Doe smiled in agreement. "So, if the space between the then and now is instantaneous, and the same goes for the future, the period you call the present simply doesn't exist."

"Do you think they'd send up a scotch if I ordered one?" asked Earl.

Doe brightened. "I've watched you scribble in your book. Little cartoon stick figures or sketches, always in the top corner of the page. How come?"

Earl smiled at a memory. "As a kid, I'd make paper movies, usually in history class, the most boring class of all. I'd draw stick figures at the top corner of my workbook. They were usually of the teacher or maybe Superman or Gene Simmons of Kiss. Then, on the next page, I'd redraw the picture again, only with slight changes. Maybe an arm was a bit higher, or Simmons' mouth was spitting more blood. I kept doing this until there was a picture in the corner of every page of the book. Then I'd pass it to my friends when the teacher wasn't looking. They would fan the pages with their thumbs, watching as the little images flicked by at high speed, revealing a mini-movie. You know, the teacher exploding into little bits or a dog taking a dump, grade school humour. Hilarious… when you're thirteen."

"Wonderful," said Doe, trying to clap his hands with stiff arms. "You've just described reality, the universe, with one simple analogy."

"I have?"

"Indeed. When humans experience the present, it's actually just a single page – the pages before are your history, the pages to come, your future. When taken as a single slice, a single page, the present is stagnant, frozen, inert, as are all the pages before or after. But here is the fun part, the pages, past and future, all exist at once, just like your comic flash movies. Make sense?"

Earl paced back and forth, gingerly stepping over cords and connecting wires. "So that means there's no free will. Nothing I can change, and nothing you can change for that matter?"

"Very good, and thankfully, very wrong. The book changes every day. Your story is rewritten every second by all the conditions that influence your page. What you call the future is being altered every second by people you've never met and never will, just as your actions affect their book. Your life evolves based on your environment and all the people and things affecting you. Cosmic laws, Earl. Environmental evolution."

"Is there blood in my ears?" asked Earl. "I feel like there's blood in my ears."

"Talk it out," encouraged Doe.

"OK. So, my future is pre-written unless acted upon by things around me, my environment. My life, my book, is broken into discrete frames, like pictures. When observed in motion, there's an illusion of time passing, it appears fluid, but it's only single frames, distinct from each other. We feel the illusion of time when we observe one frame after the other."

"Outstanding," said Doe, using his hands to rub warmth into his forearms.

"But JD, if my destiny depends on other people's actions, what's the point? Why should I try?"

"You've just solved for X, my boy. Well done."

"Huh?"

"You said, 'what's the point.' We've come full circle. Remember the entity I spoke of... the singularity?"

"Yes."

"This question, what's the point, relates specifically to *its* frame of reference, not yours. Remember the slug or fish? My question was about their perspective; what was the point from their vantage point? Well, now think of it from the singularity's point of view. What's the point?"

Earl frowned. "You said it already; to observe itself, to experience... stuff."

"Stuff indeed. To look upon its many components in order to understand *the point*. To evolve. Everything evolves, Earl."

Earl smelled something burning and realized it was coming from between his ears.

"Earl, the entity desires to experience all there is or could ever be, every dimension, every possible reality, creation, extinction, and outcome. But, and this is the important part, we are all part of the singularity. It *is* us, all of us, along with rocks and dirt and all the other stuff. You and your fellow humans are like water molecules in a vast ocean. Singular in chemical compound, but no less the ocean than any other droplet."

Earl realized he'd been holding his breath and exhaled deeply.

FORTY-ONE

Orlando listened as Eddie bragged about his all-nighter and how he had cracked the backup unit containing the massive hard drive. He boasted about his solution to the output wiring issue and how he made his own connectors, downloading the operating system from the dark web. Next to that ordeal, finding the priest pics had been a simple task. Eddie explained how he had chosen to store the images on a DVD instead of printing them since there were so many, and coloured printer-ink was so expensive. Then, he'd taken the tape unit to an acquaintance who worked at a local foundry. Minutes after, it was liquid goo.

"OK, well, that's good, I guess. Although I asked for photos. S'all good. As long as the boss can print whatever he wants."

"Totally," said Eddie with pride. "So, did'ya bring my money?"

Orlando dug in his pocket. "Five-hundred, small bills."

Eddie took the cash and stuffed it behind the counter, making no effort to count it.

*

"Here ya go, miss. This should do the trick," Stanley said, handing Mary-Lynn a black nun's habit with a white cornette.

"You don't have one with just a veil, do you?" she asked, examining the gigantic hat capable of lifting her into the sky.

"Sorry, no. I know it's old school, but most people want nuns' costumes with big hats, more traditional and striking."

Scrunching her face, Mary-Lynn lowered the cornette over her long straight hair. "Well, at least it fits."

"It does," said Stanley. "But the robe is one size fits all, so it'll be pretty big, like a potato sack. I suggest you take it in at the waist with some discreet clips."

"I'm trying to look like a nun, Stan, not Pamela Anderson. The potato sack is fine!" Mary-Lynn paid in advance for a one-day rental as Stanley placed the costume in a plastic bag.

"If you don't mind me saying, miss. If you're going for authenticity, I'd suggest changing those shoes." He pointed at her black spiked heels.

"These babies? No chance, Stan."

FORTY-TWO

Tuesday, November 17, 10:55 a.m.
Phoenix General Hospital,
Media Ready Room

Two men sat waiting for the eleven o'clock press conference. MacMann was uneasy, anxious. Watching Frank, he could tell that something about the man's demeanour had changed. For one thing, Frank seemed calm, almost reserved, lacking his typical display of uncertainty and nervous energy.

"I just asked the front desk to make a general announcement paging Earl, but I'm sure he's on his way," said Frank, staring down at his phone.

"Good." MacMann stood up to pace. He glanced inside a blue file folder for the third time.

The door to the press room sprung open, and Robert Hand's head popped into view. "All set. Ready when you are." As he disappeared, the outer door opened, and Earl walked in without a greeting, his face stone.

"It's about bloody time," said MacMann, smacking the file folder over the palm of his hand.

"Running a little late today, Earl?" asked Frank, uncrossing his legs.

"A bit, not really, just needed a little quiet time."

"Oh, aye, lad, yes, by all means, these three-hour days must be putting the boots to you." MacMann rolled his eyes as he strode toward the press room entrance.

"Alright, let's do this," said Frank.

*

Arriving at the podium, Frank wasted no time. "Today, as with previous days, we'll have a brief update from the Chief Medical Officer."

MacMann noticed that Frank had avoided using his name, which he thought odd.

"Followed by the daily update from Mr. Grey. Mr. Doe had a difficult night," Frank continued, "but I assure you we've got our best doctors working around the clock to provide excellent care. The General's renowned for having the highest level of patient care in Arizona, matched with the latest technologies." He nodded, scanning across the audience as he'd seen Earl do the day before. "Now, we'll fill you in on the medical details of the case."

Frank stepped directly backwards with not so much as a glance toward MacMann.

"Good morning, ladies and gentlemen of the press." MacMann opened his blue file folder on the podium. "As my colleague mentioned, Mr. Doe had a very rough night. It was necessary to increase his medications and introduce a machine to regulate his kidneys. Shortly, Mr. Doe will undergo exploratory surgery. One of our surgeons will perform the procedure, which examines the organs specific to the persistent internal bleeding. The surgeon will also ascertain if transplantation is an option. Mr. Doe is very sick, but as Mr. Grey will attest, he's still very much conscious and communicative… with all of his wits about him."

MacMann closed the file folder.

A dozen hands shot in the air.

"Yes," said MacMann, pointing to a young woman in the second row.

"Annie Baird, BBC World News. Doctor, judging from the tone of your comments and those of Mr. Shedmore, it would appear you've given up hope. Is it fair to say the patient is not expected to live beyond the next few days?" The reporter's upper-class accent hacked at MacMann's ancestral roots.

MacMann cleared his throat. "An astute observation, Ms. Baird. We've been working tirelessly to stabilize the patient and determine which priority to tackle first. His case is extremely complicated and unusual. From day one, it's been unclear exactly what led to these multiple and seemingly unrelated injuries. All we can do is prioritize those of an immediate threat to his mortality. The exploratory will shed light on which areas are most urgent. But I'm sorry to say, his prognosis is not positive."

"Have there been any more miracles?" shouted someone near the back.

"Other than him still being alive, I am not aware of *any* medical miracles," said MacMann, bluntly.

"Is he in pain?"

"I'm sure he's in a great deal of distress."

"Can you release his vitals, his medical reports, so we can see his exact condition?" A young journalist spoke from the foot of the stage.

"No," said MacMann. "That would be a breach of his privacy."

The young reporter added, "Yes, but how do we know you're not keeping something from us?"

"I'm not keeping anything from you," snapped MacMann, then scanned the room for another question, but the young reporter continued unabated.

"But if he's God, doesn't he belong to all of us, and we to him. What are you hiding? Does he have different physiology? How many hearts does he have?"

MacMann rolled his eyes, his Scottish blood simmering. "Look, lad, one of my top subjects in school was Mathematics. I excelled at it. So you'll have to take me at my word on this. At last count, a meticulous count I might add, Mr. Doe had only one heart. Now, if you all don't mind, I have far more important matters to attend." MacMann nodded firmly, then marched to the exit.

Frank leaned into the podium and cleared his throat. "Yes. OK. So now we'll hear from our press liaison, Mr. Earl Grey."

As Earl stepped to the mic, questions erupted before he could say a word.

"Mr. Grey? Chandrakiran Bakshi, *The Times of India*. Can we please see his photograph now?"

*

"Alright," said Earl, his arms stretched wide, palms forward. "Let me explain about the photographs. Now, before anybody gets upset, I did remember, and I did bring the request to Mr. Doe."

Earl could feel the tension rising in the room, everyone anticipating an upcoming *but*. "But, Mr. Doe is concerned about becoming the centre of the story when all he wants to do is deliver the message. He's very humble and has no desire for fame, especially posthumous fame."

"Mr. Grey," said Steve Atkins from *First Edition*, holding up his orange hand. "Try to put yourself in the shoes of a famous television reporter, such as myself. Each night we produce a show where we speak about this man who claims to be God… but without any pictures to back it up. You must appreciate the problem here – we need something."

"Oh, I get it now," said Earl, sarcasm at the ready. "I'm so sorry. Us newspaper people are oblivious to modern technologies – photographs being especially mysterious to us. We tend to opt for black and white renderings or charcoal sketches for notable events." Earl lowered his gaze to the podium, widening his eyes for good measure.

Steve continued: "I can understand that, but that's an excellent idea, better than nothing."

"What's better than nothing?" chirped Earl.

"A sketch. A sketch would suffice… for now."

Murmurs of agreement spread throughout the assembled media.

Another reporter spoke up. "It's a great idea. No direct invasion of his privacy, but we'd have an image to frame our stories around."

"Um, hold on a second." Earl wanted to explain that a sketch was hardly any different than a photograph, but no one was listening. He looked toward Frank, who simply shrugged.

"People, people, can I interject?" said Earl. "Mr. Doe wouldn't want this either."

"Earl," said Steve Atkins, simultaneously talking on the phone, "you don't get famous from a sketch. For one thing, they aren't accurate, like photographs, which have much better resolution and colours. A sketch will draw people to the story and Mr. Doe's words because pictures are attention-getters. Isn't that what he wants?"

"Hmmm," Earl nodded. "Sketches aren't photographic, are they, Steve?" He focused on the orange-hued man. "And I suppose it could encourage people to read about his words and philosophy."

Earl stepped back towards Frank and whispered something in his ear, to which Frank whispered, "No objection at all."

Earl returned to the microphone sporting a broad, arguably evil grin. "How fast can you get a sketch artist here?"

*

Earl sat in Frank's office, content with himself. Frank had poured him a dram of scotch whisky on arrival, which Earl swallowed in one motion, holding up the small glass for a refill.

"Are you an alcoholic, Earl?" asked Frank casually, tipping the bottle for a second pour.

"Oh, I wish. What an astounding profession. I think I'd be incredibly good at it."

Frank contorted his face. "You sure about this sketch artist thing?" He stood over Earl's chair, holding the scotch bottle in both hands like an attentive waiter.

"I'm not sure about anything anymore, but I love the idea. Hit me like a freight train, spur of the moment stuff. Satiate the jackals without invading Doe's privacy. Should keep those reporters off my back for a little while."

"I hope so. I'm told a freelance sketch artist who works with the Phoenix PD is on his way over. Do you have any plans after that?"

"I think so. Not sure, really. My limo driver wants to show me something. Beats sitting around here or at the hotel. I hate that hotel, Frank. Well, to be fair, I hate every hotel. Disgusting. My top dresser-drawer smells like fish. Fish! Why would that be, Frank? Why would my dresser smell like fish?"

"It must be very claustrophobic in your universe." Frank shook his head but smiled.

"Where's Doctor Feelgood, by the way?" asked Earl.

"Er… rounds… I guess," answered Frank, half a world away.

"Ah, I miss him," chuckled Earl. "He's like a personal trainer; keeps me on my toes, in full defence mode."

"Ya, he'll do that."

"You don't seem very enamoured with the Roar-man lately."

"What's to be enamoured about? MacMann's as cold as an Inuit fart and twice as hard to handle."

Earl snorted a laugh, holding his glass up for another dram. "Funny thing is," mused Earl, "I feel more positive about this whole shitstorm every day."

"Really? What on earth could you find positive about this… this… *mess?*" Frank squinted in confusion.

"I just feel I'm on the right side of the mess, ya know? Fighting the empire, defending the faith, marching to victory, or martyrdom. Frankly, I'm OK with either one."

"I wish I shared your exceptional embrace of impending doom."

"How many times can they kill us, Frank? We live in a world where the only thing more popular than a good character assassination is a redemption story. I plan to bypass the public hanging and go straight for the title of King of Second Chances."

Frank laughed. "Well, Earl, I've got a busy day ahead of me and some serious matters to address. Why don't you wait down in the press room? I'll make sure the sketch artist finds you as soon as he arrives."

"You're throwing me out?" replied Earl in mock surprise.

Frank held up the half-empty scotch bottle and swirled it around in front of Earl's face. "I can't afford you."

FORTY-THREE

Tuesday, November 17, 1 p.m.
Phoenix General Hospital,
Parking Garage

A nun locked up her car on the third parking level. Two floors above, a different nun stood, patiently waiting for the elevator to arrive. To ensure no one approached or attempted to engage, each Sister emanated an air of self-righteous determination coupled with Drill-Sergeant confidence.

*

"My name's Kevin, and I'm supposed to meet…" Kevin paused, looking down at a print out of an email, "… Earl Grey?"

Earl glanced around the small empty media room, "I think that's me, Kevin. I take it you're the sketch artist?"

Kevin, a middle-aged hippy with sunburnt toes peeking through a well-worn pair of Birkenstock's, nodded his head.

As they both sat, Kevin produced a clipboard with pre-attached sketch paper from his backpack, then fumbled around for a black pastel before reengaging with Earl.

"Alright, I'm going to ask you a few questions about the person you met, and I want you to think very carefully about each answer, OK?"

"Carefully, how?" asked Earl.

The question dazed Kevin. No one had ever asked this before. "Carefully, as in, be very sure of your description before committing, especially with things like eye colour. Like, don't just say brown if it's sandy brown with hints of grey, you see? Try to be specific. If you're off on one feature, say the nose, it can distort the entire face, ending up with something unrecognizable."

"I see," said Earl, doing his best to stifle a smile.

174

"Now, I need to understand every aspect of the subject, so don't leave anything out," urged Kevin. "For instance, in addition to facial features, did the person wear anything specific, you know, glasses or a hat?"

Earl faked a puzzled look as if deep in thought. He stared at the floor, trying not to laugh, wondering just how far he needed to go to buy JD the time he needed. "Glasses," said Earl. "Round ones."

*

"Yes, Ma'am, Catholic. I was brought up that way, but I confess, it's been a long time since I attended services or confessional." Robbie looked several feet below at the diminutive Sister Donello. Despite being a tenth of his body mass, he was surprised at how inferior and guilty she made him feel.

"My, my, young man, how disappointing. Can I assume you've led a sin-free life and see no need to confess to the Almighty?"

Robbie stared at Donello, only her face on display, an exposed oval of pale skin and dry crevasses, void of make up or recent grooming. He couldn't help but think of the Wicked Witch of the East, save for the black pointy hat.

"Oh no, Sister, not at all. I'm sure I've broken more than ten commandments along the way, but I'm not a bad guy. I'm truly sorry. And you're right. I should swing by a church for confessional to…"

"Swing by? Swing by, my boy? The church is not a drive-thru hamburger restaurant! It's a community. A community of imperfect souls gathered under God to make the world a better place. None of them swing by, young man." She smacked her hands together two times, making a loud thwack.

Can she hit me? I think she can hit me, Robbie thought. "I'm sorry, Sister, I won't swing by. I promise."

Sister Donello partially closed one eye. "No, no, you won't, young man. You'll start *visiting* again, and you'll make a point of confessing your sins regularly. Sins are not marbles, you know, not something you save up until the bag gets full, then drop them off at some," she paused, allowing her thoughts to catch up, "… at some marble selling place."

A little lost in the marble analogy, Robbie tried to find the right words to satiate the attack-nun. "I promise, Sister, on my day off, I'll go see a priest and make it all good with God. I feel ashamed."

"And well you should. Now, the patient in this room is my last of the day, so if you don't mind?"

The nun stepped around Robbie and reached for the door, only to be startled as a blue arm shot directly in front of her, palm striking the door jamb with a slap.

"I'm sorry, Sister," said Robbie, waiting for the wrath of God to smote him, "but I can't let you go in there. It's off limits to *everyone*."

"How dare you," spat the nun, twisting her head upwards with demonic precision. "You deny me access to one of God's children?"

"Oh, there's no children in there, Sister, just a patient, just a man, a man patient. And I can't let you see him. I'd lose my job."

"That's ridiculous. Why I've never heard anything so absurd in my whole life, and from a lapsed Catholic too."

Robbie's voice trembled. "I know, but my boss made it very clear; this patient can't have any visitors at all. He's very sick. He may even die. Please, just skip this one."

"Skip this one? I don't skip souls, dear boy, how ridiculous. Now remove your arm and…"

From twenty feet down the polished hospital corridor, the echoing click-clack of shoes grew louder and louder.

"Oh, I see I'm in good company," said a second, much younger, nun arriving at the scene. "I thought I was the only Sister assigned to this floor?" The second nun smiled, revealing perfect white teeth juxtaposed against flawless tan skin.

Looking the young nun up and down, the older nun growled. "What in God's name is this? Who are you? What diocese do you represent?"

Mary-Lynn readjusted her excessively large hat, scraping one wing across Robbie's face. "I'm Sister Wong. I was asked by the hospital to check on Mr. Doe's condition… to see if he needed any comforting or spiritual support."

*

In the back of the limo, Earl asked if he could have some quiet time to finish a bit of work, then watched as a miffed Orlando promptly closed the partition.

During the brief trip, Earl scanned his emails, finding nothing from Mary-Lynn. All his messages were from strangers or companies offering the world for an exclusive story or book deal. Each email was erased without a second thought.

After holstering his phone, Earl retrieved the scotch bottle and turned it repeatedly in his hands like a golden idol. "I'm gonna miss you when this is all over."

*

"Why aren't you arresting her?" demanded Donello to Robbie.

"Um, well, I'm not a cop," said Robbie.

Mary-Lynn interjected. "Arrest me? How absurd. If there's an imposter here, it's you, lady. You're not even wearing a hat." She pointed within inches of the old nun's forehead.

"It's called a cornette, and we don't wear them anymore, except for formal gatherings – something you'd know if you were a real nun."

Robbie watched as the verbal tennis match intensified. He'd managed to slide his entire body in front of the door, then leaned up against it, hoping it wouldn't fly open into the room.

"How dare you!" whispered Mary-Lynn in mock anger. "You will not speak to me in that vile street manner. Guard, take her away." She threw her arm straight out, pointing down the hall and waited for Robbie to execute the command. When absolutely nothing happened, Mary-Lynn adjusted the cornette again after it had spun sideways, exposing her long black hair.

Robbie watched her for a moment. "Oh, are you talking to me?"

Mary-Lynn rolled her eyes. "Obviously! Listen, the patient's in danger here. Who knows what this imposter has in mind. Have you frisked her? She could be carrying."

"Frisk a nun?" said Robbie wide-eyed.

"Look," said Donello, pointing at Mary-Lynn's face. "She's wearing two pounds of make-up and those shoes. Are those the shoes of a nun? They're CFM pumps."

"What are CFM pumps?" said Robbie.

"Don't ask!" both nuns replied in unison.

"Well, this is ridiculous!" Mary-Lynn exclaimed, pushing closer to Robbie. "I'm not gonna get fired because some old lady – are you actually a lady in there? – dressed up as a nun to get God's autograph. You really should check her, Mr. Guard. I think she might be a man, I mean, look at her. We both know there are no male nuns, right? Case closed."

Robbie took an extended look at Donello's face, long enough to receive the evil eye in return.

"Nuns don't get fired, you half-wit," said Donello to Mary-Lynn.

"Ah, there you go, see, proof," said Mary-Lynn. "Would a nun call someone a nasty name? Nuns are supposed to love everyone. Like I do, 'cause I'm a real nun. I love you, Mr. Guard."

As Robbie blushed, Donello spied her opportunity and leapt into action. Gaining excessive strength from somewhere, she pushed Mary-Lynn hard into the guard, who, in turn, fell backwards, knocking the door wide open.

Regaining her balance, Mary-Lynn moved to the doorway where Sister Donello stood frozen. Both nuns stared down at Robbie, spread-eagled on the floor; his phone, pepper spray and loose change now randomly distributed throughout the room.

Embarrassed, the nuns slowly raised their eyes toward the bedridden old man propped up and surrounded by machines. Doe took a long, somewhat awkward suck on a cherry-red popsicle and nodded at the two.

Donello was the first to speak. "It is with the greatest of apologies and respect that I so rudely intrude, sir. My only wish is to meet you briefly, on behalf of our church, the largest church in the world, and share in the joy and love of God."

Doe listened intently, still sucking on the red popsicle, his eyes filled with glee. He glanced down as Robbie scrambled to his feet, awkwardly retrieving his belongings. "And you, young lady, what are your intentions?" Doe looked Mary-Lynn up and down. And then up again.

"Sir, hi. I'm also a nun." Mary-Lynn curtsied. "And I'm with the same big church, and I was wondering if I, er…" she scrambled for a foothold. Donello's eyes pierced into hers as the guard stepped closer. "Oh, screw it, I'm a friend of Earl's. I just… *really* needed to meet you."

Doe raised his right eyebrow and chuckled. "That's one hell of a hat, my dear."

"Oh, you like it? You can have it if you want?"

"No, no, that's quite alright, my dear, you keep it. It looks expensive."

"I'm so sorry, sir," said Robbie grimacing, "I had it under control until…"

"Quite alright, Robbie. No harm done."

"Thank you, sir. I'll get them out of here."

"Wait," said Doe. He looked Donello up and down, and then Mary-Lynn, stopping at her shoes. "OK. Heels can stay. The little dude has to go."

Mary-Lynn grinned.

"But, sir, I beg of you, just five minutes," Donello pleaded, her hands in prayer mode.

"That's an eternity for me," smiled Doe. "But thanks for dropping by, and good luck with that big church thing."

Robbie shooed Donello into the hall like a stray kitten, then closed the door with a thump.

Mary-Lynn quickly removed the massive headpiece, tossing it onto a beeping monitor before shaking out her hair.

"My dear, you're even more beautiful in person," said Doe. "I can see why Earl enjoys your company."

Puzzled where John Doe might have seen her and his reference to Earl, Mary-Lynn took a moment to collect her thoughts. Gazing around the room, she spotted a mini-TV protruding from the wall on a metal swing-arm. "You knew who I was all along?"

"Oh my yes. For a very long time, Miss Wu."

FORTY-FOUR

Tuesday, November 17, 1:15 p.m.,
Phoenix General Hospital,
Room R2112

"You're that girl from TV, the one who thinks Christ was a tap dancer, right?"

Mary-Lynn's face reddened. "Oh… My… God… You saw that? Oh my God, I just said, oh my God to God. I'm so sorry."

"Now, let's not go there, OK? You humans and your God worship. Surely you came in here to meet *me*, right? A man. You didn't really expect to be in the presence of Almighty God, did you? Of course not. If you really thought that, I doubt you'd be wearing those…" Doe pointed at Mary-Lynn's feet.

"You heard us outside the door, huh?" Mary-Lynn stifled a laugh. "No, I suppose not. Although, it would have been freakin' cool if you *were*." She wandered around the room, searching in vain for something to sit on. "So, you know Earl's gonna kill me for crashing in like this?"

"Earl will be fine. He's very special to me, you know. And I'm glad he has a friend like you."

"Yeah, well, not much of a friend. He explicitly asked me not to see you… and I promised him I wouldn't."

"Oh, so you lied? You know, Earl's a bit fragile in that area?"

"I know, I know," Mary-Lynn said, her body deflating. "I can't tell Earl I did this."

"Oh, but you must. It would be far worse were Earl to find out another way."

"You're gonna tell him?" she burst out, her eyes pleading.

"No, I wouldn't, but you must. You can't silence Robbie or that nice old man who came in here with you."

"That was a nun. She's a she."

"Really? The whiskers were…"

"Trust me, lady nun."

"I see." Doe pondered in silence for an extended moment. "Regardless, the right thing to do is to tell Earl. Unless he's simply a tool of your profession, a means to an end? In which case, who cares, right?"

"No, please don't say that. It's not true."

"I'm glad to hear it."

Mary-Lynn fidgeted in her oversized habit. "So, I guess you're wondering what I'm doing here, huh?"

Doe shrugged.

"Well, this is going to sound silly, maybe even egotistical."

"If it's important to you, then I'm all ears."

"OK, alright." Mary-Lynn composed herself and searched for the right words. "Are you done with that?"

"Hmm?"

"The popsicle stick. The juice is running down your hand. Can I take it?"

"Oh, yes, thank you. The nurse snuck it in for me. I'm not supposed to have it, but it's not gonna kill me, right?"

Mary-Lynn smiled and tossed the stick into a garbage can, returning with a wet wipe to clean his hands.

"Well," Doe shrugged, "as for a reason to visit me, that really wasn't egotistical at all. But I agree it was a bit silly."

She giggled. "No, that wasn't why I needed to meet you. Sorry, I'm just stalling. It's hard to put this into words."

"Try… see how it goes," said Doe.

Mary-Lynn sighed. "OK. I was destined to meet you. You see, my mother always told me I was special and, yeah, I know, all parents say that. But my mom was an angel, and I believed every word she ever said. Cancer took her, but before she died, she told me I'd change the world. And that I was destined to meet someone who'd be the catalyst for that change. When I found out about you, and then Earl told me what you were really like, and the things you were saying, I instantly knew it was you. I had no doubt. God or mortal, my fate was to meet you."

"My goodness, that's impressive," gasped Doe. "OK, go on. So now what do we do?"

"Um." She placed her hands on the steel bed rail. "Well, I thought you'd know. I mean, I figured once I got in here, the rest would be obvious. We'd automatically know what had to be done."

"Well, you did clean up my popsicle mess. That was very nice of you."

"True, but I'm thinking larger scale. A little more earth-shattering."

"Oh, OK. So… do you have any questions that might lead us to something?"

"No, not really," Mary-Lynn said, disappointed. "I'm sorry, I imagined this going very differently in my head."

"OK, let's try this," said Doe. "Your destiny, after meeting me… what do you think it entails?"

"Well, I was furious about losing my mom to cancer, and I swore I'd find a way to kill the disease, so maybe that's it. Could we do that?"

"Hmm. I'm horrible with chemistry and biology. Are you any good at that stuff?"

Mary-Lynn shook her head.

"Oh, dear. Any other thoughts?"

Mary-Lynn hung her head. Then lifted it. "For my whole life, all I've seen is unfairness everywhere I look. Disgusting, cruel people becoming wealthy and successful while the innocent and vulnerable get screwed over."

"It's terrible, I know," replied Doe. "So, what did you do to make it better?"

Mary-Lynn seemed embarrassed by the question. She sat down on the edge of the bed. "Well, like I said, I knew I'd meet someone. I mean, I never thought that I alone could make a difference or that my actions could bring about change. I'm not rich, far from it, and what little I can contribute doesn't change anything. So, I haven't done anything yet. I guess I've been waiting for you."

"For me? Oh, dear, well, I hate to tell you this, but I won't be around here much longer, certainly not long enough to help you change the world. Maybe Earl didn't mention it, but I'm dying."

"No, he said you were very ill. I just thought…"

"You thought I could fix everything in an hour?"

She lowered her head. "I shouldn't have come here." She bit her lip. "Damn it, now I'm gonna cry." She closed her eyes and quickly placed the fingertips of both hands over them in an attempt to stem the flood. "This is just perfect."

"Mary-Lynn. Give me your hands," Doe said.

Mary-Lynn reached out with damp fingers and held Doe's outstretched hands, IV lines protruding from both. "I'm sorry I disturbed you. I'm sorry I barged in here like a fool." She felt a sharp tingle shoot up her arms and across her shoulders.

Doe squeezed her hands a little tighter. "Maybe I can't help. But I can show you someone who can."

*

In the back of the limo, detached from Orlando by the driver's tinted glass partition, Earl poured another scotch, then scrolled through his contact list for Mary-Lynn's number. He tapped the call button.

"Oh, hi, Earl," said Mary-Lynn at the end of the line. "I was just thinking about you."

"Hope they were good thoughts?" said Earl with a dopey grin. "Are you outside?" He strained his ears. "Or maybe jump-starting a Jumbo Jet?"

"Ya, sorry, it's very windy. I'm in a parking lot, heading back from an appointment."

"Oh, investigating, were we?" inquired Earl with trepidation.

Mary-Lynn paused. "Earl, I've got something to tell you. I did something you're probably not gonna like."

"Oh God. Let me guess – you slept with Steve?"

Mary-Lynn howled with laughter. "No, you dink. And ewww."

"So, what is it?"

"Um. Could we grab a drink tonight? I'll explain everything then if you promise not to be mad."

"How could I be mad at you?" said Earl, knowing full well there were countless ways he could think of off the top of his head. "Let me know when and where. Oh, I should probably give you my driver's number in case you can't get a hold of me." He recited it as she jotted it down.

"Awesome!" she chirped. "I found a spot to hang near the hospital. It's a short walk. So give your driver the night off. I've so much to tell you. This has been the best day of my life. Laters!" She hung up.

Earl's thoughts turned selfish, pondering the meaning of her statement. *The best day of her life?* A day that happened without him in the picture. Earl swallowed the insecurity and tapped on the partition separating him from Orlando.

"What's up, Earl?"

Earl deflated his lungs. "You ever been in love, Orlando?"

FORTY-FIVE

The limousine pulled off the main road and wound its way through a series of dusty brown undulating hills. There was little to see but the odd cactus and hearty weed clinging to life despite the relentless heat and lack of moisture.

"Orlando. What is this place?"

"We're not far from where they found your God-boy. This is Cave Creek, Regional Park. Locals know it well, but not that many tourists."

Earl looked down at his suit pants and polished shoes. "Not sure if I'm equipped for a hike today, man."

"We're not going far," Orlando said confidently.

As the car pulled around another steep corner, the vista unfolded like an IMAX movie. Directly ahead was a gravel parking area, small but well kept, a blue porta-potty standing guard in the corner. Locking the car, they headed into the desert. Orlando led the way, keeping to the trails and rocky areas to avoid getting sand in their dress shoes.

"Here," said Orlando, pointing into the middle distance. "Just up those rocks."

Earl scrambled up, around and between several boulders the size of tanks, then walked across a flat plateau towards the leading edge. He hadn't noticed the elevation change during the short hike, slow and steady, only mild grades and a few disorienting twists and turns, but as he approached the edge, two key observations struck him. First, he was standing within three feet of a vertical drop, fifty feet or more to the rocks below. Panic-stricken, Earl backed up, sideswiping Orlando, causing both men to brace themselves against the plateau's rear wall – a red sandstone pillar reaching high into the air.

Earl's second revelation was far more satisfying. Miles of desert stretched in front of him, as far as his eyes could see. Sweeping brown and gold sand, pierced by the occasional rock outcrop, random patterns rising high into the air like petrified claws swatting at white cotton clouds. Cactus and desert bush dotted the flatlands, thinning out as elevations rose, leaving only grey and purple shale, layered and stretched before the vertical red towers.

"No comment, Earl?"

"I don't know what to say," said Earl, not knowing what to say.

"Sit over here." Orlando gestured to a spot with a sloped backrest overlooking a valley sliced by a canyon.

Earl, following Orlando's directions, sat on the sandy grit next to Orlando. "This is it," he said triumphantly. "This is the most beautiful view I've ever seen."

"Yeah, I'm a city boy, born and raised," said Orlando. "But I gotta tell ya, this… this… grabs me by the balls every time."

"Couldn't have said it better," Earl smiled, glancing over at Orlando. "It's a ball grabber. It's the most ball-grabbing view I've ever seen. It expels every ounce of air from the lungs. I am completely ball-grabbed."

"Are you making fun of me?" Orlando squinted.

"No, I'm dead serious. I don't know how to express it any better. It's perfect."

"Nope, not yet," said Orlando, reaching for a travel bag he'd brought from the limo. He unzipped the top, reached in and produced two cold beers acquired from the limo's mini-fridge. "Now, go slow. I only brought six. Make 'em last."

"I humble myself to your seasoned wisdom and preparedness. Now, this is perfect."

*

The van doors opened in unison, and, like a clown car at the pontiff's birthday party, five priests of all shapes and sizes rolled out. They scampered towards the nun as she made her way up the concrete incline of the parking garage.

"That was fast," said Bellecourt, arriving first. "Did you get in? Did you see Him?"

Perturbed, Donello began pacing back and forth under a massive concrete beam. "Yes, yes, I got in, briefly."

"I can see it was brief. What happened?" Bellecourt asked, glancing at his watch.

"There was another nun."

"What? What are you talking about?"

"I was about to gain exclusive access, and, suddenly, this other nun appears outside his room."

Bellecourt grew incensed. "What other nun? There is no other nun. Father, what's she talking about?" Bellecourt demanded, looking to the portly priest to his right.

The Sister interjected. "She wasn't a real nun, I'm sure of it. She was dressed in an outdated habit. Her cornette was oversized, and she didn't speak like any Sister I've ever met. She was an Asian woman with *highly* inappropriate shoes."

Bellecourt raised his eyebrows. "But you got in, you saw him?" he spluttered.

"Yes, for a moment. We spoke. The guard wanted us out, but the patient asked each of us who we were and what we wanted."

"OK, and?"

"And... he chose the imposter!"

"What do you mean, Sister?"

"He picked her to stay. Then, the guard ushered me out of the room."

"But..." Bellecourt placed both hands on his head and began to massage his temples, hoping it might induce a little clarity. "The one claiming to be God asked the imposter nun with the inappropriate shoes to stay and kicked you – a real nun – out?"

"Exactly!"

"This makes no sense."

Donello tried to recap. "The woman was crass. She's probably never set foot in a church, and..."

"What, Sister?"

Donello grimaced. "Slutty. God forgive me." She crossed herself with her right hand.

Bellecourt closed his eyes and inhaled deeply. "Alright, so it's settled then."

"Settled?" asked Donello.

"Indeed. This man isn't God or even an emissary of God. God would've known the difference. God wouldn't select a slutty nun while casting out the real deal. This man's a phony, a fraud."

"He did seem... quite lovely," said Donello.

Everyone stared in disbelief. "Lovely?" queried the portly priest with visible surprise.

"Yes, very kind, very... benevolent. He had this aura, energy. I can't explain it."

"You actually think he's God?" Bellecourt's fingers were still in his hair, but they had stopped moving.

"No. Um, well, I don't know, I wasn't there long enough. His actions were… puzzling… but I felt like I was in the presence of… I dunno. There was something there. The room felt…"

A car quickly approached, so they moved off to the side and walked up the slope, back to the church van.

"Sister…" began Bellecourt, "… you said you'd be able to tell. Now you're saying you're not sure. We need to make a decision, and, frankly, I can't support the notion of this man being the Almighty based on him ejecting you from the room in favour of a harlot."

Donello nodded. She was suddenly very unsure of herself.

"Alright," continued Bellecourt. "I'll contact the Vatican and convey our findings. This man is no God. Agreed?"

Only the priests nodded their heads.

*

Earl, now shirtless and enjoying his second beer, sat mesmerized by the landscape. "If there's a God, this is his backyard. His go-to place of solitude and joy. And skeet shooting. Holy shit, could you imagine?"

"You don't believe in God, huh?"

"No, sir." Earl polished off the last mouthful of tepid beer. "Never have. Even as a kid, I knew it was all bullshit."

"A lot of people would disagree with you," Orlando sipped his beer. "Me for one."

"I get it," said Earl, nodding. "Maybe I'm wrong. But we've all got to decide for ourselves, right?"

"It's not a decision, Earl. I feel it." said Orlando, impassioned. "I feel him. I've done a lot of bad shit, and I know he probably doesn't think much of me. But… I did what I did to survive, nothing more. I'm sure he understands. If not, then I guess I'll see you in hell, huh?"

Earl offered a weak smile to his companion, then turned his head to trace the horizon. "A guy like you doesn't qualify for hell. Even if you're right and hell exists, you're a good man. I don't know much – but I know that."

"Oh, you know that, huh. Figured me out in a couple of days, did you?"

"Yep. You're no street thug, dude. You're articulate and intelligent." Earl nodded firmly for effect.

Orlando sat and stared at the Canadian. "And you came to this conclusion in four days, huh?"

"See? *Conclusion.* So gangsta."

"You didn't stop to think that maybe a few college words rubbed off after driving a thousand white guys around Phoenix for five years?"

"Nope."

"Really? Man, I can't figure you." Orlando shook his head and drained his beer. "Before I forget." He reached over and dug into his bag, pulling out a brown envelope and removing the disc. "Here ya go. Five hundred bucks' worth of fake priest pics."

Sunrays reflected off the disc, lighting up his face. "A DVD?"

"Ya. My guy said there were tons of pics, so he put them on this. You can print the ones you want."

"Oh." Earl sat puzzled. "So, I can't see them without a DVD player, huh?"

"Ya, and before you ask, the one in the limo's busted. Too many stag parties."

Earl nodded, then handed the disc back to Orlando. "Pop it back in your bag for now. Don't want the heat to warp it. I'll grab it when you drop me off."

Orlando placed the disc and envelope at the bottom of his bag and re-arranged his off-duty clothes on top as insulation from the heat. After centring his gun on the clothes heap, he zipped up the bag and set it in the shade.

F O R T Y - S I X

Moments later...

"Orlando, I don't suppose there's sunscreen in that bag of yours?"

"Nope, never touch the stuff. But here's a neat idea. Why don't you put your damn shirt on and come over here in the shade?"

Earl lifted his head off the sandy ground and opened one eye so he could see Orlando. "I didn't come two-thousand miles from a frosty hell to sit in the shade. This is my vitamin D for the entire winter, right here. Gotta soak it up."

"With that pasty skin of yours, all you're gonna soak up is first-degree sunburn and a dozen mellotrons."

"It's melanomas," replied Earl, closing his eye and lowering his head again. "Just one more hour, then we can head back, OK?"

"You da boss, boss. Don't blame me if you can't move later. We'll stop at Walgreens on the way home and grab you some aloe vera. Or spray-on painkiller."

"I'll be fine. Canadians do this every May to celebrate the return of summer. A ritual banishment of winter demons. It's a good pain."

"Sun's a lot stronger down here, man. Just sayin."

*

Another hour passed, and it was time to leave. Earl had fallen in love with the tiny slice of sunbleached land and asked Orlando if they could return the next day. Orlando nodded with considerable skepticism.

Sitting in the passenger seat of the limo, Earl resisted the impulse to check his emails. Insisting on his window being open instead of using the AC, he hung his arm outside to feel the wind and the last rays of the day. For a micro-moment, Earl felt more relaxed than he had in years.

Stopping briefly at a Walgreens, Orlando picked out some creams for soothing the anticipated sunburn and a bottle of Motrin to keep the swelling down. From there, it was a short drive to the Marriott. Orlando pulled the car around to the rear entrance, near the kitchen. "Call me if you need me. I'll be home tonight doing nothing," said Orlando as Earl stepped from the limo. "If you feel you're gonna spontaneously combust, just say the word. I'll drop by and sweep up the ashes."

Tipsy and reddening by the minute, Earl closed the limo door and walked around to the driver's window. "Spontaneously combust? See, there you go again with that gritty street lingo. I'll call you if there's a problem, OK? And Orlando, today was amazing. Thanks."

"Well, hold that thought until I see you in the burn ward tomorrow. You might have changed your mind by then."

Earl smiled. "Yeah, I do feel a little… pinkish. I'll head in, take a shower and cream up."

"Thanks for the visual."

"Night, bud. See you at 8:30."

Orlando slowly shook his head. "Goodnight, Earl."

*

Bellecourt strained to hear the man on the other end of the phone. The connection was weak, and there was a delay between sentences, resulting in each man talking over the other.

"I understand, Cardinal Olmstad. But with the greatest respect, we've tried those approaches. We simply can't get alone time with the patient." It was only the second time in his life that Bellecourt had spoken to a Cardinal.

"Father Bellecourt, try to comprehend the big picture? We're still reeling from John Paul's death, and Benedict's so green he's barely memorized the route to the bathroom. On top of that, he's German. So God forbid you're late for a meeting. We're completely swamped here at the Vatican. So I'm depending on you. This absurdity is spreading worldwide, a complete embarrassment to our new Holy Father. It's time to put an end to it. I expect to see an official statement from you indicating your final judgement on the matter, which is that this man is not our saviour, or anyone else's, for that matter. On behalf of the Church, you will attest to meeting with the patient and have fully discounted his claims. Am I clear?"

"Cardinal, please, you must understand…"

"What I understand is your baffling refusal to comply with Vatican wishes. You are leaving yourself open to Church judgement and our definition of appropriate punishment. The question is… do you understand?"

"How can you ask me to sign something I can't support with fact. How can you ask me to lie?"

"By your own admission, you feel the patient's actions are unbecoming of a holy man. Perhaps if you hadn't sent a nun to do a priest's job, you'd have already confirmed this."

"Sister Donello feels differently about my conclusion. She believes there's something to this. She felt… something."

"Is that right? Well, that proves nothing. Didn't you say the patient threw her out in favour of a young woman defiling the habit?"

"That's why I don't believe this man is God, Your Eminence. But I can't support a statement concluding he's a fraud without ever meeting him. Regardless, surely a lowly Monsignor such as myself is inadequate to represent the Church in such matters? Shouldn't a Cardinal such as yourself address the global press, or at the very least, a Bishop?"

"We have no intention of escalating this farce by sending in the big guns. That would only serve to validate the media's mania." The Cardinal lowered his voice and slowed his speech. "You have twenty-four hours to see this man with your own eyes. If you haven't made the declaration by then, you and I will discuss your next assignment. It is my understanding that Anchorage is in dire need of a Monsignor."

Bellecourt closed his eyes and exhaled. "Very well, Your Eminence," he mumbled in defeat. The Cardinal had already hung up.

FORTY-SEVEN

Tuesday, November 17, 6:15 p.m.
Phoenix Marriott Hotel,
Room 624

Earl stood in front of his hotel room's window, scanning the scene below. People milled about near the main entrance and congregated in a small park across the street. The Phoenix General, wrapped in concrete and glass, appeared close, large and imposing. He watched as a helicopter lifted from the roof, swooping left toward the city centre as the sun sank mercifully in the west. A much-needed reminder that nature was still in control.

Earl's room was uncomfortably hot. Slightly drunk, he removed his shirt and dropped his pants where he stood. Standing by the open curtains in black socks and stretchy orange boxers, he adjusted the thermostat from sixty-nine to fifty-five because it seemed like a suitable number.

As he walked past the TV, a sudden terrible thought sprang to mind. The DVD of the priest was still in Orlando's bag. Earl hastily dialled his phone. "Hey, man, didja get far? I forgot the damn DVD."

"Shit," spat Orlando. "With the pharmacy stop and all, I plain forgot. Too late now, dude; I've already dropped off the car for the night. But, relax, the disc is safe in my bag."

"OK, OK, no biggie. I guess it can wait till tomorrow."

"I'll give it to you when I pick you up, OK?"

"Yeah, OK. That's cool," said Earl, furious at himself. "Have a good night, man."

Frustrated, Earl peeled off his socks and walked to the bathroom, turning the big silver faucet handle until the pointer was in the red. After checking the temperature with his palm, he dropped his underwear and stepped into the bathtub. Pulling the glass door shut, he turned the knob that diverted the tap flow to the showerhead.

At the hotel's front desk, recent Philosophy graduate Amy Dixon answered the phone. She listened carefully, jotting down a few crucial points on a yellow notepad, then assured the guest that everything would be taken care of immediately. Hanging up, she hurried into the back office, where the night manager was preparing for his shift. "Gary?"

"S'up, Amy?" asked Gary, a hardened hotel management professional in his mid-twenties.

"I just got a call from a Mrs. Holt in 625. She says there's a man in the room across the hall, screaming like a banshee."

*

"Oh my God," laughed Mary-Lynn as Earl approached her bistro table near the back of Mickey's Bar and Grill. "What happened to you?" She tried very hard to cover her giggling with her hand.

"I may have got too much sun," said Earl, gingerly mounting the stool.

"Ya think?"

"This sun is apparently stronger than the one we have in Canada." He dabbed his forehead with a cocktail napkin. "I'm a little crisp."

Mary-Lynn tittered again, then shifted to concern. "Oh, Earl, it looks like it hurts… a lot? Is it… *everywhere?*"

"Thankfully, I kept my pants on. But yeah, my chest and arms and neck are pretty bad."

Mary-Lynn pouted. "And me jonesing for a hug."

"Yeah, that could snap a limb or two; not the best idea."

"Aww." She jumped off her stool and came around beside him. Gently she placed one hand on his red forearm and slowly leaned in, kissing him on the cheek, hesitating so he could feel her eyelashes flicker on his skin. "Better?"

Earl's red face kept his blush well hidden. "A miracle," he whispered.

Mary-Lynn giggled and returned to her stool. "There go my plans for an all-night sex-fest," she said, holding a straight face.

Earl's eyes and mouth fell wide open, a reflex that hurt a great deal. "If you've got any humanity at all, please tell me you're kidding?"

She broke her stoic expression with a teasing shrug of her shoulders.

"That's unhelpful."

"Big baby."

"Sorry I'm so late." Earl moved the conversation along. "My shower took a bit longer than anticipated, as did the police interview."

"Say again?"

"Yeah, the hotel called the cops when I became a little vociferous after drenching my crispy upper half in scalding hot water."

Mary-Lynn closed her eyes and grimaced.

"Yeah, so anyway, I'm dying. And one of my ears is sweating. At least I hope it's sweat."

"Men! Suck it up. You're not dying."

"That remains to be seen. But let's get to your amazing day," urged Earl, changing the subject again and motioning Mary-Lynn to tell all.

"OK, sure. Shit. I need another drink." Mary-Lynn signalled the bartender.

"Oh, just tell me," said Earl. "How bad could it be?" He stiffened in expectation of how bad it was going to be.

With her hands in her lap, Mary-Lynn fixed her gaze on the floor. "I saw *him* today."

"Saw him? Saw who?" Earl sat puzzled until the answer surfaced near the back of his skull. It swam across his sunbaked brain to the shallow end before emerging and evolving legs. His jaw unhinged. "Oh no!"

Mary-Lynn nodded, her eyes welling in the corners.

*

Orlando confidently stepped from the No. 13 bus at the corner of Camelback Road and Nineteenth – Phoenix's version of the projects. After a lengthy dinner at Chang's All You Can Eat, jeans swollen, he sauntered towards his building, one of twenty identical brick boxes with no balconies. Not that there was anything to look at – only rows of concrete monoliths lining both sides of the I-17 corridor.

Orlando had stuffed his uniform and gun, a small Smith and Wesson revolver, into his duffel bag, his black driver's hat wedged between the handles. His street clothes, a tee-shirt, baggy jeans, white runners and a baseball cap made him instantly invisible in the neighbourhood. Just one of a thousand commuters, plodding their way home after another day of subservience.

Orlando's mother had been strict about his vocational options and made it clear that earning money at the end of a gun barrel was not one of them. Still, in addition to safety, the Smith and Wesson doubled as a security blanket and massive ego boost, adding a virtual two feet to his height.

His apartment was a short walk from the bus stop, precisely why he rented it in the first place. After reaching his door on the second floor, he dropped the duffel bag like a sack of oatmeal and rifled his pockets for keys.

Something was different. Orlando could sense it, maybe smell it. The hallway looked the same as always: dingy, overhead fixtures long extinct – the only sound and light a dull red glow from a buzzing exit sign at the far end of the hall. Orlando's most dependable sense was number six, and it pleaded with him to reevaluate his lack of high-calibre preparedness. But he shook off the feeling as fast as it came. Chalking up the queasy sensation to standard paranoia, he keyed the door locks, two keys for two different deadbolts.

Once inside, something indeed felt different. The apartment was very dark and smelled of musty, curried chicken. *All good so far*, thought Orlando. But something remained alien about the environment, something foreboding, and then it hit him – a breeze.

Flicking on the light switch resulted in absolutely nothing happening. Quickly shifting his eyes to the kitchen, Orlando checked the digital clock on the stove. The usual flashing twelve now black and lifeless.

Orlando ran the logic through in his mind. *Exit lights are on in the hall. Other apartments seemed to have power. There's music playing nearby. It must be just me*, he deduced. *And the breeze – where the hell is that breeze coming from?*

After taking a few cautious steps into the living room, the source became obvious. The double-hung window leading to the rear fire escape was wide open, a faded curtain billowing into the room like a fat yellow ghost.

His eyes struggled to scan the room for damage – new damage – something he might be responsible for under his cleaning deposit. But nothing had changed, other than the open window.

Orlando's next thought came fast: his gun. He turned, glancing back toward the bag in the hall.

"Orlando, we finally meet. Please take a seat," said a disembodied voice somewhere behind a gun barrel pointing from the blackness of a recliner.

FORTY-EIGHT

Tuesday, November 17, 9:30 p.m.,
Orlando's Apartment

After quickly assessing the situation, Orlando brought his heartbeat under control. Instinctively, he had turned sideways, striking a martial arts pose. "You've got some honkin' balls breaking into my apartment," he shouted toward the seated shadow. Edging closer, Orlando tried to catch a glimpse of the man hidden in darkness. *Was it Danny, the loan shark, thought Orlando, or maybe Fat JJ? No. The voice is all wrong – this guy's white, very white.*

"Orlando, sit down. I'll make this quick. Can I get you a beer?"

Orlando's face contorted. "You're offering me one of my own beers?"

"Nope, I brought my own. When I didn't find what I was looking for, I stepped out to the Circle K, grabbed a couple of six-packs and came back here to wait for you. You work crazy hours, dude."

Orlando moved slowly in the darkness, past the dancing curtain to the front of the sofa. Sitting, he studied the figure's silhouette. White for sure, thin too. "I'll skip the beer if it's all the same. What do you want?"

"You've got some videos that don't belong to you, little man. Dangerous stuff. Could shorten a guy's life. Better if I take them. You're in way over your head." The figure paused, looked Orlando up and down, then added, "No disrespect intended."

"Fuck off!"

"Yes, of course," the shadowman replied with a chuckle. "Hand me the backup drive, and I'll fuck off with pleasure. Can I assume it's in your snazzy bag over there on the floor?"

Orlando glanced at the silhouette of his duffle in the hall.

"Come on," sighed the intruder. "I'm in no mood to play games." As Warren lit a cigarette, his face burst into view with highly defined orange and yellow hues.

"You're not good at this, you know," said Orlando.

"At what?"

196

"This whole intimidating, secret villain thing you got going on. You kinda suck at it."

"Look, Orlando…"

"And how do you know my name?"

"Oh, that was easy. After I found out you'd fucked off with the backup, I simply asked for your description. Easy-peasy. A four-foot black guy imitating a courier from some tech company…"

"Iron Mountain," added Orlando.

"Yes, Iron Mountain. Vince Carter, brilliant. It was easy to track you down."

Orlando clenched his fists. "So, why do you want the back up?"

"Not your issue, little man. Just hand it over, and I'll be on my way."

Orlando's brain was quickly catching up to the present. He stalled for time, hoping he could invent a suitable escape plan. Standing up and edging toward the kitchen, he said, "Actually, I think I will have that beer."

Warren flinched. "No prob, dude, but stay right there where I can see you. Sort of. I'll get one for you."

"Alright," said Orlando casually.

Warren kept his eyes on Orlando as he fetched two cans from a brown paper bag sitting on the kitchen counter next to a window overlooking the main street. Orlando studied the man as he moved in and out of the yellow glow from the flickering streetlight. About five-foot-ten, slim build, 175 pounds at best, dirty blond hair, dark grey jacket, blue jeans, black cowboy boots. A Sig Sauer 226 semi-auto in his left hand. *Stupid choice for a gun,* thought Orlando. *Total rookie.*

Warren swiftly returned with two warm beers, placing one on the beat-up coffee table between them. "Knock yourself out," he said, returning to the recliner and opening his own. "Sorry, they're not very cold. No power."

Orlando cracked the tab and took a long swig. "So… I'm guessing if I tell you I don't have the backup drive, violence will follow?"

"Oh, but you do have it, my friend. I am quite sure of it. And since I've been through your apartment with a fine-tooth comb, I'm also sure it's not here. So, that leaves two possibilities. One, you gave it to someone, in which case I'll need a name. Or, B, it's in your knock-off designer bag over there in the hall. Being a betting man, I'll put thirty-to-one on the big bag in the hall." Warren smiled smugly, knowing full well Orlando couldn't see him.

"Well, you'd lose that bet, Sherlock. I did have it, but it's gone now." Orlando nodded and took another gulp.

"Ah, so I should take your word for it, should I? Look, man, I got no beef with you, but I either leave here with the backup drive, or I leave with your head. A peace offering for my boss."

"The back ups don't exist. They're toast. Couldn't give 'em to you if I wanted to. My job was to get the backup drive and destroy it so no one could ever see what was on it. Love to help, since you seem very pleasant and civilized, but you're shit outta luck."

"Uh, huh," said Warren. "Well, then, I'm sure you've got no issue with me peeking in your bag." He lowered his gun and pointed it towards Orlando's head.

Orlando laughed loudly. "Man, I've seen a lot in this line of work, but you take the cake. You've never killed anyone in your life. Ain't got it in ya. Your moves are stolen from every cliché mob movie ever made. You're a poser. Now… get out before you make me angry."

"You forget who's holding the gun and who's holding the beer."

"Yeah, and that's another thing: who taught you to carry a semi-auto in this kind of work? What's up with that?"

"What's wrong with… my gun?" queried Warren, glancing at the silhouette in his hand. "I like my gun."

"Jesus, dude. What happens when you fire that thing?"

Warren thought about the odd question for a moment. "It goes bang and fixes problems."

"Yeah, OK, Rambo, and what else happens? The gun goes bang, and the bullet comes out the little hole. And what else?"

Warren became visibly frustrated. "I dunno; the barrel gets hot? The next bullet loads itself? What do you want me to say?"

"What happens to the casing from the last bullet fired?"

"Oh, OK, gotcha, it shoots out the side here. So what?"

"And what's on those casings?" Orlando began to slowly pace by the coffee table, his hands now clasped behind his back.

Warren strained at the thought. "I dunno, the brand name, the calibre?"

"Your fucking fingerprints, idiot!" Orlando shouted.

Warren sorted the words into a visual of himself loading each magazine. Pushing each round into the clip with his thumb and index fingers. "Oh, right."

"Oh, right. You've shot nobody, man. You suck at this! You need a coach before someone blows your head off – or the cops get around to picking up your brass, which you basically autograph. Look, man, you're not the enforcer type. I see a guy who likes the business card but not the business."

Warren stood up slowly, remaining in front of the easy chair, gun still pointed at Orlando's head.

"OK." Orlando tried a Hail Mary pass. "I'll give you a freebie. There's a gun in my bag, a real gun, one that leaves no evidence, much better suited for our line of work. But there's no giant metal backup drive in there."

Warren edged towards the hall, keeping his gun trained on Orlando. Kneeling, he moved his hand over the top of the bag, discarding the hat and unzipping the zippers. He pulled the flap away and plunged his hand inside, stopping instantly at the first item encountered – a revolver. He turned it around in his hand, feeling the metal and the ribbed rubber handgrip. "Huh, cute."

"It's not cute, you fuck, that's the perfect weapon."

Next, Warren pulled out a small pair of pants followed by a chauffeur's jacket, a belt and a black pair of shoes. "Also cute."

"Fuck off!" Orlando gave a dismissive wave and climbed up on the couch, attempting to look unfazed.

With the bag near empty, Orlando watched as Warren flipped it upside down and shook it violently. All was quiet but for the thunderous boom of a brown-paper envelope crashing to the ground in slow motion. "Well, well, what's this?"

"It's porn," shouted Orlando. "And I'd appreciate it, one dude to another, if you didn't judge me for it."

Warren slid his hand inside the envelope, his fingers tracing the unmistakable shape of a DVD. "Aren't you the clever one?" He looked at Orlando's silhouette, fidgeting on the couch. "Download the bits you need. Smarter than I gave you credit."

"It's just porn!"

Warren stashed the envelope inside his grey jacket and picked up Orlando's gun with his free hand. "Huh. No spent cartridges covered with fingerprints, eh?" *Click.*

Orlando jumped several inches in the air.

Following the click came the sound of marbles bouncing on a hardwood floor, scattering in every direction – six oblong marbles spinning to a stop. Warren gathered the bullets, shoved them in his jacket pocket, then flipped the gun's cylinder closed with a snap of his wrist. Casually, he dropped the revolver back into the bag. "It's been a pleasure, Orlando. I won't forget the cooperation or advice. You're OK, little dude." Warren opened the apartment door, stepped into the hallway and closed it in one fluid movement.

Orlando shouted towards the door from the darkness of his living room. "Hey, dickhead! What about my electricity, how do I turn on the…? Goddamit!"

FORTY-NINE

Tuesday, November 17, 9:50 p.m.
Phoenix
Mickey's Bar and Grill

"I trusted you." Earl was aching – an ache that dwarfed his sunburn.

Mary-Lynn wiped away a tear. "Please, listen. I didn't do it to hurt you. And I didn't do it to scoop you."

"But I asked you not to see him. And not 'cause of the media liaison bullshit. Don't you see, I'm not interviewing him; I never did. We're… talking… helping each other. I'm discovering a lot about myself."

"I know. He's healing you, isn't he?"

"What?" Earl was taken aback.

"Healing you, don't you see? Same for me. I was there for less than an hour. Not as a reporter, but as a… patient."

Earl shook his head and studied his drink, eventually lifting it to his mouth. "I asked you to stay away."

Mary-Lynn sighed and swallowed all of her Chardonnay at once. "Listen to me, Earl. There's part of me that stops at nothing to get what I want, steps on anything… and anyone. Chalk it up to my childhood, people keeping things from me for my own so-called good. Tell me no, and I'll go right ahead and do it, damn the torpedoes. All I hear is, I dare you."

"Soooo…" elongated Earl. "I'm just another authority figure you need to defy?"

"No, no, well, yes… kinda. At dinner, I told you I needed to meet Doe because it was my *destiny*. And I wasn't wrong. Earl, I didn't interview him. And I have no intention to tell anyone I ever met him. That's the truth."

Earl pondered if it was unfair blaming Mary-Lynn for his sizable collection of interpersonal trust issues. Besides, he wanted and needed to believe her, and this *was* a highly unusual situation. He reached out and cupped her hand in his. "What exactly did you mean when you said he's healing me?"

"Haven't figured it out yet, huh?"

"I've figured out that every time we talk, Doe triggers these latent emotions or pain points, bringing them to the surface… where I don't want them."

"He's fixing you, Earl. He told me so. He said you're very special to him."

Earl felt a sudden warmth unrelated to the biting sunburn. His stomach and shoulders sank in unison. "I think I've known that from the start. It's just surreal to say it out loud, you know?"

"Yes, I do know. *Now.*"

"What did he say to you?"

"I told him about my past, about loss, anger and my self-inflicted mission to change the world. And he just listened, you know, the way therapists listen and never say a friggin' word?"

Earl nodded.

"He asked me what I'd done with my life, and I felt like running out of the place. I felt ashamed. Within minutes he'd crushed my defences, burned down my façades. Then he said there was someone I needed to meet, someone who knew my future and what I needed to do."

Her eyes welled up. "Doe asked me to look in the drawers. You know, the ones along the wall, across from his bed, where they keep the files and extra pillows? He said I'd find the contact info in the top right drawer. And do you know what was in there?"

Earl nodded, "A mirror."

Her teary eyes went wide with astonishment. "Yes. How did you…? You knew about this?"

"No," he assured her. "But it couldn't be anything else."

The waiter arrived with a pint of beer and another large glass of Chardonnay. Mary-Lynn asked him to keep them coming and ordered a stack of napkins. "Am I that transparent, Earl?"

"Not at all, just a common theme among us outlanders. It's a wonder we made it this far in life without ever meeting ourselves, isn't it?"

Mary-Lynn nodded enthusiastically. "Doe told me I was running. Running from anything that might result in failure. And the goal I'd set for myself, for my mother, *save the world,* was so monumental it paralyzed me. I set myself up for failure, Earl. No one could ever live up to those expectations." She gulped a mouthful of wine. "Now I know where my low self-esteem comes from."

"It's about not blaming yourself anymore, right?"

"Wrong," she smiled. "It's about not blaming anyone *but* yourself, yet still loving yourself despite everything you've done. Truly loving yourself, but not for the wonderful things you've done, that's pride and ego, but for everything else. Everything we hate about ourselves because it's a massive part of who we are. It's about acceptance." She leaned over the table to hug him.

"No, no, no." Earl backed away, palms outstretched in front of him.

"Ooo, right, right. Sorry."

"Not half as sorry as I am, believe me."

Mary-Lynn's stoic look broke into a giggle. "You'll have a lovely tan… in a few days."

"Yes, true, right after the snakeskin peel."

"You say the most romantic things."

"It's a curse."

"Earl… Doe's on the same journey as you. He's trying to help."

"I know. I see it. *Feel it…* there's something… binding us. Still, I'm struggling to understand why anyone would care enough to bother."

"Don't you see, he's just practising what he preaches, thinking of others instead of himself. Focusing on your personal evolution. Becoming a better person by helping you."

"I don't feel worthy of his help. I mean, why me, you know?"

"Earl, do me a favour. Go find your own mirror and fall in love, OK?" She smiled and squeezed his hand tightly.

*

As Earl rode the Marriott elevator to his floor, Mary-Lynn's words roamed throughout his head, colliding with the events of the afternoon. As each floor passed, his life changed forever. Earl had wanted so desperately to kiss Mary-Lynn when she dropped him off outside the hotel, but something, a thought, told him to wait. A tipsy, sunburnt, first kiss in a shitty hotel lobby was not the romantic anecdote he wanted to tell their grandchildren.

Unlocking the door to his room, he shuffled inside to discover winter had come. The room was sub-zero, dusty white flakes spewing from the AC unit by the window. Against his burnt skin and high body temperature, the effect was heart-stopping. He could see his breath.

Knowing that windows don't open in high-rise hotels, he racked his brain for a solution, knowing he couldn't call the front desk after the banshee incident. Since lighting a fire was probably discouraged, he turned the thermostat up as far as it would go, sparking the heating unit to life. To hasten the thawing process, he let the bathtub fill with hot water while he lay under the duvet, watching as steam billowed forth from the bathroom. Turning on his Blackberry with shivering fingers, he checked for messages.

The first message in his inbox was from his editor, the polite tone triggering immediate suspicion. Earl examined the note for clues, and, sure enough, his editor had replied, cc'ing *all*, assuring the message was visible to the media group's Board Members.

Earl, I've discussed your idea for a book with our management group. They stand behind the idea 100 percent but pointed out that, since you're a paid employee of the Telegraph, the book's content remains our intellectual property. So, we're counting on you to double profits, Earl. And I'm very much looking forward to having you back in my office.
Ed.

Earl laughed out loud at the thinly veiled intimidation.

The remaining messages fit into the tap and delete category, leaving Earl thoroughly fatigued. He turned off the water in the tub and let it sit, steam hovering several feet from the ceiling. Rolling back into bed, he lay still and considered the potential effects of condensation on smoke detectors.

FIFTY

The Story of Nog: Part V

Sunday, November 15, 12,042 BC, 12 p.m.

As Numa napped, Nog roamed the cave, studying the many beautiful works of art adorning the walls. He especially enjoyed a section near the back of the cave where Numa, he presumed, had stencilled a single handprint on the wall. Apparently, the old man knew the technique of blowing powder over his hand while holding it flat against the wall, creating an outline. Once finished, dabbing a little water around the stencil was enough to make it permanent.

Nog moved back to the pedestal where the jewelled bag lay at the centre. He watched as the sun shifted another inch above the cave, catching new fissures in the rock ceiling. A beam of light sprang from a tiny hole now aligned with the noon-day sun. It coalesced on the bag's surface, focusing on the many gems and polished stones on the top side.

Nog was transfixed at the spectacle as the light swelled with technicolour intensity.

Seconds later, all hell broke loose.

To suggest the cave was bright was an understatement, like saying the sun's surface was warm or that Stalin was temperamental. The cave lost all definition, all context. Even the walls vanished in the white haze of nuclear radiance.

Nog threw himself against the wall, only four feet from the pedestal, his eyes glued shut as the blinding light stabbed at his brain and attacked his senses. His skin burned, his ears plugged, and everything smelled like sulfur. Sinking to his knees and elbows, Nog buried his eyes in his forearms. Still, the light's intensity only grew as his consciousness faded, slowly drifting away. Then blackness.

*

As Nog floated in nothingness, he summarized his first impressions as a way to dispel the mounting anxiety. First off, there was this blindness thing, total blackness all around, deep and penetrating, with no sense of proportion. Even placing his hand in front of his face revealed nothing. He knew his arm was there, but there was no way to visually confirm it.

Next on the checklist was sound. Of which he heard none. A simple test came to mind. Nog opened his mouth and screamed… Nothing. *Well, that's great, deaf, too. This could prove to be a tedious afterlife.*

Condition three was easy to measure and equally unsuccessful. There was no smell, and since Nog had no desire to taste anything at that particular moment, this only left touch. And it was touch that rapidly became his greatest concern. Nog couldn't feel himself. He couldn't touch his own body. And there was no sensation from his surroundings, no ground under his feet, just floating without the sensation of floating.

Pondering his circumstance, Nog concluded that death could be a lot worse. All he needed to do now was to find a place to sit or stand or be. He considered his fate for some time, or no time at all. He wasn't sure. Which revealed a much bigger problem. There was no sensation of time. As far as Nog could tell, he'd been in this place forever and only just arrived seconds ago. He couldn't tell if anything was happening, or nothing, nor for how long either of them hadn't been happening, if they were.

Then it occurred to him to try a different approach. Instead of thinking and answering his own queries, he could reach out and ask the void for answers, not with his mouth, which apparently didn't work, but with his subconscious.

Nog concentrated on one clear, targeted thought…

Where am I?

An immediate reply echoed throughout the ether. **You are everywhere.**

That's helpful. Nog tried again. *Why am I dead?*

You are not dead.

Nog was unsure if this was good or bad since being alive in this state would suck.

Why am I blind?

You are not blind. You can see everything from here.

Huh. I guess it's night-time for everything, Nog thought to himself. *All I see is blackness.*

Is that a question?

No, more of a statement or panic-stricken observation.

Silence ensued.

Nog tried a new approach. *I would like to see or feel something. Can I do that?*

You are everything that exists. What do you wish to see and feel?

Ah, now we're getting somewhere. I want to see Numa's cave. Right now!

When is now?

That's a damn fine question, thought Nog. *I want to see it the moment after the demon light-bag attacked me.*

Instantly, Nog's senses exploded. Light, sound and smell, everything erupted into existence. He was back in Numa's cave, his world rushing toward him and away at the same time. Fog drifted everywhere, replacing the very air itself. But after a quick glance around, Nog realized that he wasn't back in the cave at all. He was just viewing it. Two blatant clues led to this conclusion. One, he was roughly five feet off the ground and floating. Two, Nog's physical body was lying on the ground, four feet from the devil bag, face buried in his forearms with no signs of life. Slowly, Nog drifted on, uncontrolled, slipping through a cave wall and outside, moving west toward the valley and an ominous bank of black thunder clouds.

Oh, shit. OK, OK. Nog quickly forced another thought. *I want to view something else.*

A bit vague, what do you wish to view?

I dunno, a happy place. Wait, no, a safe place.

Where?

Anywhere, anywhen. I don't care, Nog shouted in his mind. *Pick a favourite spot of yours; just do it quickly.*

Nog's senses exploded once again, an atomic blast of light, sound and smell. He was indeed somewhere, but it was no place he'd ever seen before – inexplicable, alien, and overwhelmingly green.

FIFTY-ONE

Earl slept poorly for the fourth night in a row. His sunburn made it impossible to find a position that didn't result in some degree of pain, crimson skin protesting the slightest movement. His dreams were scattered, primarily scenes of various days in hell, usually summertime, extreme humidity with sulfuric thunderstorms and a total lack of frozen cocktails. Dehydrated, his body had no reason to wake up for midnight urinations, leaving him tossing and turning until the clock radio released him from his fitful slumber. As consciousness took hold, it became apparent that the bed was on fire. Not literally, but as close as he cared to imagine without actual flames rising from the sheets. Salty sweat poured from every inch of his body, further antagonizing the burns. He dabbed at his face using the top sheet, moving it very gently so as not to remove all the skin from his skull.

After kicking the sheets and pillows to the floor, he lay spread-eagled, staring out the window and catching a glimpse of the thermostat control on the wall. "Oh, hell no!"

He rolled off the bed and stepped to the window, focusing on the digital read-out. As suspected, it displayed an ambient room temperature exceeding the average daily output of the sun. Pressing the off button, he staggered to the bathroom and sat down in the now tepid bathwater. He bathed his lower extremities and under his arms, deciding his head and torso could wait another day. Towelling off was laborious and painful, quick enough around the lower regions but bogging down at the arms and back. After soaking his crispy bits in aloe vera, he dressed quickly, knowing he had only minutes before the overwhelming heat rendered him bath-worthy again.

*

"You don't look as bad as I thought," Orlando said with a laugh as he looked into the rearview mirror. The limo lurched away from the curb.

"I'll survive," Earl said as he reached for the scotch before remembering the time. "Soooo, give me the DVD, man," said Earl, his voice serious. "I want to have a look as soon as I get up to MacMann's office."

Orlando was tempted to omit the details of the previous night's break-in, figuring what Earl didn't know wouldn't hurt him. Still, he knew there was no other way to explain where the DVD had gone, the same DVD Earl had held just hours before.

"Earl." He spoke with softness. "I had a visitor at my apartment last night. An unwanted visitor. I found him sitting in my living room with a gun."

"What?" Earl snapped out of his anti-morning mood and leaped to the forward couch, directly behind Orlando. "Who? Holy shit, are you OK? What did they want?"

Earl's genuine concern surprised Orlando. "Yeah, s'all good, I'm fine. The dude was an amateur, no real danger. He just wanted the backup drive from the hospital."

Earl sat stunned. The consequences of this news were enormous. He stared at the leather seat beside him, slowly shaking his head back and forth. "Oh shit, shit, shit. Someone knows I'm after the videos. So, they know I'm looking for the phony priest. They must think I sent you. Did they get the DVD?"

"Kind of," said Orlando, embarrassed.

Earl's face puckered up. "Kind of? What sort of answer is *kind of*?"

"Yeah, he took the disc. But I got my crew working on it. They'll find the prick. I got a good look at his face, a local for sure, white trash cowboy, seen too many gangsta movies."

"Is this some new definition of *kind of*, I'm not aware of?"

"He won't get far," repeated Orlando, ignoring the sarcasm. "Besides, this is way better than having the pics in the first place."

"Better? Jesus, dude, this is bad. Somebody knew you had the back ups, and it couldn't be the hospital or the cops. They don't operate that way, breaking and entering and all. Or do they? I'm not accustomed to this highly-armed society of yours."

"Earl, listen to me. Just chill for a second and listen. The dude said I was in over my head. He said I was stepping into some heavy shit, dangerous stuff. But, to be fair, he was pretty nice about the whole thing."

"Nice? What the hell, man? He robbed you at gunpoint in your own home."

"He's just a pawn. He brought me beer, and he didn't kill me. That's nice. And he was more nervous than anything. He just wanted the backup videos."

"Ah, well, that's good. I'm glad it's all settled then. The nice man robbed you, took the pics I paid big money for, and dropped off some beer. Not the worst evening one can have, I suppose."

Orlando laughed. "I know the game, OK? I'm not a rookie. There was no danger. Anyway, I'm sure this won't lead to you. My bet is the IT nerd sold me out. But, this is better, Earl. This will lead straight to your phony priest."

Earl cocked his neck at Orlando in confusion.

"Earl, pay attention. A fake priest visits Doe in private. Then, suddenly, there's this great interest in the security video for that day, which would, of course, have the priest on it. But I come along and grab the tapes first, only to get screwed over by some low-level bag boy who rips me off. Therefore...?" Orlando watched Earl's eyes, waiting for the moment of realization.

"Go on..." said Earl, blank-faced.

"Jesus, I thought you said you were a reporter."

"I never said I was a good one."

"Earl. Don't you get it? We don't need the DVD anymore. Tracking my cowboy friend leads us straight to your priest. Simple shit."

Orlando watched Earl's brain as it caught up, out of breath.

"Anyway, just chill, Earl. I put the word out right away. People I know who know people. We'll find him. Then we'll watch him like a hawk until he leads us to the priest."

Earl sipped on the tsunami of new information as Orlando parked the limo. "Orlando, if this guy's bad mojo, as you say, we shouldn't antagonize him. We should find out who he is and then decide what to do."

"Sorry, we're way past that point. Shit's personal now. Break into my fucking crib and steal from me? Nah-ahhh, no way. Pics or no pics, this is my house. These people need to learn some respect."

Earl pondered the latest wrinkle in his severely distorted shit-quilt of poorly-sewn plans. He threw Orlando a sober look. "Just be careful, OK?"

The pair walked from the limo to the staff elevators and waited for the doors to open. Orlando told Earl of his busy day ahead and how his chauffeur role would need to play second fiddle to more important tasks. Then he reassured Earl that he was only a call away if there was an actual emergency.

Unclear about their next move, Earl asked Orlando not to mention the late-night break-in during his daily report to MacMann. To which Orlando replied with a definitive "Duh," as he walked away, slightly offended.

*

"Well, there he is," said Frank, greeting the red and clammy Earl Grey as he stepped through the big glass doors of the administrative offices. "How are ya, stranger?"

"Toasty, but none the worse for wear," said Earl, grimacing.

"I see you've been enjoying our state's perpetual sunshine." Frank chuckled.

"Yeah, enjoyed it – past tense. Paying for it now."

MacMann slid into the waiting room as if his shoes were greased. "Have you lost weight?" he inquired, staring at Earl. He tried his best to stifle a laugh and failed.

"Maybe a bit. I tried this new sauna treatment last night. Melts the fat away."

MacMann pursed his lips. "Well, you best be finding something to do with yourself today, lad. For one, I'd suggest avoiding the sun."

"Why's that?" said Earl bemused.

"Don't be daft. You'll only make that burn worse and do some permanent damage."

"No, why should I find something to do today? What do you mean?"

"Oh, aye, well, Doe is pre-op now, being prepped for exploratory. You won't be visiting him this morning. And I doubt he'll be in any condition to see you later."

"Oh," said Earl, disappointed. "So, no press conference?"

"Oh, aye, there'll be a presser. We need to explain the details of Doe's procedure. You should be there too, if for no other reason than to present the artist's sketch."

Earl winced a little. "Yeah, about that, I worked with the artist yesterday, and I'm pretty happy with the results... but I'm not sure you guys will be totally on board."

"On board?" mused Frank.

"Well, I figured I was doing you both a favour."

"Ah, Jesus," said MacMann. "When it starts like that, ya just know someone's gonna take one up the chocolate speedway."

"Can I assume you... *embellished* a little as we discussed?" asked Frank, ignoring MacMann.

Earl sat down on the leather sofa. "I may have exaggerated a bit. The sketch may not be entirely... realistic." Earl winced.

"You knew about this?" MacMann looked at Frank. "And just how does that help us?"

Earl interjected. "Look, this whole thing can't last much longer. Doe's health won't let it. If he dies, I suspect most people will move on, but some – let's call them the conspiracy-loving type – will chew on this like a dog on a bone. They won't be satisfied until they've seen him in the flesh. Dead or alive. So, we must give these idiots a more, shall we say, fictionalized version of Doe's likeness. It protects the hospital, and it won't have the staying power of an accurate depiction. Remember, Doe could be anybody. He *is* somebody. And we may not like his true identity when it comes out. This way, we maintain a bit of artistic licence, a little cover."

MacMann paced his office and thought about Earl's words. "That's not the dumbest thing I've heard all day."

"Um, thank you?" said Earl.

"On stage, Earl asked me if he could get creative with this," Frank added. "A way to diminish the potential of us getting sued for exploiting a person with mental health issues."

"I like it," said MacMann. "I approve."

Earl rolled his eyes. "Oh, thank God."

"You're a wee tit," said MacMann as he glided out of the room, his doctor's coat flapping behind him like Batman's cape.

Robert Hand watched the doctor depart, then sidled through the door opening and scurried up to Frank. "I've got the Board Chairman on line four for you."

FIFTY-TWO

Five minutes later...

Frank held the phone tight against his ear as David Arlington, Phoenix General's Board Chairman, spoke for nearly five minutes without a pause. "Yes, sir," said Frank, "2 p.m. is fine. Yes, I remember the place; we had a meeting there regarding the harassment case." Frank listened further, frowning at the instructions and overall tone of the call. "Yes, for sure. Thank you, David. OK, goodbye."

"Shit!"

*

The daily presser began on time with MacMann describing the various techniques the surgeon would use during the exploratory procedure. Some were only mildly intrusive, while others required significant invasion and surgical precision. He explained that Doe would be under a general anesthetic for several hours and, once conscious, would be spending an undetermined amount of time in recovery before returning to his room.

Many questions surrounded the procedure. Some reporters inquired about the examination of organs and the best and worst-case scenarios for each. Others asked for more details surrounding the results from the continuous blood work and fluid tests. Orange Steve from *First Edition* asked why the 'p' in pneumonia was silent but not the 'p' in pulmonary, then inquired if Doe would be awake during the general anesthetic.

Twenty minutes later, Earl took to the podium. "As you now know, I don't have any updates for you today, but I'm happy to continue our discussion from yesterday. Are there any questions?"

Many arms shot into the air. It seemed, in the space of twenty-four hours, reporters had not only published their stories but also received many questions and comments in return. Feeling more comfortable in his role, Earl addressed each query directly, confident of what Doe would have him say. In fact, he was starting to enjoy public speaking – a marked change from when it represented his second greatest fear in life – the first being change-rooms with group showers.

Halfway through the Q&A, Earl ventured down a rabbit hole regarding the nature of pain and suffering and why God allowed it to exist. "Life by its very nature is experiential," said Earl, as if delivering a philosophy lecture. "You see, everything's relative, and this applies to our senses and circumstances as much as it applies to the laws of physics. Without black, how could you determine the state of white? Without hot, how would you begin to understand the concept of cold? Pain and suffering are the flip side of joy and happiness, inseparable. Now, suppose you believe that time is infinite, as Mr. Doe suggests. In that case, even a short period of physical pain is meaningless. A necessary experience to understand the relativity that exists in everything."

Some reporters took notes. Others stared in incredulity, dismissing Earl's ramblings as unnewsworthy. They knew the public would view Earl's ramblings as nothing more than philosophical gibberish.

"If you knew your consciousness would exist forever, what importance would you place on a few years of suffering, even at its worst? Without a dark side, a negatively charged counterweight, how would we learn, how would we grow?" Earl completed the rant with a nod.

Three reporters clapped.

Quickly realizing he may have jogged down the philosophical equivalent of a dead-end street, Earl abruptly changed the subject. "Now, I have with me today the sketch of Mr. Doe you requested yesterday. It's the original drawing. I've had no time to make copies. So, with your permission, I'll place it here in front of the podium where you can photograph it."

An over-excited murmur swept through the crowd as Earl removed the drawing from the envelope and placed it upright against the front of the wooden pulpit. A hundred camera shutters exploded like a giant flock of birds, all taking off at once.

MacMann stepped down from the stage and walked in front to view the drawing first-hand. After staring at the sketch for a few seconds, he shot Earl a stunned look of disbelief.

Frank stepped to the microphone again and called the room to order. The camera clicks dwindled as many reporters had already left the room, breaking news in hand. "This concludes today's press conference. Tomorrow's conference will commence at the scheduled time. Thank you all."

Before Frank could back away, one hand rose at the front of the room, directly in front of the sketch.

"Yes?" said Frank, pointing to a reporter from ABC news.

"Um, maybe it's just me, but this sketch here, I mean, is this for real? Are we being asked to accept that God is a dead-ringer for Albert Einstein?"

Frank raised an eyebrow then stepped off the stage, intent on getting a look for himself. "Huh, yes, despite the buzzed hair, that's pretty close, I must agree. Earl, would you mind offering a few words about Mr. Doe's facial features and this remarkable coincidence?" Frank, and the remaining reporters, scanned the room, but it was quickly evident Earl had disappeared.

*

Earl was surprised to see an empty hallway outside of Doe's room. Equally disconcerting was the absence of Robbie, the guard.

As Earl stepped into Doe's room, he was struck by an ambiance of frigid sterility. Not a sanitary sterile, more akin to the absence of a soul. Sunbeams streamed through the gap in the curtains, but instead of providing warmth or comfort, the room felt dead and desolate. Earl's chair was back, so he settled in with a local newspaper he found resting on one of the machines.

Naturally, the headlines were about John Doe, along with several articles analyzing the words and concepts Earl had relayed to the reporters. A few pages into the paper was a feature article surrounding the philosophy of Jeremy Bentham and his theory of Utilitarianism. After that, a full-page article on Collectivism, presenting several quotes from Plato, Kant and Hegel. The author railed against the notion of oneness, calling it a communist plot. He warned the reader that ideologies of this nature only produce monsters like Stalin, then ended the article with a statement. *"Only through individualism and freedom can America, nay, the world, reach the pinnacle of equality and liberty."*

Earl devoured every word, shaking his head in annoyance, then tossed the paper aside, wondering what Doe would think of this counter-ideology, the opposite of oneness and togetherness. Every man for himself.

Frustrated and itchy, Earl stood and left the room in search of a cell signal. After wandering for ten minutes, he found himself in the doctor's lounge, where he was quick to email Orlando – *"Please tell me you're having a better day than me?"*

*

In the heart of the old city centre, Frank stared up at the imposing grey building, old and stately, a bank at one time back in the twenties – cold, solid and impenetrable. There were no signs anywhere, no company name or logo, not even a street number. A series of stone steps led toward two large oak doors where the words *Gutta Cavat Lapidem* dominated the curved headstone.

Familiar with Latin, like most in the medical profession, Frank knew the translation but was undecided on the intent: *A water drop hollows a stone.*

Once inside, a matronly woman at the front desk guided Frank to the second floor of the grand building and into an ornate meeting room. Leather-bound books lined every square inch of the walls, stacked to the ceiling. An antique ladder on wheels stood in a far corner should anyone desire a high-altitude medical journal from the seventeen-hundreds. A massive oak table packed most of the floor space, surrounded by a dozen chairs on each side, high back thrones accenting each end.

On the far right side of the room, seven men sat staring at Frank, not one of them rising to shake his hand. In the middle of the seven sat David Arlington, Chairman of the Phoenix General's Board of Directors. Tanned and fit, David Arlington sported a jet-black Hugo Boss suit and crisp white shirt. The shirt's collar was massive, engulfing his expensive pink silk tie, perfectly knotted and tucked inside the expensive jacket. Arlington's straight back and intense stare screamed police commissioner or politician – robust, bold and highly combative. He motioned for Frank to sit directly across from him.

"Let's get right to business, Mr. Shedmore. You already know everyone here." A series of nods orbited the table. "After our conversation last night, I took it upon myself to convene the Board to discuss the events that have led us to this point. That meeting was concluded this morning, after which we had lunch." Around the table, several murmurs acknowledged the deliciousness of lunch.

"Our concern surrounds the hospital's reputation," continued Arlington. "Your initial assurance that this unusual situation could shine a positive light on our facility is now in question. Many of the articles we read in the press are less than flattering."

"Yes, David, I think…"

"Let me finish, Mr. Shedmore."

"Oh, I'm sorry." Frank bowed his head.

"So, as I was saying, our concern does not stem from your efforts to improve the image of the hospital in general. No pun intended." Everyone on the east side of the table guffawed in unison. "But we are concerned about the abrasive attitude of Dr. MacMann, and the irreverent musings of one…" Arlington shuffled a few papers in front of him, using his forefinger to locate the needed name, "... Earl... Grey."

Several murmurs decried the desire for a nice, hot cup of tea.

"Let's start with Mr. Grey. We've noticed... a reluctance. He appears to be actively blocking inquiries and avoiding anything to do with what one might expect a liaison to do. Also, he emits a rather condescending attitude toward the media. His sarcasm and obnoxious mannerisms reflect a poor representation of the hospital. Exactly why do we continue his tenure as spokesperson? Surely, we could find someone more... suitable?"

Frank nodded but remained quiet.

"You may respond, Mr. Shedmore."

"Oh. OK, thank you. And it's nice to see you all again. You all look well." Nobody smiled, nobody responded, and most of them did not look well at all. Frank cleared his throat. "As to your question, Mr. Grey's a quirky man, for sure. He is, in fact, Canadian."

A murmur of collective understanding, and much nodding, filled the room.

Arlington wrote down a few words that Frank couldn't see due to the table's vast breadth. "Mr. Shedmore, need I remind you that the last Chief Administrator left our organization under... *regrettable*... circumstances? We haven't fully recovered from that debacle, and we desperately need to improve our image and public awareness."

"Yes, sir. I've got extensive plans to do just that."

"Mmm," exhaled Arlington. "I'm sure you do."

Frank continued. "I see now that this situation has not had the desired outcome we envisioned. But I believe we've managed to maintain a professional image and the highest ethical standards throughout, and..."

"And that brings us once again to Dr. MacMann," Arlington interjected. "In our collective opinion, the doctor has displayed far too many unprofessional outbursts for a man of science. His actions show that he is clearly more interested in his career than he is in the hospital. As such, he is in breach of our guidelines on proper public decorum. And we've counted a dozen situations where his comments and attitude violate our code of ethics. May I assume you've reprimanded him for each of these occurrences?"

Frank felt his sphincter tighten. "Not as such."

"Oh? Is there some reason you believe it acceptable to ignore our ethical standards and policies, Mr. Shedmore?"

Frank was at a crossroads, an ethical fork in the road. He had wanted nothing more than to reprimand MacMann. But with MacMann's ability to throw anyone under the bus to save his skin, he had thought better of it.

"David, as you know, I'm only the *acting* Chief Administrator. I technically don't have the power to reprimand one of the doctors. That would require the convening of an Executive Oversight Committee. However, Chief Medical Officer, Dr. MacMann, is a permanent member of this committee and would be present to vote on any and all items of reprimand. If passed, which seems unlikely due to MacMann's stature with the committee, the motion would proceed to you, the Board, for final approval. And frankly, gentlemen, the last thing I want is to escalate issues of this nature to the Board. You would instantly lose all legal deniability. As such, I believe it's important to keep our problems at the operational level."

Frank was building steam, his confidence in full flow. "As a side note, gentlemen, if we appointed an *official* Chief Admin, that person *could* reprimand any employee as a private HR matter. There'd be no need to escalate anything to the Board's attention."

Arlington slowly nodded. An act repeated by the six other Board members. "We must fill the vacancy immediately," agreed Arlington.

Murmurs of agreement echoed around the room.

Frank took charge of the conversation. "Yes, indeed. We need to find a candidate willing to join us while turning a blind eye to what has already happened. This candidate must be of impeccable trustworthiness. I'm sure you can imagine the mess if an outsider joined and then decided to expose everything we've done to the light of day."

The chairman looked shocked. "Everything *you've* done, don't you mean? This whole thing was your idea, wasn't it?"

"My intentions were for the betterment of the hospital and its reputation," lied Frank. "As well as that of the patient, of course. The leaks, wherever they initiated, were not of my doing or responsibility. I've done my best to turn an unexpected situation into a great opportunity for the General."

Arlington raised his voice, "Yes, well, great opportunity or not, where the hell do we find a Chief Admin on such short notice? One who can corral MacMann while willingly representing the hospital in the middle of a PR crisis not of their doing? Nobody's going to accept that responsibility, Frank. We might as well advertise for a fall guy."

Frank played the card of silence.

The directors began whispering amongst themselves for several minutes until finally, Arlington delivered his verdict. "Mr. Shedmore." He paused, deliberately improving his tone. "Frank, we have a proposal for your consideration."

FIFTY-THREE

Wednesday, November 18, 3 p.m.
Downtown Phoenix (the seedier side)

It was only the second time Warren had visited the Albion hotel, but he was even less impressed than the first. Two police cars were parked by the main entrance and a coroner's wagon off to the side. His anxiety was already high enough without the added presence of the law.

Warren parked his Jeep in the middle of three open slots near the main entrance, its giant off-road tires rendering the other two spots unusable. Climbing down from the massive vehicle, he locked the doors and walked into the hotel, ignoring the handicapped parking sign crushed under the front of his Jeep.

"Hey," said Warren, addressing the same clerk he'd met the day before. "Thanks for calling me."

"Where's my money?" said the clerk, forgoing the usual, 'good afternoon, sir, what a pleasure it is to have you back with us again'.

Warren pulled a twenty from his jeans and tossed it on the table.

The clerk snatched it, adding dryly, "Room 266. He's waiting for you."

"He is?" croaked Warren. "You told him I was coming?"

"He's a guest. You're just some guy looking for him," rationalized the clerk.

"OK, so where do I..."

"Stairs are over there. Elevator's broke."

*

"Well, good day, young lady, that was quick!" said Stanley. "You're fast becoming my favourite customer."

Mary-Lynn dropped the nun's costume on the counter. "Well, don't get used to it, Stan. I don't live here. When I leave, you're gonna miss all this off-season revenue."

218

"That I am, miss. Although you'd be surprised how many people rent costumes throughout the year."

"No, I wouldn't," laughed Mary-Lynn. "I'm not as innocent as I look."

Stanley searched for a response that wouldn't incur a slap. "None of my business, ya know. It's a crazy world."

"That it is, Stan."

"Is there anything else I can get for you at this time?" Stanley inquired.

Mary-Lynn chewed on her lip and thought for a second. "As a matter of fact, there is *something* I need."

*

With the heavy drapes drawn, the hotel room at the Albion was on the black side of dark. Warren strained his eyes to make out a chair in the far corner where a man sat, a silhouette outlined by the minimal light rolling in from the hall like fog.

"Hello, sir. I've got good news."

"Indeed?" encouraged the silhouette.

"I have the video from the security cameras, and the originals are toast."

"Is that so?" questioned the outline in a deep voice.

"Yes, sir, the files were overwritten at the hospital, so there's no problem there. But some dude stole the backups."

"I see." The shadowy man pulled a heavy drag from his cigarette, allowing his face to glow red, his sick and cruel smile revealing deep facial crevices.

"So, yeah. This dude copied the videos onto a DVD and destroyed the originals. So, all I had to do was relieve him of the disc and voila."

"Warren." The dark man stood. "Close the door, then come here... where I can see you."

Warren, puzzled by the conflicting command, proceeded as instructed, walking to the door, closing it, then blindly stepping back into the blackness of the room.

"Sit down."

As far as Warren could tell, the bed was the only option. He chose the edge and awkwardly sat down.

"Tell me something, Warren. Why are you so confident the hospital overwrote the files, and how do you know the backups are gone?"

Warren shivered. "Well, the techie at the hospital told me, and I had him pretty rattled. He wasn't lying. And the dude who stole the backups was very cooperative, as people tend to be with a gun shoved in their face. I'm sure this is the only copy of the files."

"Are you, Warren? Well, that's good, isn't it?"

Warren quivered.

"May I have the disc, please?"

Warren pulled the brown envelope from his jacket and handed it into the darkness, where a hand emerged to retrieve it.

Warren listened as the envelope was opened, then discarded.

"So, is my face clear in the videos, Warren?"

"I don't know, sir. I wanted you to have it as soon as possible. So, I haven't seen it – no DVD player at home." Warren garbled on.

"I see." A moment passed while the man lit another cigarette. "So, for all you know, it could be blank or something completely different?"

Sudden panic attacked Warren's cerebral cortex as he remembered how Orlando insisted it was porn. "I'm certain it's what you're looking for, sir." His voice trembled.

"Certain? Well, certain's good, isn't it?"

"Yes, sir."

"Excellent. Well, Warren, as you might imagine, fine establishments like the Albion don't provide their guests with DVD players. So, you've brought me a piece of useless plastic. You'll forgive my delay in congratulating you until I've viewed it."

"Yes, sir."

"Very well. Leave now."

Warren didn't need a second invitation. Rising from the creaky bed, he hurried for the door.

"Oh, and Warren?"

Warren stopped inches from escape.

"If this isn't the video of my visit, and someone can still prove I was at the hospital, I will be very… disappointed. Do I make myself clear?"

Warren's heart crashed into his stomach. "Yes, sir."

Flinging open the door, Warren wasted no time hitting the stairs, sprinting through the lobby and outside to his Jeep. After slamming the door closed and starting the engine, he peeled out of the lot, dragging the handicapped parking sign beneath him.

*

As Warren fled the parking lot, a stranger smoking a cigarette watched from the curb opposite the hotel. His clothes appeared typical for the rough neighbourhood – jeans, black biker boots, a tee-shirt with sleeves cut back to the shoulders, and a Raiders ball cap. But everything was spotless, like it had all been bought that morning. The shirt was pristine white, and the jeans were stylish, predesigned holes everywhere, nothing earned from a life of abuse and neglect. The stranger's sunglasses were too expensive for the neighbourhood, and his bare arms were tattooless. The man's grooming habits were even more curious – squarely trimmed collar-length hair with a thick jet-black moustache set against a clean-shaven face. As Warren sped away, the stranger spat the cigarette from his mouth and dialled his cell phone.

"Got 'im."

FIFTY-FOUR

Wednesday, November 18, 3:35 p.m.
Phoenix General Hospital

With no place to go and no driver to get him there, Earl strolled back to the administrative wing, happy to discover a complete absence of priests, doctors and administrators. *Do hospitals have bars?* he thought. *After all, this is America.*

An email update arrived from Orlando. Earl paced around the empty reception area as he scanned the details. Orlando's message was vague, explaining that he had new information about 'our guy'. *Completely unhelpful*, thought Earl. He dialled Orlando's number and listened as it rang seven times.

"Uh-uh?" mumbled Orlando softly.

"Dude, it's me, Earl," he replied in a whisper, although he had no idea why.

"I'm undercover, Earl. Whatcha need?"

"Any chance you can come get me?"

"Not the best timing, man, but hang tight. Be there in twenty."

*

Orlando stopped the limo at the far end of the parking garage on the main level, blocking four expensive vehicles. Moving from the driver's seat to the back, he readied two glasses with ice.

"Good to see you," offered Earl, climbing in the back of the limo with a sense of relief. "I felt trapped in there. So, whatcha got?"

"OK, check it out. One of my guys knew a guy who knew a guy. Anyway, my intruder's an urban cowboy, just like I said. Dude's name is Warren Peel, a low-level stoner and local courier turned trouble-maker. I asked my guy to hang out on his street and watch for him to show up, and he did. After that, we watched him every second until *bingo* – Albion Hotel. Mega shit-hole downtown. Wouldn't recommend it to a dead rat." Orlando poured a generous shot of scotch in both glasses and handed one to Earl.

"You think our phony priest's staying there?" asked Earl.

"I know it. After Peel left the hotel, my guy went inside and bribed the desk clerk, some dude named Iceberg. He was happy to tell us who Peel visited."

"Wait, wait. The clerk's name is Iceberg?"

"Earl, don't judge a culture you know nothing about, OK? Yeah, Iceberg."

"Sounds like a Jewish rapper," said Earl swigging a healthy two fingers from his drink.

Orlando rolled his eyes. "So... our priest registered at the hotel under his real name, Tony Del-Monte."

"How do you know it's his real name?"

Orlando stopped. "Well, I don't. But that was the name MacMann told you, right?"

"Yeah, but that doesn't mean it's his real name. Did you check him out?"

"No, Earl, I didn't. I was rudely interrupted by some dick who was bored and needed a ride to nowhere."

Earl conceded the point.

"But here's the even gooder news. Now that I know where Peel lives, I can go have a little chat with him... in his own fucking living room."

"Don't be an idiot," said Earl frowning, "you'll get yourself whacked... or whatever the word is."

"Dude, please. Have a little faith. I know what I'm doing. This Peel guy's green. Pre-school. I can handle it. In the meantime, what do you want to do about Del-Monte?"

Earl scratched his neck and instantly regretted it. "I suppose I could tell Frank and MacMann... or go to the police."

"That's it?"

"Well, yeah. Isn't that what most people do when they uncover the identity of a criminal?"

"That's what most stupid people do," said Orlando, shaking his head. "Earl, you don't know a thing about this phony priest – he could send his people after you, people who'd shut you up permanently. Besides, what are you going to tell the police? 'Officer, there's this guy; he's impersonating a priest at the hospital where I'm interviewing God. This guy met with God and wasn't very nice to him. So, I decided to conspire with an ex-con to steal the hospital's security footage and track him down. Now, I'd like you to arrest the guy for...'?"

"Isn't it a crime to impersonate a priest?"

"No, Earl, I don't think it is."

"Well, it should be."

"Look, Earl, listen. If you want this done the right way, we do it my way. We go through Warren Peel. He'll tell us who the phony priest is, and then we'll actually have something to go on. If you're gonna go off half-cocked, you're just gonna end up in jail or dead. OK?"

"That's a strange expression, don't you think?"

"What is?" Orlando stared at Earl like he was growing horns.

"Going off half-cocked. Seems rude."

Orlando snapped his fingers in front of Earl, who was lost in an inappropriate thought. "Christ, are you even listening?"

"Of course I am. That's how I heard you say half-cocked."

"I think you're losing your shit, dude. It's just a saying. It means your gun fired in the half-cocked safety position when it shouldn't have."

"Serious? That's what that means?"

"What the hell did you think it meant?"

"I thought it was about premature ejaculation or something."

Orlando put a hand over his eyes and rubbed aggressively. "Alright. You go back to doing your reporter thing. I've got detective work to do. Once I get more info, we can figure out what to do next, OK?"

FIFTY-FIVE

Wednesday, November 18, 3:45 p.m.
Phoenix General Hospital

Dr. MacMann and Frank Shedmore sat in the hospital's administration wing, pouring over the exploratory report recently delivered by Doe's surgeon, Dr. Higgins.

Frank sat reclined in his chair, lost in thought. His mind searched for a way to get MacMann to resign on his own accord, without fuss or lawsuit. The Board was emphatic on the matter: Frank's new permanent Chief Administrator role was tied solely to MacMann's immediate departure. The Board had chosen their fall guy, and a lanky Scotsman was he.

"Look here, Frank," said MacMann, pointing to a paragraph where Higgins had detailed the condition of Doe's liver. "He didn't capitalize Subhepatic, and again, here with Enteritis. Kid's a hack."

"You've deemed his medical skills valueless based on his writing ability?"

"I'll have a word with him," said MacMann, flipping over to the next page.

"No, doctor, you won't. He's doing fine."

MacMann lowered the report and crossed his arms. "What's with you lately?"

"What do you mean?" said Frank, staring through MacMann. He did his best to avoid the doctor's glare.

"I get the distinct impression you're… *bailing*. Need I remind you, you're in this thing up to your arse, just like me. Partners to the end, laddie."

"I'm not your partner," said Frank angrily. Spittle reached the far side of the desk, his eyes locking onto MacMann's for the first time.

"O-aye, you most certainly are, Frankie. And the sooner you get used to it, the better. We've got a perfectly good scapegoat in Grey. No need for us to be tearing at each other."

Frank said nothing. He turned his head to the view out the window.

"Aye, well, I can see I'm not wanted." MacMann rose, tossed the surgeon's

225

report across the desk and stormed through the open office door, making a point of slamming it shut as he left.

*

"Good morning," said Earl grinning, nearly colliding with the departing doctor. MacMann passed with no reply or eye contact.

Earl watched as MacMann walked to the elevators. "You too. Have a wonderful day, bye-ee."

"What was all that about?" Earl asked, taking a seat in Frank's office.

"Who knows," said Frank, "mano-pause?"

"God help us! Any word on Doe?"

"Yep, a few. None of them good."

Earl's cheery disposition changed instantly. "Oh."

"You can have a look if you want." He pointed to the scattered file on the desk. "Not sure you'd understand it, though."

"I see," said Earl. He made no effort to reach for the file.

"We were expecting as much. Maybe not the severity."

"I know. I was just hoping for, I dunno…"

"A miracle, Earl?"

"I guess. Something like that. Are you going to release it to the press?"

"Doubt it, but we have time to consider."

Earl nodded in dejection.

"Speaking of the press, Earl… Albert Einstein?"

Earl lifted his shoulders and opened his palms, feigning innocence. "Like it? I gave him Wolf Blitzer's hair."

Frank shrugged. "I guess. Lord knows no one's gonna recognize Doe by that sketch. No chance of anyone identifying him."

"All I was trying to do was ensure his true likeness didn't become the next Last Supper or sitting Buddha."

Frank looked puzzled.

Earl explained, "Doe doesn't want to be associated with his message. He doesn't want to be an idol or leave a legacy, a legacy that might turn into something even worse than Scientology."

"Ah, I see," said Frank. "So, instead, you turned Einstein into a deity?"

"Einstein and Wolf Blitzer. It's the glasses, take them off, and it's Blitzer." Earl half-laughed. "Besides, it's not likely to stick."

Frank managed a slight chuckle. "Who am I to second guess your strategy, Mr. Grey? You've kept this all together so far."

Earl observed Frank's body language. The man had changed. *Is this sincerity?* "Thank you, Frank. That's very nice of you."

"I'm not trying to be nice, Earl. Out of all of us, you've maintained your integrity. You didn't sell out. More than I can say for myself."

Earl tilted his head. "What did you do, Frank."

Frank shook his head slowly. "Earl, you're looking at the new Hospital Chief Administrator."

"Wow, congrats Frank, nice going."

"Yeah, I think someone said that to Judas too."

"What's wrong? Don't you want it?"

"Of course. I've worked my whole life for this. It just feels… hollow."

"Is this what's up MacMann's ass?"

"No, I haven't told him yet."

"Oh," said Earl puzzled.

"Have you ever dealt with a board of directors, Earl?"

"Indirectly, yes. Though it's something I've tried to avoid."

"As you should. Nasty buggers, think *Lord of the Flies*."

Earl laughed.

"Earl, with my promotion, comes an order to clean up this mess. The Board wants a graceful exit. Do you know what happens in graceful exits? Some poor bastard takes a not so graceful fall."

"Holy shit," said Earl piecing things together. "Did you just can MacMann?"

Frank shook his head. "Not yet, but, well… you get the picture."

"So, when does the axe fall?"

"That's just it. I'm not allowed to axe him. They don't want the lawsuit or a PR disaster. I've got to find a way to have him quit on his own."

Earl shook his head. "Good luck with that. No chance he just walks away."

"Maybe… unless he thinks it's the lesser of two evils. Unless he believed this whole thing's going to come down on him and him alone."

Earl absentmindedly scratched his sunburnt neck again and winced. "You know, I might have the perfect guy for this. Leave it with me for a bit," he said, heading for the door. "Right now, I'm gonna see if Doe's back in his room, but I'll circle back with you on this, OK?"

Frank stood and nodded his approval. Then watched Earl as he jogged down the hallway toward the elevators, every overhead fluorescent flickering like a strobe light.

F I F T Y - S I X

Wednesday, November 18, 4:35 p.m.
Phoenix General Hospital,
Room R2112

"Robbie, you're back!"

Startled by Earl's stealthy arrival, Robbie abruptly ended his call and stuffed the cellphone in his pocket. Sheepishly, he turned and smiled. "Hi, Mr. Earl. Yeah, they brought him back about fifteen minutes ago. He's asleep. I think they said they're gonna keep him asleep for a while. Can they do that?"

Earl nodded. "I'm sure it's intentional. Probably for the best."

"Poor guy. Had all these tubes and wires sticking out of him."

"Is it OK if I go in?"

"Mr. Frank said you could go in anytime. But Mr. Doe won't be able to talk to you."

Earl smiled. "I know, Robbie. I'd still like to see him."

Earl stepped into the dimly lit hospital room. The clouds outside the large window were grey and thunderous, filling the space with premature twilight. He was surprised at how few machines remained, unsure if it was a good or bad sign.

"Hello, JD," Earl whispered, placing a hand on the old man's shoulder. "It's me, Earl." He had no idea why he needed to be there or if Doe could hear him or sense his presence, but it felt right. "I hope you're feeling better?"

Earl pulled the chair closer to the head of the bed and sat down. Reaching under the bed rail, he gently took Doe's hand, conscious of the many tubes. Earl needed nothing more than someone to talk to, not with. A captive audience with no ability to respond, advise, lecture or opine. He had a lot to say, and it required no interruptions.

"JD, it's important I explain about my history, my childhood…" He took a deep breath. "So here goes… never in my life has there been anyone like you. I've never allowed anyone is probably closer to the truth. I guess there were my parents, but that's a long story that ends with me owning a grand set of ugly luggage and an inability to function around people. It wasn't until college that someone made the first attempt to excavate the peat bog I call a mind. His name was Sawchuck. He was my writing and history professor, and I never thanked him for his wisdom and insight, all of it falling on deaf ears. Perhaps I just wasn't ready to hear it. He passed away eight years ago, but I was too busy or lazy to fly down for the funeral."

Earl used his free hand to wipe his eyes. "I lost my chance with him. But I won't lose it with you. I guess what I'm saying is, in these past few days, you've become very special to me. In fact, it feels like I've known you my whole life. So… while you're still here, I don't want to miss the opportunity to tell you something, coward that I am, you laying there unconscious. What I'm saying is…"

"Oh, hello, I'm sorry to intrude," said Dr. Higgins, barging into the room, his eyes distracted by the charts on his clipboard. "The guard told me you were in here, but I didn't know I was interrupting a private moment. I'm so sorry."

Earl, startled, turned towards the doctor. "Oh, no, that's fine, doc, we were just, well, I was just talking to him. I know he can't hear me." Earl could feel the dampness of his cheeks but didn't care.

Dr. Higgins moved closer. "Well, we don't know that for sure. There've been many studies on the subject, nothing definitive, but I'd like to think that they can."

Earl shook the doctor's hand, sizing him up and wondering if the puberty fairy had paid a visit yet. "I'll get out of your way," said Earl.

"No, no, stay. I just came in to check his vitals."

"How's he doing?"

Higgins looked at the numbers on the various machines. "Still the same. Look, Earl, I won't sugarcoat this for you. The internal injuries are consistent with someone who's undergone massive trauma, like a major car accident. It's not that I haven't seen this type of injury before; it's just I've never seen anyone with this level of damage still breathing. By all accounts, this man should not be alive."

Earl shook his head slowly. "How does he handle the pain?"

"I have no idea," Higgins responded. "I don't understand how he's remained conscious. It must be pure agony. What's more, the body should be in shock, which to a great degree it is, but the fact he's been aware and communicating is unbelievable. His internal organs are non-functional. His esophagus and stomach are intact, but they're not connected to anything. This is not a functional biological unit."

"Jesus," exclaimed Earl, not knowing where to look. "Will he ever regain consciousness?"

"For his sake, I hope not. But if he does, I've ordered high dosages of morphine."

Earl couldn't hold back his tears. "So that's it? We'll never talk again?"

"I don't know, Earl. We may lower the sedation in a few hours and see what happens, but, depending on the pain level, we may simply decide to put him back to sleep."

"Well, I don't want him to suffer," said Earl shuffling awkwardly. "But if he's awake, can I come back?"

"Yes, of course, we'll let you know. But I wouldn't count on that happening."

"I understand."

"Alright, well, the nurse will be in shortly to check on him. You can stay as long as you'd like."

"Thank you." Earl rose to shake Higgins' hand before watching the young doctor leave, then leaned over the bed and whispered into the old man's ear. "Please don't go yet, sir."

*

As six o'clock neared, Earl left Doe's room, taking time for a last goodbye, certain they would never speak again. Earl had talked to Doe for what felt like an eternity but, in reality, had only been several hours. He had spent the time revealing his history to Doe, entertaining the unconscious man with stories of embarrassment and perpetual failure. Of soul-crushing summer camps, hopeless jobs, and failed romances. Of his ill-conceived wedding, divorce, and his subsequent breakdown and chronic depression. Through it all, Earl held fast to Doe's hand, feeling an overpowering sense of unburdening. Finally, exhausted, Earl wrapped up his confessions, noting a pleasant clear-minded sensation that bordered on vacant – but in a good way, as in, he still knew how to drive.

Earl arrived in the parking garage with no recollection of the walk, lost in an inner universe of self-reflection. The last thing he wanted now was human contact. Solitude was mandatory but unlikely. His hotel room was the only sanctuary he could conceive of, the only place he could hide behind a locked door with little chance of interruption.

Throughout the afternoon, Mary-Lynn had sent several texts, all of them apologizing for her schedule and her need to work late. Earl was relieved. The thought of a lengthy dinner filled with flirtatious gamesmanship was too much for his current state of mind, even though he desperately needed a Wu-shaped hug.

Earl watched as Orlando arrived, driving the limo into the garage area and running it up along the curb, directly in front of him. The window rolled down, revealing the driver's smiling face, which instantly sobered after one look at Earl's expression. "Oh shit. Is he gone?"

Earl bit down hard on his lip but couldn't stop the water from welling in his eyes.

"As good as…"

"I'm sorry, dude. I don't know what to say."

Earl nodded while composing himself. "Can you take me to the hotel? I need some… *time*."

"You bet, man."

They spent the short trip in silence, Orlando stopping at the rear of the hotel, beside the dumpsters as always.

"Thanks, my friend," said Earl, stepping from the car.

"Anything you need, you just call, OK? We can catch up tomorrow morning."

Earl nodded. He reached inside the driver's window and squeezed Orlando's shoulder in appreciation.

*

After locking his hotel room door, Earl ran the chain across the groove, triggering thoughts of Mary-Lynn. Moving to the window, he pulled the thick curtains together tightly, blocking the evening sun. Dropping his clothes where he stood, he crawled into bed, desperate to stem the unrelenting deluge from his newly awakened inner voice. It was as if his cranial radio, normally mistuned and staticky, had suddenly locked on the perfect station. A hundred-thousand-megawatt signal that pumped unrelenting commentary deep into his psyche. Minute by minute, streams of buried memories and emotions rose to the surface. Once exposed, they were duly sorted into categories then dragged out into the daylight for immediate attention.

Holding back the mental flood, Earl promised himself he would address every Pandorian package in due time. But for now, wanting only sleep, he laser-focused his mind on an imaginary desert island. There he sat, alone, on a white sandy beach facing the setting sun, his back to the world's biggest all-you-can-eat pizza buffet. Contented, sleep came fast.

FIFTY-SEVEN

Wednesday, November 18, 9:15 p.m.
Downtown Phoenix,
Warren Peel's Shitty Apartment

Orlando drove the limo into a cracked and heaving concrete lot and parked at the rear of the apartment building, out of sight. The four-storey structure had seen better days, basic cinder block construction with a stucco façade, chipped and broken in spots, revealing a rusty wire mesh. The main doors were unlocked, allowing Orlando free access to the second floor. He wandered up and down the hall until he located Warren's apartment fronted by a solid wood door with peeling paint and the faint outline of 213 stencilled near the top.

Noting the absence of a peephole, Orlando rapped on the door, then waited, gun cocked.

"Who is it?" came a distant, muffled voice.

"Ya, hi. I got a pre-paid pizza here for Alonso, 3-1-3," Orlando shouted through the door.

There was a moment of silence. Orlando knew Warren was probably calculating the odds that a pizza intended for the apartment upstairs would be delivered to him via stupidity and serendipity. The sound of a deadbolt filled the hall.

"Yeah, right here," said Warren, as the door swung wide.

Orlando stood, legs apart, gun gripped in both hands, pointed up at Warren's head. "Hello, Huckleberry," he offered with a grin.

Warren glanced down at Orlando, then looked up and down the hallway with a frown. "So… no pizza, huh?"

*

Earl slept like he was dead, not moving an inch, curled up in the same spot where he had passed out. His sleep was restorative and cleansing. A slumber of rejuvenation, repair, and resurrection – albeit for only three hours.

An aggressive knock on the hotel room door roused Earl from an undecipherable dream about ruling a desert kingdom named Pizza Hut.

"You gotta be kidding me," mumbled Earl, partially opening his eyes and checking the digital clock on the nightstand. 10:35. He glanced at the curtains, checking to see if any light was leaking in. There was only blackness. *10:35 p.m. Jesus!*

"Who is it?" he yelled, then dropped his face into the pillow.

"Phoenix PD."

*

"Don't do anything stupid," Orlando urged, shooing Warren back into his nest. "No one'll think twice about a gunshot in this neighbourhood."

Warren raised his palms a few inches from where they dangled. "Dude, can we do this some other time? I've got a lotta shit on my plate right now."

"Back, back, back," jabbed Orlando with the revolver, herding him further into the apartment. He swung the door closed behind him without looking. "Now, where's your gun?"

"I dunno, it's around here somewhere." Warren motioned with both hands.

"Where's the fucking gun, Warren?" This time he yelled and targeted the barrel of his revolver at Warren's balls.

"Alright, alright, it's in the bedroom. On the crate beside the bed." He pointed the way with both index fingers.

"Sit down. Put your hands on your knees. Don't move." Orlando walked sideways toward the bedroom door. He glanced inside and immediately spotted the Sig where Warren said it would be. "Alright, good," he said, walking back to a ratty old couch. "Now, we've got a little business to take care of."

"Dude, I don't got your DVD. I gave it to my boss."

"Oh, I see," said Orlando. "Alright, well, thanks. I guess I'll be on my way."

"Really?" said Warren, smiling.

"No, not fucking really, you douche. You stole from me. You broke into my place and held a gun on me. It's payback time, motherfucker."

Warren cringed, his pupils dilated. "What are ya gonna do?"

"You need to learn a lesson about breakin' into a brother's crib. I figure it's worth a kneecap, at least."

Warren's eyes popped. "Are you crazy? You're gonna cripple me for some stupid DVD?"

"I don't make the rules, bro. I only play by them. You'll never learn if you don't feel the consequences of your actions." Orlando spun the chamber of his gun, watching the bullets rotate.

"You're... insane."

"Perhaps," Orlando said dryly, revelling in his control over the moment.

"Look, I feel shitty about busting in on you, but you don't understand how big this is."

"If you say I'm in over my head again, I'll pop you right now."

"Maybe not, but I am. I'm in deep. This guy, my boss, needed some dude taken out, and I saw the chance to make big bucks. I was gonna skip town right after, go straight. Head to the coast, maybe go to computer school or just chill." Warren was rattled, shaken, his legs bouncing rapidly on the balls of his feet.

"How big are these bucks?" asked Orlando, lowering the gun slightly to ease Warren's tension, playing the friend card.

"Ten-K upfront. Twenty on the back-end."

"Big score, dude. Let me guess, John Doe was your mark?"

Warren nodded.

"And your boss is the priest who went in to see him?"

Warren nodded again, looking at his feet.

"So, summing up. The boss-man doesn't care if *you* show up on the security video. He just wants anything connected with him erased. Right? That makes you a fucking patsy, cowboy."

"I'm screwed, aren't I?"

"Only if *screwed* is much, much nastier than you're making it sound."

*

What fresh hell is this? thought Earl. He willed himself out of his cozy cocoon and begrudgingly trudged to the door. "What do you want?" he said, seeing nothing through the peephole other than the door across the hall.

"Phoenix PD, Mr. Grey. We'd like a few words with you. Please open the door." The voice was female but forced into a lower octave to sound authoritative.

"Show me a badge," said Earl, his brain booting back into reality. Thoughts of Orlando's home-intruder popped into his mind.

A silver flash appeared in the peephole, a shield of tin with the words Phoenix Police Department embossed around the edge, framing a bald eagle, wings spread in attack.

Earl removed the chain and turned the handle, pulling the heavy door towards him. The officer pushed her way inside, her sidearm brushing his underwear as she passed. Turning, she smiled and removed her cap, allowing her long black hair to spill down the front of her uniform.

FIFTY-EIGHT

Orlando pocketed his gun as an act of trust. "So, who is he? What's God's real name?" Orlando asserted aggressively.

"Ah, well, I don't have a name," mumbled Warren.

Orlando pinched his eyes closed. "You just said you were supposed to kill him, but you don't know his name?"

"That's not uncommon in the hitman business," Warren said.

"Oh, for Christ's sake, Warren. You're not a hitman. Drop the bullshit. You've never killed anyone in your life."

"I'm just sayin', us pros don't use names. Safer that way. I had photos, you know, some basic information. A time and place to nail him. That's all I needed."

"Except you didn't kill him. Although, from the sound of it, you laid quite the beating on the old dude."

Warren didn't reply. He squirmed, focused on the floor and slowly shook his head. Orlando wasn't sure if Warren was struck with remorse or embarrassment.

"Warren, start from the beginning. Tell me *everything*. What did you do after you got the info on your mark?"

Warren sat forward, placing his elbows on his knees.

"The mark was playing golf that afternoon, way out of town, at the Renegade Golf Club. So, I got directions and worked out a plan to grab him," Warren began.

"Grab him? You weren't gonna shoot him at the golf course?"

"No, too public, too many people. My plan was to snatch him in the parking lot, assuming he had no bodyguard."

"Bodyguard?"

"Yeah, apparently he's some important rich-ass dude – big money. So, I arrive well ahead of him, taking up a good spot in the parking lot. I knew the car and

236

plate to look for, a silver Mercedes. And, right on cue, it pulls in. As he parks, I pull my Jeep around and block him in. But then this dude gets out who looks nothing at all like my mark. He was like twenty years old, if that. Then I realized it was the valet."

Orlando shook his head from side to side.

"So, my next plan was to wait for him to finish his round and come back to the car, but I wasn't sure if he'd return to the parking lot or call the valet. So, that was a problem."

"Uh-huh."

"So, I figured, if the valet came to get the car, I'd follow it out of the club and pick a secluded spot on the drive to force him off the road. Shoot him. Then grab some drive-thru."

"Makes sense," said Orlando, with more than a hint of sarcasm.

"I waited for five hours. Very boring. While I waited, I used a map program to mark several spots to run him off the road and complete the hit. I've got a knack for computer stuff, studied it in school before I dropped out."

"Uh-huh."

"So anyway, none of that was necessary, 'cause my guy shows up, walking down the path to the parking area, dressed up in this wicked cool suit. I guess he must have showered inside or something; he had one of those tote bags over his shoulder, Nike, I think. No clubs, so I figured he was a member or something, or maybe he rented them. So, I park the Jeep right behind his car again, and he glances over at me, then goes back to workin' the door handle. It was then I noticed he was swaying and stumbling."

"OK, Warren. Perhaps I should've been more specific," said Orlando shifting uncomfortably. "I was looking for the short version here, not a play-by-play."

"Well, I skipped over the five-hour wait in the car."

"Thank you for that."

"So anyway, I realize he's piss-drunk and could hardly stand. In that state, there's no way the valet would've brought him his car. The guy didn't even have his keys. I briefly thought of shooting him right there, but there were still cars around, and someone could have shown up any second."

"How professional of you."

"Yeah. So, I get out and say, 'Can I help you?' and the old dude turns and says he can't get his car door open, but he's got to get to a dinner meeting. And then he kinda vomits. Not full-on, but that gross kind of spit-up. So, I say, 'Come on, I'm heading back into town, and you're in no condition to drive, I'll take you.'"

"How convenient."

"Yeah, even better. He climbs into my passenger seat and passes out. Dead to the world. Easiest 10K ever… or so I thought…"

*

Earl could think of a thousand better ways for Mary-Lynn to discover his preference in underwear. It was enough she'd already seen his bare ass, and God knows what else, but this was almost worse. Earl felt utterly vulnerable as he stood in the darkened room, his silhouette enhanced by the orange glow from his jockey shorts. Mary-Lynn, by comparison, stood with pride, thumbs hooked in her gun-belt and giggling with glee.

Earl's mouth fell open as if to speak. "I… uhhh…"

Mary-Lynn laughed out loud. "Gotcha, mister. Whatcha think? Not quite as sexy as I wanted. They only had a men's small, way too baggy on me."

Earl stepped to the side of the bed and retrieved his pants. A small effort to even the playing field. "Mary-Lynn, what are you doing here? What's going on?" he said sternly.

She unleashed her most lethal weapon – a full-on pout, complete with glistening lower lip. "You're not happy to see me?"

"Yes, yes, of course, I'm happy to see you. It's just that I was sleeping. And you startled me. Well, scared me. I've got enough anxiety without cops busting in."

"When we talked before, you sounded so sad. So, I figured this ensemble would cheer you up, and it gave me easy access to get up here. I just wish it fit a bit better. Do you like the gun?" She drew the handgun and struck a Charlie's Angels' pose.

"Jesus, careful with that thing," said Earl, startled.

"Ha, it's not real. Feels real, heavy enough, but just plastic, see, no hole in the end." She pointed it at him.

"Don't! Don't point it, Jesus."

"Oh, Earl, ya big grumpy bear. Come here, let Officer Wu hug it out."

Earl obeyed the officer, and they embraced. She smelled as good as ever, leading him to reflect on how bad he must reek and that he hadn't brushed his teeth in nearly sixteen hours.

"Earl?"

"Yes?"

"You can let go of me now. If you want."

"I don't want to." Earl thought about Doe's last words, his theory of time. No present, just a single page in a flipbook. He wondered if there was a way he could stay on this page forever.

Mary-Lynn squeezed him again as she balanced on the tips of her black combat boots.

Reluctantly, Earl relinquished his grip.

"You're not OK, are you, mister?"

"It was a rough day." Earl stepped back from her and dropped his arms to his sides.

"Oh, Earl, I know."

"You know? How do you know?"

"Orlando told me."

Earl shook his head and slumped down on the edge of the bed. "Should I even ask how that came about?"

Mary-Lynn smiled sweetly. "I called Orlando to find out where you were. I wanted to surprise you after I finished work today, that's all. He told me about your visit today, about Doe's condition, and how distant and sad you seemed. It broke my heart. I can take off this stupid costume if you want. I only used it to get up here? I've got boy shorts on underneath and a bra. It's not like I'm naked."

Earl laughed. "Yes, that would make things so much better. Then I could concentrate on my self-pity."

"He means a lot to me, too, you know. It's an awful situation. I hate it."

"I know. But I can't think of anyone I'd rather be with right now," said Earl, smiling.

She stood over him, bent down and kissed the top of his head. "So, what do we do now, mister?"

FIFTY-NINE

"It took me a little over an hour to get to the spot," said Warren. "I grew up around here, so I know every square inch of the place. I'd already decided where to do the deed. No one would find him for months, maybe ever. He only woke up once during the whole drive, asking me where his ball had landed and if it was OK to piss in the cactus patch. Then he took a huge drink from a water bottle in his bag. But it smelled like booze. I think the guy might be an alcoholic."

"Ya think?" Orlando rolled his hands over and over like an eggbeater. "OK, moving on."

"Right, so I drove in the back way of the Cave Creek Park, miles from any roads or cell service. I know the mini-mountains like the back of my hand. The Bluffs, we'd call them as kids. A tough climb if you're coming in across the flat. But I know a better way by heading further east then backtracking through the wilderness reserve. Takes a lot longer but no climbing. I stopped the Jeep near the edge of a steep drop leading down to the valley."

Orlando gave him the eggbeater hand roll again.

"OK, OK. So, I walked around to the passenger side, opened the door, and the dude just fell out. Face-plants right on the ground. He staggered to his feet and looked around. 'This isn't downtown. What the fuck?' he shouts at me. So I say, 'I know. I've been hired to take you out'. Then I waved the gun in his face."

"Classy!" said Orlando. "Real Hollywood quality you bring to your hits."

"Yeah," said Warren, oblivious to the sarcasm. "So then he says, 'Whatever you're getting, I'll double it'. And I'm like, 'Nice try'."

"Uh-huh."

"Yeah, so he says, 'Do you have any idea who I am?' And I say, 'Nope,' nor do I care. Just doing my job. Then I raise my gun. And I'm an excellent shot, dude. I aim right at his head, couldn't miss at that range."

240

"And then you don't shoot him?"

"Right. I don't."

"Right, so how do we get to the part where you beat the living shit out of the poor drunk bastard?"

Warren sat down, cavalier adventurism draining from his body language.

"Orlando, have you ever shot anyone?"

Orlando waited a moment, unsure of Warren's sudden change in tone, maybe a trap or diversion. He put his hand in his jacket pocket, around the rubber handgrip of the gun. "Yep, a couple of times."

"Did you kill them?"

Orlando didn't like the question. "Nope. Mom would've freaked out in heaven."

"Ah, OK. Well, neither had I."

"I'm stunned."

Warren nodded. "Truth is, I've never shot anyone, ever. But, here I was, three feet from this old dude who I don't know from Adam… about to blow his head off."

Orlando nodded back. "It's a big fucking deal, isn't it, Warren?"

"Yeah. Yeah it is. So, I hear this voice saying, 'OK, I'll give you a head start. Start running'. Then I realize it was my voice. I guess I was hoping it would be easier to shoot him if he was running away."

"And did he? Did he run?"

"Yeah, he did. In his drunken stupor, he ran right over the edge of the cliff. It was pretty ugly."

"Hell-no," exclaimed Orlando. "Seriously?"

"Yep, and if this guy had any luck in his life, he'd used it all up. Like Wile E. Coyote, this guy hits every boulder, rock and jagged piece of shale on the way down, missing a dozen soft sandy spots. Just one gut-punching impact after another. I couldn't look away, you know?"

Orlando shook his head.

"I mean, dude, this guy must have bounced down fifty feet by the time his body skidded to a stop."

"So, you left? Figured he was dead?"

"Yep, no sense in climbing all the way down to put a bullet in him. The body lay at the cliff's halfway point, on a thin but wide plateau near the old sandstone formation we used to call Big Dick. You know, 'cause it looks like a big dick? If the old dude was still breathing, he wasn't going anywhere."

"But, somehow, he *survived*?"

"A fucking miracle, Orlando. Impossible if you ask me."

"Then you went back and told your boss the deed was done. And to cover your cowardice, you implied you shot him," Orlando concluded the story.

"Yeah, but now he knows that ain't true. Guess that's why he insisted on seeing Doe with his own eyes at the hospital. No bullet wounds."

"And now he won't pay because you didn't actually kill him? Even though Doe's not gonna make it."

"You get it. My twenty grand's long gone. I'll never see it. Probably gotta give the ten back too. And I'll be lucky if that's the worst of it. This dude's no average criminal. He's like evil, totally black."

"Something wrong with that?" said Orlando raising a lone eyebrow.

"No, Jesus, I mean, there's an emptiness there, no light. He's like a walking talking demon. It's hard to explain. I'm not gonna walk from this, Orlando. This dude's gonna kill me."

Orlando nodded, a twinge of sympathy poking him in the gut. "I guess we better get you outta town, cowboy."

*

Earl stood up and returned Mary-Lynn's kiss, this time on her soft lips. "Got something I need to tell you."

"This is never good," she frowned.

Earl flashed a crooked smile. "Just let me get through this, OK? Mary-Lynn, I think the world of you. I admire you, your passion, intelligence, and your *take no prisoners* attitude."

"Earl…"

"Shhh, let me finish. I know I'm not fooling anyone, least of all you. I've got these feelings for you. Mushy, messy, fucked-up feelings. And I'm trying to embrace them, however…"

"There's always a however," she said, stepping back.

"Shhh, man talking here."

She punched him in the bare arm.

"OK, OK," he laughed. "Just listen. I spent the afternoon telling Doe exactly who I was. Not who I appear to be, or who I've convinced myself I am, but who I really am. OK, he was unconscious, but that's not the point. The words were for me, Mary-Lynn. The very second I walked into his room, something compelled me to just tell him *everything*."

Mary-Lynn shuffled closer, softly taking his hands in hers.

"But during my... confession... I realized I'm not that person anymore. I'm not even the person you first met."

She nodded her head, still holding his hands at waist level.

"For instance, my entire physical essence wants you right now, wants to know every part of you, every curve and... every... other curve. All the curves."

Mary-Lynn's eyes lit up like sparklers.

"But... for once in my stupid life, I'm gonna wait for the right moment. And this... here... now... isn't it."

Mary-Lynn gulped.

"I've got to know this is real. I need to feel it without all this other sensory bullshit bombarding us."

She let go of his left hand and wiped her eyes. "Oh my God."

"Do you kinda understand? I'm desperately bad at this. Not even sure I understand. But..." Earl let his thoughts run on...

Mary-Lynn pushed his chin up, kissed him softly, then rested her head on his chest. She whispered faintly. "Remember this moment, Earl. When this is all over... we'll pick up... right here."

She stood on the tips of her combat boots again and kissed Earl as time stood still.

Earl's chest heaved as he let out a long, satisfied sigh.

"*We,*" she stressed the word, "will tackle the world tomorrow... together... OK? But, I want you to get some sleep..."

Arriving at the door, Earl opened it like a gentleman, then turned to face Mary-Lynn. She took his head in her hands, kissed him again, then pulled his forehead to meet hers.

"Boy shorts, huh?" Earl whispered.

"Robin's egg blue with frills," she replied, releasing his head and stepping into the hall.

"I hate you," Earl said, grinning.

The door across the hall opened ever so slightly. An elderly woman peeked out into the half-light of the hallway and surveyed the odd scene.

Mary-Lynn nodded to the woman. "Nothing to see here, ma'am. He checks out fine. A full cavity search revealed nothing. Sleep well."

S I X T Y

Stretching from overnight stiffness, Earl lay in his hotel bed thinking about the previous evening. An involuntary smile crept to his lips. He could feel a sense of pride rising. Pride in his self-restraint and, dare he say it, maturity. It was 8 a.m., and Earl felt well-rested and surprisingly free of anxiety.

Earl used the remote to turn on the TV then immediately lowered the volume, preferring to watch in silence. He propped up the pillows for a better view, ignoring the urge to reach for his phone and check messages. Peace and quiet were a priority. And his hotel would fit the bill, safe and warm, surrounded by a protective half-inch of drywall.

At 9:30 a.m., Earl opened the curtains and raided the mini-fridge. Two chocolate bars and an orange juice: the breakfast of third runners up. He showered and dressed, then skimmed the day's newspaper, left as ever in the corridor outside his room. The paper was dominated by stories about God, and Doe, with several of Earl's statements misquoted and abused. He lay down again and tried to relax, but restlessness grew. No longer able to ignore the outside world, he turned on his Blackberry for the first time that day.

*

Warren slept poorly again, a condition he knew would either lead to his passing out from exhaustion or spending a few weeks in Loonyville. He pondered if Loonyville was safer than Phoenix.

Sleepwalking through a coffee and two slices of toast, Warren stared out the window in a trance, pondering what to do with his day. He had reduced his options to two: jetting to Fiji for a few decades or investing all his money in plastic surgery.

244

Warren's phone vibrated in sync with his stomach.

"Hello, Warren," said a low, raspy voice. "I trust you slept well?"

"Yes, fine," Warren stuttered through the lie. "How are you, sir?"

"I've got good news, Warren. I've decided to forgive you for all the screw-ups. After all, you're only human, right?"

"Thank you, sir." Warren inflated with relief.

"But there is, as always, a catch," said Anthony Del-Monte. "I think you'll agree that I have every right to deny remuneration based on your incomplete and botched services. After all, you didn't complete the task I assigned in any way, shape or form."

"Remuneration, sir?"

"Payment."

"Oh, oh, I see." Warren felt the vibrato in his voice as he spoke.

"But I'm a fair man, Warren. I only require you to return five thousand of the down payment. You may keep the rest."

Warren felt oddly OK about the proposal. A reprieve. Forgiveness being far more valuable than five grand. He'd already spent the other five on knobby tires for the Jeep and a new gun, a Smith and Wesson Revolver, just like Orlando's.

"Warren, it seems my old friend at the General isn't long for this world. Therefore, I've decided to head home. My work here is done. But I require one last meeting with you, where I expect you to return my five thousand dollars."

"That's very fair of you, sir," said Warren, realizing he wasn't lying.

"Good. You'll meet me tomorrow at noon. I've selected a little place outside of town, nice and quiet. We'll complete our transaction there. Then, I'll be on my way."

That's odd, thought Warren. *Why not the Albion right now? It could be over and done within the hour.* His nerves began to rattle again. "Um, where is this place?"

"It's called The Black Canyon Greyhound Park, just off Interstate 17. Boarded up and abandoned."

Warren shivered. "I know it well. I used to hang there all the time. Hard to get in now, all fenced up."

"You'll get in."

The line went dead.

*

Orlando sat in the back of the limo flicking through the latest edition of *Sports Illustrated*. He'd just finished reviewing the basketball stats when his phone rang. "Slow down, slow down, Jesus, Warren, take a breath. Start again from the beginning."

Orlando listened to Warren's frantic recollection of the Del-Monte phone call and his demand for a meeting. "You know the dog track, Orlando. You could lawn-bowl with hand-grenades out there; no one would hear a thing. I gotta get out of town, man."

"Calm down, OK?" interjected Orlando. "I'm working on it. I can get you set up in Mexico if you want out that bad. I just need a bit more time."

"Dude, he wants to see me *tomorrow*. I gotta bolt, like… right now."

"OK, just chill. Give me thirty minutes. Let me talk to some people and see what I can arrange. Where are you now?"

"My apartment."

"OK, throw a bag together, grab your gun and get the hell out of there. If I was able to find you, anyone can. Head toward the hospital, and I'll call you soon. We'll figure this out, cool?"

"Cool."

Warren sprang into action. He grabbed a canvas bag and a huge backpack, stuffing them with anything of value, which wasn't a lot, mostly dirty clothes, country and western CDs and toiletries.

Tossing the apartment keys on the couch, he shouldered the backpack, picked up the canvas bag in his left hand, and used his right to open his door one last time.

The man standing in Warren's doorway seemed startled, frozen, fist up in the pre-knock position.

Warren jumped backwards into the room.

"Warren Peel?" asked the moustachioed man. He wore a sports coat over a white tee-shirt and jeans.

"Who's asking?"

The man removed his Oakland Raiders ball cap, turning the insides toward Warren. The hallway lights reflected off a silver badge fastened inside. "FBI. Mr. Peel, I have a few questions for you."

*

Earl opened an email marked urgent from Frank, scanning through it like a speed reader, expecting the worst. At first glance, several words like *incredible*, *unexpected*, *amazing* and *wide awake* leaped out. He lowered the phone, steadied himself with a few deep breaths, then re-engaged, forcing himself to read slower.

Earl, Doe's wide awake. It's unbelievable. The nurse went in this morning to check on him, and he just opened his eyes and said, 'Hi, how am I doing?' It defies medical logic. To say the very least, this was completely unexpected. Can you get over here right away? We're about to have a quick presser – no need for you to attend this one, but we'll have another after you've spoken to Doe. Frank

Every cell in Earl's body was tingling, celebrating, energized. Hitting speed dial for Orlando, he mumbled to himself while waiting for an answer. "Come on! Come on!"

"Sup, man?"

"Orlando, I've got to get to the hospital right away. It's urgent."

"Shit, what's wrong? What happened? Are you OK?"

"What?" Earl paused, confused over the odd vector the discussion had taken. "Yes, oh, yes, fine, it's not me. Doe's awake and talking. I gotta get over there."

"Holy shit! OK, I'm not far. Head downstairs now. It won't take me more than two minutes to get there."

Earl hung up, then moved back and forth across the carpet, looking for something specific, with no clue what it might be. "OK, hotel key, wallet, Blackberry, OK, OK!" He threw a change of clothes in his carry-all bag and hurried out the door, leaving it to close by itself.

Once in the elevator, Earl stood watching the floors go down as he bounced on his feet, smiling wide, his thoughts frantic, scattered, chaotic. *It's not a miracle,* he repeated in his mind.

Orlando drove in as Earl arrived at the loading bay. "Floor it, buddy," said Earl, pulling the door shut and sitting in one motion.

"What happened?" cried Orlando. "You basically read me his eulogy last night."

"No clue. Who knows, maybe the doctors got it wrong. Maybe he's still got time left or something. Maybe Doe's time is different than ours. I don't know. I don't know anything. It's insane. I can't process a damn thing right now. Can't we go faster? We're just sitting here?"

"Earl, we're at a red light."

SIXTY-ONE

Warren looked at the badge in the hat, then the ID card in the man's hand. It looked legit, he thought, an odd wave of relief sinking in, the better of two evils standing in his doorway. The ID read, Special Agent Aaron Cooper.

"Do you mind?" said the agent, walking into the room. "Looks like you're heading out somewhere? Leaving town, Warren?"

"Um, what? No, I, well, I was going camping."

Agent Cooper nodded with a blank stare, perching himself against the back of the couch. "Warren, I've got a few questions to ask you regarding your affiliation to one Anthony Del-Monte."

"Affiliation?"

"Your connection, yes. How do you happen to know him?"

"Um, I think you've got me confused with someone else, officer."

"It's Special Agent. And it's a felony to lie to the FBI."

"Oh," said Warren, scrambling.

"I watched you visit him at the Albion Hotel," Cooper said, pinching his nose and scratching his face.

"Ohhhhh, *Tony*. Yeah, you threw me off with that Anthony thing."

"Uh-huh. So, how do you know *Tony*? Good friends?"

"Oh, no, well, he's kinda new to the area. I was just trying to help a dude out, ya know?"

"That's very considerate of you, Mr. Peel."

"Right?"

"And, are you aware of the line of work Mr. Del-Monte is in?"

"Um, he said something about the cleaning business, contracts and stuff. Couldn't help him much. I'm not in the same line of work myself."

"Is that right? And what line of work would you be in, Mr. Peel?"

"Me? Oh, you know, odd jobs, favours, I do a lot of work with... " Warren stalled, looking around the room for help, "... backpacking. You know, hiking, sightseeing, tourists."

"I see. Must be very strenuous work, lugging those bags around, especially in this heat."

"Oh, it is. But that's not all for hiking. It's laundry day too."

"Is it?" The agent straightened up, seemingly increasing his height by ten inches.

"Yeah, yeah. So, what can I do for you, Agent Cooper? What's this all about?"

The agent stepped inside Warren's comfort zone. "It's about you negotiating contracts to kill people, Warren. It's about you going to jail for a very, very long time."

*

Rezipping his shoulder bag, Earl pushed at the sides to ensure it was balanced and secure. After exiting the limo, he jogged to the elevators, brimming with an indescribable energy. Electing to bypass the admin offices, he tapped Doe's floor number, then waited impatiently.

As the elevator staggered upwards, the fluorescent ceiling light above Earl flickered wildly. Briefly distracted, Earl's focus drifted to thoughts of Professor Sawchuck and his multiple attempts to impart sage advice. The professor's voice emerged between Earl's ears.

"Earl, there most certainly is meaning to existence, a point to all of this. However, life insists on hiding it in the corners, the cracks, and the edges where we seldom look. You appear to be waiting for it to pop out and hit you in the face instead of rummaging through the hiding spots, the forgotten relics, and the back of Grandma's dresser drawer. Answers, Earl, are provided for those who dig, not those who demand."

Earl blinked away the memory as the elevator door pinged open. Breaking into a sweat as he sprinted down the hall, he slid to a halt, using Robbie as a backstop. "Robbie, is it true? He's awake... talking?"

Robbie grinned. "See for yourself, Mr. Earl. He's been cracking jokes for the past hour."

Earl opened the heavy door and stopped fast. The small room was filled with people. Frank was at Doe's bedside, MacMann too, and Higgins, all deep in rumbling conversation. Nurse Morallas was fluffing the bed pillows, much to Doe's delight.

"Earl!" exclaimed Doe. Joy spread across his face. "Come here, my boy. I've been asking for you all morning."

Earl stepped through the small crowd and reached for Doe's nearest hand with both of his. "I'm so sorry, I didn't expect…"

"Gave up on me, eh?"

"No, no, not at all, I, well, OK, maybe a bit, but *they* said you were in grave condition." Earl made an accusatory head nod toward the white-robed doctors.

"Oh, they're not wrong. It's a bit of a mess in there." Doe nodded at his belly. "But you and I aren't done yet. And I said I'd stay for as long as it took."

"A walking talking bloody miracle if you ask me," said MacMann looking at Earl. "Quote me on that, and I'll deny every word."

"Simply no medical explanation, Mr. Grey," Higgins added. "I can only caution you that it's a reprieve, perhaps a reaction to the morphine. Nothing's changed internally. I'm sorry to say, Mr. Doe's injuries are beyond repair."

Doe smiled as if this was good news.

"Are you comfortable?" asked Nurse Morallas.

"Oh yes, very much so. Thank you, my dear." Doe patted her on the arm.

"Anything else you need?" she asked.

"No, no. But it would be wonderful if Earl and I could have some alone time, just the two of us. We've still much to discuss. And if I'm as temporary as the good doctor says, I don't want to waste a second. You all understand, right?"

Frank was quick to speak. "Yes, of course, if there's no medical urgency, let's leave them alone." He motioned for the others to follow and left the room.

MacMann shot Earl a menacing nod before turning his gaze to Doe. As he opened his mouth to speak, the doctor suddenly froze, as if he'd forgotten something. After an awkward empty stare, MacMann cleared his throat, smiled politely and walked out the door.

"My goodness, Earl, what an eventful twenty-four hours," said Doe as the door closed with a click.

"Quite the understatement." Earl pulled up the only chair in the room.

"I must tell you, they're quite right about the plumbing in this old shell. Shot to hell, frankly."

Earl grimaced. "But the pain…"

"Pain is all in the mind, just bioelectrical signals. And most of those stopped last night. But all I really need is brain activity at the crudest level and two reasonably flexible lungs to push air across the vocal cords. So it's much easier for me now, less moving parts. Although I may appear to be a bit less… lively."

Earl shook his head in amazement. "Alright then," he chuckled. "So, where did we leave off?" He looked around the room, finding a pen and a stack of medical printouts that he flipped to the blank undersides.

"You'd just finished a detailed account of your difficult childhood and the many unfortunate occurrences plaguing your adult life. You were also saying something about how much you cared about me. Of course, I was in no condition to reply at the time, but I must say, I was extremely touched."

Earl stared at Doe in disbelief. His face turned an intense shade of red.

*

The FBI.'s interrogation room at the Phoenix field office was located on the fifth floor of an aging windowless building.

Warren had never cared for the feel of handcuffs: ice-cold, harsh and unforgiving against cartilage and skin. This being his third experience, he was convinced that every time felt worse than the last. It was also apparent that Agent Cooper had missed the FBI. training film on blood flow and its essential role in ensuring a suspect's hands didn't fall off.

"Warren, do you know how much trouble you're in? Our wiretaps alone could put you away for twenty years." Baseball cap removed, moustache real, Agent Cooper looked every inch the stereotypical FBI. agent.

Warren nodded. "I want a lawyer." Warren didn't know why he wanted a lawyer or what a lawyer could do for him, but he'd seen enough cop shows to know it was something you should ask for."

"We've got you a lawyer. We just wanted a quick chat before she gets here."

In addition to Cooper, two other people sat across the table. A stern-faced blond woman of about fifty years, who seemed to be very much in charge, and a younger man who had placed a tape recorder directly in front of Warren. The room itself was bare, beige and smelled like asparagus. "The Phoenix FBI. have been watching Del-Monte since he arrived in Phoenix. I hope you won't take offence, but we don't give a shit about you."

"No offence taken."

"We've been struggling to nail him with something that will stick when suddenly you show up. A gift basket. Dumped right in our laps. A rare loose end, still walking, talking and breathing. We don't often get breaks like this."

Warren swallowed.

"Here's the deal, Warren. We have a plan to dig you out of your deep hole and help you re-establish yourself as an upstanding citizen. Consider it a second chance at what you miserably call a life."

Warren felt beads of sweat rolling down his neck, back and arms.

"Warren, have you ever heard of the witness protection program?"

"That deal where you rat someone out, and the government makes you disappear?"

Agent Cooper nodded. "Crude, but essentially spot on."

"Is that what this is about?"

"Judging from our long list of intercepted phone calls, we don't believe you've killed anyone yet. And we're aware Mr. Del-Monte... *Tony*... is extremely unhappy with your bungled efforts. We've got enough to charge you with conspiracy to commit murder, but that's something we'd be willing to overlook were you willing to... comply."

Warren shook his head violently. "He'll kill me. You don't know this guy. He's got eyes everywhere. He'd find me."

"Warren, if Del-Monte is as connected as you say, capable of finding anyone anywhere, what makes you think you'd be safe in prison? I'm guessing that's the one place where you'd be certain to feel his... influence... no?"

Warren briefly wallowed in the notion, then appeared to perk up. "That's a pretty good point." He nodded again, completing his thought. "Do I get to pick where I live?"

*

"Don't be embarrassed, Earl. It was genuine, real and wonderful," said Doe with a grin. "A splendid... confession."

"Yes, but like most confessions, it was supposed to be private and self-reflective." Earl shook his head.

"Regardless of intent, I heard every word, and you've got a pretty good grasp on the truth, young man."

Earl forced a small laugh. "But..."

"Look, son, you said what needed to be said. Your words had purpose. And you held my hand. You said precisely what you needed to say... and I'm so glad you did."

Earl felt a lump emerge in his throat. "I thought you'd gone. I thought I'd never speak to you again. But I kinda hoped you could hear me."

Doe sighed peacefully. "You've come a long way. It's not very often one gets to eulogize the living to their face. Truly touching."

SIXTY-TWO

"Jesus, Warren," said Orlando over the phone. "So, now you're Jack Reacher? You know it's a trap, right? You know he's gonna pop you, and there'll be no one there to help you."

"I know the track, and I'll scope it out before I go in. I'm not scared. I can do this."

"No, no, you can't. Not without help. I'm going with you."

"No!" Warren snapped, firm and authoritative. "I gotta do this alone. I'll explain later. You just can't come, OK?"

Orlando listened intently, trying to tease a clue from Warren's words, something to explain the sudden bout of courage. "What if I wait in the car?"

"Orlando!" Warren was emphatic. "Look, I'm sorry I robbed you, but please listen, I've got this covered. I don't need you. I'll be fine, OK? You can buy me a beer as soon as it's over. Alright?"

"Alright, fine, you wanna get yourself killed, go ahead. I'll have that beer in your memory, OK?"

"We'll drink together!"

The phone went dead. Orlando stared at the screen for a few seconds, then pitched the phone on the floor of the limo. "Idiot."

*

"It was written in the flip cards, Earl. I had to choose you. It should be obvious by now that I'm not the man in this bed," said Doe, with no hint of his normal lightheartedness. "This body is dead, although, for now, it remains a viable portal for me. Maybe *connection* is a better word…"

"So, who are you then? If you're not the man in this bed?" asked Earl in wide-wonder.

"Earl, at first, a little deception was necessary. The God label is always useful at getting attention. And frankly, none of this, none of *us*, Earl, would've been possible if I hadn't assumed that... persona."

"But... you're not God!"

"I suppose if you took every human definition of God, every description of a deity, and merged them into a common description, I wouldn't be far off. But the truth is, you already know who I am. Reach into your mind, Earl, access everything we've talked about so far."

Earl wished he could flip through his notes. Instead, he pondered infinity for a moment. "You said we're all part of the one, the singularity. Connected like water drops in the ocean. But we're only aware of our own story, from our own vantage point. We can't see the bigger picture of who or when we are."

"Well said."

Earl snapped another piece of the puzzle in place. "But if we're all part of the singularity, then the concept of one of us, such as you, being superior to the others makes no sense."

Doe grinned and nodded for Earl to continue.

"You spoke of this other realm and the notion of visiting us many times. Plus, you claim absolute knowledge and awareness of all that exists."

"Keep going."

Earl suddenly popped to his feet. "Jesus... *Christ*."

Doe laughed. "Yeah, he had a similar moment."

"You're..."

"Say it, Earl. Tell me. Who am I?"

*

'Two doctors and an administrator walk into a bar...'

"Scotch... rocks," MacMann barked at the bartender as he pulled out a stool.

"I'll just have a coffee," said Higgins, selecting the middle stool and ignoring MacMann's exaggerated eye roll.

"Is it too early for a beer?" Frank asked no one in particular.

It was too early, and the little bar was empty. The only employee, the bartender, was busy restocking a refrigerator.

Frank took a shot at articulating what they were all thinking. "Suffice to say, no one's ever seen anything – *anyone* – like this before, right?"

The doctors nodded in unison.

"But, there must be a logical explanation. It's not a miracle. It can't be… right?" Frank acknowledged the bartender as he set down a bottle of beer.

MacMann chirped in loudly, emboldened by the first sip of scotch. "What we've got here, lads, is a talking corpse in a state of decay. It's shut down, dead."

"You concur with that, Dr. Higgins?" asked Frank.

The young doctor nodded his head wearily, emptying two low-cal sweeteners into his coffee. "There's a heartbeat. And there's no denying he's awake and conversational. But the body has expired. I don't think he ever came back from the code blues. Which makes all this biologically impossible."

Frank looked past Higgins and down the bar to MacMann. "Rory, what about the press? How do we explain this?"

MacMann stared straight ahead. "Aye, the word… zombie… comes to mind."

"Dr. MacMann!" exclaimed Higgins.

MacMann drained the scotch and swirled his finger over the glass until the bartender nodded.

"Rory, we've got to go back to work today," said Frank coldly.

"Fuck off, Frank."

"Why not put out a press release?" Higgins interjected. "Delay the press conference until after Earl's chat with the patient. You could state there's been no change in the patient's condition, which is true. Let Earl handle the rest."

"That's a good idea, Paul," said Frank appreciatively.

Steam was building in MacMann's lungs. He opened his mouth to speak just as the bartender leaned in front, delivering the second scotch. MacMann glanced at the drink, then Frank, and then at the young doctor hunched over his mug. "Fuck this." He dismounted, downed the drink, and stormed out of the bar.

"Sorry, Paul. He can be a real asshole sometimes."

SIXTY-THREE

The Story of Nog: Part VI

Sunday, November 15, 12,042 BC, 12:06 p.m.

Nog's eyes strained as he attempted to take in his new surroundings. Anyplace – Anywhen. His sudden arrival in this strange location felt both real and surreal. From an inside-out perspective, it appeared as if he was walking, except he couldn't feel the ground or the wind or any sensation to corroborate his belief that he was in motion. Yet still, he moved. He glanced side to side and then at the ground, then a prolonged look at several puffy clouds. None appeared to be thunder clouds, which lessened his anxiety a bit, but not entirely.

The ground beneath him was a deep green, and there was no sand, no baked dirt anywhere to be seen. In the distance, on every horizon, were terrifying shapes, unnatural and imposing – giant cliffs with impossibly smooth sides. Rock faces made from tiny identical stones stacked upon each other and rising into the sky. Two of these impossible monoliths rose into sharp points and appeared to puncture the clouds.

He walked, uncontrolled, up a slope and into an area choked with flowers – shitty useless flowers with no edible berries. It was quickly apparent he was not commanding his body to do anything. He was simply along for a ride, inside someone or something else.

Up ahead, two ape-like creatures with hairless faces sat in conversation; their skin differed, one bronze, one pale. Their legs were covered in some sort of cloth, and their chests were odd colours, one red and the other white with tiny black dots up the centre like a bug parade. Lacking toes, both creatures had smooth odd-coloured feet, the older male's dark brown while the younger's were bright white.

Nog had no desire to approach the odd creatures, yet his body moved closer nonetheless, walking straight up to the two males and stopping. The males paused their discussion and looked up, leaving Nog speechless. He couldn't understand the strange sounds they made, so all he could do was stare. The older male had a certain glow about him, a radiant light. Perhaps it was the way the sun reflected off the top of his bald brown head, but there was something peaceful and benevolent about him.

It was at that moment that the younger male, seemingly annoyed, shouted something unknown at Nog. Nog, unwilling to initiate any aggressive moves that might lead to conflict, nodded and moved on, or at least that's what his body did without any need of encouragement.

Disturbed by the bizarre scene and unfamiliar surroundings, Nog refocused his mind on one clear thought… *Take me back to Numa's cave.*

In an instant, he was back, and he was alive.

He could see, smell, hear, think, touch, and, damn, did his body hurt. The aches and pains were bearable, but his eyes felt like toasted sandpaper. Crawling to his feet and shaking off the sand, Nog consciously sidestepped the little jewelled bag of death and staggered across the cave to where Numa was sleeping. Kneeling down to wake the old man, Nog gently prodded his shoulder before slowly realizing that Numa, his new friend, was cold, unresponsive, and stiff.

SIXTY-FOUR

Thursday, November 19, 10:15 a.m.
Phoenix General Hospital,
Room R2112

Earl stared at Doe's smiling face. "You're serious?"

Doe forced a nod.

"I'm in a hospital room in Phoenix, Arizona, having an informal chat with the... singularity?"

"Pleased to meet you."

Earl moved in a tight circle, pacing. Then paused and walked back in the opposite direction. Then said, "um," three times, followed by nothing.

"Sit down, Earl. You're making me dizzy. Let me take you a little further."

Earl sat down on his pen.

"As I've mentioned, the singularity, me, was just a quantum ball sitting in nothing – a singular point. Then, by a stroke of genius, I expanded myself into this... universe. Simple, really. From your perspective, I am quite literally everything, Earl. All the energy, all the matter, all the space, and every *thing* that inhabits it. However, when I created this universe by scattering myself, it quickly became apparent that there was a fly in my primordial soup. I lacked the ability to observe every part of myself without incurring a significant time delay. Distance equals time, you see. So, I needed to find a way to fix it."

"You're the singularity," said Earl, wide-eyed.

"Um, yes. Earl, should I continue?"

"Uh-huh."

"The plan was elegant. I'd amplify my thought realm, the area where I think. This is hard to explain without implying an actual location. If I asked you to point to the part of your body where you think, you'd naturally point to your head, but it isn't that simple for me. There isn't this big squishy brain floating around in my personal universe."

258

Earl decided he should document something of this historic moment. He wrote down *big squishy brain* using the good half of his broken pen.

"My thought realm is outside of time, always has been. But I created a way to tap into every creature's mind across my universe without distance getting in the way. The solution was to decrease my thought frequency enough to sync with an individual's material mind. My goal was to access feelings, sentient emotions, without the subject knowing. Call it… remote viewing."

"You're saying there are sentient creatures all across this universe?" Earl's mouth went bone dry, as did his brain. He could feel his communication skills fluttering away like a swarm of butterflies in a wind tunnel.

"Indeed, Earl. Countless species, all within me. Adorable little self-replicating clumps of energy. Most of them are less advanced than your species, but a few would consider humans… trivial. But rest assured, I have a tender spot for my little hairless primates, disgusting and dangerous as you are."

Earl looked humbled. "Thank you. I think."

Doe continued. "You see, the seeds of life and the mechanics of evolution are everywhere. It's the norm, not the exception. But here's the thing, Earl. My universal bubble, my body, if you will, is massive. I should probably cut back on the carbs."

"Hmm?"

"Sorry, bad joke. Anyway, I'm so big that I continuously produce billions of beginnings. The perpetual seeds of life. Which begin to evolve at the instant of incarnation."

"That's wonderful," said Earl. "A universe full of living creatures."

"Wonderful, yes, but there's a catch. It's a numbers game, really. Do you like statistics, Earl?"

"Nope."

"I thought not. So I'll frame it up like this. For every one hundred places where life gains a foothold, ninety-nine are wiped out before reaching an advanced level of intelligence. This leaves us with one in a hundred. Not bad when you're sampling from trillions. But then we have to look at those life forms that evolve in conditions unsuitable to producing beings of complex thought. Out of the remaining one percent, ninety-nine percent never make it out of the ocean, never form a thumb and never perfect complex speech patterns. Most importantly, they never create defensible societies, a precursor to cultural intelligence."

"You're getting low on planets?"

"Indeed, but the worst is yet to come. A minuscule amount of life forms manage to crawl out of the water, avoid the comets, evolve logic and the all-important thumb. They form societies based on a shared language, then bang the rocks together to make fire, which, I should point out, really pisses off the rocks. Eventually, some reach the tool stage. However, very few of these civilizations make it past the nuclear tool stage, either because they use up their precious natural resources or mutually destroy each other. It's hardwired, Earl. Those evolutionary traits that allow a species to form societies are the same inherent qualities that ensure societal groups annihilate each other. Civilizations fail because they're inherently uncivilized. In your case, human beings evolved globally, but human culture evolved locally."

Earl stared, blank-faced, fear welling inside him. "But couldn't you…?"

"No, Earl, I'm a victim of physics, just like you. I don't have the physical presence to intercede everywhere in the universe at once. Besides, I've got enough to do, fending off those cancerous black holes eating away at me."

"So, we're doomed?" said Earl, overwhelmed at the prospect.

Doe's face went stony. "There have been a few civilizations that survived by banding together," he said diplomatically.

Earl considered his next question and if he actually wanted to know the answer. "So? Do we?"

"Do we?"

"Do we survive it? You're the one holding all the future flipbook cards. Do we get beyond our adolescent self-destructive stage?"

"As of this moment, it appears the dandelions shall inherit the Earth. But as I said, the future's written in dry erase marker."

Earl made a strenuous effort to compose himself by cracking his knuckles and turning his head around until his neck made a popping sound. "You've intervened, so I… so we could change things for the better?"

Doe sighed. "Earl, selfish as this may sound, for me to continue to enjoy all these experiences, I need more civilizations to move beyond their own extinction phase."

Understanding suddenly swept over Earl like a spider in a dishwasher. "So, your desire to see civilizations advance is self-serving, based on you running out of playgrounds?"

"A bit harsh. If anything, I'm playing with myself."

"I won't write that bit down."

"Hmm?"

"So, you're here to help?" Earl grinned like he'd won something. "By changing our future."

"The cards constantly shuffle, Earl. However, simply watching your species through remote viewing is not interactive; it changes nothing. I can only watch and feel what a subject watches and feels."

"OK," said Earl. "So, an obvious question comes to my foggy mind. If you've been remote viewing us up until now, then what are you doing here, in the flesh, so to speak?" Earl glanced at Doe's body and grimaced.

"I deemed this little visit necessary because it was important for me to reach *you*, Earl. So far, every time I've tried, I've failed." Doe laughed, which sounded a bit like a bagpipe played underwater.

"This connection, right here, my discussions with you, means the mind of the singularity is right here in this room? And nowhere else?" asked Earl.

"That is true, Earl. But you and I are not connected right now, not really. I'm simply just… *here*. Although I can't stay long, there is lots of crap piling up while I'm away, you know how it is? In truth, my boy, there are several ways I can connect to the mind of a subject," said Doe. "If I'm physically present, like right now, and the subject's mind is open and willing, all I need do is touch them. I use this method sparingly because, as I said, it requires physical travel on my part. I hate travel. But, more importantly, it's not a viable communication conduit. Yes, the subject can instantly experience my realm, but it's a poor way to have a lengthy discussion. I'd have to be here, in a physical body, and nowhere else, all the time, just to maintain the connection. That's why, for the most part, I prefer the remote viewing option, although the subject never knows I'm there."

Earl listened in a trance, absorbing every word.

Doe closed his eyes and rested for a moment, summoning strength and clearing his throat. "But there is a third, deeper connection I reserve for special occasions," he said, smirking. "I arrange to have a connection device, innocuous and unassuming, introduced into the subject's timeline. This device could be anything; it's unimportant. But it must be something that attracts their undivided attention long enough for me to focus my energy on them, thus connecting us. I've left these things all over the place." He nodded for effect, and something cracked loudly.

Doe continued. "With the subject's attention now deeply engaged in the conduit device, there's a brief unpleasant jolt, a little bit like touching the tip of your tongue to a lightning bolt, followed by some disorientation. But the subject quickly regains their senses. From that point on, a two-way thought portal remains open forever. And the subject begins to understand far more than they've ever experienced or learned during their lifetimes. Some do nothing with it, but a few go on to become great teachers, philosophers and change agents."

"Ah-ha, so that's it. You wish to open up my portal?" Earl squinted at his own poorly chosen words.

"Indeed, my boy. You're going to be my agent in the field. You're going to help me nudge the human species beyond their extinction barrier. You're going to be a very special primate."

Earl swallowed hard. "Um, I've seen what happens to your field agents throughout history, JD, not a pretty sight. Most of them met with very painful ends."

"Pain is merely a state of mind, Earl. And biological death is irrelevant in the big picture."

"Oh, don't get me wrong, I'm not afraid of death. But the process of getting to that point, the suffering part, scares the living shit out of me. You have no idea how fragile I am, how susceptible to pain and injury. For Christ's sake, I once cut my finger inserting a suppository."

SIXTY-FIVE

Moments later...

"So, how does this work?" asked Earl, recomposing himself in his chair.

"When I open portals, I typically employ an elaborate and dramatic blindsiding of the subject. In other words, they never see it coming. You probably won't either, but at least you'll recognize it for what it is, thanks to this little spoiler. You, Earl, are going to help me infuse a societal change focused on the oneness of humanity."

"It's been tried."

"In a way, yes, several have tried. But the communication mediums they had at the time were weak or non-existent. The ability to connect with everyone on the planet wasn't there."

Earl thought about the many seers throughout history: Prophets and shamans, preachers and wise ones, medicine men and futurists – none of them possessed the sheer power of modern-day communications, the ability to reach everyone on Earth.

"So, you're saying you have faith in me," Earl chuckled. "Were you not listening when I spilled my guts yesterday? I've spent an entire life cutting my losses with a dull knife. At the risk of questioning your cosmic intelligence, are you sure there's no better choice than me?"

"I *know* you can do it, Earl."

"Great. Looks like fifty percent of the room is on board."

"Earl, listen. Every connection I've ever made or will make has one trait in common. Each subject was a natural-born messenger, curious, inquisitive and capable of explaining any concept, regardless of audience. Adaptable and relentless, they possess the greatest skill of all, observation. They were all natural-born reporters."

"Reporters, JD? That's why you chose me, 'cause I'm a reporter? Dude, did you ever misfire on this one."

"Perhaps. But, Earl, you'll have the one thing the others didn't; you'll have me. None of them had the pre-awareness I'm giving you, and none of them came equipped with a mentor."

"JD, trying to make a prophet out of me is like putting moisturizer on a mummy."

"It's not about prophecy, Earl. It's about your ability to create optimism."

Earl looked like Charlie Brown lining up for a field goal. "This feels a lot like the discussion we had about belief. It seems to me that optimism isn't something you fake. It would be evident to the onlooker."

"Optimism is a commodity, Earl, not a trait. It's not ingrained. It's something you find."

*

Dr. Higgins' arrival was well-timed. Doe had become distracted and uncomfortable, and Earl figured a break was overdue. Leaving Doe with the doctor and Nurse Morallas, Earl headed down to the cafeteria for his first coffee of the day, a fact his brain had been protesting for hours. He sat at a table by the window, staring at the sun as it climbed to a dominant point overhead.

With his mind churning, Earl needed a distraction to bring him back to Earth. He checked his emails, finding nothing of importance. Then he messaged Orlando to let him know he was free for a bit.

A reply pinged immediately.

Sup, Earl? Shit's getting weird here. Our boy Warren's gone all 'O. K. Corral' with Del-Monte. Couldn't talk him out of it. Dude's as good as dead. They're meeting tomorrow.

Earl raised an eyebrow and typed a quick response:

Is this guy stupid? Should we call the cops?

That wouldn't help him. Warren's in the middle of a world of hurt. Nowhere to turn, no positive outcome in sight. Screwed if he does, screwed if he doesn't.

What happened last night. Did you two go at it?

There was a pause before the next email.

Can we speak…?

Earl hit the speed dial for Orlando. "Hey."

"Earl. First of all, I don't know who raised you, but grown men don't say 'Go at it,' OK? And, no, there was no fight, we just… talked."

"Ah, OK," laughed Earl. "So, I guess I really don't understand your world. A guy breaks into your place, and instead of calling the cops or beating the crap out of him, you have a good talk?"

"Don't try to figure it out. Different planet, OK?"

"Fine. So, why's Warren going after Del-Monte?"

"If we'd had more time this morning, Earl, I would have explained. Del-Monte is the one who paid Warren to take out your God guy. Warren's the guy who fucked Doe up in the desert."

"What? That tears it. Now we're calling the cops, for sure."

"No, that's not what we're doing, Earl."

"You're protecting this guy?"

"Short answer is yes. Look, Earl, Warren's not the problem, OK, he's just an idiot who bit off more than he could chew."

"But he tried to kill Doe?"

"Tried being the keyword. But my boy couldn't do it. And, whoever Doe is, he sure as hell isn't a mountain climber. Dude messed *himself* up. Fell off a cliff."

"And you believe that?" said Earl, incredulously.

"As a matter of fact, I do. And you should too. Warren's an honest dude."

Earl laughed into the phone. "Now that's funny."

"I'm not laughing, Earl. There's *street*, and then there's *bad*. Warren's a street kid, but he ain't bad. He doesn't deserve this. When the time came, he couldn't kill Doe, and that says something. So, I'm gonna help him. And you're not gonna call the cops."

"This is so confusing!"

"Earl, how long have we been friends?"

Earl was surprised at the question and the sincerity in Orlando's voice. "Umm, twenty, thirty years now?"

"Do they think you're funny in Canada? Here's the deal. We're friends. And a friend never hangs another friend out to dry. It's part of the code. Now, I don't know a lot about Warren, but I know he's OK. He's not a bad man. They could have sent much worse after me."

"You should get a horse."

"'Scuse me?"

"Yeah, you know, like the Cavalry or John Wayne. Riding in at the last minute to save the day."

"Earl, do I look like the horse type to you?"

Earl pondered the question for several seconds. "They make these steps so kids can mount them."

"Remind me to kick your Canadian snowballs next time I see you."

"Will do." Earl laughed. "And you remind me that I have a new assignment for you later. Something you'll enjoy."

"Is that right? 'Cause I'd enjoy kicking you in the snowballs, so is it better than that?"

"Oh yes. Tartan balls."

SIXTY-SIX

Thursday, November 19, 2:55 p.m.
Phoenix General Hospital,
Room R2112

It was nearing three in the afternoon, and Earl paced outside Doe's door as members of the medical team went about their tasks inside the hospital room. After a long nap, Doe was undergoing a battery of medical tests along with a complete change of oil, lube and filters.

"Robbie," pondered Earl. "A week ago, I was sitting in a cubical writing a story about snow tires and seriously considering stepping off the pointy bit of a crane. Now, I'm here, in the middle of a worldwide spectacle, kneeling at the feet of mysticism. Life's not funny, man. It's goddamn hilarious."

Robbie watched Earl orbit around him, quickening his pace. "I don't know this Miss Tescism or her feet, but I know that guy in there is pretty special."

"That he is, Robbie."

"Right? It's like everyone who comes out has this weird look on their face. Like they've just found Jesus or something."

Earl nodded a lot. "Bigger than Jesus, my friend."

"Yeah. I mean, even the nuns were blown away. And..."

"Nuns?" Earl interrupted.

"Ya, the two nuns that visited."

Earl stopped pacing. "Didn't I ask you to call me if anyone tried to see him, anyone out of the norm?"

"Ya, you did. But there were no Norms. Oh, but one tall dude tried to get in dressed as a doctor. I sent him packing. Then these two nuns show up the next day."

"And these were real nuns?" Earl said suspiciously.

"Oh ya. Well, the old one for sure. She scared the shit out of me. The other one was too beautiful to be a nun. She was really hot."

A glimmer of understanding struck Earl. "Describe the hot nun… and don't leave out any details."

"Oh, easy," nodded Robbie. "Very friendly, about five-foot-five, plus a two-foot hat. She sounded American, but I think she was oriental."

Earl cringed. "I think you mean Asian?"

"Asian? Ya, well, she could have been that too."

"Let me guess," deduced Earl. "The other nun was like cryptkeeper old, really short, and looked like she could shove her bony fingers inside your chest and pull out your soul?"

"Ya, that's her. Like she'd spent her life wrestling demons. And not winning."

"OK, I know who that is – a member of Bellecourt's God-squad. And I suspect your fake doctor was too."

"Maybe," said Robbie, looking over Earl's shoulder and blinking for focus. "Why don't you ask him yourself? Here he comes."

*

"Mr. Grey, I'm glad I finally caught up with you," announced Bellecourt. "I think it's high time I meet John Doe. And I don't expect any more interference from you."

Earl looked the tall man up and down. "Were you the one who came here disguised as a doctor?"

Bellecourt broke eye contact and looked at his shoes. "Umm, well, yes. But you don't seem to understand the urgency of the situation."

"I think I do," said Earl. "Let me summarize it for you. You're a priest."

That's pretty good so far, thought Robbie.

"And as a man of modest constitution," continued Earl, "let's pretend that I open that door and usher you in; what happens next?"

Bellecourt was unprepared for practical questions. He'd readied himself for an ideological fight that didn't seem to be materializing. "Mr. Grey, it's my duty, my mission to…"

"To what, to debunk all of this? To discredit the man's words and message? Words about caring for each other and how we're all connected? Or how we need to shelve our selfish desires and become a collective to ensure humanity survives?"

Bellecourt froze, his mind searching for a counter-argument to the philosophy he had preached his entire life. "Earl, the message is, well, it's very nice, spot on, I guess, but we can't have people making unverified claims that they're God."

"Why not?"

"Because…" Bellecourt paused.

"Because proof would destroy the very foundation of your religion," interjected Earl emphatically. "Belief would be obliterated by certainty. You've never been interested in the truth. You're only here to protect your job."

Bellecourt shook his head. "I've no quarrel with you, Earl. I'm sure you can understand how claims of this nature happen all the time and are very detrimental to our organization."

"Organization? You speak like you're with the UN or NATO, or the Boy Scouts of America."

"You know what I mean." Bellecourt threw his arms up in frustration.

"Sadly, I do. Look, you seem like a dedicated man, someone who truly believes in what he does."

"I am, and I do."

"So does he." Earl pointed at the door to Doe's room. "And both messages are the same. But instead of capitalizing on this worldwide attention, you'd rather prove him an imposter. You never came here to determine his authenticity in the first place," said Earl, pushing the point hard with his index finger. "Your job has been, and no doubt remains, to squash all claims of divinity that arise without any genuine investigation to the contrary."

The priest's aggressive body language and facial expression signalled his desire for denial. But he remained silent, watching as the last member of the medical crew left Doe's room.

"Fine! You know what?" said Earl. "Let's go in and see him, huh? Let's go meet the imposter."

SIXTY-SEVEN

One minute later...

Doe looked much worse. His eyes droopy, his lower lip sagging slightly, dry and blistered. His demeanour brightened only slightly as Earl entered. "There you are," he mumbled.

"Your pit crew needed more time than they thought," said Earl, noting that the room had taken on a stale feel, like sterile sadness.

"Ah, yes, Dr. Higgins, such a nice man, very thorough. And who's this tall fella with you?"

"Oh, sorry," said Earl. "May I introduce Monsignor Matthew Bellecourt? Monsignor Bellecourt, this is John Doe."

Bellecourt stepped further into the room. He leaned in and offered his hand. "It's good to finally meet you, Mr. Doe."

"You too, Matthew. Please forgive. I can't shake hands very well right now."

"Of course, I completely understand."

"Here," said Earl, pointing to his usual seat. "Sit down, make yourself comfortable, Father."

Bellecourt tried to sit in the chair, a long way down for him, his knees buckling then collapsing into his chest like an awkward, oversized child.

"JD," Earl commenced. "Monsignor Bellecourt has remained steadfast in his efforts to meet you. I believe it's probably in our best interests to allow him a few moments of your time."

Doe looked down from the bed, fixing a stare on the robed stranger. "What's on your mind, Matthew?"

Earl took a few steps back towards the door and opened his phone, checking for any aggressive emails that might have evaded the hospital blocking devices.

Bellecourt cleared his throat. "Yes, well, I suppose I should get right to it. I'm sure you can guess why I'm here?"

"Last rights?"

Bellecourt fell silent with surprise. He looked over his shoulder at Earl.

Earl glanced up from the phone. "He's teasing you. He's got a spectacular sense of humour."

"Oh, I see. I thought… well, I know he's very sick."

"You have a lovely voice, Matthew," interrupted Doe. "I'm sure anyone in need of last rights would be happy to receive them from you. Very comforting."

The Monsignor nodded. "Well, I'm glad we're not at that point, sir."

"Oh no, not at all. Way, way past it."

Earl smiled to himself at the back of the room.

"Past it? I don't understand?"

"No. No, I don't suppose you do. You see, Matthew, this body is dead. It's been dead for a while now. Ghoulish as it sounds, I'm just using it for a little while. I needed a way to chat with Earl. It's been difficult to get the boy's attention. Atheists – too cynical to take a hint."

Bellecourt looked back and forth between the two men, his firm foundation cracking. "I don't understand. You're clearly not dead. I mean, you're talking, you're… moving."

"Matthew, did you take biology in high school?"

Bellecourt blinked, hoping it might reset his stability functions. "Yes, of course, but I…"

"Then you're aware that a small electrical current attached to a dismembered frog-leg will cause it to jump, correct?"

"Yes, that's true, but…"

"Consider me a big frog, Father. Easier to comprehend that way."

"A big frog? Are you telling me that… you're God… using a dead body to communicate with us?"

"I am indeed speaking through a dead man. As for the God part, that requires a bit more explanation."

"Sir, it's my job to ascertain your divinity. That's my purpose." Bellecourt pushed forward to the edge of the chair.

"That's a fine purpose. And by divinity, I presume you mean the Catholic version of the one true God?"

Earl rolled his eyes without looking up from his Blackberry.

"Worded like that, it sounds a little foolish, but that's essentially the idea. My job is to determine if you are God, as defined by the ones who sent me."

"Matthew," said Doe. "I hate to disappoint you, although I suspect I won't, but I'm not the God they seek."

Bellecourt let his head slowly drop into his chest. "Well, I suspected as much, and I do appreciate your honesty. But I won't lie, when these situations arise, there's always a part of me that wants it to be true."

"And why's that, Father?"

"Mr. Doe, I know God exists. I've felt Him. But I've often wished for one unifying event capable of bringing us all together. A revelation from God would do the trick."

"Matthew, there's something fundamental you need to understand. Otherwise, you'll remain part of the problem."

"You think *I'm* part of the problem?"

"Oh, indeed." Doe shifted his head three inches to the left, an effort that appeared to take every ounce of his energy. "You came here to determine if I were God. Sadly, your quest was quixotic from inception. Your question should be, *is* there a God?"

"Mr. Doe…" Bellecourt stated emphatically, "… I won't debate whether there is a God or not. The fact is, there *needs* to be one."

"Matthew, your God is a human construct, designed to explain the unexplainable and define the metaphysical. These facts have been well documented and continuous throughout history. You, above all, should know that. There was never a God from the start, my friend. Perhaps humans needed one once, but not anymore."

Bellecourt shook his head. "Say what you will; humans need God."

"No, son, humans need to *seek* God. Problems begin when they find one."

Silence overwhelmed the room.

Doe lightened his approach. "You humans have a delightful phrase. I believe it goes like this: 'It's the journey, not the destination.' Is that correct?"

"Yes, that's right," said the priest, staring intently at the bedridden man.

"Well, Matthew, your *Bible* states, *Seek ye first the kingdom of God*, does it not?"

"It does."

"But it doesn't say find him. It doesn't say 'find ye the lord' or 'what's wrong with you people, how hard can it be to locate a God.' No, it just says seek. Salvation, happiness and joy are found within the experience of seeking, not finding."

Bellecourt frowned. "I seek God every day because I know he exists."

"Alright, let's try something, shall we?" suggested Doe. "Matthew, place your hands on my arm."

The priest did as asked. "It's cold."

"Yes, I'm sorry about that, but please leave them there for a moment. Is it true what you said? Do you really wish God would show you a sign? Your mind is open to that?"

"I would not lie about such a thing."

"Very well, then close your eyes and free your mind. Focus only on your belief and your need for a sign."

Curious, Earl lifted his head up from his phone. He watched as the priest closed his eyes. Within an instant, Bellecourt's body tightened. And then relaxed.

Seconds later, his cheeks wet, Bellecourt opened his eyes and removed his hands from Doe. With pleading eyes, he looked up at Earl but said nothing.

Earl smiled. Try as he might, he couldn't possibly dislike Bellecourt at that moment. Here was a man who'd spent his entire life defending a simple concept, the indisputable fact that his God was *the* God. Yet there he sat, a humble man in a humble chair, who'd just glimpsed everything there is or ever was, all of eternity, and found it lacking a creator.

Doe spoke softly. "Matthew, the blind pursuit of a specific God can only end in destruction. A man of your influence could change that. Change the world if he wanted to. Our friend Earl here is about to try. Will you help him?"

Bellecourt wiped away a stream of tears, knowing there was no possibility of composing himself after what he just saw. He looked up into Doe's eyes and nodded.

*

After escorting the Monsignor out into the hallway, Robbie held him steady against the wall.

"Robbie, please wait with him until his friends arrive," said Earl. "He's been to the edge of the universe and back, so he might be jet-lagged. I'll be back in a bit… no one sees Doe, got it?"

Robbie nodded, then turned his attention to the sagging priest, unable to stand up. "I hope they send the pretty oriental nun," said Robbie. "The tiny old nun might have trouble walking you out."

SIXTY-EIGHT

Thursday, November 19, 3:40 p.m.
Phoenix General Hospital, Doctor's Lounge

Once in the doctor's lounge, Earl grabbed a tepid coffee and a day-old donut. Several messages from Orlando brought Earl up to speed on the Warren/Del-Monte situation: that being that nothing had changed so far. Mary-Lynn had left a total of three messages, mostly ranting about her exhaustion and working too many hours with the 'Orange Ken Doll'. Earl replied, suggesting she was overdoing it, then told her they'd meet in the morning as he wasn't sure when he'd be leaving the hospital.

As he pocketed his phone, Earl's thoughts wandered back to his recent vocational change – saviour of the human race. He realized the concept didn't frighten him in the slightest. Unlike his old self, who'd be searching for a thick rope and a sturdy beam, this new mission felt exciting. He was borderline euphoric, especially knowing Doe had his back. As Earl began to envision what his new role might look like, his thoughts were interrupted by a tall man standing next to his table, clearing his throat.

"What are you doing in the doctor's lounge?" demanded MacMann. "This place is for doctors only. Clue's in the name."

"I needed some space to… decompress. And the room was empty," Earl said.

"Consider yourself decompressed. There's a presser at five. Let's go."

"In a moment." Earl waved a dismissive hand at MacMann. "You've just reminded me of something important. I need to make a quick call, then I'll meet you in the ready room. Cool?"

"We're not all here by your command, wee lad." MacMann stormed away.

Earl hit the speed dial for Orlando.

"Sup, Earl?" said Orlando.

"It's been another remarkable day, Orlando. Things just keep getting stranger and stranger."

"What now? He walk on water or something?"

"Might as well." Earl chuckled. "I just watched Doe convert a devout priest in under a minute."

"No shit?"

"Yep. But listen, man, I gotta hang here for a while longer. Got a press conference, then back in to see Doe. I'll probably stay late, maybe even sleep here. Don't worry if you don't hear from me, OK?"

"Alright. You know best."

"And Orlando, about that little job I mentioned."

"Tartan balls? What's up with that?"

"I need you to call MacMann first thing tomorrow morning."

"OK. And?"

"And tell him that Earl's gonna spill the beans. Tell him you heard me speaking to someone on the phone and that I'm going to reveal everything to Mary-Lynn Wu. Confess the whole sordid mess, so it looks like I'm the good guy. Tell him I plan to wait for Doe to pass on, then give Mary-Lynn an exclusive TV interview."

"Jesus. OK, if you're sure. Any specific time?"

"I'd say nine, gives me time to figure out what's going on with Doe first."

"Gotcha."

Orlando pressed 'end' then resumed his urgent task, his hands clad in blue latex gloves. Carefully he extracted the last bullet from its box and placed it into one of three speed-loaders – little plastic clips that held six rounds in a circle, allowing shooters to reload a revolver in seconds. Once finished, he reread the description on the top of the empty ammo box: *hollow-tipped mushrooming rounds – armour piercing*. In street lingo, 'Cop-Killers'. Although Orlando knew there would be no cops around when these babies went off.

*

Earl hoped his pre-presser meeting with MacMann and Frank would be brief. "Don't know what to tell the press this time, guys. Impossible to put Doe's comments into words. The concepts are too… deep."

"And you'd be the measurement of deep concepts, would ya?" said MacMann, laughing like a jackal.

Earl ignored him. "It's best I prepare them for Doe's demise. Try to combine his teachings with his desire to shed his broken body and rejoin the collective. How does that sound?"

"Like a *Star Trek* episode," said MacMann.

"It sounds fine, Earl," said Frank, resigned to the events. "Just go with that."

MacMann made no attempt at disguising his eye roll.

Earl slowly nodded. "Yeah, and Frank, I have a question. Something I've been thinking about for some time,"

"Is it, where do babies come from?" MacMann grinned.

"When Doe passes on…" said Earl, once again, ignoring MacMann, "… can you make the announcement. I don't think I can do it."

"I wouldn't ask you to, Earl. Don't worry, I'll do it."

MacMann made for the door. "Well, I see I'm not needed as usual. You're on your own, big man," he said, staring at Frank before storming out.

Earl broke the silence. "This is gonna get nasty."

"Already is. Did you come up with any ideas?" asked Frank.

"Just one. But it's a wicked one."

*

"Ladies and gentlemen," said Earl. "There's not much to report today. I won't beat around the bush. Doe's condition is grave, and I should prepare you for his imminent demise."

A loud murmur rippled through the crowd. "Is he in pain?" a sombre voice inquired.

"He is aware of the physical pain but says he's blocked it out," replied Earl. "But he has a final message for us. Something the world needs to know."

Pens went to paper as microphones were thrust closer and higher.

"Our human lives are extraordinary," began Earl, clear and confident. He could picture all the right words laid out in front of him. "We exist to experience the physical world. Sometimes wonderful, other times tragic. The entity we exist within, God, if you wish, feels joy and sadness through us. Wondrous experience or horror show, your life, all of it, is so very important to God. Your physical lives are merely a blink, so you can and will make it through because God needs you to. *We* need you to, all of us, collectively. You are not God's messenger, relaying feelings and physical interactions. No, you're God's senses, touch, smell, vision, and, most of all, mind. You are literally how God feels."

In room R2112, Doe looked away from the small television set towards Nurse Morallas. "My dear, please fetch Earl as soon as he's finished," he mumbled softly, his eyes dry, face pale, and his body motionless as a stone.

SIXTY-NINE

Thursday, November 19, 5:45 p.m.
Phoenix General Hospital

Earl came to a stop in front of Robbie and patted him on the shoulder. "Did the Monsignor find his way home?"

"Oh yes, Mr. Earl. Another priest came and collected him, little fat dude. And that Yoda nun came too. Terrifying."

"I'm sure it was. Nobody has been inside?"

"Nope. Just the nurse."

"Good stuff, thanks, Robbie." Earl pushed open the big door. "JD, I came as soon as I heard you needed me. How are you feeling? Or is that a redundant question now?"

"Thank you, Earl. Yes, it's getting hard to maintain this meat sack." He motioned with his head and eyes at the motionless torso attached to him.

"Is it time, sir?" Earl's voice cracked.

"Almost. This vessel is decaying rapidly now."

Earl stood by the bed rails. "Can I get you anything? Would you like a drink?"

"I'd love a *real* drink."

Earl smiled, then retrieved his bag. Unzipping the top, he prodded among his emergency clothes until he found the bottle of thirty-year-old ambrosia. "Will this do?"

Doe's thickset eyes lit up. "What a magnificent specimen. Acquired at great difficulty, I presume?"

"Nah, it was just lying around in the car. No one will miss it. Tragically though, I've no ice, but I can cut it with some water if you wish."

"Heresy, my boy, wouldn't think of it."

Earl scanned the room for a glass.

"And that would be our next compromise," said Doe. "Only paper cups in here." He pointed to the counter along the wall. "But, I suspect the lack of crystal won't kill us."

277

Earl poured healthy portions into two paper cups, holding one to Doe's lips and tipping slowly. "Good?"

"Nectar of the Gods. Exquisite."

Earl poured a little more. "So, what happens to you after this, JD?"

"Technically, I'll still be right here. And in the flower vase, and these bed rails, and that alarmingly large dust bunny in the corner."

"To dust bunnies," said Earl, holding his paper cup in the air. He closed his eyes as he drank, feeling the warmth from the whisky seep into his body cavity. "You know, JD, you never explained how you tried to reach me?"

"Ah, yes. You were a tough one. Most people notice 'in your face' signs or at least question the odd occurrences around them."

"Streetlights!" Earl shouted. "Blown out streetlights, right?"

"Indeed, that was one, although unintentional. You see, when I remote view through an intelligent creature, there's an overflow of my energy into its body. In order not to harm the subject, this excess energy must be dissipated, like lightning. The viewers I had surrounding you were prone to the odd discharge. Depending on the location, it could do quite a number on the local power grid."

Earl nodded but had already moved on from the streetlight explanation. "Sawchuck?"

"Much more than a viewing portal, Earl."

"Oh my God," said Earl, his eyes roaming the room for something to fix on. "I just thought he was an eccentric professor." Earl's emotions swelled. "I didn't pay attention."

"As I said, Earl, you were a tough one to break."

"I'm such an idiot."

"Perhaps, but I'd argue a completely normal one for your species. Self-awareness quickly leads to self-centricity."

"I want to tell him how sorry I am. Can you tell him I'm sorry?"

"You just did."

Earl's head spun, his legs bending like balsawood tent-poles. "Maybe we should discuss my new role now before I drink any more."

"Earl, as my messenger, you must walk a rocky road. Some will fear you, try to lock you up, or have you committed. You know, for your own good. They'll say you're a cult leader. Religions will denounce you, call you a heretic or the spawn of Satan. For millions, you'll be as popular as the vegetarian booth at a Houston Rodeo."

Earl nodded, analyzing all the wrong words for significance. "So, there's a Satan?"

Doe rolled his dry eyes. "The only one I know personally on this planet is Flavio Satan. Peruvian guy. He's a baker."

"An evil baker?"

"No, mostly bread and pastries."

"Ahh."

"Earl, pay attention. Your success depends on your ability to energize a movement. To institutionalize optimism. Creating a base of unstoppable followers."

"Followers, huh?" laughed Earl. "The minions of a pawn. Frankly, sir, I've always felt safer as a follower. You know, fewer knives in the back."

Doe struggled for a breath before replying. "You underestimate the power you'll have at your fingertips."

"Power? Really? What will I be able to do? Strike down my enemies?" Earl laughed, a little too maniacally.

"Earl, I…"

"I'm kidding, sir. I'll only kill a few."

"Earl, I'm talking about the power of knowledge, a power so immense I must confine it to the intelligent and pragmatic, hiding it from the passionate or rebellious. Power, much like revenge, is best wielded by the smart, not the emotional."

"You're saying I'll have influence because of my knowledge?"

"Not your knowledge, Earl, your *access* to knowledge."

Despite the growing haze between Earl's ears, another puzzle piece snapped into place. "I'll have access to other people's histories and futures."

"Immense power, wouldn't you say?"

"Dangerous power."

"In the wrong hands, yes."

"I meant dangerous to me. People won't like it when they find out that I know more about them than they do. They might wish to, I dunno, get rid of me."

"Not with your ability to see their past secrets or future actions. Any nemesis would be an open book to you."

"Now that's a game-changer."

"I'm glad you approve, Earl." Doe coughed as he snickered. "You happen to possess the right intellect, along with a good heart. A rare combination… on this planet, at least."

*

After a brief lapse in consciousness, Doe's reentry to Earl's reality was far more challenging than before. His eyes blinked as he coughed, the body motionless but for the odd facial twitch, and his limbs were cold and rigid. He managed a whisper. "Earl? Still here?"

"Yes, JD, right here." Earl stood and leaned over his face. "Right in front of you."

"I'm afraid I can't see very well. Just a dull gray mist now. The puppet strings are snapping."

A storm surged through Earl's stomach. "There's no need to strain; just take your time."

"Time, time, time, yes. Take some, give some, waste some, live some. What time is it, by the way?"

Earl gently patted Doe's arm, icy hard, like a stone. "It's 2 a.m.," he replied, checking the clock on the wall.

"Ah, good, it's tomorrow already. The day has come. So, Earl, later on today, I want you to head out into the desert."

"The desert?"

"Yes, you know the way. You were so close the other day."

"The State Park? Will I find you there?"

"Find me. Find you. What's the difference? But you've got to finally open that mind of yours all by yourself. Then, and this is important, you must walk alone until you find a cave. You'll know it when you see it. It's pretty obvious; the cave's guarded by a somewhat rude-looking rock formation."

"Rude?"

"Yes, it's a rather large monolith. Kinda looks like a…" Doe shifted his eyes toward his swimsuit area.

"Um, alright. But which direction? It's kinda big out there."

"You'll know. Walk like a ray of light. Follow gravity. Trust your internal compass."

"But… I still have so many questions."

Doe tried to shush Earl, but the sound came out like a breeze drifting through a trumpet. "No more questions. Just seek."

"OK, JD."

With satisfaction, Doe's eyes slowly closed, then abruptly shot open as if zapped by a hefty current. "Oh, and Earl…"

"Yes, sir, still here."

"Make sure you wear sunscreen this time." Doe's eyes closed again, and he slipped into an unconscious state.

Earl sat back in the chair.

Hector, the night guard, entered with a pillow and blanket, followed by a night nurse who checked the monitors. She frowned.

Earl, head still mushy from the scotch, waited for them to leave and then curled up in the small chair, his pillow wedged between himself and the wall.

SEVENTY

Friday, November 20, 6:55 a.m.
Phoenix General Hospital,
Room R2112

There's a certain kind of pain associated with sleeping incorrectly. It's a pain that lingers, stays with a person all day. The sort of ache that says your body has limitations, no matter how young you think you are. Limitations easily exceeded after too many motionless hours in a yoga position.

Earl coaxed his legs to work, stiffening under him, raising him to a semi-bipedal stance. Leaning in with trepidation, he looked closely at Doe's face – a doppelganger for every coffin occupant he'd ever seen.

Earl sighed. Stepping away from the bed, he fished a change of clothes from his shoulder bag and hobbled to the small bathroom. After freshening up, he dressed and combed his hair using wet hands. Feeling ready to face the inevitable, Earl stepped back into the room then gasped in surprise. Doe lay still in the same spot as before but his eyes were wide open and staring at Earl.

"Jesus, you scared me," said Earl, two octaves higher than usual.

Doe whispered something too quiet for Earl to hear. Earl moved in and leaned over the bed. "I'm here. What did you say?"

"I said, I can't see a damn thing."

Earl, startled but relieved, said, "To be honest, JD, I wasn't sure you'd be here this morning."

"Hadn't planned on it. I was gonna let this poor bugger's body go last night. But I forgot to tell you something."

Earl pondered the absurdity of an omnipotent being with a sketchy memory. "What is it, sir?"

"I've got something for you, something for your journey. Over there, in the top drawer, where the nurse put my clothes and shoes. It's an old bag. Stones adorn the outside, and inside there's rocks and sand and ash."

Earl raised his eyebrows. "You want me to have it?"

"It's not a gift, Earl." Doe's breath came in short bursts with long pauses between comments. "Take it with you. Protect it."

"Protect it? Is it valuable?"

"Absolutely not. Completely worthless." Doe wheezed.

"OK," Earl smiled. "Regardless, I'll treasure it."

"Fine, but you'll need it too, in the cave. It only works there."

"Works?" Earl scrunched up his face. "Alright, consider it done, my friend."

"Good." Doe closed his eyes. "Earl, meeting you has been a cosmic pleasure."

Shivers ran up Earl's spine like ripples in a pond as the room grew cold and shapeless.

"JD, meeting you has been the greatest honour of my life," Earl said, his voice warbling.

"Earl," Doe rasped. "Every part of you is a part of me. I can't think of you as something separate, something distinct." Exhausted, Doe went quiet for a few seconds, forcing energy into the decaying body, animating it for a few more precious seconds. "It is impossible for us to be apart. You'll see."

Earl burst at the tear ducts.

"It's time for you to go, young man. There's nothing left for you here."

Earl smiled as the tears streamed down his face. "I believe we'll meet again, JD."

"Yes, Earl the believer. And meet we will, son. So, I'll simply say, *au revoir*?"

Earl's throat closed. His lips trembled, nose full and dripping on the bed. He placed a hand on either side of Doe's face and took a deep breath. "A*u revoir*, JD."

Monitors went wild as the ceiling lights popped out of existence.

SEVENTY-ONE

The Story of Nog: Part VII

Sunday, November 15, 12,042 BC, 12:15 p.m.

Nog was very familiar with death, be it animal or human. He'd seen enough. He knew that when a person ceased to be, their chest didn't move anymore, and their drumbeat stopped. The thought left a hollow sensation in his stomach and many questions in his throbbing head.

Sitting next to the lifeless man, Nog thought, *Numa must have been to the dark place. His teachings must come from first-hand knowledge of this other world.*

Very clever, Nog, Numa's voice echoed in Nog's native language.

Nog spun about on his knees, looking around the cave for the source.

I'm inside your head, Nog. I'm using this voice because it's familiar to you.

For some ridiculous reason, Nog felt no fear. Everything seemed normal, almost expected. He stared at the body of Numa, much like he'd stared at his own while he was inside the void.

"Darra me, chhoo, Numa, narra, do lama duckk," said Nog. *I am sad about your death, Numa, but delighted to hear from you.*

There was a faint chuckle.

You must replace me, Nog. Make me proud. Oh, and please do something with my old body there before it spoils.

Nog was well aware of what happened to bodies once they stopped moving, and it was pretty gross. This was why the elders began burning those who'd stopped participating. A special fire that made the body vanish, leaving only sacred grey ash.

By nightfall, Nog had wrapped Numa's body in his bedding and dragged it from the cave, gently placing it in the middle of a funeral pyre he'd built with sticks and dried grasses. After learning of Numa's passing, a dozen local men arrived to assist Nog. They sat together in silence, watching as the purple and orange flames faded to black.

Once back inside the cave and unable to sleep, Nog forced a thought in the darkness.

Still there?

Where else would I be, Nog?

Now content, Nog smiled, then instantly slipped into a deep sleep. A sleep without nightmares or fears, just a deep-seated connectedness to everything around him. A dream-filled sleep of strange beings, impossible structures and endless curiosity.

*

Sleeping in well beyond his usual time, Nog awoke with a start. He heard sounds. Scampering to the cave opening, he peeked outside to discover more than two dozen males, females, and children had assembled in front of the cave and were milling about aimlessly.

Nog ducked back inside and considered the situation. Glimpsing Numa's robe lying in his sleeping area, a thought formed.

Yes, Nog, said an inner voice. **It's your turn now. Comfort them. Show them beauty. Grow this community, for they are one within me.**

Nog took a deep breath. Two days ago, a task of this nature would have been unthinkable, but now he felt a mounting excitement. He moved to the robe and put it on, tying the jewelled bag to the belt as Numa had done. With no plan or idea what he might say, he headed for the door, only to stop abruptly. Something was calling. And it wasn't the voice of Numa this time. He looked around, finally focusing on the wall with the handprint. It was calling him, drawing him in like a magnet.

Moving quickly, he selected a bowl of powdered red ochre from Numa's paint supply, along with some water from a large misshapen bowl. He placed his right hand on the cool rockface and blew the paint powder through his left fist. After admiring the outline, he dabbed a little water on top to set the powder to a paste without any streaks or runs.

Finished, he cleaned off his hands and focused on one clear thought.

Are you with me?

The response was instant. ***Always.***

With a grin as wide as the horizon, Nog crawled from the cave, emerging between the two boulders. Taking a deep breath, he rubbed his hands together briskly, then set about to climb the shady side of the mushroom-esque monolith.

Arriving at the top of the red rocket, Nog carefully moved to the front edge. He gazed over the small crowd standing below, their necks craned, smiling back with acceptance and welcome.

For a brief moment, Nog assessed what he was about to leave behind. His old cave, his possessions, his past life. But no sadness arose. His mind was crystal clear. None of it mattered anymore. He was now part of something bigger. And although he had little understanding of what that might be, it felt crucial, essential and life-affirming. A feeling of history welled inside him, generations, ancient bonds rooted deeply in the planet's primeval soil.

Nog scanned the faces in the crowd, some content, others distraught over Numa's passing, and instantly knew what to say. It was innate. This was his time.

Raising his arms straight out from his sides, he smiled and announced, "Shaaa-rattt," then dropped them back to his sides with a snap. And there was much hugging.

SEVENTY-TWO

Friday, November 20, 7:35 a.m.
Phoenix General Hospital,
Room R2112

Sitting on the bed, Earl held Doe's cold face in his hands.

Doctor Higgins rushed in along with Nurse Morallas, quickly addressing a series of emergency checks and life signs. Higgins shook his head and looked up at the room's clock. "Time of death, 7:36 a.m. I'm so sorry, Earl. My condolences," he said, placing a comforting hand on Earl's shoulder.

Earl nodded, his expression blank and grey.

"Earl…" started Nurse Morallas. Then she simply hugged him, squeezing his shoulders for a long time before letting go.

"Thank you," said Earl, offering a shaky smile.

"Do you wish to stay a little longer?" asked Higgins.

"I, I don't think so. What will happen to the body? Where does it go?"

Higgins lowered his head. "Well, that's always a difficult one," he said. "As with all John Doe cases, the body will reside in our morgue for a few days until the next of kin, if any, can claim the body. Failing that, the state's policy is cremation."

"I see," said Earl solemnly, Doe's words crashing to the shore of his near-term memory. *This face must not be remembered.*

"Are there any specific requests?" said Higgins. "It appears you're the only one who knew him."

Earl stared at the body as Nurse Morallas pulled a top sheet over Doe's head. "Actually, I never met the man."

Morallas smiled as Higgins nodded in understanding.

"I need to go," said Earl, picking up his bag and heading for the door.

"Take care of yourself," said Nurse Morallas. Her lip trembled as she attempted a smile.

In the hall, Earl came to a quick halt. "Oh, Robbie. Yes, Robbie." Earl fumbled, then sighed. "Um, I have to go now."

Robbie acknowledged with a nod. "When will you be back, Mr. Earl?"

"Back? Oh! I'm afraid I won't be coming back, Robbie." Earl watched the guard's face shift as understanding overcame him.

Robbie paused to compose himself by counting ceiling tiles. "Well… I guess I better make some calls or something."

"Robbie, where I come from, Canada, it's common for people to hug each other, even strangers, even men to men. Would it be OK if…"

Robbie arched forward, extended his big arms, and engulfed Earl, pulling him in close. "Goodbye, Mr. Earl."

Earl patted the big man's lower back. "Goodbye, Mr. Robbie," he whispered through collapsed lungs. "Make me proud, OK?"

*

Earl leant against the wall at the back of the parking garage, between a laundry van and a steel-blue SUV, waiting for Mary-Lynn to answer her phone.

"Earl, this is an early surprise. Just stepped out of the shower. Everything OK?"

"Hi, Mary-Lynn…" Earl's voice was low and sombre; he paused as the lump returned to his throat. "He's gone."

"Oh, Earl. Oh, Earl. Where are you?"

"At the hospital. In the garage. I gotta get out of here."

Mary-Lynn broke down and began to cry. "Were you… with him?"

"Yeah, I…" Earl rubbed his eyes with his free hand. "I really could do with a… Wu hug."

"Oh, Earl."

At that moment, it was evident to Mary-Lynn that everything had changed. This was the end of the big story. God was dead. "I'm coming to get you, OK? Sit tight. I just need to make a few calls and excuses first, or quit… or something."

Mary-Lynn's comment triggered an idea in Earl's mind, a eureka moment. He craned his neck and stood up straight with purpose as a plan flickered to life.

"No, no, don't quit," he said. "In fact, bring your camera crew with you."

*

"Good morning, Rory," said Frank, stirring a coffee and staring out the window of the doctor's lounge.

"Not for everyone." MacMann grabbed a cup, poured his own, and then stepped back to the table to sit with Frank.

"Oh?" Frank questioned.

"John Doe. He's gone. Higgins just pronounced."

Frank hung his head, a sad sigh escaping his lips. "Does Earl know?"

"Aye, he was there."

"Oh, good. I mean, it's good someone was there."

MacMann stared coldly at Frank. "Anyway, there are bigger issues afoot. Our boy Earl's gone and sold us out."

SEVENTY-THREE

Friday, November 20, 8:22 a.m.
Phoenix General Hospital,
Parking Garage

A white panel van pulled up to the side of the hospital's main parking garage, a small satellite dish with the *First Edition* logo clamped to the luggage rail on the roof.

Mary-Lynn stepped down from the van's passenger side as Earl jogged out from the darkness of the garage. He engulfed her in a hug. Mary-Lynn grabbed Earl's head, bringing it close to hers, then kissed his lips repeatedly. As the pair untangled, the van's side door slid open, revealing James, the cameraman, eating a breakfast burrito.

"I brought everyone and everything we have. We can live-feed or go direct to tape, whatever you wish."

Earl hopped in the back of the van, shaking hands with James and nodding towards Andy in the driver's seat. The van, retro-fitted with enough electronics to microwave a man-sized set of testicles, had barely enough room to sidestep down the middle. Between the editing machines, recording devices, booms, lighting, light deflectors, microphones, and a vast array of cameras, there was nowhere to sit. Earl wedged his way to the back. "This looks safe."

Mary-Lynn shouted from the passenger seat. "Either kneel or sit on the floor. Grab hold of the metal shelf legs. They're attached to the van. By the way, where are we going?"

Earl wrapped his legs around a brace that held up a shelf laden with big cameras. "First, my hotel, around the back, kitchen entrance. I have to pick up some stuff from my room. It won't take long. Then a scenic drive."

Mary-Lynn looked back at Earl and raised an eyebrow. "I've got something you need to see," Earl added. "And, more importantly, something very important to tell you."

290

*

True to his word, Earl was mere minutes in his hotel room, returning with his roller bag, bulging with content.

"Moving out, Earl?" asked Mary-Lynn, puzzled at his need to bring all his luggage.

"Relocating for a bit." He offered a weak smile. "Andy? Can you take us to Cave Creek Regional Park? I just looked it up; it's an easy drive. Get on 17 north, and keep driving. It's just over an hour."

After 75 minutes of traffic-free driving, the van pulled into the park's deserted gravel parking area. Andy instinctively parked next to the blue porta-potty, believing a long day was ahead of them. Quick to jump out, Mary-Lynn opened the sliding side door for Earl. "How are you feeling?" she asked.

"Odd." Earl kicked at the gravel, raising a little dust. "I thought I was prepared for his death. I knew it was coming, and yet… I didn't see it coming. But, also, I'm relieved. I can still… feel him."

She smiled and rubbed his forearm up and down. "All natural feelings, Earl. Feelings! You know, those things we humans have."

He tried again to smile. "He wanted me to find myself and then find him. Somewhere out… there." Earl motioned his hands towards the vast expanse of land stretched out in front of them.

"That's why we're here?"

Earl nodded. "But first I'd like to go for a walk with you. I need to show you something. Will your boys be OK for a while, unsupervised?"

She laughed. "They've got snacks. They'll be fine." Mary-Lynn surveyed the enormity of the landscape before her eyes. "So, where are we going?"

"A little piece of heaven," Earl replied.

*

"What are you talking about? Earl would never sell us out." Frank leaned forward, his elbows on the small cafeteria table.

Aware of other people sitting in the lounge, MacMann whispered. "Do you remember this little table, Frank? This is where our plan came together."

"Your plan!" snapped Frank. "I seem to recall the words, 'Leave everything to me.'"

"Can't say I'm surprised to hear that."

291

Frank tried to personalize the moment. "Look, Rory…"

"Don't *look Rory* me, Sonny Jim. I've been flying solo for days. It's time I find out where you stand because *we* have a big fucking problem. Your golden boy's outed us to the media." MacMann was furious.

"What? Never!" replied Frank, quick to realize that this was obviously Earl's attempt to scare MacMann into bailing out.

"Oh, aye, and it gets better. Grey's given his gal-pal an exclusive tell-all, and that's exactly what he's gonna do. Tell *all*. He's gonna dump this whole thing on us, Frankie."

"I can't believe it. Who told you this?"

"Oh, you'd better believe it. I've got a reliable wee mole. Drop-dead accurate."

Frank pondered. It was clear that Earl's calculated leak had triggered MacMann's self-preservation mode. Now all he had to do was maintain pressure on the doctor before offering him a tiny opening. "If this is true, then you're in a heap of shit."

MacMann, eyes wide, put down his mug with a smack, launching steaming hot java into the air, then pointed a finger directly at Frank. "Me? I'm in shit? You run this place. You're solely responsible for what happens here, regardless of who initiates it. You're up to your arse hairs just like me, Mr. Shedmore."

"You're right about one thing, I am in charge. And when I conduct the investigation, it will be my conclusions and recommendations that the Board uses to affix blame and punishment to whoever's responsible."

"Don't be daft, ya pooner. You can't do that. You're only the acting admin. It'll go to the Exec Committee, then the Board. They're gonna fry you over the coals."

Frank found the moment exhilarating, strengthening. It was the first time he had ever felt capable of handling conflict, and he was relishing it. With his backbone straight, fingers entwined, and composure approaching jet pilot status, Frank squared up with MacMann. "Rory, that's not how the process works with a Chief Administrator in place."

"Aye, I'm aware, but we're absent one of those, so your ass is haggis."

"I see you're unaware of the Board's recent appointment?"

After a brief paralysis, MacMann's tall frame deflated. He exhaled, "When?"

"Yesterday… officially," said Frank, straight-faced.

MacMann nodded, breaking eye contact to stare at the microwave oven. "You know I'll never work again, right? They'll strip my licence."

Frank's chest deflated. "I don't want that to happen, Rory. And I think I know a way to ensure it doesn't."

"I see. You're Billy-big-balls now, are ya?" MacMann rapped his fingers on the plastic tabletop, still staring at the oven.

Speaking with legal precision, Frank summarized: "If Earl's gone to the press, as you say, then I'll be tasked with an investigation, initiated by the Board of Directors. My findings will be intentionally vague, blaming a series of random mistakes and odd coincidences. I'll ultimately announce a series of policy changes, including security protocols, privacy procedures and a few sacrificial terminations. The General will survive."

"And I won't. Correct?"

"If I'm not mistaken, Rory, you've been talking about retirement for some time." Frank steered the doctor towards the Get Out Of Jail Free card. "I'd suggest you make it common knowledge, so we can plan a nice going-away party. Perhaps even assist you, should you wish to maintain a private practice after leaving."

MacMann nodded, then started to laugh. "Aye lad, touché. Well done! Are ya sure there's no plaid running through those thin veins of yours?"

Frank remained calm. "I'm willing to go on record as being aware of your retirement plans long before Doe's arrival. Your departure, although oddly-timed, will be depicted as something unrelated to this incident. All I need is a suitably backdated letter of intent stating your desire to end your tenure at month-end. Your involvement in the John Doe matter could be spun as superficial."

MacMann thought for some time. He went through Frank's machinations in his mind, then rose from the table like a phoenix. "Yes, I remember sending you that letter, Frankie boy. I'll reprint a copy for you within the hour." His fake smile slipped into a sneer.

"That would be most helpful," said Frank, remaining in his seat. "I must have misplaced my original copy."

"Right, then. I'll be on my way. But before I go, perhaps I could write you a prescription, something for the pain?"

"What pain?" Frank looked up, puzzled.

"The carpal tunnel, lad," snapped MacMann. "Perfecting those backstabbing skills must have really fucked up your wrists." A little spittle escaped, landing in the middle of the small plastic table.

SEVENTY-FOUR

Friday, November 20, 10:15 a.m.
Cave Creek Regional Park

Earl led the way. Mary-Lynn held his hand during the more tenuous parts of the hike. The heat was overwhelming, far hotter than his previous visit with Orlando, the unfocused horizon rippling with mirages. Earl helped Mary-Lynn navigate several sandstone boulders then circled his way towards the south. "Not much further. Don't worry, there's shade up there."

Arriving at the same plateau as Earl and Orlando had visited, Mary-Lynn gripped Earl's hand tight as she stared at her phone in the other. "Earl, my phone has no bars. There's no signal out here. At least I had a weak one back at the parking lot."

"Wonderful, isn't it?" Earl smiled, pointing at the view as he walked toward the edge of the plateau. Mary-Lynn crinkled her nose and pursed her lips, implying a disconnected phone was somewhat less than wonderful. Following Earl to the perilous edge of the plateau, her frustration disappeared in an instant as the view ahead engulfed her senses. Her mind scrambled for the right words. She inhaled deeply. "Wow."

"Spoken like a seasoned reporter," laughed Earl. She punched him in the arm.

"This was the scene of my own personal barbeque," Earl said, pointing to a spot near the eastern edge. "I sat over there, in the open, with all those cosmic rays. Today, I think I'll sit over there, in the shade, if that's OK with you?"

Mary-Lynn followed Earl to the monolith's base, choosing a flat, sand-free spot to sit down. "Earl, this is magnificent. You can see forever."

Earl remembered his narrow-minded comment to Doe about cloudless skies. "Not quite forever, but a good twenty miles for sure." He nodded at the scene with approval.

Mary-Lynn, covering her face from the sun's gaze, looked to Earl. "I see why you'd want to show me this. Very inspiring."

"I'm not sure you do," said Earl. "I mean, inherent beauty aside, there's another reason I brought you here."

"Doe?"

"Partly. He's out here. Well, out there." Earl pointed toward the higher elevations, and the cliff faces dotted black by countless cave entrances.

Mary-Lynn could see that Earl's emotions were busting at the seams, pulling him in every direction. She understood grief, but there was something else, an emotion within Earl she couldn't pinpoint. She watched him slowly pace about, staring in one direction, then suddenly turning, moving to another spot, looking for something, looking beyond the scenery. "Are you alright? Do you want to sit down?"

"In a minute, yeah. I've got a lot to tell you."

"You're scaring me a little. Are you having a nervous breakdown? I think you should come sit with me."

"Doe came from here. They found him out here. Not the man in the hospital, but the entity inside him, hitching a ride."

"Yes, Earl, I've gathered that. And I understand why you want to be here, but…"

"Mary-Lynn, this is hard to explain. We're at a turning point, a crossroads."

"Are you dumping me?" She raised an eyebrow.

Earl sat down, his feet dangling perilously over the edge of the plateau. He smiled and shook his head. "The *we* I'm referring to is all of us, humankind. We're close to extinction, self-induced oblivion. But it doesn't have to happen."

"Earl, please, just get away from the edge. You're freaking me out. Come sit with me, tell me what Doe said. Tell me what he wants us to do?"

Earl paused for a moment in thought, then joined Mary-Lynn in the shade. "It's OK, Miss Wu. I'm not losing my mind. There's a lot you don't know about this whole story. And about me… the *old me.*"

"Tell me."

Earl considered all the entry points for his story, but there was no suitable spot to dive in. His childhood, failed marriage, the last-minute trip here with no serious intent to work. He could start with Doe's words and what comes next, but out of context, without hearing them come directly from Doe, they sounded ridiculous, even to him. "I don't know where to start."

"OK, then tell me why you wanted the TV crew here today. What does that have to do with all of this?" She nodded toward the horizon.

"It's simple, really. This day has two possible outcomes. One, where you help me broadcast Doe's message to the people of the world before it's too late. The other, where I reveal what I'm caught up in, then you slap my face and walk out."

*

Trying Earl's phone to no avail, Orlando figured Earl was still at the hospital, and the signal blockers were wreaking havoc with his phone's reception. After two more calls, Orlando gave up and, with no alternatives, left a voicemail.

> Hey, Earl, it's me. I'm gonna be busy for a few hours. Truth is, I can't leave that big dummy Warren to fend for himself. He's gonna get killed. Now, don't go freaking out. I'll be fine. I'll call you when I'm done. Look, I'm sure you're going through hell right now, and you don't need me adding to it, so just focus on Doe. I'll be fine. You take care, Earl.

Ending the call, Orlando made a point of turning off his phone, so GPS couldn't track his location. Turning onto the interstate, he checked his watch for the fourth time.

*

In the press room back at the hospital, Frank walked to the podium, followed by Higgins. The usual crowd of reporters and journalists looked on, atypically quiet, sensing an ominous change.

"Good morning, everyone," said Frank, making no eye contact with anyone. "It is my sad duty to inform you of the passing of John Doe at seven thirty-six this morning. Present was our liaison, Mr. Earl Grey. Mr. Grey has asked me to speak on his behalf today as he is having… difficulty with the news."

Frank paused for a few breaths as the room remained in respectful silence. "The attending physician, Dr. Higgins, will answer your questions as Dr. MacMann is also absent today, making arrangements for his upcoming retirement." Frank gestured toward the young physician, then stepped away from the podium.

"Good morning, everyone. My name is Paul Higgins. This morning John Doe succumbed to his injuries and ailments. As Mr. Shedmore said, time of death was recorded at 7:36 a.m. I'll try my best to answer your questions."

An NBC News reporter in the front row cleared his throat. "Doctor, this is indeed sad news. Do you have any more information about his overall injuries or how they came to be? Also, what were his last words?"

Higgins nodded. "Mr. Doe had severe internal injuries, the type you'd expect to find after a horrific car accident or other high-impact events. The damage was ubiquitous and, in many areas, irreparable. In layman's terms, Mr. Doe's body was not functional. However, remarkably, his ability to think and convey ideas appeared to be unaffected by his physical condition, which, as I said, was not viable or sustainable."

"Is this a miracle, Dr. Higgins?"

"It's unexplainable. I've never seen a miracle, medical or otherwise, but I've never seen this either. The body and Mr. Doe's... essence... seemed totally independent of each other."

The reporter nodded, his pencil vibrating as he recorded the doctor's comments in shorthand. "And his last words?"

"I wasn't witness to his last words. Only Mr. Grey was present." He paused briefly, glancing at Frank. "Mr. Doe's body has been moved to the hospital morgue."

Higgins struggled through two more questions related to the philosophy of Cartesian Duality, the theory of mind-body independence, and the ability for either to exist without the other. Sensing a theme, the young doctor gracefully backed out, yielding the podium back to Frank.

"Before closing," Frank announced, "an additional speaker has requested a moment with you all to comment on his recent interaction with John Doe. This impromptu and unplanned meeting took place yesterday, and our guest was privy to the insight and mind of John Doe. May I present to you... Monsignor Matthew Bellecourt."

*

"Slap you? Earl, what's goin' on?"

"Mary-Lynn, it's time I told you everything."

An ominous look highjacked her face.

Earl's head felt tight; not a headache, more like a swollen brain or contracting cranium, growing pressure aching to explode. "I haven't lied to you. I couldn't. But there's some stuff I... left out."

Mary-Lynn turned slightly to Earl. "Get it all out, mister, clean the slate."

"OK, here goes."

Earl began by detailing his flight to Arizona and his unwanted appointment to media liaison via malevolent lottery win. Mary-Lynn laughed as he revealed his actual function at the *Telegraph*, his mediocre journalistic career and his desire to perpetuate an all-expense-paid vacation.

"I tried to resign, but MacMann and Frank had pre-confirmed everything with my snake of an editor and already booked the first presser with no time for me to bail out."

"I called it!" Mary-Lynn thrust her open hand into the air.

"I thought I could beat them at their own game. But then it all kinda got away from me."

"But… you never quit?"

"No." Earl broke eye contact and shook his head shamefully. "It wasn't long before I found genuine joy and purpose in talking with Doe. I didn't want it to end. I'm so stupid, Mary-Lynn." He closed his eyes tight and lay back against the huge monolith.

"Earl, I've only known you for a few days, but I know you're a good soul. When we first met, you looked into my eyes, in front of the whole world, and said, 'This is about a poor sick man in a hospital bed'. I would have had your baby at that moment, Mr. Grey." She chuckled.

Earl went on to explain Doe's message of oneness, timelessness and the flip-book universe, and as he spoke, Mary-Lynn soaked up every word. "I remember," said Earl with a broad smile, "when Doe finally revealed who he really was, the moment we actually met for the first time."

Mary-Lynn's eyes went wild with curiosity.

"I am the singularity, he said, just like that, Mary-Lynn, like he was choosing a pizza topping."

She squealed. "Oh my… *God?*"

"Not God, Mary-Lynn. *Everything.* And, here's the best bit, when he says everything, he means everything, every photon, every molecule, every slice of pepperoni. He is the universe. You and me, all together, we're part of him. We… are… him."

Mary-Lynn shivered in the heat. She squeezed Earl's forearms while gently bouncing with excitement.

Earl continued. "He told me he'd come to Earth to meet me, and he'd been trying to establish contact with me my whole life. Apparently, I'm oblivious to signs."

"But why you?"

"Great question, one I'm still struggling with," said Earl. "JD said I was the right person to deliver his message, whatever that means." Earl proceeded to explain the details of Doe's plan. How he intended to alter humanity's course, hopefully ensuring its future and allowing sufficient time for evolution to take humankind to the next level.

"And JD's death wasn't an end, Mary. It was a beginning. My journey begins here, *now*."

Mary-Lynn probed his eyes, looking for clues. "You're... leaving?"

Earl nodded. "Not for long. You see, apparently, I'm not ready yet. I must have an open mind to connect with him. I must lose myself... and then find my true self out there, in a cave." He pointed to the endless rolling landscape, complete with hills and rock outcrops. "Doe said, when my mind is ready, we will be connected again."

"There are thousands of caves, Earl. How will you know?" Mary-Lynn scanned the horizon, her face scrunched with confusion.

"Huge dick!"

"'Scuze me?"

"Near the cave. Doe said there's this unmistakable monolith. Looks like a big dick..."

Mary-Lynn raised an inquisitive eyebrow. "Did he say how long all this would take, how long you'd be gone?"

"No."

She threw her arms around Earl, holding tight until he shattered the moment. "How's my deodorant holding out?"

Mary-Lynn pushed him away at the chest. "Jerk."

They sat in silence, crossed-legged, staring at the hills and valleys and the black dotted pockmarks of the distant cliffs. "So, what happens now?" Mary-Lynn said, her eyes locking on Earl's. "Where do we go from here?"

The sun crept around the front side of the monolith, casting a halo over Earl's reddish-brown hair. He smiled and took in a deep breath. "Well, Miss Wu, since I haven't been slapped, let's hike back and tell Andy and James to set up their cameras right there in the parking lot. We've got one hell of a story to tell, don't you think?"

SEVENTY-FIVE

Seemingly dropped in the middle of nowhere, the Black Canyon Greyhound Track stuck out like a sore thumb. Few visitors ventured this far north of Phoenix but for the occasional hiker or ATV rider. But certainly not to attend greyhound races at the long-shuttered and crumbling facility. Now abandoned for over twenty years, the desert had reclaimed the actual racetrack, invisible under weeds and brush. A few remaining light standards curved around unseen corners or hidden straightaways, now just rusty monuments to a bygone era. Most structures had collapsed. The only exception was the white-washed cinderblock walls of the main building and viewing stands. Inside, theatre-style seating rose thirty rows to a foyer that once housed betting windows and a small café.

Warren had arrived at the dog track near eleven. An hour before Del-Monte's planned arrival. Fidgety and nervous, he paced about the abandoned building, rehearsing his lines. His FBI handlers had spent hours going over instructions and concealing the microphone transmitter underneath a state-of-the-art Kevlar vest, unnoticeable beneath his plaid button-down shirt. Warren rehearsed his lines as well as the traps he needed to spring, knowing he'd only have one chance to say what the Feds needed him to say.

Warren tugged at the right side of his shirt near the beltline, the hip holster for the Sig digging into his skin. Convinced the bulge was noticeable, he flared the shirt out, hoping it would settle in a nondescript way without revealing an outline. He was sweating. The viewing gallery was stifling hot, the windows facing the track broken for years. Walking up and down the concrete steps several times, he studied the room dynamics for hiding spots should he need one. Each row was lined with folded-up plastic chairs bolted to the concrete floor. Partial cover, but Warren knew most handguns would shatter the seats like glass.

A sudden wind whipped across the flat track area and into the viewing stands, stirring up garbage and dried brush. Warren returned to ground level and rechecked the envelope in his back pocket, making sure the five thousand dollars were still there. *This is a bad idea*, he thought, *possibly my worst ever.*

Agent Cooper had stressed the need for Warren to remain calm and natural.

"You've got to get him to talk," Agent Cooper had said. "Ask him why *this* hit, why *this* man, what was so important that he had to come to Phoenix personally. Ask him if you can be of further assistance after he leaves, what else you could do for him."

Warren's mind flooded like a root cellar. Too many instructions, too many things to go wrong. He glanced around for the right place to sit, settling on the first row, an aisle seat in the middle of the viewing gallery. This way, regardless of which entrance Del-Monte chose, there was a clear path of retreat.

Warren glanced at his watch for the eighteenth time – five minutes to noon. His pulse quickened as more sweat formed on his forehead. *I'm gonna die*, he thought.

The sound of Del-Monte's BMW arriving was distinct and unmistakable – the low throaty rumble of a European muffler. Seconds later, Del-Monte entered left of the stands, spying Warren instantly and holding ground. After looking up the stairs and into the rafters for signs of a trap, he took a few more steps, halting by the first giant window and standing in a pile of broken glass. A disgusted expression erupted as he examined his shoes for damage.

"Hello, Warren," Del-Monte said casually, atypically dressed in jeans, a black tee-shirt and a light windbreaker, unzipped and blowing in the breeze. A black logoless baseball cap covered his head, dark reflective sunglasses wrapped around to each ear. Only his shoes were unchanged, butter-brown Oxford's, Gucci's best.

"Hello, sir, good to see you again," Warren said, rising to stand.

"Yes, yes. I suppose it is. However, I've no plans to conduct this meeting under the threat of violence, so I suggest you remove that gun from your side and toss it somewhere far away. I'm unarmed, and until you're the same, I will not conduct business."

SEVENTY-SIX

Friday, November 20, 11 a.m.
Phoenix General Hospital,
Media Room

"Good morning, everyone, and may God bless you on this beautiful day."
Monsignor Bellecourt gripped the sides of the podium with two steady hands.
"I asked Mr. Shedmore if I might say a few words, and he very graciously agreed."

Frank nodded.

"Through an unusual set of circumstances, I was permitted a few moments
with Mr. Doe last night, and I wanted to impart..."

"Father..." interrupted a reporter, "...does this represent the official position of
the Catholic Church? Are you speaking on the record?"

"Ah, well, not as such."

A murmur vibrated through the room.

"Truth be known, I *was* sent here by the Church and instructed to meet with
Mr. Doe to verify or denounce his claim of divinity. Last night, I was fortunate to
spend a few minutes with the man," Bellecourt paused and inhaled all the oxygen
in the room, "...and I can indeed verify his credibility."

The crowd erupted – a verbal surge of ubiquitous sound.

"Please, everyone, please. Let me explain."

A begrudging lull came to the storm.

"I'm not here to express the official position of the Catholic Church. This is
more about Mr. Grey and what he's been trying to relate to you all week. I was just
lucky enough to verify it with my own eyes and ears."

"You, a priest, just confirmed that John Doe *is* God," a reporter yelled
indignantly.

Bellecourt frowned and cleared his throat. "What... is a God?" he exclaimed
into the microphone like a Baptist preacher.

A blanket of silence fell upon the room.

302

Bellecourt dug deep inside himself, mustering a memory, a sermon he'd once saved, never believing the day would ever arrive. "What is a God?" he repeated, his voice echoing. "Tell me, what's the likelihood that all of you would agree on the answer to my question? Zero," he shouted. "Each of you has differing opinions gathered from sacred books, writings and upbringings. Your needs are different; thus, your expectations of God differ as well. Look around you. In this room alone, you'll find those who believe in a personal God, or a vengeful God, or a stubborn God, or a merciful God who brings justice and peace. Some of you require a God of pure goodness, leaving evil to be explained elsewhere, perhaps in the hearts of man. But others need a God who created good *and* evil, even a devil. Some of your Gods prepare a place for you after death; others prepare two places. Some of your Gods smite your enemies, while others offer olive branches. But there's one commonality throughout. Do you know what that is, my friends?"

The reporters looked around, hoping someone might have an answer or was willing to engage in an impromptu ecumenical debate.

"All of your Gods represent the beginning." Bellecourt let his words hang in the air for a few seconds. "All of them represent creation, the alpha, the life, the universe, yes, *everything*." He held quiet, letting the line sink in.

"OK…?" A reporter broke the wordless stalemate.

"The man I met, the body in that hospital bed, the *man* you call John Doe, was not God."

Further uproar ensued. "You just confirmed that he was."

Bellecourt continued undaunted. "No. The man in that hospital bed never made that claim. That crushed and broken body never spoke with anyone. I met someone – *something* – else."

Confusion engulfed the room.

"The entity that Mr. Grey and I met was a mind, with no physical presence in the room whatsoever."

"You're saying the mind you met, and the person Mr. Grey spoke with, was not physically here," stated a radio reporter in deep baritones, adding ominous overtones to the inquiry.

"I am."

"And you're saying that mind, was the mind of God?"

"God by our collective definition, yes."

"Father?" asked a journalist near the back of the room, hopping up and down to be seen. "As a Catholic, is it your position that you met God, here at the hospital, in possession of a patient's body?"

"That is what I experienced, yes."

"And this God was the same Christian God you worship?"

The silence was deafening, one collective breath held as if the last lottery ball was falling.

Bellecourt leaned into the mic. "No! It was *the* God, all of our Gods, a beginning with no end, a timeless entity, a body to which we all belong and always will. This God has no religion. This God was… *everything*."

Boom!

Phones dialled, runners ran, cameras cameraed, and writers wrote.

Frank leaned in toward the priest, cupping his hands around his mouth, and whispered, "And so begins World War III."

Bellecourt turned to Frank. "Not if Earl and I can help it."

SEVENTY-SEVEN

Friday, November 20, 11:45 a.m.
Black Canyon Greyhound Track

Three turns after exiting Interstate 17, Orlando cruised down a dusty back-road, drifting past his ultimate destination several times, scoping out the area. Driving past the facility, Orlando eyed the empty parking lots, waves of sand, interspersed with bare spots of heaved concrete. He noted a large open section in the fence near the main entrance and signs of recent activity surrounding the opening. Most tire tracks appeared to belong to dirt bikes or ATVs heading north toward the Black Hills. However, a couple of deeper car tracks ran straight toward the central facility.

On his third pass of the racetrack, Orlando turned the limo in to the grounds via the makeshift entrance and drove cautiously toward the main facility. He swore each time the limo vaulted over a concrete parking barrier buried under the sand or craggy bush.

Believing Warren and Del-Monte would meet at the back of the main facility, hidden from the road, Orlando felt secure parking in front of the main doors. As he stepped from the limo, he noted the complete absence of tire tracks other than his own. Moving slowly, he edged around the limo towards the building, checking every sightline and hiding spot. *After all*, considered Orlando, *Del-Monte probably brought help*. After adjusting his jeans and baseball cap, he removed his revolver from its holster. Then, unzipping the fanny pack, he double-checked the speed-loaders to ensure he had instant access.

Other than the boarded-up entrance doors, the entire front of the building was white cinder block, covered in graffiti, a faint outline of the original lettering still visible along the length of the wall. Only two words remained prominent, painted over many times, welcoming all to the DOG CRACK.

Edging down the length of the building, Orlando stopped at the first corner. He dropped to his hands and knees, then executed a ground-level peek around the

305

building's edge, a valuable skill learned from watching action movies. Nothing. Standing up, he moved on, stepping lightly down the short, shaded side of the building to the next corner, which led to the track and viewing stands. Another low-level peek revealed two vehicles, as expected, at the far end of the stands. The Jeep appeared empty, but the BMW's windows were tinted black, so there was no way to tell if anyone was inside.

Orlando stayed low, revolver in one hand, the fingers of his other hand tracing the block wall for balance. After twenty feet, he arrived at the central opening – a massive façade, once glass-enclosed, tiered seating now exposed to the elements. His first glimpse was of Del-Monte, facing him dead on, about forty feet away. Orlando snapped his head back from the edge and stood still, his back against the concrete block. Nothing happened and continued not to happen.

Inching back to the edge, he angled his head, his right eye far enough out to see inside. Del-Monte was talking near the exit on the far end of the gallery, and Warren's back was visible, standing twenty feet from Del-Monte, in front of the first row of seats. *I've got a clean shot*, thought Orlando, forcing his breathing to slow while examining the gun, ensuring it was jam-free, the cylinder spinning with ease. Cocking the hammer in the firing position, he moved back to the opening and raised the gun to eye level.

Del-Monte inched closer to Warren, who, for some inexplicable reason, had just placed his gun on the ground and kicked it off to the side.

Orlando's aim was dead on. His finger inched to the thin metal trigger, then hesitated. Seconds passed as the wind whipped and faded. Then Orlando gently removed his finger from the trigger and placed it back in the safe position along the side of the gun. *A prudent move*, he thought to himself as chills vibrated down his spine from the cold gun barrel now lodged in the back of his neck.

*

"Alright, guys, look alive. We've got a lot of work to do." Mary-Lynn clapped her hands as if calling a kindergarten class to attention. On the walk back to the van, Mary-Lynn had suggested that Earl record three sixty-minute interviews to video rather than broadcast live. James would then edit the videos as much as possible using the equipment in the back of the van. Once complete, they would offer the first part of the story to the TV networks the following day. Part one would be a teaser, vague questions implying profound answers to come. The second and third segments would entice networks, cable channels and maybe a few fledgling internet news sites to pick up the story.

James set up the camera near the parking lot, ensuring the porta-potty was out of frame. After which, he positioned two chairs so Mary-Lynn and Earl could chat overlooking Arizona's panoramic desert landscape. Andy would operate a second handheld camera, giving them two vantage points and a slicker edit.

Mary-Lynn sat with Andy and James and explained what was about to happen and that they were free to leave if they wanted. She also revealed that she'd resigned that morning, right after Earl's call. Neither man was concerned, figuring that the Doe story, if true, would make them both legends. But James did voice a nagging concern.

"Earl," James asked, seemingly puzzled. "If you want the world to hear this story, why this approach? Why not just call another press conference? Explain it live."

Earl was quick with an answer. "I've already seen what the press does with my words. Your own employer used the headline, 'Foreign Reporter Grills God On U.S. Soil'. My words have been chopped up, re-edited, and even overdubbed. And the press never runs the important parts, only the most sensationalized. They even add commentaries and new segments produced entirely out of context. In this world, James, the medium really is the message."

"Earl's right," Mary-Lynn added. "And we must control that message – all of it. If there's editing to be done, it will be ours. This interview will be aired intact." With that, she grabbed Earl by the hand and walked him over to the chairs.

"OK, Earl, here's the deal. Just be yourself and speak from the heart. Speak directly to me. Forget the cameras are there."

"Gotcha," said Earl, rolling his head around, loosening his stiff neck muscles.

"Alright, guys," shouted Mary-Lynn. "Let's do this thing."

*

Orlando instinctively lowered his gun, bringing the hammer back to safety, then letting the revolver fall to the dirt. Glancing over his right shoulder, he noted that nothing – such as getting shot in the head – happened, so he shifted, turning all the way around. The view was much worse from this direction. A large black gun barrel hovered an inch away from his nose. The barrel was attached to an equally large assault rifle with a long-curved magazine jutting out at the bottom. Attached to the gun was a man and, although pretty much every man was big to Orlando, this one was a truck. Tactical gear, flak jacket and pants with a thousand pockets.

The man didn't speak but motioned with one arm for Orlando to move. With no desire to debate the matter, Orlando followed the silent instruction. Stepping past the man, Orlando walked back toward the corner of the building. Then, after turning right, he met several more gentlemen in flak gear, all of whom encouraged him to lie down on the dirt and keep all movements to sub-atomic distances.

*

After two hours of answering Mary-Lynn's leading questions, Earl was getting into the swing of the interview.

Mary-Lynn had expertly led him down specific paths while avoiding others or mentally filing them for later use. Earl bounced from memory to memory, subject to subject, at times drifting into silence, thinking of Doe's words, still fresh in his mind.

"Earl?" she asked on a break.

He was miles away, staring at the blue hills in the distance. "Hmm?"

"This is going great, but something's nagging at me. Anyone can see you're sincere and that you've gone through a life-altering event. But what's missing is collaboration. What, if anything, can you tell the audience that they'd accept as factual? How can you prove you didn't make this all up or that you're not crazy?"

Earl shook his head. "I don't know what to say."

"Maybe this'll help a little," said James, flipping through his phone messages.

"Whatcha got?" asked Mary-Lynn as she approached James.

"Take a look." He handed her the phone. "The media's going nuts."

Mary-Lynn took the phone, reading the first few Breaking News emails.

'Senior Official Breaks With Catholic Church.'

'Monsignor Claims Meeting With GOD.'

'Priest Confirms The Almighty Was Present At The Phoenix Hospital Incident.'

Her head shot up. "Holy shit. Um, Earl?"

SEVENTY-EIGHT

Friday, November 20, 12:05 p.m.
Black Canyon Greyhound Track

"Kick it over there, as far as you can," said Del-Monte, pointing to Warren's gun on the floor. "It's not that I don't trust you," he paused, "OK, well, I guess that's exactly what it is, but whatever."

Warren remained calm-ish. "Sorry. I forgot it was there." He gingerly set the gun on the concrete floor then sideswiped it with his foot, sending it spinning into a pile of glass and debris.

"Very good." Del-Monte moved closer to Warren, his hawkish eyes scanning for the slightest movement. "Let's make this quick, OK? I've got a long trip ahead of me."

"Of course," Warren replied with a warble.

"Well?" asked Del-Monte.

"Oh, the money, right." Warren reached behind with his left hand, pulling the envelope from his back pocket. "It's all there. You wanna count it?"

"Of course not," replied Del-Monte, scanning the periphery again.

The two men were six feet apart, but Warren made no effort to step forward. Arching over with his arm straight out, he tentatively held the envelope in mid-air.

Del-Monte stepped forward and snatched the envelope, immediately stashing it in his jacket pocket.

"I'm really sorry about all this, sir. You paid me to finish a job, and I didn't. I didn't kill our guy like you asked me to."

Del-Monte stared through Warren. "What? What are you... doing?"

"Sir?"

"What are you babbling about?"

Warren shivered. "Just nervous. I don't like disappointing you. Just wanted to apologize for messing up the hit you hired me for."

Del-Monte raised a suspicious eyebrow.

Warren continued, "I'm annoyed at myself for screwing up the hit. I wanted to impress you. I was kinda hoping you'd have more jobs for me, you know – stuff I could do for you while you're out of town?"

Del-Monte looked around the big viewing area, taking time to focus on blind corners and half walls. He sniffed the air. "Warren, I only hire professionals. You are not a professional. You are an idiot."

"I honestly thought the guy was dead."

"Dead? You mean after you didn't shoot him?"

"Stuff went wrong. But rest assured, I covered everything for you. There's no trace of you ever being here."

"Ah, no trace – like there's no video placing me at the hospital, right?"

Warren stood silent and confused.

"I watched the DVD you gave me, Warren."

"Are you happy with the result, sir?"

"Oh, it's delightful. But that's right, you haven't seen it. Would you like to borrow it?"

"Um."

"Well, I'll save you the trouble. It's roughly three hours long and chock-full of priests."

"Priests? Meaning you?"

"No. Sadly, I don't seem to appear on one single frame of video. But, rest assured, it's full of other priests. All of them prancing about the halls, meeting in various offices or the cafeteria. Two adventure-packed days within the priesthood. Why there's even a cool bit where they all get together with a nun and pray. I was spellbound, Warren."

"I… I don't understand."

"I'm not on the fucking DVD, you idiot. No trace! No evidence of my visit. I'm guessing you kept those bits to blackmail me with or maybe to send to the cops."

"What? No, never. I'm so confused." Warren scrambled for a foothold. "But the backup drive is gone, so even if you're not on the DVD, there's nothing left of your visit. No other copies were made, I promise you."

"I'm tired of this, tired of you. In my entire life, I've never come across anyone so… imbecilic."

With that, Del-Monte moved his right hand inside his jacket and produced a revolver. In one swift move, he took two steps forward while raising the gun. "Bye-bye, dummy."

Time stood still as a booming voice descended from the heavens, echoing throughout the viewing stands.

"Freeze, FBI. Drop your weapon."

Del-Monte whipped his head upward toward the foyer as three tactical agents emerged from old betting booths, rifles trained directly on his body.

Del-Monte glanced at Warren, "Motherfucker!" then swung his arm up towards the tactical team, squeezing off one ear-piercing round after another.

The noise was deafening. Warren dove for cover on the floor of the second row as agents wildly returned fire.

Del-Monte ducked behind the first row of seats, emptied his gun's cylinder and reloaded. He reached over the seats, fired three more shots, then scampered up the first two concrete steps and down the row toward Warren, who lay face-up on the ground, knees raised to protect himself.

Del-Monte dropped low, using the seatbacks as a shield, and raised his gun, levelling it on Warren's prone body. Once again, the shots were deafening, in rapid succession, one, two, three, followed by four, five and six. In mere seconds, Warren emptied his shiny new revolver, clamped between his hands and fired through his open legs into Del-Monte.

Del-Monte's body slid down two steps and rolled to a stop. Then, everything went quiet.

SEVENTY-NINE

Endless seconds later...

Time accelerated to normal speed as two FBI agents bounded down the concrete steps, descending on Del-Monte's body like baboons on a Twinkie. Agent Cooper hurdled over several rows of seats and reached Warren in seconds.

"Hey Coop," said Warren, lying flat on his back, staring at the ceiling.

"Were you hit?"

Warren patted down his body, looking for holes. He shook his head. "Del-Monte?"

"Dead. And handcuffed."

Warren laughed in relief. "Good. Can't be too sure."

"Would you mind telling me where you got that other gun? The revolver?" asked a flustered Agent Cooper. "All of us took a collective shit when you kicked the Sig away."

Warren raised his arm off the floor so he could see his gun, holding it above his face. "I like my new gun. Feels good. No brass flying around. Very clean."

Agent Cooper slowly shook his head and stood up from his crouch. "What a mess." He grimaced. "Harris, update?"

A large, heavily-armoured man kneeling over Del-Monte's body replied, "I called it in. There's a wagon on the way with a clean-up crew."

"Forensics?"

"Also, on the way."

"Where's Caldwell?"

"Up in the foyer, with the prisoner."

Agent Cooper keyed the microphone on his chest. "Caldwell, bring down our guest."

Agent Cooper's radio squawked. "Roger that."

From his prone position, Warren could hear scuffling and awkward steps. Then a voice, escorting another much louder voice down the stairs. "Christ, is he dead? Tell me he isn't dead, you fuck! I could have stopped this. Where is he?"

Warren smiled at the sound of Orlando's expletive-laden rant.

Hands cuffed behind his back, Orlando stared down the aisle at Warren's body lying parallel to the seats, unmoving. "Is he…"

"Hey, buddy, nice of you to drop by. I figured you couldn't stay away," said Warren, popping his head up just high enough to see Orlando.

"You stupid piece of shit!" Orlando tried to pace, but a large uniformed arm held him in place. "I thought you were…"

"I'm fine, man. Everything's under control."

"Everything under control? You idiot. You could have got yourself dead."

With Agent Cooper's assistance, Warren stood up. "Never in danger, my friend," he said, unbuttoning his shirt in the middle, revealing grey body armour.

Orlando rolled his head in astonishment. "And if he'd shot you in the head? Bad guys shoot people in the head, Warren. Or didn't your new pal here tell you that?"

Warren scrunched up his face and turned his head to Agent Cooper. "Is that true?"

Agent Cooper shrugged innocently. "You can uncuff him," he said, nodding to the big agent holding Orlando in place. After raising a skeptical eyebrow, the agent rummaged for a key.

"Yeah," said Orlando. "Damn right. And I'll have my gun back too."

"You're not getting your gun back," said Agent Cooper dispassionately.

"What? That's my private property. You got no right."

Agent Cooper rolled his eyes. "The gun is our property now, confiscated at the site of a felony. Besides, a two-time loser like you should be thanking your pal Warren here. He's the one who figured you'd show up and refused to cooperate unless you got immunity from prosecution. And you should be thanking Agent Caldwell here for stopping you before you shot Montagna. If you did, we couldn't have honoured Warren's deal," said Agent Cooper.

Orlando paused to process the details embedded in Agent Cooper's words. "Who the hell's Montagna?"

"The guy you knew as Anthony Del-Monte…" explained Agent Cooper, "… is actually Vincent Montagna. Biggest crime boss in the Midwest."

Orlando looked down at the dead guy on the floor covered in dust. "That's the biggest crime boss in the Midwest?"

"Was."

Orlando turned to Warren and kicked him. "You idiot!"

Warren nodded, looking at his feet. "Yep."

"Mr. Peel agreed to enter the witness protection program in exchange for his testimony after the arrest of Montagna," said Agent Cooper. "He also agreed to work with us on this takedown, wearing a wire to get Montagna's confession."

"Witness protection program, huh?" said Orlando, pulling down a seat and settling in.

"Told them I wanted to live in Orlando." Warren smiled.

Orlando rolled his eyes. "So, you're letting my boy walk?" he asked Agent Cooper.

"That's the plan."

"OK, but wait…" said Orlando, trying to work everything out. "Something's missing. Del-Monte, or whatever you called him…"

"Vincent Montagna. Runs the second-largest crime family in America, stretching from his base in Chicago, all the way to California," said Agent Cooper.

Orlando looked back at Montagna's dead body and squinted.

"So… who the hell's John Doe?"

"Giovani Amicarelli," said Agent Cooper, unzipping his jacket. "Big shot mobster based in California. Fingers stretching as far as Texas. Big golf nut. Spends more time playing than running the family business. He used to be part of Montagna's stable but bailed out and went rogue several years ago. We've had our guys in California tailing him for months… then all of a sudden, he disappears."

Orlando was stunned. "The guy in the hospital room… the guy Earl's been speaking with… the guy who's got the entire world hanging on a string… is a mob boss?"

"The irony's delicious, huh?" said Agent Cooper with a smirk.

"And you knew this?" said Orlando turning to Warren.

"No, I didn't. I didn't even know his name. He was just some dude in a fancy suit."

"This is nuts," said Orlando. "The press is gonna freak. Everyone's gonna freak. Oh, Christ, they'll fry poor Earl alive."

Agent Cooper shook his head slowly. "They'll never know. Your hospital saviour stays anonymous. When he passes, they'll give him a nameless cremation and dump the ashes."

"How can you be so sure?" said Orlando.

The agent grinned. "We've had a well-placed informant inside the hospital the whole time. A very loyal and… patriotic young man."

"So, you're gonna allow the entire world to go on thinking the guy's God when he's actually a mob leader?" Orlando struggled to find the right words. "That's messed up."

"Is it?" said Agent Cooper. "I see no harm. John Doe's message isn't incendiary. He doesn't promote hatred or religious division. He just says we should all get along because we're connected. Seems OK to me. Look, if we reveal that Montagna came down here to put a hit on Amicarelli, then died in some mysterious shoot-out, there's gonna be a holy war between mob families."

"So?" said Orlando. "Let 'em wipe each other out."

"It's the innocent that suffer in mob wars, Orlando. Trust me, I've seen a few."

"Kinda playing God, aren't you?" said Orlando.

Agent Cooper chuckled. "Wouldn't be the first time."

*

Orlando received a stern warning from Agent Cooper, which included the direct threat of jail time should he ever reveal the happenings of the day.

As the FBI concluded with Warren, Orlando stepped up beside him. "You went out and bought the exact same gun as mine?" he whispered.

"It was your advice, man."

"Dude, that's messed."

Warren laughed. "I'm heading back into town. The G-men want my official statement, specifically about how I didn't shoot anybody."

Orlando nodded. "Alright. Find me when you're done. You owe me a beer, remember."

*

As Orlando drove closer to the city, processing the events of the last few days in his mind, he turned on his cellphone and speed-dialled Earl. The call went straight to voicemail. Worried, Orlando tried Mary-Lynn's number, but it too went straight to voicemail. He hung up without leaving a message.

"Goddamit, what's going on?" he shouted at no one.

EIGHTY

Friday, November 20, sundown.
Cave Creek Regional Park

Mary-Lynn and Earl spent a few minutes dissecting the impact of Bellecourt's announcement. Both were thrilled with the added authenticity and validation the Monsegnior had injected. Mary-Lynn decided additional interview footage was needed where Earl would describe the exact moment of Bellecourt's conversion in emotional detail. Once complete, she happily declared the interview over just as the sun slipped behind the nearest rock outcrop.

"We've got a huge night ahead of us, Earl," said Mary-Lynn, packing up her equipment. "Plus, we're on West Coast time. It's gonna be an all-nighter if we plan to launch the teaser tomorrow."

"Why the urgency? Why not take a day to polish it?" asked Earl.

"Oh no, we need to strike while Bellecourt's revelation is still front page. It's gotta be tomorrow. It's got to be part of this news cycle."

"OK, you're the boss." Earl winked. "Well, I guess that just leaves the one task I've been delaying all afternoon."

Earl removed his Blackberry, frowning at the signal meter as it toggled between zero and one bar. He dialled Orlando's number, then closed his eyes in frustration as the call went straight to voicemail. "Damn it." He hung up.

"What is it?" asked Mary-Lynn, stepping closer.

"I wanted… needed… to say goodbye to Orlando before I left. But he didn't answer."

"Leave him a message."

"I can't. After everything we've been through, I can't just leave a voicemail and walk off into the desert." Earl drew a deep, controlled breath, then let it out slowly.

Mary-Lynn put her hands on his shoulders. "I will call him, OK? Just tell me what you want to say."

"That's just it; how can I possibly put it in words? If I heard his voice, it would be easier. I think… I mean, how do you tell someone they're a true friend, and they've changed your life immeasurably?"

"What you just said sounds pretty good to me."

Earl nodded slowly. "Yeah. OK. Can you tell him that?"

"You got it. I'll tell him where you're going and what you said."

Earl broke eye contact and nodded, the moment suddenly taking on a train station feel, departure whistles blowing.

Mary-Lynn stepped close to Earl. "Which way will you go?"

Earl turned to the northwest and pointed at hills in the distant, glowing orange and purple in the evening sun. "Those caves, over there… I'll start there."

"We'll drive you."

"No, please. Don't make this harder than it already is. I've got all I need for a few days. I'll be fine." Earl swung his bag around his shoulder.

"How will I know when you're back?"

"Well, I never learned how to make dinners from scorpion's tail and mud, so, a couple of days at best. I'll stay until I've found myself, I guess. Or until Doe finds me."

"Make it quick, mister," said Mary-Lynn with a sad smile.

Earl nodded apologetically. "Miss Wu, there's something I need to say."

Mary-Lynn quickly placed two fingers over his mouth. "Not now. Don't make this worse than it already is."

Earl nodded again.

Mary-Lynn wrapped her arms around him and whispered in his ear. "Remember at the restaurant, our first dinner? Remember when I told you about my destiny, how important it was for me to meet Doe – how my entire life was leading to his arrival?"

"I do, of course," whispered Earl. "I remember every word."

"Do you?" Mary-Lynn continued to whisper. "Well, I was wrong. I got it all wrong."

"What?" Earl tried to pull away, but she held him tight to her chest. "What are you talking about? We're living it, your childhood prophecy."

"Oh, we most certainly are. It's all coming true. Except for one thing. I told you my destiny was to meet someone who'd change the world, someone who'd ignite my passion, change my direction, complete my lifelong search."

Earl froze, firmly embraced in Mary-Lynn's arms.

"Don't you see, mister? It wasn't Doe I was supposed to meet; it was… *you*."

EIGHTY-ONE

Moments later...

Earl took a tall drink from a short water bottle then thanked Andy and James for all their help, shaking their hands.

"Well," he said, sauntering over to Mary-Lynn, who was staring out across the desert.

She placed a hand over his mouth. "I'm serious, Earl. We're not gonna do this. It's just a few days."

He smiled, taking deep breaths to control his emotions. "Makes sense. Just a little break, a short walk with no destination and no survival skills. Should be good."

"Yeah, don't remind me." She grimaced.

"Mary-Lynn, this is all according to Doe's plan. And it's kinda romantic in a way, right? You know the old saying, if you love something, set it free, if it gets lost in the desert and dies, well, I guess you didn't love it enough to stop the stupid endeavour in the first place."

She frowned. "I hate you."

"I know you do," he said, chuckling. "But I should go now. It's time." He allowed Mary-Lynn's hand to slip from his, took a deep breath, then walked off into the desert. Stopping after ten feet to tie his shoelaces.

*

Hours passed as Mary-Lynn, Andy and James worked in the cramped quarters of the *First Edition* van. Mary-Lynn focused on segmenting the footage into three episodes and writing and recording voice-overs for critical parts. By morning, she planned to work the phones, calling East Coast broadcasters. She would work her way west until she had a national partner or several key partners for segment one. Her head spun with a hundred priorities; however, one ranked above the rest. She called Orlando.

"Christ, where are you guys?" said Orlando answering the phone. "Is Earl OK? I'm at the hospital. Just heard about Doe and what Bellecourt announced. Holy Shit. Is this whole thing for real?"

"Earl's safe, Orlando. He's with me. Well, he was. And, yes, it's all for real. I've seen it with my own eyes. This is really happening."

"Wait, whatdya mean he *was*?"

"It's complicated. Earl needed some alone time. He's gone for a walk, well, a hike, in the state park, the area you showed him. He asked me to contact you with a message."

"What? Earl's no hiker. He can barely tie his own shoes. It's not safe out there at night."

"I know, I know, please don't remind me. I'm trying not to think about it."

"This is messed up, Mary-Lynn. We need to go get him." Orlando paused. "What message?"

"Earl tried to call you. He wanted to thank you. And to tell you how much it meant to spend the week with you. He said you changed his life."

There was silence on the phone.

"Orlando?"

"Yeah, I'm here."

"He's coming back, you know. It's just a few days."

"OK. So, where are you now? Should I come out there, wait for him?"

"No, me and my crew are heading into town shortly. We taped several hours of Earl speaking about Doe and his message. We used the editing machines in the van for a rough cut. Tomorrow, I plan to highjack the airways with the greatest story ever told."

"Are you sure that's a good idea?" said Orlando. "Perhaps you'd like to know who Doe really was first?"

EIGHTY-TWO

Friday, November 20, 8:55 p.m.
Mary-Lynn's hotel

Mary-Lynn set up her computers, crawling around on the hotel room floor to find suitable power outlets. During the ride back, she'd internally wrestled with the fall-out from Orlando's remarkable mob story. She had always known Doe was not the man in the hospital bed, but a mob boss was certainly an unexpected twist. Mary-Lynn grew anxious at the thought of what might happen if word got out that the mystery man was really a mob boss from California.

The van's radio was abuzz with breaking local news about a police shoot-out north of Phoenix. Orlando had said the FBI would leak a fake story about a drug deal gone wrong, with no mention of any connection to the John Doe story. She nodded in appreciation of the FBI's speed in crafting the story and their innovative use of misdirection.

As the night progressed into early morning, Mary-Lynn put the finishing touches on the Earl interview, part one. It didn't need to be perfect. In fact, she was pleased with the lack of polish, noting how the *Blair Witch* production values added credibility and impact to the story.

By 7 a.m., Mary-Lynn had settled two agreements, one with CNN and another with NBC News. Both networks had agreed to air the interview simultaneously. They had also conceded to Mary-Lynn's demand that the first segment be released online immediately after it aired. Although NBC expressed their firm belief that internet news was a passing fad.

Mary-Lynn stepped out for some air and a drive-through breakfast, finding herself at the hospital parking lot out of habit. With the press army now decamped from the main lawn, she decided to go in, feeling compelled to give the hospital a heads-up about the imminent broadcast.

Robert Hand moved quickly around the corner into the lobby of the

320

administration office, appearing startled to see Mary-Lynn standing by the glass doors. "Can I help you, Miss… Wu… isn't it?"

"It is. Yes, is Mr. Shedmore in?"

"He is." Robert hesitated. "Do you have an appointment?"

"Oh no, not at all," Mary-Lynn insisted. "But I do have a story airing shortly that Mr. Shedmore really needs to know about."

Robert's face turned a whiter shade of pigeon droppings. "I'll be right back. Please, make yourself seated. I mean, seat yourself comfortable or whatever. Just stay here, don't move."

As she waited, Mary-Lynn picked up the morning newspaper. The front page was dominated by the Bellecourt story and John Doe's passing. It wasn't until page three that she found vague details of the FBI shoot-out, mostly rumour and innuendo. She smiled to herself, knowing the mob story would be buried by the massive media storm surrounding Doe's death and Earl's announcement.

Within a minute, Robert reappeared, looking winded. "Mr. Shedmore's waiting for you in meeting room three, down this hall, first door on the right."

"Thank you," Mary-Lynn said, tossing the newspaper back on the coffee table. She glanced at her watch. In twenty-five minutes, Earl's interview would be splashed across every CNN and NBC screen in the country.

"To what do I owe the pleasure, Miss Wu?" Frank held the chair out for Mary-Lynn as she entered the meeting room. "Robert tells me you've something important to share?"

Mary-Lynn was too tired to be polite. "I felt I should give you a heads-up regarding a story that will air in a few minutes. Without a doubt, you're going to be contacted for comment."

Without waiting for Frank to say anything, Mary-Lynn leapt into detail about the interview with Earl and their broadcasting plans. Then went on to describe Earl's mission to spread the word about the vital and pressing need for the world to come together as one.

Frank nodded throughout the remarkable story. After everything he had witnessed, he instinctively knew it was the gospel truth.

"Earl's a good man, you know," he said affectionately. "I hope he succeeds. That's a message we all need to hear."

"Thank you, Mr. Shedmore."

"Please… call me Frank."

"Thank you, Frank. Now," Mary-Lynn announced as she looked around the room, "if you've got a TV here somewhere, perhaps we can watch history in the making."

EIGHTY-THREE

Saturday, November 21, 6:15 a.m.,
Big Dick Rock

Morning arrived, as it often does, all bright and frisky and annoyingly full of hope. Another day dawned on the wickedly slow pace of planetary evolution. The earth rotates one more time. The moon disappears, and the sun resumes sunning – cyclical blessings from the patron saint of second chances.

After an incredibly dull and uneventful trek through the desert, Earl had located the cave at the base of what the locals called Big Dick Rock, just after midnight. He'd spied the rock from a distance, conspicuous by its enormous phallic shape reaching high into the air.

Despite the potential dangers of snakes and bugs, Earl had slept incredibly well. There were no wake-up calls, no worries, no traffic, no cell signal, no hangovers, and no midnight visits from Spymaster Wu.

He'd woken only once with the eerie feeling that people were standing over him, talking in hushed tones. Confirming he was alone, he faded back into the soil's cradle, so simple yet so huge, a smile of satisfaction bonded to his face.

Morning brought the spectacle. An amber light show flickered on the west wall of the cave. Not yet above the highest peaks of the hills, the sun caught the first few fissures in the cave ceiling. It was enough to flood the west end of the grotto with orange spots that shimmered like distant campfires. The cave floor meandered in random patterns of shifting sand, heaving and plunging in burnt umber waves, dirty little dunes concealing long-buried rubble.

Disoriented, Earl stood up and bounced his head off the low ceiling. He sat down again, regrouped, then stood back up in a hunch, watching as the sand poured from his pant legs and sleeves. Glancing around, he noticed that the cave appeared more extensive in the daylight, extra nooks and alcoves, unseen in the blackness of the previous night. Clearly, the cave was old, but several signs of modernity existed in the guise of fresh footprints, an empty liquor bottle, and vast amounts of wall graffiti. Directly under a bright spotlight, three wooden golf tees had been inserted into a mound of sand and arranged like a miniature crucifixion.

"What a dump," Earl said to himself, aware that someone or some thing had visited recently. Random holes, dug by hand or paw, scattered throughout the cave – some against the walls, others near the centre of the room, and one containing a single small jewel or bead of glass. Beside each hole, excavated sand lay in every direction, the wind having no time to smooth it into ripples. In the middle of the cave, a trench had been dug around an upright rock formation resembling a smooth beige pedestal. Human handiwork was evident across the pedestal's flat top – tiny chips and grooves where a chisel once passed.

Hungry but happy, Earl decided to stay in the cave for the day to see if anything magical happened, such as finding himself. Failing that, he would hike back to the city, likely dying of heat exhaustion along the way. Doe's words echoed in his mind. *One can find the most significant emotional experience at the precipice of disaster.*

By noon, the sun was high overhead, filling every crack and opening in the cave ceiling. Earl sat on a firm rise of sand, eating one of the many chocolate bars he'd stolen from the hotel mini-fridge. Moving about the cave was awkward. Earl wasn't a tall man, yet he was too big to walk fully upright in most parts. Those areas where he could stand erect were traps – brief interludes of forgetfulness before smacking his head on something extremely hard.

At first, the graffiti was of no interest, but as the day wore on and boredom rose, Earl began to study the symbols. He was pretty confident in his deciphering skills with the more modern pieces such as Fuck You, Big Dick Rules, and Angela's A Douche. But there were others, less obvious, hidden at lower levels or in scraggy corners, faded or partially covered by contemporary art. These drawings were far more challenging.

He sidled along the rock face, hunched down like a strawberry picker, carefully examining the faded pictures both in and out of sunbeams. This wasn't graffiti, he realized, nor recent. A horned beast, a tree in front of a cave, a humanoid face like Santa Claus *sans* the hat – each step introduced another hieroglyph. *It's a story,* concluded Earl.

Reaching an illuminated section near the back of the cave, he froze, staring blankly at the stencilled outlines of human hands. The images started well under the sand at the bottom and rose to the very top of the cave – hundreds of hands.

One intriguing aspect of the hands was how they differed in colour and intensity, perhaps due to varying paint compounds or dissimilar methods used over the years. As Earl instinctively placed his right hand on top of a stencilled

323

hand, a wave passed through his body, less of a shiver, more of a floating sensation. The handprint was connecting, speaking from history, long ago yet timeless and omnipresent.

Gently, Earl placed his hands on other prints, a slow rhythmic game of patty-cake, respectful of each connection, each human who'd left their mark. With each touch, the rock felt alive, flexible, pulling him in like a magnet. And each time he removed his hand, there was a snap in consciousness, a disconnect, like a blown fuse or popped light bulb. More than a physical disconnect, he felt emotionally drained every time he broke contact with the wall. But one thing was clear, the feeling was of loss, not gain. A pleasant loss, devoid of grief, more like a jettison, the feeling one gets after a spring house cleaning or a trip to the dump.

Earl felt his energy level and mood improve – strength returning despite being lost in the middle of nowhere with minimal food and water. Disconnecting from a handprint, he thought of Doe's words: *Optimism is a commodity, not a trait. It surrounds you, ready for harvesting.*

As Earl stared at the hands, feeling their attraction, their desire to speak to him, a hunger pain broke the moment. He glanced at his backpack. *So much for spacing out the candy bars*, he thought. *At this rate, I'll be out by dinnertime.* He grabbed the first Snickers bar he came to and unwrapped it while scanning the remaining contents of the backpack. Spying the ragged old bag encrusted with cheap gems and coloured glass, Earl fished it out for a look.

A gust of wind whipped through the cave entrance, stirring up grains of sand into a miniature funnel cloud. Light beams shifted slightly as the sun took a few steps to the left, a ray of light catching the corner of Earl's eye. Squinting, he inspected the bag, removing the contents and sifting through the smaller stuff. There was nothing of note, some common rocks, sandstone shards, and fine grey ash. Refilling the bag, Earl tied the top, then rolled it over and over in his hands like a beanbag. He examined the exterior stones and the empty spots where long-lost gems had once been attached. The surviving stones were tied tightly to the bag by cross-thread stitching from the inside out. Earl was intrigued at the bag's immaculate condition, despite it being, he assumed, many centuries old.

Earl shifted himself, placing the bag on top of the small pedestal at the cave's epicentre. He smiled, thinking of Doe's insistence that he accept the bag, not as a gift, but as an obligation.

The sun moved again, breaching a new hole in the cave's ceiling, a small, perfectly round shaft that had thus far eluded any rays. A tight beam quickly grew at floor level, engulfing the jewelled bag and the surrounding pedestal.

That's pretty, thought Earl, a split-second before the bag erupted into beams of blinding light. All the colours of the spectrum, bleaching, searing, penetrating every crevice, nook and eyeball in the cave.

Earl fell backwards, slapping his palms to his eye sockets and rolling away from the violent photonic eruption. Crawling on his knees and elbows, he tried to find a corner or indent for cover. Even with closed eyes, the lights were still visible – dancing, burning, each spectrum morphing to the next, unrelenting and brutal. Writhing in agony on the floor, he buried his face in the talcum sand as the intense light burned through his back and neck as if his clothes didn't exist. As consciousness started to fade, Earl could feel the light invading his very mind.

After several seconds of abject discombobulation, a stray cloud blocked the sun, providing enough time for the barely conscious Earl to scamper to the pedestal and knock the bag off. Then, exhausted, he rolled into a dark corner and lay gasping. "Like touching the tip of your tongue to a lightning bolt, huh?" he scoffed to nobody.

Hours passed and Earl sat with his back against the cool stone wall. His head was raging, as was his sunburned back and neck, but his eyesight had thankfully returned. On the floor, near the cave entrance, the bejewelled bag sat staring back at him, all innocent and benign.

Still shaking, Earl crawled over to his inanimate assailant and made a quick scooping motion, simultaneously lifting and moving the little bag back into his bigger bag. Zipping the knapsack closed, he gave it a swift kick for good measure, which felt thoroughly petty and unsatisfying. Then a realization struck him like a freight train, and he giggled out loud.

Anger.

That's what was missing.

That's what had been lost, excised or forgotten.

Anger!

Perilously close to a moment of Grinch-like redemption, Earl staggered back to the wall of hands. But this time, he hugged it, the whole wall, arms stretched out, face against the stone as it pulled him in. And it felt so good. Not because his physical ailments had improved, but because he wasn't angry anymore – at himself.

As the sun sank on the day, the last rays clung to tall rocks like fingers on a cliff edge, then slipped away, along with Earl's entire history. And he was giddy with what remained. Convincing himself there was enough food for another day, he readied for bed.

That night, Earl slept the best he'd slept in years. Decades. He slept with commitment. He slept without care or stress, the sleep of acquiescence. He dreamed of voids, galaxies and impossible creatures – of sitting inside an atom and on top of a black hole.

Rising with the sun and the cyclical light show on the west end wall, Earl pondered what remained of his mental baggage and was forced to concede there was none. His history still existed in all its dusty detail, but it was unimportant, forgettable. Instead, Earl felt very large and very interconnected. A mental connection that stretched from the cosmic to the atomic. Yet, despite this feeling of infinite reach, his new world felt private, personal and peaceful. It was as if he'd stumbled over an answer he wasn't even looking for, but one that made every other question irrelevant.

After a less than satisfying Snickers bar, Earl spent the morning in meditation, although not traditional by any standards. There were no crossed legs or monotonous chanting, as he still couldn't get Bananarama out of his head. But he was able to contemplate the condition of being one with something – everything.

"You're there, aren't you?" he asked out loud into the cave, startling himself with the gruffness of his voice. Earl grinned like a schoolboy as the instant reply echoed off the walls of his mind. He nodded with glee and decided to remain one more night, just because.

The sandstone caves held heat well into the night, and Earl slept again, the sleep of the dead, but with sufficient breathing. On the third day, he rose, hungry but well-rested. The rations were down to one Snickers bar, a stray Oh Henry! and half a bottle of water. Enough calories to get him back to civilization, but certainly not enough water. With no survival plan coming to mind, he ate another chocolate bar and peed in the corner. Urination, for men, represents quality thinking time. And a thought did indeed pop into Earl's mind. Moving to the centre of the cave, he gently opened his knapsack so as not to disturb the precious little bag of death rays. Rummaging around inside, Earl located a black marker, medium tip, usually used for doodling in his notepad. *Let's hope it's permanent like the label says*, he thought.

Kneeling in front of the wall of hands, Earl placed his right hand on a blank spot and joined a very prestigious club. There was no sudden clap of thunder, angelic choir, or shaking ground. But, he did have an enormous sense of completion as he stared at his handprint on the wall. *This was enough*, he thought, putting the cap back on the marker. Suddenly, Earl felt compelled to say something in honour of the moment.

"This is where I'll always be, no matter where I go. I will never leave this place."
Then Earl promptly left the cave.

Crawling from the cave exit, Earl stood up, stretched, and squinted until his body agreed to operate within normal parameters. After glancing around, searching for a suitable vantage point, he set about to climb Big Dick Rock. Once at the curved surface of the summit, he moved to the front edge and sat down in a deep groove. For many hours after, the sun arced lazily over his burning scalp, eventually dropping low in the west without incident or comment.

However, in Earl's mind, he'd spent the entire day gingerly poking around in his newly discovered universe. He found that if he focused intently, he could feel and even see individuals. But if he lost focus, a sudden overwhelming wave would hit – too many thoughts, too many visions. He'd instantly bail and head for the exits and the safety of his own physical reality. Once recovered, he would edge back into the universe with rising confidence and explore a little more.

It wasn't very long before Earl realized he could spend months within the thoughts of another, then pop out to find only minutes had passed. Earl replayed Doe's words over and over in his mind. *Time is eternal, each moment an eternity, existing forever.*

Learning fast, Earl realized that if he produced each thought in the form of a request, it would instantly manifest before his eyes. Heroes replayed their finest hours with courage and dignity. History's villains lived again in duplicity. Future timelines sprang up at his bidding.

Making a conscious effort to further open his mind, Earl expanded his thought requests, pushing his knowledge and creativity beyond his comfort zone. Only then did he discover that his universal back-stage pass was 'all-access'. His reach stretched far beyond the confines of humanity and planet Earth. Once the stuff of childhood sci-fi novels, Earl's fanciful thoughts would instantly reveal strange and exotic worlds populated by even stranger inhabitants. There was literally nothing he couldn't see or experience – anywhere – anywhen.

As the day wore on, his curiosity raised an interesting query. From inside the cosmos, Earl questioned the void.

Can I still call you JD?

The answer came instantly and softly, with the benevolence of a parent.

Of course, my boy.

That was enough. That was all he wanted for now. Earl settled back inside himself and reentered reality.

Climbing down from the rudely-shaped rock, Earl walked the perimeter of the extensive plateau, absorbing the beauty that stretched out for miles, more apparent now than ever before. His eyes traced the silver linings of clouds and the subtle hues of sand, grass and cacti. The view was infinite. Ahead of him, a tangerine dream, deep purple at his back.

Suddenly, without warning, tears streamed down his cheeks, uncontrollable, unstoppable, flowing to his chin and beyond. But this time, there was no emotional trigger, only apocalyptic waves of sand slamming into his body as a helicopter landed in front of him.

A Cessna had circled overhead several times during the afternoon, likely confirming that Earl was a lost dishevelled human and not the remains of a lost dishevelled human. The rescue helicopter was big and green, a large Red Cross emblazoned on the side. A massive metal door flew backwards, coming to a halt with a sharp clang as if the Hulk had grown bored with a crib toy. It was difficult to make out, but the rescue technician, clad in an olive jumpsuit and aviator's helmet, appeared to have jumped just before touch-down. With rotors in full decapitation mode, the medic made a hunched run toward Earl.

"Are you OK?" said the technician, her identification badge whirling and spinning on a string, rudely slapping Earl's face.

Earl squinted, trying to make out the technician's face through the vortex. His short-term memory banks processed the image and triggered a smile of recognition. "I need to brush my teeth."

The technician placed her hands around his head and drew him close. The kiss was passionate, long and tender, both sealing their eyes as a page in time stopped forever – an eternal kiss, a bond, a connection. Two flip books merged into one timeline, future pages mixing like playing cards in the hands of a grand magician.

Mary-Lynn opened her eyes and smiled. "Hello, mister. Now, where were we?"

Acknowledgements

Writing *Nothing Sacred* took the better part of a year. But the story and characters congested my brain and notebooks for over a decade. However, if you're wondering, no, I am not Earl; Earl is slightly shorter.

The *Nothing Sacred* storyline evolved from my continuous search for cosmic understanding and personal meaning. Despite my lifelong love of physics and philosophy, I found it difficult to find personal meaning within these arenas of pure reason. Conversely, I've never been satisfied with religion's simplistic answers, audacious claims, and conflicting parables that habitually conclude with **God did it**. Especially when this same omnipotent, loving God bequeathed us with evil talking snakes, global floods and eternal hell. So, *Nothing Sacred* represents my effort to reconcile both sides of the science/religion debate – an audacious attempt to make everyone happy. It should be noted that the current odds of my success in this endeavour are 1 in 10^{42}. So yes, there is a chance.

For those readers who love hidden references and inside jokes, you will find many in *Nothing Sacred*. For example, I went out of my way to drop references to musicians, groups, and songs that top my eclectic list of favourites. Keen-eyed readers may also discover a few factual tidbits regarding mythology, anthropology, cosmology and Arizona (one of my favourite places on Earth).

I owe a great deal to many people, but mostly banks. However, those who have helped me write NS through their encouragement, support, love, and constant nagging deserve, at the very least, a shout-out.

To my family:

Olive, my Irish mother, and **Anthony**, my British father. Thank you for my sense of humour, education, open mind and stunning good looks. This book

329

would have been impossible without a mother's passionate zeal and father's wit, and unrelenting support.

Karen. Somehow, you managed to put up with me through the worst. God knows why. Thank you for your kindness, support, and my two beautiful children.

Karissa, my daughter, first proofreader and staunch believer. Thank you for the best words ever spoken, "Hey, this reads just like a real novel."

Matt, my son. Thank you for your faith in me, your unabashed hugs, your laughter, and for creating the name Frank Shedmore.

Christopher (Shecky) Hayes, my son-in-law. Thank you for your contributions in building me a granddaughter. And, almost as important, your craftsmanship in building me a kick-ass electric guitar.

Charlotte Featherston-Hayes. My granddaughter. There are bad words in this book, Charli. **Don't read it until you're forty.**

Molly and Norman. Thank you for protecting the house, eating the leftover pizza crusts, and chasing the squirrels from the yard.

To all the great people that put this book together:

To my exceptional editor **Malcolm Croft** of Bristol, England: Our chance meeting and perfect pairing led to a novel of which I'm genuinely proud. Thank you for your priceless guidance, sense of humour, encouragement, and for chasing the squirrels from the yard.

The great people at Matador Publishing and Troubador Books for their extraordinary efforts:

Production Controller – Joshua Howey
Marketing Controller – Jonathan White
Digital Controller – Andrea Johnson
Senior Designer – Jack Wedgbury

Cover Illustration – Dave Hill, www.davehillsart.co.uk

Author cover photography – Jessica West Photography, Elora, Canada.

Website Creation – Stuart Grant, www.digitalauthorstoolkit.com

And last but not least, my friends, early editors, and heroes:

These beautiful people urged me to go for it, insisting I make every effort to expose the real me (which is still legal in parts of Europe). To save a few of them further embarrassment or culpability, I've used their prison nicknames.

Rob, my oldest friend (he's 117), Taz, Harold, Dan, Lynnie, Angelo Amicarelli and **the family**, Lori, Sparks, Jack Daniels, Fenchurch, Kaz, Ron's Auto Service, and the brilliant and deeply missed Warren Zevon.

ABOUT THE AUTHOR

Before belly-flopping into the deep end of the writing pool, Martin moderately enjoyed a career as a corporate executive and part-time lecturer at Montreal's McGill University.

Now, free from politically correct corporate-speak and the obligation to wear pants, he writes short stories and fictional novels from his home in Canada.

Born in Rugby, England, Martin was snatched from the crib and quickly immersed in all facets of British humour. He spent his childhood looking for the meaning of life through a lens dominated by Goodies, Pythons and Galactic Hitchhikers. So, it should be no surprise that, as a grown man, his global perspective remains a tad bent.

Unable to skate, Martin was considered an outcast in Canada and summarily banished to the small village of Elora, Ontario, where he is outnumbered by cows. As such, he has embraced a dietary policy of 'no red meat' to pacify the more militant bovines in the neighbourhood. His hobbies include Amateur Radiology, Ardvarkian Philosophy and collecting pottery-based weapons.

Martin is a citizen of both the U.K and Canada and plans to leave everything to his great grandfather.